UNLOCK THE MYSTERY OF THE HEART
WITH

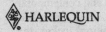 HARLEQUIN

INTRIGUE

The place for
BREATHTAKING ROMANTIC SUSPENSE!

To introduce you to our expanded publishing lineup,
we have collected stories from some of our
outstanding veteran authors and paired them with
brand-new stories from our most promising rising
stars. In these four fantastic volumes, sample the
best of the Harlequin Intrigue brand of excitement.

"Harlequin Intrigue gives readers
the best of both worlds—page-turning suspense
and sizzling romance.... Readers who love their
romance spiced with suspense need look no farther
for a thrilling read."
—*Romantic Times* magazine

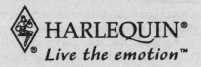

HARLEQUIN®
Live the emotion™

www.eHarlequin.com

GAYLE WILSON

Five-time RITA® Award finalist and RITA® Award winner
Gayle Wilson has written twenty-seven novels and two novellas
for Harlequin/Silhouette. A former high school English and
world history teacher of gifted students, she writes historical
fiction set in the English Regency period and contemporary
romantic suspense. She has won more than forty awards and
nominations for her work. Recent recognitions include the
Daphne du Maurier Award for the Best Historical of 2000
for *My Lady's Dare,* the first of the SINCLAIR BRIDES
trilogy. *My Lady's' Dare* also won the 2000 Shining Star as the
overall winner in the Sooner Area Romance Writers Rising Star
Awards. Her 2000 Intrigue novel *Renegade Heart* was a finalist
for the prestigious Romance Writers of America's RITA® Award
for Best Romantic Suspense, a category in which Gayle has
been a finalist for the past three years. Another of her Intrigue
titles, *The Bride's Protector,* won the RITA® Award for the Best
Romantic Suspense novel of 1999. Gayle still lives in Alabama,
where she was born, with her husband of thirty-three years and
an ever-growing menagerie of beloved pets. She has one son,
who is also a teacher of gifted students. Gayle loves to hear
from readers. Write to her at P.O. Box 3277, Hueytown, AL
35023. Visit Gayle online at http://suspense.net/gayle-wilson.

JULIE MILLER

Julie Miller attributes her passion for writing romance to
all those fairy tales she read growing up, and to shyness.
Encouragement from her family to write down all those
feelings she couldn't express became a love for the written
word. She gets continued support from her fellow members
of the Prairieland Romance Writers, where she serves as the
resident "grammar goddess." This award-winning author and
teacher has published several paranormal romances. Inspired
by the likes of Agatha Christie and Encyclopedia Brown,
Ms. Miller believes the only thing better than a good mystery
is a good romance. Born and raised in Missouri, she now lives
in Nebraska with her husband, son and smiling guard dog,
Maxie. Write to Julie at P.O. Box 5162, Grand Island, NE
68802-5162.

KEEPING WATCH

Gayle Wilson
Julie Miller

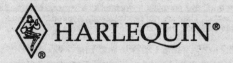

HARLEQUIN®

TORONTO • NEW YORK • LONDON
AMSTERDAM • PARIS • SYDNEY • HAMBURG
STOCKHOLM • ATHENS • TOKYO • MILAN • MADRID
PRAGUE • WARSAW • BUDAPEST • AUCKLAND

ISBN 0-373-83594-9

KEEPING WATCH

Copyright © 2003 by Harlequin Books S.A.

The publisher acknowledges the copyright holders
of the individual works as follows:

HEART OF THE NIGHT
Copyright © 1997 by Mona Gay Thomas

ACCIDENTAL BODYGUARD
Copyright © 2003 by Julie Miller

This edition published by arrangement with Harlequin Books S.A.

® and TM are trademarks of the publisher. Trademarks indicated with
® are registered in the United States Patent and Trademark Office, the
Canadian Trade Marks Office and in other countries.

Visit us at www.eHarlequin.com

Printed in U.S.A.

CONTENTS

FOREWORD
by Anne Stuart

I've always considered the creation of the Harlequin Intrigue line to have been one of the best things that ever happened in my career. I started writing in the Dark Ages, when Gothic romances were just dying out. I was a mere child, but I loved stories of feisty governesses and brooding heroes and lost heirs and big old mansions and storm-whipped nights. Romance was all well and good (and my favorite part of any story), but I liked the spice of suspense and danger to make things more interesting.

Unfortunately in my exuberant youth I failed to realize that Gothics were way past their prime, and I managed to come in only on the very tail end of the craze. Since I loved the relationship between the hero and heroine, I concentrated on writing romance rather than moving over into mystery when Gothics were no longer selling, but I still missed that streak of danger and suspense. I did what I could to incorporate it into my Harlequin American Romance books, but I had a wistful longing for a nice dash of violence.

And then blessed Harlequin came up with the idea for the Intrigue line: mystery and suspense woven through a cracking good love story. I was in seventh heaven. I wrote my first one in twenty-eight days, on the first computer I ever owned, and it was probably only my passion for the book that kept me from taking a sledgehammer to my brand-new Kaypro.

Tangled Lies was burning a hole in my brain and Harlequin Intrigue gave it a happy home. Even to this day I still adore that book.

It was followed by an adorable cat burglar, an insane puppeteer and all sorts of fascinating creatures. Fifteen years after the launch of the line I was even able to a take one of my old unsold Gothics and rewrite it for Harlequin Intrigue, where it ended up winning all sorts of awards (including the RITA® Award) and being reissued countless times. Obviously the line and I were a perfect match.

I made it through the hard times, when Harelquin Intrigue was having trouble defining itself. There were times when we couldn't have political intrigue, couldn't have guns, couldn't suspect the hero of being the villain (which I always thought was half the fun). But in the end chicken-hearted rules flew out the window in favor of great stories and fabulous writers like Gayle Wilson and Julie Miller. And the line keeps growing stronger and more popular, going from two books a month in the beginning to a commanding six!

I'm writing the same books I've always written, whether they're Regencies, historicals, series romance or mainstream contemporary novels. They're all romantic suspense, full of intrigue and passion, and blessed Harlequin Intrigue has always given me a happy home and a place to showcase some of the wonderful writers out there. Long may they prosper!

Anne Stuart

HEART OF THE NIGHT

Gayle Wilson

For Mona Kathrine, my heart's daughter,
who was supposed to be called Mona Kate, and
who instead, somehow, became our beloved Katsy,
and for her daughter Katelyn Joy.

Prologue

In a darkened room in Atlanta, Georgia, Thorne Barrington put the phone back in its cradle. It took a conscious effort to force his fingers to unclench from around the receiver. He raised his left hand to run it tiredly through thick black hair, a habit left from childhood, used then to subdue its stubborn tendency to curl. He became aware that he still wore the latex gloves with which he had handled the letter.

He stripped them off and laid them on the table beside the telephone. He shivered suddenly, although, even with the efficiency of central air, the brutal heat of the Georgia summer had invaded the house. Finally he closed his eyes. There was nothing to do now except wait. He had had a lot of experience waiting during the last three years. As he had endured the rest, he would endure this, but the waiting was always so hard.

IN AN OFFICE a thousand miles away, Hall Draper also put a phone back in its cradle and sat for a moment reliving the triumph of last night's game. They were in the play-offs, and Trent had gone two for three and then made a diving grab of a shot down the middle that no one had any right to expect a ten-year-old to catch. Tonight would be the test. The Sox were the best in the league, and everyone knew it.

Trent was pitching, and although Hall was nervous as a cat, he knew the boy wouldn't be. Trent would be keyed up, looking forward to the game, the challenge, but he'd be okay with a loss. It would give him more time for other things. It was a long season, and the kids were always glad when it was over. It was the adults who suffered the letdown, who cared how it all turned out, who held the bitterness of defeat into the coolness of fall.

Hall had often vowed he'd never be one of those Little-League parents, but that was before it had been his kid up at bat, *his* son on the mound. The adrenaline started flooding, no matter what he told himself. Jackie wouldn't even go to the games anymore. It made her too nervous. He just hoped for a win so he could sleep tonight.

"Mail," Claudia sang out as she came through the door that separated his office from the small reception area. An eternally cheerful woman, a little heavy and beyond middle age, his secretary had previously worked for an attorney who had just retired. Hall sometimes thought she knew more about running a practice than he did.

He had come to it late, had postponed the dream because of a lack of money and an early marriage. Trent had arrived before they were on their feet financially, and Hall had worked days and attended classes at night. It had taken far longer than it should have before he had his degree and had passed the bar, and it had been a struggle since. He hadn't attracted the interest of any of the big firms, his résumé unimpressive by his own standards. Even now, they were just barely getting by. Jackie was still working, but she didn't seem to mind.

Life was good, he thought, a little surprised by the introspection. He was not by nature an introspective man.

"A couple of remittances, a bill and a package. You want me to open it?" Claudia asked, a matter of form, they both knew. It was always slow enough that even the mail was an event in his day.

"Who's it from?" he asked, using his thumbnail to split one of the envelopes. It was a check from a client. A dollar-down-and-a-dollar-a-week law practice—he knew that's all he had. But at least this one was still sending his dollar.

Claudia turned the package, pretending that she hadn't already read the return address.

"Thornedyke Barrington," she told him. "It's marked personal. You know him?"

"If I do, I can't remember where. It sounds familiar. Just leave it, and I'll get to it later."

"You remember I'm taking Mother to the doctor? I'm taking the rest of the day off. I swear I dread it. That woman wears me out. You'll be okay, won't you?"

"Unless we get a rush. What are the chances of that, Claudia, do you think?"

They smiled at each other.

"Good luck tonight," the secretary said, turning to retrace her steps to the door. "Tell Trent I said to knock 'em dead."

"I don't think that's what you tell a pitcher—especially in Little League, but I'll try to convey the thought. Be careful on the way home from the doctor's."

"I will. See you tomorrow."

The door closed behind her, and Hall's thoughts moved back to the game. He thought about calling Jackie and asking her to run out and pick up some Gatorade. He decided finally that he could stop on the way home and then she wouldn't have to get out of the house in this heat.

He got up and walked to the windows behind his desk. He lifted one slat of the blind that was closed against the summer sun and looked out on the deserted street in front of his office. It was too hot for anyone to be out if they didn't have to.

He turned back, and the package caught his eye. Thornedyke Barrington, he remembered, but he turned it around so the address faced him and read it for himself. He had heard the name before, but for the life of him he couldn't remember where. He'd never been to Atlanta. Probably something to do with a client.

He took his old Boy Scout knife out of his top drawer and slipped it under the string that bound the brown-paper-wrapped box. He pulled the blade up sharply against the twine and cut through, the string releasing with a small twang. He turned the package over, his mind again slipping away to the familiar scene under the lights of the ballpark. He slid his thumb under the taped triangular flaps on the back and lifted the paper away from the box.

He had wadded the wrappings in one hand before he thought better of it. He probably should save the return address, he decided. He straightened out the crumpled sheet and laid it carefully on his desk. He put both hands on the box, one on each side, and the lid slid upward in one smooth motion.

As soon as the top had cleared the upright sides, just as the maker of the bomb had intended, the world exploded before Hall Draper's eyes. He was dead before his body slammed into the chair behind the desk and then fell heavily to lie on the blood-splattered floor of his office.

Chapter One

"Your boy did it again."

"My boy?" Kate August questioned, her blue eyes flicking up to meet her editor's as she opened the bottom drawer of her desk to put her purse back in its accustomed place. She'd just returned from a long and pleasant lunch with a college friend, and she had not yet refocused her mind on the newsroom. She didn't understand the reference. At the moment she could not, in any context, be accused of having a "boy."

She bent to fumble awkwardly under the desk, one-handed, trying to locate the comfortable shoes she'd worn this morning. The black heels she was now wearing, which she had put on for her luncheon appointment, had been carried in to work in a Rich's bag. There was something about meeting a friend you hadn't seen in a while, no matter how old or how good a friend, which demanded a little extra effort, a conscious decision to mask the evidence of years passing and the concessions that had inevitably been made to their passage.

So Kate had put her long, sun-streaked chestnut hair up today, had worn a little more makeup than usual and her best suit, but all the way back from the restaurant she had thought only that she couldn't wait to get the shoes off, no matter what they did for her ankles.

"Jack," Lew Garrison said, his usually smiling brown eyes serious. His thinning gray hair was disordered as if, distracted, he'd run his fingers through it. "Jack hit again."

Kate's hand, which had been searching in the black hole where her flats had apparently disappeared, froze. Her cheek still resting on the metal surface of the desktop, she allowed herself a deep breath and then straightened to meet Lew's eyes.

"Damn," she said softly. "It's not near time…" The comment trailed. There was no point in voicing the obvious. The consensus had been that the mail bomber, whom the press had begun calling Jack the Tripper almost two years ago, was working according to a careful schedule. Twice a year some unsuspecting victim opened his mail and died.

Doctor, lawyer, Indian chief. Ridiculously, the children's rhyme ran through Kate's mind, which was still trying to deal with the shock of Lew's announcement. That was one of the many puzzles of this story she'd been working on the last four months. There seemed to be no connection between the recipients of Jack's mail bombs, at least none anyone had yet figured out. Only his timing had been consistent. Until now.

Shoes forgotten, her fingers quickly lifted above the edge of the desk to flip backward through the revolving calendar. She was right. It had been late March, a little more than three months ago. She didn't need the notation to remember where. Austin, Texas. She had gone there. With the help of Detective Byron Kahler, her "in" with the Atlanta police, she even had been allowed to view the carnage in the boarding house where the device had exploded, killing an old man. Such a *nice* old man, everyone had told her. She closed her mind to the images from that devastated room, denying their impact.

"Who?" she asked.

"A small-time lawyer in Tucson. A guy named Hall Draper."

Kate felt a small surge of excitement. "A lawyer? Like Barrington."

She couldn't remember exactly when the press had made the connection between the first bombing here in Atlanta and the others. The police had not originally discussed the Barrington case in conjunction with the rest—because, of course, there was one obvious and very important difference. Jack the Tripper had screwed up. One intended target, an Atlanta judge named Thornedyke Barrington, had survived.

The Barringtons had always been prominent in civic affairs, cultured, educated at private Southern schools or the Ivy League. In Thorne Barrington's case it had been Tulane and then on to Harvard Law, followed by a return to Atlanta where he'd gone to work in the DA's office. And why not? Kate thought. Heir to one of Georgia's largest fortunes, he didn't need the income from some Peachtree partnership.

The surprising thing had been how good he was. A lot of people in Atlanta had waited for Thorne Barrington to fall flat on his face, believing his academic successes had resulted from his father's generous contributions to the schools he'd attended. Smart, dedicated, and realistic, he had proved the doubters wrong, and the most remarkable thing was that he hadn't even seemed to be aware he needed to.

Barrington had risen quickly through a stream of successful convictions, and when a judgeship had come open, his record and family name had secured it. If his daddy had used his influence, no one thought at that point to question the rightness of its use. Thorne Barrington was already being mentioned for the state Supreme Court when Jack's package arrived.

"There's no justification in linking this guy and Barrington," Lew said. "Maybe if all Jack's victims were involved with the law—"

"Barrington was a judge; this guy in Tucson's a lawyer.

It seems a pretty obvious connection to me. Don't try to tell me that you didn't at least think about it.''

"What about the six in between? Besides, the law those two practiced was poles apart. Apparently Draper had a hole-in-the-wall practice, mostly wills and simple divorces. And he wasn't born with a silver spoon in his mouth.''

"Just because we haven't *found* the link between Jack's victims doesn't mean there isn't one," Kate said. This wasn't a new argument. The cops' idea that the bomber ran his finger down the pages of a phone book to choose the next recipient of his package had never made much sense to her. Other serial killers might be forced to depend on opportunity. Because of his method, Jack wasn't limited by that. He chose his own victims, and Kate was convinced they were chosen for a reason.

"Random selection," Lew said. "You know that's the usual rule. You just think your theory makes for a better story.''

"Makes more sense, you mean. You think he'll talk to me?" she asked, keeping her voice casual. It took a second for Lew to sort through the possible *he's*, but he was bright, and of course, he knew Kate very well.

"Barrington? You think Barrington's going to talk to a reporter?''

"Yeah. Maybe," she amended. "Under the right conditions. Maybe the bombing today brought something back, triggered some feelings. Maybe I'll get lucky and catch him in a moment of weakness. You never know until you ask.''

"Trust me," Lew said, "Barrington's not going to talk to the press. Today is only going to drive him a little further into that shell he crawled into. He doesn't see anybody. Not since the bomb. He didn't even go to his father's funeral last year.''

"Was he disfigured?" It was a question that had bothered her since she'd begun the series, one there had been no information about. There was not a whisper about Barrington's injuries in the published reports. Only a lot of money could buy *that* kind of privacy.

"He'd have access to the finest plastic surgeons in the world, and it's been three years. Surely by now, *whatever* injuries he sustained..." Lew shrugged.

"Then why? Why disappear?"

"How would you react to someone trying to blow you up? Especially someone who has succeeded in blowing up everybody else he's targeted."

"Jack's only failure. You think he's afraid the bomber will try again?" Kate asked. She had become fascinated with the Tripper case and the cast of characters she'd studied so carefully during the past four months. And, she admitted, especially fascinated with Thorne Barrington.

"He hasn't changed his address. He hasn't run." Lew shrugged. "He's just..."

"Stopped living," she said. "More than three years ago."

"How would you react?" Lew asked again. "How can any of us know how we'd react to something like what happened to Barrington?"

The same thing that had happened again today in Tucson, Kate thought. Another human tragedy, its humanity lost, somehow, in the familiarity of its violence. By the national telecasts tonight, she knew and accepted, the coverage of the bombing would have been reduced to a four-minute segment, complete, if possible, with a glimpse of members of the grieving family, the real cost of today's events etched starkly in their faces—providing, of course, that the local affiliate came through with the tape.

AFTER SHE LEFT the office that night, Kate was reluctant to go home, too keyed up by the events of the day, by thinking about Jack and the series she was doing on the bombings. So she found herself heading once more in a now familiar

direction. During the last three months she must have driven
by the Barrington mansion a thousand times.

It was in a section of Atlanta that had been the city's
most exclusive before the turn of the century. Only the Barringtons had never moved out, refusing to give in to the
urban decay that had slowly surrounded the house during
the last fifty years. This is where the Barringtons had chosen
to live, and to hell with anyone who believed they had made
a bad decision. The irony was that the area was coming
back. The homes that were left, huge and hard to maintain,
expensive to heat and cool, were being snapped up and
renovated into exclusive apartments.

She slowed as she approached the house, only its shape
and size visible, the distinctive Victorian tower and irreg-
ular roof lines jutting against the night sky. The one concession to the changing neighborhood that the family had
made some time in the last thirty years was the high,
wrought iron fence that surrounded its narrow grounds, the
gate always securely locked against intruders. There were
lights visible deep within the house, their glow diffuse and
distant.

As she held the Mazda to a crawl along the street that
paralleled the grounds, she saw that the front gate was
standing open. That was unprecedented, and on today of all
days, it seemed almost bizarre. Kate pulled the car up to
the curb.

A golden retriever sat forlornly near the open gate. She
could see the light-colored lead securing him to one of the
tall spikes of the fence. There seemed to be no one around,
and as Kate watched, the dog lifted his head and howled.
The aching misery of the cry raised the small hairs on the
back of her neck. She cut off the engine, but it took another
plaintive wail before she opened the door and stepped out
onto the street in front of the mansion.

The dog strained toward her, whimpering in his frenzy
to free himself and to once again secure the safety of human

companionship. It was obvious that he had not been placed here to serve as a watchdog. He was far too glad to see her, a stranger appearing out of the night, to be effective at that.

The retriever was almost beside himself by the time she knelt down to smooth her hands over his head, scratching behind the silky ears and eventually cuddling the reaching nose against her chest. Despite his size, she could tell he was still young, just an overgrown puppy.

Apparently someone had begun the dog's evening walk and then returned to the mansion, leaving the gate open. The only problem with that reasonable scenario was what she knew about Thorne Barrington's obsession for privacy.

Was it possible that the retriever had been brought out here deliberately to get him out of the way? she wondered suddenly. That idea was melodramatic, perhaps, but why was the gate standing open? Today of all days. Against her will, Kate again remembered the room in Austin and before she could talk herself out of it, she reached to release the puppy's lead from the fence.

As soon as it was loosened, the leather loop was pulled out of her fingers, and the dog, trailing the lead, disappeared into the darkness inside the fence, far more eager to escape her company than she could have imagined based on his previous delight. Kate hesitated a moment, and then, following the retriever, she entered the grounds through the gate she had not ever, in all her trips by the house, seen standing open.

Trespassing, she reminded herself, climbing the stairs to the front porch. *This is trespassing.* She had no right to be here, no logical explanation for the compulsion she felt to investigate.

The front door stood ajar. There was a faint light from inside, dimly visible through its heavy beveled glass panels. She put her palm against it and the door swung inward, almost inviting her to enter. *Breaking and entering* flashed into her head, but she ignored the mental warning because her sense that something was very wrong, a feeling that had begun before she'd ever gotten out of her car, was now too strong to deny.

The crystal tears in the chandelier overhead tinkled softly in the draft from the open door, and hearing them, she automatically stepped inside, closing the door behind her.

The faint light she had seen from the porch seemed to be coming from the back of the house, from behind the massive staircase that climbed to the upper stories. She walked to the foot of the stairs, and looked up, her gaze following their rise. Four stories of railings spiraled upward, like some Escher drawing, into the darkness at the top of the house.

It was as still as death except for the faintest strain of music drifting into the foyer like fog. Even the sounds from the street had disappeared behind the thickness of the materials that had been used in the mansion's construction.

"Hello," she called, her voice too tentative to reach the back of the house or upstairs, the most likely places to find the inhabitants. Still she waited, listening. Even the crystal teardrops were silent now.

"Is there anyone here?" she called again, holding her breath. She had wanted to meet Thorne Barrington, but somehow, despite her legitimate concerns about the deserted puppy and the open door, she knew this was a bad idea. She had invaded his privacy on the flimsiest of excuses: his front gate was open on a day that Jack the Tripper had claimed another victim, more than a thousand miles away.

It would be better to leave and call 911 from her car phone. The police could come and check. An anonymous call from a concerned citizen who had seen the dog and the opened gate. She wondered if they'd send a car if she refused to give her name. Or better than that, she should call Detective Kahler, who would certainly understand the strangeness of the situation. Kahler had been the officer in charge on the Barrington case, long before anyone had realized they were dealing with a madman.

Instead of following any of those sensible avenues, she found herself surveying her surroundings. There were four sets of closed double doors, two on each side of the long entrance hall. She crossed the foyer to stand before the first set on the right. She fumbled for a knob in the dimness, realizing finally there was none. What her fingers discovered was an indentation by which the door could be pushed open. The half of the door that she touched slid almost noiselessly to disappear into the wall beside it.

Through the opening created by the sliding door, she saw an empty ballroom, lights from the cross street behind the tall sweep of windows providing enough illumination to allow her to determine, without any doubt, the room's purpose. Both sets of doors on this side led into this ballroom. In the stillness, she could almost visualize couples swaying on the floor that still gleamed softly, as if awaiting their return.

She stood a moment, caught by the ghosts her mind had created, and eventually she realized that the faint echo of melody was not part of the fantasy. The music was very real and had been there from the first, softly whispering into the darkness. Leaving the ballroom doors open, she moved back across the foyer to those on the opposite side.

The doors there operated the same way, sliding just as noiselessly to hide themselves in the wall. The design was such, she realized, that all four sets could be opened at once to create an enormous space, encompassing the wide foyer and the rooms on both sides, suitable for the lavish entertainments the Barringtons had been famous for. Now the house itself was as lonely as the man who inhabited it. So different from its past. So different now from his.

The music originated from this room, much louder now than the eerie whisper it had been before. She stepped into what had obviously been the downstairs parlor, the familiar shapes of the Victorian furniture indicating that it had stayed unchanged from the century before. In the dimness she couldn't see the fabrics that covered the scattered chairs and couches, but she could imagine their richness.

Despite her fear, despite the sense of urgency that had compelled her to enter tonight, she had been caught by the house's timelessness. Thinking only about the slow, deliberate gentility of the life that had been lived in these rooms, she was totally unprepared for the voice which spoke from the shadows gathered thickly to the left of the fireplace.

"What the hell are you doing in my house?" Thorne Barrington demanded.

Kate could see nothing of his features. Her eyes had not adjusted to the gloom after the faint light of the hallway. She doubted, even when they did, that she would be able to distinguish details about the man who sat in the darkest part of the room. There were no streetlights on this side of the mansion to provide even the faint glow that had unveiled the splendor of the long-deserted ballroom.

There was something, however, in the deep voice, an authority bred from generations of privilege, that made her very sure the questioner was Barrington himself.

"The gate was open," Kate said. It was why she'd stopped, but as she said it, she knew it didn't begin to answer his question.

"Obviously," Thorne Barrington said. "I asked why you're in my house."

"I saw the dog. He was tied to the fence, but he was upset, and then I found the front door wasn't closed. I thought something was wrong. I was worried…" She hesitated, considering all the things she couldn't tell him. All the real reasons she was here. *Because I know the gate shouldn't have been open, that it never is. Because… because I know all about you.*

"Where's Elliot?" asked the voice from the shadows.

"I don't know," she said. Who was Elliot? Did he expect

her to know that? "There was no one here. I called, but no one answered, so I thought something must have happened."

"Because the gate was open?" The question was derisive.

"Because of the dog. The front door," she added, trying to sound convincing. It was the truth, and she wondered why it sounded so specious.

"Who are you?" Thorne asked.

Kate hesitated, but she knew she had no choice but to tell him. He might ask to see an ID and besides, she doubted he'd recognize her name. People read a thousand stories without ever looking at the byline.

"My name is Kathrine August."

"August. I should have known," Barrington said, his soft laughter sardonic. "Don't you ghouls ever give up? Feeding off other people's pain like vampires. Doesn't what you do keep you awake at night?"

There wasn't much doubt after *that,* Kate thought, that he had recognized her name. So much for playing a long shot. "People have a right to the news, Judge Barrington," she argued, fighting to keep emotion out of her explanation—one she truly believed. "You know that. It's one of the most fundamental rights in this democracy."

"A fundamental right," the dark voice repeated, still mocking. "Does seeking to provide them with that 'news' give you the right to break into my home. I'm not 'news,' Ms. August. Not anymore. Get out."

"I'm afraid I can't agree with that. I'd like to talk to you about what happened in Tucson today. About—"

"Get out," he ordered softly, but there was no denying the threat. For the first time, Kate felt more than a sense of unease. More than embarrassment for having done something which she knew was wrong. For the first time, she was afraid. There was so much anger in the quiet command.

"You can't hide forever," she said. It was something she

had thought since she'd realized what his life had become. How empty. Hiding. That was the truth, and maybe one he needed to hear, but as she said it she knew *she* had no right to tell him what he should do. Lew had been right. Who could know how they would react if faced with the lack of trust Thorne Barrington must deal with every day for the rest of his life? She couldn't imagine how opening a seemingly innocuous package and having it blow up in your face would color your view of the world.

"Hide?" he repeated. His voice was louder now, stronger in the darkness, apparently furious with what she had suggested.

The puppy whimpered at his tone, and Kate realized the retriever was sitting beside Barrington's chair. Her eyes gradually adjusting to the darkness now, she could make out their shapes, a darkness against the surrounding shadows. Barrington's hand rested on the dog's neck, the animal pressed as closely as possible against the chair in which the judge was sitting.

"Is that what you think I'm doing, Ms. August? Hiding?" Barrington asked again.

It was what everyone thought, Kate knew, but given the anger in the dark voice and her situation, she hesitated. Apparently he had never realized what people believed about his disappearance.

"I don't think anyone blames you for that. I can't begin to imagine…" She hesitated. "I don't know how I'd react to—"

"I'm not *hiding,* Ms. August. Now get the hell out of my house before I call the police and have you arrested for breaking and entering."

"I didn't *break* in. The door's open. The gate. And your dog…" she paused, wondering for the first time how the dog had gotten in here. Obviously, there was another entrance.

"Elliot was supposed to…" He stopped whatever explanation he had begun when the retriever whimpered again. The puppy shifted position, uncomfortable with the anger, pushing his head against his master's hand. "Look, none of that's your concern," Barrington said. "Just get the hell out of my house."

"I would really like to talk to you. It doesn't have to be tonight, but you have a different perspective on the bombings than anyone else. I'll meet with you anytime you say. I'm doing a series. You may have read—"

"No," the voice from the shadows said. "I won't talk to you, Ms. August. Not tonight. Not ever."

"It's understandable, after all that's happened, if you're afraid, but surely you must realize—"

She never finished whatever idiotic advice she was about to offer. In the darkness she didn't see him press the button of the speaker phone which was on the table beside him, conveniently near at hand. By the time she'd realized that he had, he was speaking to whoever had responded.

"This is Thorne Barrington. I have an intruder. She doesn't appear to be dangerous, but I want her out of my house. Please send a patrol car."

"You're going to have me arrested?" Kate asked, stunned. She had played the good Samaritan because she was concerned about his safety, about breached security, and he was calling the cops.

"*Afraid*, Ms. August?" he asked mockingly.

Unable to believe it was really happening, she heard in the distance the siren of the patrol car. Apparently when Thorne Barrington asked for the police, he got them. Immediately.

Son of a bitch, she thought resignedly, wondering what in the world Kahler was going to do to her for pulling this stunt.

WHEN THE OFFICERS had gone and silence again reigned in the familiar darkness that surrounded him, Thorne Barrington closed his eyes. He recognized the perfume the woman had worn, floating to him from across the room. His mother had worn Shalimar, and the fragrance haunted the room now, reminding him. Smell was the most evocative of the senses, and he wondered how the reporter could have known what to wear to create the images that were moving through his mind. Images of life as it had once been lived in this house. Images of what his own life had once been. Angered again, he pulled his thoughts away from the past and back to the reporter who had invaded his well-guarded privacy.

Kate August. She was the one who had written the series of articles on the bombings. He should have known. God, he should be better prepared by now. After what had happened today in Tucson, someone was bound to try. Usually the fence was enough to deter the curious. Either she was very determined or she had somehow convinced Elliot to let her in.

Where the hell is Elliot? he wondered for the first time. He hadn't escorted the policemen into the parlor. They must have entered through the door she had claimed was standing open. In his fury at her intrusion, he had totally ignored what Kate August had said, discounting her explanations as lies. Was it possible that something *had* happened to Elliot?

He stood up suddenly to stride across the dark parlor. He knew these rooms by heart. Not a piece of furniture was ever moved. Nothing ever changed in the house.

Except tonight, he thought. Tonight the house was different, its aura subtly disturbed, because the elusive fragrance she had worn moved before him now through the once again silent, deserted rooms.

Chapter Two

The cops had been businesslike and impersonal. They acted as if escorting a female reporter out of Judge Barrington's mansion was part of their nightly routine. By the time they'd arrived at their precinct house, Kate was completely humiliated by her own stupidity, but she made the call to Detective Kahler, praying he would be in and at the same time dreading the possibility. And Kahler didn't let her down.

He looked long-day tired, slightly rumpled, with the collar of his oxford-cloth shirt unbuttoned, rep tie loosened as a concession to the heat. Kahler was pushing forty, but his face was good, the lines around the eyes and tonight's slight shadow of beard not detracting from its attractiveness.

It was, however, his voice Kate liked best. The transplanted Yankee speech patterns had softened just enough to take the edge off. He was a good-looking man, and she had begun to think of him as a friend, but it was obvious he wasn't feeling friendly tonight and his usually pleasant voice was coldly furious.

"What the hell made you think you had the right to walk into the man's house at night?" he asked. "You're damn lucky he didn't shoot you. I would have. What the hell were you thinking, August?"

"I've already told the cops all this. I saw the dog tied outside and the open gate. It's never open, so—"

"How do you know Barrington's gate is 'never open'?" he interrupted the reasons she'd attempted to offer before. "You take a survey of his neighbors? They tell you that if the gate's open, there's a crime in progress? The bomber always leaves it open when he visits? If you really believe something's wrong, August, you call the police. You don't waltz in on your own. It won't wash. You just wanted to talk to Barrington about what happened today, and so you break into his home and—"

"I didn't break in. The damn door was open. How many times do I have to tell you that?"

What she didn't tell him, would never tell him of course, was how she knew the gate was always closed. She wouldn't admit the number of times she'd driven by Barrington's home. Kahler's reaction was making her question what she had done. Not tonight—she knew what she'd done tonight was beyond the bounds—but before. To question her growing fascination with the central character of the story she was working on.

She even had a file folder of material she'd collected on Thorne Barrington. But if she didn't admit the number of times she'd driven by his mansion, she certainly wouldn't confess the number of times she'd studied the black-and-white photographs that folder contained.

Maybe Kahler was right. Maybe she needed to back off, maybe even get Lew to assign someone else to finish the series. She had broken the first commandment, the prime directive. She had become personally involved with this story. She was no longer objective. Not about Barrington. And not about the bomber.

"You broke a trust, August," Kahler went on. "I agreed to talk to you, against my better judgment, I have to tell you. And then you go and pull something like this."

Kahler had been up-front from the first about his and the

department's motives in agreeing to help her with the series of articles she was writing about Jack. *"Anything that will draw this joker out is okay with me,"* he had said. *"Just remember that we're using you, August. Not the other way around."*

So they had shared some dinners, all of which she'd put on her credit card, a legitimate business expense since they had talked about the bombings, with only an occasional foray into how the Braves were doing. And he took her calls, patiently answering her questions and guiding her series into something that might, they both hoped, spark a response in someone who had information about the bomber that they didn't realize might be important. And in the process, she had come to consider Kahler a friend. Only gradually had Kate begun to wonder if the look she had occasionally surprised in his hazel eyes was rooted in the growing personal interest she'd been attributing it to.

"I didn't mention your name," she said defensively. "Barrington doesn't know you've talked to me. He won't ever know. All he knows is I'm a reporter. He called us vampires."

That comment had bothered her. *Feeding off other people's pain.* She knew there was a lot of truth to the accusation. It just wasn't the way she usually thought about her job.

"The media frenzy might be one of the reasons Barrington chose to disappear. Somebody sneaked into his hospital room and took pictures a couple of days after the bombing."

She hadn't known that. Those photographs weren't part of the collection in her file, of course. Those were all pre-Jack, from the social pages or stories about his courtroom, his family.

"What happened to them?" she asked.

"You want to publish them?" Kahler asked sarcastically.

"They'd be spectacular, all right, released now, given the timing with the one in Tucson."

"You know better than that," Kate denied hotly. "You know I'd never do anything like that. Lew wouldn't."

"How could Barrington know? *Somebody* took those pictures. A reporter for some scum of a paper. At a time when he was..."

Kahler paused to gather control, but Kate wouldn't let her eyes fall from the accusation in his. She knew how people felt about journalists. None of this was new to her, but it hurt to find out this was what Kahler thought. The same things Barrington believed.

"Did Barrington call you today?" she asked. A change of subject seemed prudent since, after tonight's escapade, she wasn't exactly in a position to argue the ethics of her profession.

"As soon as his mail was delivered."

"Minutes before Draper got the package," she guessed. The bomber's revenge for his one failure had been a subtle torture. Before each bombing a warning of what was about to happen was delivered to the one man who had escaped, but never in time to allow the authorities to prevent the bombing.

"He's added a new refinement. The return address on the package sent to Draper was the judge's."

"Barrington's address?" she repeated in surprise. "Why would he do that?"

"You're asking me why Jack does the things he does? I don't have any answer, August. Maybe to put the press back onto Barrington. More punishment. Like the warnings. Interest in the judge has died down, and Jack probably doesn't like that. Maybe he knows how much Barrington hates publicity, and the news of the return address is bound to generate a lot if the authorities decide to release it."

"What did Barrington tell you when he called?" she asked.

"Same as always. That Jack was going to kill again. That it would be in Tucson. And that he had sent Barrington his best wishes for another pleasant day."

Kate tried to imagine receiving such a message, and knowing, better than anyone else, exactly what was about to happen to the next victim. Being unable to do anything to prevent it. Seven warnings, all delivered to the one man who survived.

"Did you ever wonder if he deliberately spared Barrington to be his messenger?" she asked. "To taunt the police."

"Maybe Jack was still learning," Kahler said. "He screwed up, and Barrington didn't die. If anything, that mistake caused him to move on to overkill. He's making sure now there's no chance anyone will survive."

"Have you ever seen Barrington, Kahler?"

"He calls me. He sends me Jack's letters. He's meticulous about protecting whatever evidence they might provide, but I don't meet him, August. Nobody sees him. Not since the bomb."

"But he always calls you."

"He thinks he's obligated to reveal the contents of the notes. They created a pretty strong sense of duty in their boy."

The Barringtons and their golden boy, their only son and heir. There had been a younger child, she remembered, but something tragic had happened. An accident involving the family swimming pool. Then there had been only one son, the focus of all the Barrington ambitions, and all that very old money.

"Did you ever wonder what it was like growing up as Harlan Thornedyke Barrington IV?" she asked.

"I don't have that big an imagination."

She didn't know much about Kahler's background, but enough to know there was no old money there. In answer to her question about how he'd gotten into law enforcement, he had told her he'd joined the Marines at seventeen and ended up an MP, but other than that single piece of personal information, Kahler had been as reticent about his own past as about the case he had worked on for the last three years.

"The Barringtons are way out of my league, too," Kate agreed. "They used to make the papers a lot. Only it was on the social pages then. I guess they didn't hate reporters so much in those days." There was a trace of bitterness in the comment. She had finally met Thorne Barrington, the man in the pictures she'd collected, but it hadn't gone exactly like her daydreams about it.

"The guy's been through hell, August, and people like you want him to relive it, to satisfy the public's lust for all the gory details. 'How did it feel, Judge Barrington, to have a bomb explode in your hands? Can you tell our viewers how that's affected your life?'"

"I told him he was hiding," Kate admitted. Put it all on the table, all the *mea culpas*. If Kahler wanted to despise her, she'd give him the right reasons.

"Maybe he is," Kahler said. "Maybe I would. Maybe you. Who knows? But it isn't your right to question how Barrington reacts to what happened to him."

"You know better than that," Kate said. "He's news, Kahler, and he will be until Jack's caught."

"You're as bad as the rest of them," Kahler said in disgust. "Leave him alone, Kate."

There wasn't much left to say. No high moral ground to take in what she'd done. Neither of them credited her claim that her actions had been motivated by real concern for what she'd seen when she'd driven by. She didn't particularly want to explain that driving by had become a normal part of her routine. Kahler thought she'd gone there to question Barrington about today's bombing. The judge thought she was there because she was just like whoever had sneaked into his hospital room to take those pictures. A ghoul. A vampire.

"Can I go now?" she asked when the silence between them grew beyond comfort.

"You can go. I'll try to get Barrington to drop the charges."

She thought about telling him not to bother, but she wasn't sure enough about the consequences if the judge wanted to pursue it. Between being taken in by the patrol car and Kahler's fury, she was beaten down enough to be afraid. Of what Lew would say. Of eventually ending up in jail.

"Thanks," she said. She waited a moment to see if Kahler's anger would allow him to relent enough to say goodnight.

"Your car's in the north lot. I had them bring it in."

"Thanks," she said again, glad he seemed willing to allow her to escape. To run home and hide. *To hide.* That's what she'd accused Barrington of doing, she suddenly realized, and all that had happened to her—

"Don't bother him again, August. Stay away from Barrington. I want your word on that."

"You've got it," she said. "But it wasn't what you thought. It wasn't what *he* thought. I swear to you I wasn't there because I wanted an interview." She didn't wait for a reply. She walked out of the small room with its revealing glass walls where she'd waited for Byron Kahler's arrival and endured his fury and disgust. Then she went out through the Saturday-night confusion of the station house.

The heat hit her when she opened the heavy outside door, but she stopped a moment before she started down the shallow steps. She'd tell Lew tomorrow to give the series to someone else. She wasn't sure she'd tell him all the reasons. It was enough that she'd lost Kahler's trust. She knew she would have to endure a similar lecture from her boss when he heard what she'd done. She'd blown it, big-time, and maybe it was just as well. But she wouldn't pass on the file, she thought, embarrassed by the pictures she'd acquired. Like some kind of groupie. *That* she'd throw away. No one would ever know about that secret collection.

She almost bumped into the man who came hurrying up the steps, briefcase in hand. Despite the haste with which he brushed past her, she had no trouble recognizing Barton Phillips. She wondered what one of Atlanta's highest-priced attorneys was doing in a neighborhood precinct house this late at night.

She glanced at her watch, surprised to find that it was almost eleven. She fought the automatic urge to follow Phillips inside, her instincts telling her that if he was here, something was going on, but for some reason she didn't even want to know what. It could be the biggest story of the year, and all she wanted to do right now was go home. She started down the shallow stone steps, feeling more depressed than she could remember.

When she reached the street, she had to stop and think what Kahler had told her about her car. North lot. She turned right and had taken several steps before she became aware of the black Mercedes paralleling her movement down the sidewalk. The windows, closed against the heat, were so heavily tinted that she couldn't catch even a glimpse of the occupants.

She didn't become concerned until the Mercedes turned into the parking lot, pulling to a stop before her, blocking the path to her car. Her heartbeat began to accelerate, her mind dredging up all the stories of carjackings and kidnappings she'd heard in the last few months. This was a police station. Surely…

The rear window glided down smoothly, but she jumped at the unexpectedness of its motion.

"Ms. August." It was the same voice that had spoken out of the shadows tonight—Thorne Barrington. "I'd like to talk to you," he said. "Would you get into the car, please?"

The invitation was the last thing she'd expected. In view

of what she'd just promised Kahler, it couldn't have come at a worse time. Except she hadn't sought Barrington out. He had found her. However, considering the fool she'd made of herself tonight, she knew it was better that she apologize now and then do what Kahler had told her.

Reluctantly, she put her hands on the top of the glass, bending her knees to look into the car. She could barely see Barrington, a silhouette against the blackness of the glass behind him, its tint dark enough to prevent the parking lot security lights, almost as bright as day, from really penetrating the car. He would be able to see her clearly enough, she knew, with one of the powerful lights just above her head.

"Judge Barrington, I can't tell you how sorry I am for what happened tonight," she began. "I know it's no excuse for entering your home, but I really thought—"

"Ms. August, I would be deeply grateful if you'd just get into the car," Thorne Barrington interrupted.

Kate hesitated a moment longer.

"Please," he offered finally.

There was something compelling in that single syllable. She suspected that Barrington seldom asked favors. That *please* had sounded as if it had been wrung from him against his will.

While she was trying to decide what to do, Barrington reached across the wide back seat and, releasing the latch of the door, pushed it slightly open. He leaned back against the opposite door, waiting.

Kate knew somehow that he wouldn't ask her again. *This is what you wanted,* some inner voice reminded her, but it wasn't, of course. Not this way. Not under these circumstances. Kahler had supplied all the abuse her frayed conscience could handle for one night. She didn't want another lecture, so she was a little surprised to find herself crawling awkwardly into the back seat.

Despite the size of the car and the width of that seat, she

felt very close to Barrington. He was a big man—six-four, she remembered from her notes—and she was very aware of his size. In the diffuse light that filtered into the car from the lot's security light, his features were revealed for the first time. He looked just as he did in the pictures taken before the bomb. If there had been facial injuries, they were no longer apparent—at least not in the dimness of the car's interior.

"Would you close the door, please?" he asked.

She took a deep breath before she complied, and then listened to the window slip up again as soon as she'd done what he'd asked. The tinted Plexiglas panel between the driver and the back seat was already closed.

"It appears that I owe you an apology," Thorne Barrington said. His voice was soft in the enforced intimacy, holding now none of the anger it had held before. The accent was still there, familiar and comforting, caught below the overlay of years he'd spent up North. A Southern gentleman.

Kate's lips lifted suddenly in relief. He was apologizing to her. "The gate was open," she said.

"Elliot had fallen. He had left the dog and had come back inside, but then he fainted. The dog's too much for him. I should never have…"

Kate waited, but he didn't complete the explanation.

"Elliot?" she asked.

"My butler. He's a little…beyond caring for a puppy. Especially one that size. I should have realized it before now."

"Beyond?" she repeated.

"He's almost ninety. A vigorous ninety, but still…"

Again the soft voice faded. Guilt and regret for what had happened to the old man was clear in his voice. Yet despite his concern, Judge Barrington had taken the time to find her, to apologize to her. Only…she wasn't sure she deserved an apology. Had her motives in going inside his house been as straightforward as she'd indicated to Kahler? Or had her judgment been clouded by other emotions? Even now she wasn't completely clear about that.

"Is he all right?" she asked finally.

"Just a small cut on his forehead. He's been treated and released. I took him home."

"So...I was right. Something was wrong."

"Yes," he admitted.

"You don't intend to press charges."

"No."

"Thank you," Kate said.

"It seemed the least I could do. To apologize. I'm afraid I didn't even listen to what you tried to tell me. When I heard your name..." Again he hesitated, and Kate remembered what Kahler had told her about the hospital photographs. "When I realized you were a reporter, I prejudged your motives. I simply wanted to tell you that I'm sorry. I was wrong."

Leave it alone, her head argued. Accept his apology, be gracious and forgiving. Let him take the blame. *I was wrong,* he had just confessed, letting her off the hook.

"Not about everything," her mouth whispered instead.

"I beg your pardon?"

"You weren't wrong about...everything."

The silence lengthened. "I see," he said finally.

"No, you probably don't," Kate said, knowing she could never really explain, "but it doesn't matter. I'm not as guilty as you thought, but I'm also not as innocent as I would like to believe. Some of what you said tonight..."

She had intended to say that some of what he'd accused her of was true, but she couldn't seem to bring herself to admit it. Not to him. He had been through hell, just as Kahler said, and she *had* wanted to stick a tape recorder under his nose and ask, if not the mocking questions the detective had suggested, others just as hurtful. Just as invasive.

"I'm sorry," she said. "For everything."

There was no answer from the man on the other side of the car. She found the handle of the door and stepped out. The Mercedes didn't move until after she had backed the Mazda out of its parking place and was driving across the lot. She turned south and in her rearview mirror, she watched the taillights of the big car, which had headed in the opposite direction, disappear behind her into the night.

SHE MANAGED TO UNDRESS down to her bra and panties before the phone rang. A little apprehensive, not only because of the lateness of the hour but also because of all that had happened since she'd left her desk, she let it ring a couple of times. Had Barrington called Lew at home or had Kahler thought of another sarcastic remark that couldn't wait until he saw her again? She finally picked up just before the sixth ring, which would trigger the answering machine.

"Hello," she said, trying to sound as normal as possible.

"I just thought you'd sleep better if you knew there won't be any charges," Byron Kahler said. There seemed to be no residual anger in the deep voice.

"That's wonderful," Kate assured him. Apparently, the judge hadn't admitted he'd already talked to her when Kahler had, as he'd promised, asked him to drop the charges. Letting Kahler think he'd arranged for her rescue might put her back into his good graces, and she needed all the help she could get.

"Thanks, Kahler. And thanks for letting me know."

"As much as I'd like to, I can't take credit for the dropped charges. Barrington had a change of heart. It seems…"

When Kahler hesitated, Kate's lips involuntarily curved into a small smile. It seemed the detective was also having a hard time admitting that he now knew her story to be true.

"There *was* a problem at the house. The gate and the door were open and, under the circumstances, he decided to give you the benefit of the doubt," he finished.

She fought the urge to say "I told you so," and awarded herself a few character points for finding the willpower.

"Whatever the reason, I'm grateful. I'd already decided to tell Lew to put somebody else on the story. I didn't think I could be too effective having been arrested for breaking and entering one of the victim's houses, no matter how innocently that happened."

Kahler's laugh expressed his disbelief. "I can't see you giving up that easily, August. Once you've got hold of a story, you're not going to let go. You'll be there at the bitter end."

"Which for this one is soon I hope. You going to Tucson?"

"Yes," Kahler said.

The voice had become official, putting distance between himself and that unpleasant task. Kahler had visited all the scenes, talked to all the victims' families, all the business associates. He had been the officer in charge on the Barrington case, and the Atlanta bombing, like all the others, was still open, the investigation ongoing.

"I hope you find something," Kate said softly. "I hope this time he screwed up. I hope you catch him, Kahler."

There was a silence on the other end. She knew she'd said something so obvious it didn't require an answer. Kahler lived with that hope daily. It probably intruded even while he worked on his other cases. Then every six months—except this time, it hadn't been six months.

"Why do you think he hit early?" she asked.

"Who knows? Who knows how he thinks or why he does what he does? I don't have any answers for you, Kate."

"I know. It was just a thought. I'll talk to you when you get back?" It was a question. *Will our arrangement still hold despite your anger, despite what you revealed tonight about your opinion of what I do, of my profession?*

Again there was a brief hesitation, and she held her breath.

"You must have made a big impression on him, August."

It threw her. It made no sense in the context of the conversation. He couldn't mean Jack, so that left... *Barrington?* He thought she'd made an impression on Barrington? Maybe, she conceded, but not the one she would have liked to make. She couldn't even keep her mouth shut about her motives in entering his home. She just blurted that out with all the other confessions she been forced to make tonight. Too many years of Sunday school. Confession's good for the soul. Yeah, right.

"Impression?" she said aloud.

"He sent Phillips to take care of you."

"Barton Phillips?" she asked, remembering the hurrying figure on the stairs. Apparently, like the Atlanta police, when Barrington said, "Jump," Phillips simply asked, "How high?"

"Esquire," Kahler agreed. "Quite an impression," he repeated, some nuance in his tone she had never heard before.

She wondered what she was supposed to say. Was he jealous because Barrington had come to apologize? *My God, Kahler's jealous,* she thought in wonder.

"He just realized he was wrong," she said. "Southern gentlemen always apologize. Their mamas teach them how in the cradle. You should try it sometimes," she suggested.

"There're only two things wrong with that plan, August. I'm not Southern..." He paused to allow her to finish.

"And you're not a gentleman. What a shame."

"*You've* just known too many of both. You might consider broadening your field of knowledge. That's what an education is all about. I'll see you when I get back from Arizona.''

He had hung up before she could think of anything witty—or even halfway witty—to say. That had definitely sounded like an invitation, and not one to continue the strictly professional relationship they had shared up to this point. She wasn't sure how she felt about that. She had avoided thinking about Kahler in that light. For a lot of very good reasons.

She took a quick shower and put on her nightgown. She walked back to the kitchen and poured herself a glass of milk. She stood by the refrigerator drinking it, feeling the pleasant coolness of the tile floor under her tired feet. Unbidden, under the fluorescent brightness of her kitchen light, came the remembrance of the man who had sat alone listening to music tonight in the darkness of that dead mansion.

She carried her milk with her into the living room. She set the glass down on the table beside the couch while she opened its drawer and took out her collection of pictures. She sat cross-legged on the sofa. She forced herself to finish the milk, slowly, before she would allow her fingers to open the folder and spread out the contents on the coffee table in front of her.

She knew them by heart. The dark eyes laughing down into his mother's. In a tux at somebody's wedding. Always taller than the people around him. Dominating. *Too good-looking for his own good,* her grandmother would have said. He was surrounded in one shot by smiling debutantes, who looked up into that handsome face with something approaching her own fascination. *You must have made quite an impression,* Kahler had said. Not exactly the one she had daydreamed about making.

She knew there was something weird about looking at pictures of some guy she didn't know. Like a teenager putting posters of a rock star on the wall. She was thirty-two years old. Way too old for this kind of crush. *Crush,* she repeated. That's exactly what this felt like, and it was so stupid. So childish. Crazy.

Tonight she had met him. Twice. She had even sat beside him in his car. She closed her eyes and allowed herself to remember. To think past the embarrassment and the fear to remember what it was like to sit beside him. To remember how he had smelled. Not cologne. Just clean. Soap. Male.

His voice had wrapped around her in the dark. Soft and very deep. Southern slow. He had been near enough that she could have reached out and touched him. *Crazy,* she thought again, deliberately breaking the spell of the memories.

Finally she pushed all the pictures back on one side of the folder and closed it. She hid it again in the drawer and turned off the light on the table. The apartment was dark except for the lamp she'd turned on in her bedroom, its soft glow inviting her down the hall. Even when she crawled into bed and switched off the lamp, creating total darkness, the images from the pictures, superimposed over the reality of the man she had met today, were still there. It took her a long time to go to sleep.

Chapter Three

Kate overslept on Monday, arriving in the office a little late, feeling pressured and behind schedule. She hated to have to rush in the morning. It made her feel disorganized and out of sorts the whole day.

Lew greeted her with his usual mind-on-something-else lack of awareness, and she was relieved. Apparently no one had called him to complain about the incident on Friday night. She listened to his suggestions about the things she was working on, jotting down quick notes she'd have trouble deciphering later. A typical day, and after Friday, normality was a relief.

She worked a while on the Tucson bombing, which had pushed up the deadline for the next victim profile. Since she had started, the series had contained other types of articles: the FBI's psychological profile of Jack, a brief overview on the other well-known mail bombers, and some carefully screened information about the technical aspects of Jack's explosives. She was also planning to do a segment about the agencies and officers involved in the hunt. Lew had arranged to have a stringer contact each local police department which, like Atlanta, had open cases on the bomber's victims to gather information on the officers in charge of those investigations.

Working on that would have been far more pleasant than

doing a profile of another victim. They were the hardest to
write, chronicling the poignant details of the seemingly ordinary lives. But it was from Kate's profiles that the police
were hoping some reader might make a connection, might
provide a reason, a new direction for them to pursue. Hoping for anything.

The story on Barrington had started her obsession with
him, what had become her secret collection of the newspaper's photos at first simply a legitimate attempt to gather
information about the only survivor. She had carried the
pictures home after she'd finished the article, and that, of
course, had been her mistake.

She cleared Thorne Barrington from her mind and tried
to pull all the available information on Hall Draper together.
On the surface there didn't seem to be anything in this guy's
life that should result in his becoming a target for a killer.
Too ordinary. Like the old guy in Austin. She couldn't
imagine any skeletons in those closets to attract Jack's attention.

Maybe the cops were right. Maybe the bomber just found
an address in a phone book. Maybe the victims weren't
related, and if that were true, they might never find Jack.

Most serial killers were caught only by happenstance or
if they made a mistake, an action that went against the
routine that had worked in the past. They were usually
bright, at least the ones who succeeded for any length of
time. A couple had been on the inside, knowing how the
system worked. That had allowed them to escape detection
longer than the guy on the street might.

Others had been "interested observers," seemingly fascinated with the case. *Why shouldn't they be?* she thought.
They were at the center of it. Often that's what gave them
away—the desire to let someone know they had the starring
role. The urge to take credit and to have their brilliance
admired eventually became overwhelming. Or maybe it was
the urge to get caught. Maybe something inside said they

had caused enough carnage. Maybe those things the police labeled mistakes or happenstances were really pleas for someone to stop them.

Kate realized she'd been staring at her screen for a long time, not composing and not editing. Just thinking about Jack, wondering when he'd reach his saturation point. Distanced from the reality of what he did, would he ever give them the means to identify him, ever become overwhelmed by what he was doing?

"You got some mail, Ms. August," Lew's nephew announced. Trey was this summer's office gofer. A nice kid. Polite.

"Thanks, Trey. Put it down anywhere you can find a clean spot," she instructed, glancing up to smile at him while putting her fingers back on the keys.

Trey surveyed the clutter on her desk. Finally he grinned at her, handing a package and some letters over her computer. Automatically, Kate reached up to take them.

"I don't think you've *got* a clean spot," he said truthfully.

"I think you're right," she acknowledged, smiling at him.

"You working on the bomber?" he asked, watching her pile the mail he'd given her on top of the wire releases.

"Trying to. I think I've run out of things to write."

"Cops don't have anything, do they?"

"So they say," Kate agreed. She sometimes wondered if Kahler knew as little as he said he did. Occasionally there was something at the back of his eyes that made her question his claim to have come clean on everything they had. People like Kahler always knew more than they told you.

"You think they'll catch him?" Trey asked, his face serious.

The public's right to know, Kate thought again. "Eventually. He'll make a mistake or somebody will remember something. Or somebody will see a link between the victims that will trace back to Jack. They'll catch him.''

''I guess you're right,'' he said, sounding relieved.

After he'd moved on to deliver the rest of the morning's mail, Kate allowed herself a small smile. She supposed she was some kind of authority figure to Trey, someone in the know. If she thought they'd catch Jack, that was good enough for him.

Fingers still resting on the keys, she glanced at the package he'd given her. It was wrapped in brown paper and tied with white twine. She turned it around to be sure that the return address said what she thought it did. Thorne Barrington.

What in the world would Thorne Barrington be sending her? she wondered. Even as she thought it, she knew. He was a man who had been reared in the old school. *Well brought up* was the phrase. A Southern gentleman, as she had thought Friday night, and there was a code that went along with that training.

She would have thought he'd send flowers—roses, maybe. But he didn't have to be caught in the Dark Ages. Just because he lived in that mausoleum didn't mean he wouldn't know something beyond the traditional dozen roses. Maybe candy. Godiva chocolates. In a box this size that would be a hell of a gesture.

Which he could well afford, she thought, opening her center drawer to take out her scissors. She couldn't find them, so she pushed her chair backwards on its plastic pad, putting the package in her lap. That gave her more room to open the drawer, and she found her scissors at the very back. She snipped the cord and put it on her desk. She turned the box over and slid her fingers under the taped, triangular flaps, lifting them free. The paper had not been taped together where it met at the center back, so it slipped off easily. The box was not the distinctive gold foil she'd half expected. It was plain white cardboard, a little heavier than the kind you bought at Christmas from Wal-Mart, five for a dollar ninety-nine. She turned it over and eased the top off.

The explosion wasn't that loud. No more startling than a backfire or a distant gunshot, she thought later—when she was capable again of coherent thought. Only it had gone off in her lap, literally under her nose. Whatever exploded had enough force to propel the lid out of her hands and across the room. And enough force to carry the metallic red confetti the box had contained almost ceiling high, so that it rained down on her desk, showering her hair and the surrounding area like some kind of crimson fallout.

Kate didn't realize she had moved, but the chair she'd been sitting in banged into the desk behind her, and suddenly she was standing, knees trembling, the remains of the package scattered over her feet and the plastic square she was standing on.

"What the hell was that!"

She was aware that the comment came from Trey. She even knew when someone pulled the chair back and helped her sit down in it. She thought she responded to the questions about whether she was all right. Someone handed her a small cup of water from the cooler, but she couldn't hold it. She was embarrassed by how much her hand was shaking. Finally Lew was there to take the paper cup away, to stop the icy drops from sloshing out to mark the pink linen dress she was wearing.

She wanted to put her head down on her desk and cry, to scream, to do something. Instead she kept saying to the gathering crowd that she was all right. "I'm all right," she said over and over, wondering if she would ever really be again.

"It was with the other mail. I couldn't remember where I'd heard the name before. I didn't make the connection."

Trey's voice, explaining. Some part of her mind was still working, still functioning on a rational level. The other part

was looking for a cave to hide in. A hole to crawl into.
Who could know how they'd react, Lew had asked. Now
she knew what it felt like. At least on some minimal level
she knew.

"I didn't recognize the name," Trey went on, enjoying
the limelight, maybe, now that it was obvious no one was
hurt. When he'd come charging up to her desk, his face
had been as blanched as Kate supposed hers was. "Thorne
Barrington. I knew I'd heard it, you know, but I couldn't
exactly remember where."

I didn't put it together either, Kate thought, *and I had a
lot more reason to than you, Trey. Only I never suspected...*

What did she suspect? she wondered suddenly. That Jack
had sent her a fake bomb? A warning because her insightful
series had hit too near home? Yeah, right. She and about a
thousand other journalists who were cooking up stories
based on the bits and pieces which were all they had on
Jack.

The bomber was *real* worried about what she was revealing in her articles, which, when you got down to it was
nada, nothing, zilch. Jack the Tripper wasn't worried about
Kate August. Which meant, of course, that he hadn't sent
the package. She knew who had filled a box with red confetti and some kind of explosive and had it delivered to her
office. *You want to know how it feels to have a bomb go
off in your hands, Ms. August?*

The bastard had even put his return address on the package. He had called her a vampire, feeding off the pain of
other people, and he had apparently decided to arrange a
taste of what it was like to be those other people. She had
been lulled into believing his apology. She wondered if she
would have been fool enough to have opened the package
if he hadn't apologized Friday night. She would like to
think she wouldn't have been this stupid if she hadn't had
that personal contact.

After all, she was one of the few people who knew about

the return address on Jack's last package, something the police hadn't made public. So Barrington couldn't know, of course, that she'd been told. The return address wasn't supposed to trigger any red flags. He had even asked her Friday night, mockingly, *"Afraid, Ms. August?"* He had wanted her to feel as terrified as she'd accused him of being, and so he'd arranged a demonstration of exactly how that terror felt.

She opened her bottom drawer and took out her purse. She was aware of the confusion of voices around her, but her head was remarkably clear, her mental processes functioning very well, she thought. Considering.

"Excuse me," she said to whoever was standing over her chair. *Lew,* she realized, looking up. "I have to go now."

"Relax, Kate. The police will be here in a few minutes. I've already called Detective Kahler. They'll want to talk—"

"I have to go *now*," she interrupted, insistent. She pulled her arm away from his hand. "I *have* to go. Please, Lew, I really have to go."

Maybe he could read the building hysteria. Not just fear any longer. Anger. She was so furious she could strangle Thorne Barrington with her bare hands for making her feel this way. Especially when she remembered how she'd daydreamed about him, practically drooled over his damn pictures, for heaven's sake.

"At least let me drive you home. Kahler can meet us at your apartment. You're in no condition to drive," Lew argued. His voice was quiet and reasonable, like someone talking to a child who was afraid of the monsters under her bed.

"I'm *fine*," she said again, walking past him. She was relieved no one else attempted to stop her. The room was perfectly quiet now, a silence unnatural to its usual frantic atmosphere. With every step she took, pieces of red confetti fell out of her hair, off her shoulders.

When she reached the hallway, away from the watching eyes of the people in the newsroom, she stopped. She shook her head, aware of the resulting shower of metallic bits. She glanced down at them, scattered over the flat charcoal of the commercial carpet. Several caught the light from the ceiling track, glittering like freshly spilled droplets of blood. She picked off a couple that had clung to the damp spots on her dress.

A newsreel picture of Mrs. Kennedy climbing the stairs of the airplane that day in Dallas, still wearing that blood-splattered pink suit flickered into her head. Blood. That's why he'd made them red. Like the room in the boarding-house in Austin, she thought, and then she was forced to block the image.

Did he think this was some kind of joke? Even given the fact that she'd entered his home, invaded his damned privacy, did he believe she deserved this? How sick could you get?

Pretty sick, her subconscious jeered. From the mail she'd gotten since she'd started the series, she certainly had cause to know that there were a lot of very sick people out there. Only she had never before believed Thorne Barrington was one of them.

SHE SHOULD HAVE KNOWN the gate would be locked. She had pulled up to the curb exactly as she had on Friday night, but today the security system was clearly back in place. She wondered briefly if Barrington had been expecting her.

She opened the car door and stepped out, the heat rising around her from the street and the sidewalk. There had to be a bell or a buzzer, something to let the inhabitants of the house know they had a caller. She found it beside the gate, almost directly above where the dog had been tied Friday night.

As she waited for some response to her jab on the button, she looked over the wide, tree-lined street to watch the construction crew working on the ruined house that stood directly across from the Barrington mansion. It had been the victim of a recent fire, windows charred and the glass blown out. In some places the damage was enough that she could see into the exposed rooms, their walls literally burned away.

Heat waves shimmered off the pavement between the two old mansions, despite the scattered shade of the oaks, and she wondered how the workers could continue to labor in the sweltering heat.

"May I help you?"

Apparently there was no intercom. An old man stood inside the fence, waiting for her response to his question. He was thin and stooped, wearing...what butlers wear, Kate realized with a trace of amusement, despite her anger. Like something out of a thirties movie, those old black-and-white society comedies. He looked like Carole Lombard's butler.

The sparse white hair was neatly combed, but clearly visible under its sweep was the flesh-colored bandage on his forehead. Elliot, she thought. This was Elliot. And Barrington was right. That big lummox of a puppy would certainly be too much for this fragile old man.

"I'd like to see Judge Barrington, please," she said, smiling at him. She hid her anger, but it took a great deal of effort. First she had to get in; then she'd tell that bastard exactly what she thought about his sick prank.

"I'm sorry, but Judge Barrington is not receiving guests," the butler said. He placed a trembling, liver-spotted hand on the crossbar of the gate, as if to steady himself.

It bordered on criminal to send this old man outside into today's inferno, Kate thought. Why didn't Barrington answer his own door, or at least hire staff that didn't appear to be at the point of death? "Are you all right?" she asked.

She wondered what she'd do if he fell again. She wouldn't even be able to get inside to help him.

"Oh, indeed, miss. I'm fine, thank you."

"Would you please tell the Judge that Kate August is here? I'd like to...thank him. Would you tell him that, please?"

"Of course, but I must warn you, miss, that he doesn't see visitors. He hasn't for years."

"Please," Kate begged, smiling at him again, "just ask."

She wondered why she was bothering. Barrington wasn't going to let her in. Why should he? He had to know how angry she would be. Her only hope was that he might personally want to gloat over the results of what he'd done.

"Do you have a card, Miss August?" the old man asked.

"Of course." She fumbled in her purse and then handed him her card through the wrought iron bars. His hand trembled so much she was afraid he'd drop it in the transfer, and she knew if he did, he'd never manage to bend over to pick it up. However, he finally grasped it and turned to totter up the walk. She held her breath as he climbed the steps to disappear into the house, shutting the glass-paneled door firmly behind him.

Kate took a breath, letting it out almost in a sigh. She was still angry, but the flight or fight adrenaline that had brought her here was beginning to fade, and she wondered if she'd be able to get up enough steam to say all the things she wanted to express to Thorne Barrington. *If* she got in, and that appeared to be a very big if.

KATE AUGUST, he thought again, looking down at the card Elliot had handed him. She'd come to thank him for dropping the charges, he supposed. At least he thought the old man had said something about thanking him.

He hadn't listened too carefully after he'd heard her name. He had surprised himself by agreeing to see her, but his responses to being told she was here had surprised him even more. Anticipation. And something else, stirring deep and hot in his body. A feeling that he had almost forgotten.

Despite the situation Friday night, he hadn't been able to forget her. He had especially liked her voice. Low and husky. A "whiskey-voiced" woman was the old expression. And he had remembered her perfume. Released by her skin's warmth, its sweetness had invaded the room. As it had later in the car. All the way home, he'd savored the lost pleasure of being surrounded by a woman's perfume.

When he woke last night, it had not been the familiar nightmares, not those scenes of devastation that the media celebrated, which had pulled him from sleep. Instead, her softness had been under his lips, the familiar fragrance, the smooth texture of her skin tantalizing. His body had responded to the dream. A hard, aching response. It had taken him a long time to go back to sleep, and he had remembered it all this morning. He had lain in bed, remembering the dream. Remembering Kate August. And now she was here again.

IT WAS PROBABLY ten minutes before the front door reopened, and Kate watched the old man retrace his slow journey down the walkway. This time he carried a black umbrella, still furled. Kate found herself wishing he'd use it as a walking stick, but he carried it with the crook over his forearm. Her card seemed to have disappeared, but she was gearing herself up for another polite Southern argument if he refused her admittance.

"I'm so sorry to have kept you waiting," Elliot said, releasing the latch on the inside of the gate, "especially in this terrible heat."

Unbelievingly, Kate watched as he pulled the gate inward, inviting her to step inside. Then the butler carefully reclosed the gate and checked the lock. He turned to her with a smile, opening the umbrella to hold over her head.

"I thought that a little shade might be welcome," he said.

"Thank you. That was very kind of you," Kate responded, biting the inside of her cheek to prevent a smile.

"My pleasure. Judge Barrington sees so few visitors. I must confess," he said, "that I was a little surprised when he agreed to see you. Please don't misunderstand. I was very pleased, of course, but surprised. Since that terrible, terrible explosion, you know." He paused and glanced at her face.

"I know," Kate said.

She was trying to slow her pace enough to match his and to stay under the umbrella he carried. Anything else would have been rude, and no matter how angry she might be at Barrington, she could never be unpleasant to this old man. Since the butler was at least two inches shorter than she, Kate was finding it difficult to accommodate his umbrella.

"I worry about him being so alone," Elliot confessed.

So did I, Kate thought bitterly, *until he pulled his little stunt today.*

"I'm so glad you've come, Miss August," Elliot said, as he opened the door for her, inviting her into the coolness of the dark interior. He carefully closed and refurled the umbrella and then placed it in the stand by the door. "Mr. Thorne is in the parlor. He said you would know the way. If you'll excuse me, I think I'll fix some iced tea. That would go nicely on a day like this, don't you think?"

Kate's own training was too strong. She knew all the things she was supposed to say, and she found herself saying them without effort. "Tea would be wonderful, but please don't go to any trouble."

"No trouble at all. I'm delighted you're here. You go right in, Miss August. Mr. Thorne is waiting for you."

Somehow in the enforced intimacy of the shared umbrella, Barrington had become Mr. Thorne. She had been accepted. By Elliot, at least, who was now going to make them some iced tea.

And then they could have a tea party. Just Thorne Barrington and her. That was okay. She probably would, she thought on reflection, work up quite a thirst telling him exactly what she thought about the way his mind worked. Surprisingly, she found she was dreading this confrontation. She was still angry, but somewhere in the back of her mind, she remembered all the things she'd said to this man. She'd accused him of hiding, and maybe he was, but who had given her the right to judge?

What gave him the right to do what he did today? To make a fool of me in front of everyone. To scare me to death.

She pushed the sliding door open. The room was dim, an artificial twilight, the heavy shades all pulled to keep out the afternoon sun and its heat. It reminded her of her grandmother's house in Tupelo, always darkened against the oppressive invasion of the summer heat. People had kept cool that way in her grandmother's day, but here she could hear the air conditioner's efficient hum in the background. Apparently the darkened parlor was simply another anachronism, clinging to the dead past.

"Ms. August," Barrington said from across the room. "You asked to see me?"

He was standing. The perfect gentleman. She was a little surprised to see that he was wearing jeans and a dark knit shirt. Somehow she had expected a suit. Because of the butler's formality, she supposed. But there was no reason, of course, for Thorne Barrington to be formally dressed in his own home.

His shoulders were broader than she'd expected, and his chest filled the cotton shirt, its muscled width tapering to a flat belly and slim hips. She'd seen his physique often enough in the photographs, but as he had last night, he seemed a little larger than life in person. A little overwhelming.

His eyes were very dark, surrounded by that sweep of long lashes. His coal-black hair was longer than in the pictures and maybe touched with gray at the temples. Something new, but what was he now? Thirty-seven? Thirty-eight, she thought. Old enough to be graying. The same strong nose and square chin. The individual features weren't that remarkable, but taken together—

"Ms. August?" he interrupted her inventory, questioning.

"Why would you do that to me, you bastard?" Kate asked.

That wasn't what she'd intended to say, but it was the crux of the matter. Why would anyone, no matter what he thought about what she did for a living, do what he had done today?

"I beg your pardon," Barrington said.

"Did you want to make me afraid? Is that what it was all about? Because if you did, I think you should know how well you succeeded," Kate said.

She moved closer to him, almost across the width of the room, to hold out her hands. Despite the time that had passed, they were still shaking. Seeing that, she could feel the anger Elliot's kindness had tempered beginning to rebuild. The dark eyes left hers to move downward to her trembling fingers.

"I couldn't even hold the cup of water they gave me," she told him, wanting him to understand what he'd done. Suddenly she clenched her hands into fists and brought them back to her sides. She regretted showing him her trembling fingers, regretted giving him that satisfaction.

Furious, more with her own fear than with what he'd done, she forced herself to look up. His dark eyes were slightly narrowed. She was close enough that she could see the small lines around them. There was a whitened scar on his temple. And she had been right about the graying. Even that looked right. Perfect. *Too good-looking for his own good,* echoed in her head.

"I didn't deserve that," she said aloud. "No matter what you think about what I do for a living, I didn't deserve what you did to me today."

"Ms. August, forgive me, but I don't have any idea what you're talking about. I thought you were here because of—"

"Don't you *dare* pretend you don't know. Your name was on the package. Your return address. Don't you dare pretend. At least, admit that you—"

"The *package?*" he interrupted.

That had certainly gotten a response, Kate thought with satisfaction. Even his voice had changed, no longer polite. No longer pretending he didn't know what she was talking about.

"The package you sent me," she went on. "The exploding one. The red confetti. It worked just like you intended. It blew up in my face and shot that damn red crap all over the office, and I was *scared,* Judge Barrington. Real scared. I really thought for a second that I was dead. Is that how you wanted me to feel? Is that what you wanted? To make me understand what you felt?"

His face hadn't changed. He was still watching her with those too-dark eyes. Almost black, she thought. She'd never seen eyes that dark.

"I didn't send you a package, Ms. August. Not of any kind. Not today. Not ever."

"I accused you of hiding, of being afraid, and maybe that bothered some image you have of yourself. So you got even. Only that's really sick, you know. Especially for someone…" She paused, whether for breath to go on or because he was watching her so intently, she wasn't sure. He didn't speak into the sudden silence, so she tried to pick up the thread of her anger.

"Especially with Jack out there, *really* blowing people up. Sending death out with your return address—" She stopped abruptly. She shouldn't have told him that she knew his address was on the last bomb. It wasn't public knowledge, and he would wonder how she knew. "It was sick. For *anybody* it was a sick thing to do, but especially for you," she finished lamely.

She had run out of steam, faced with his lack of response. The lines of his face revealed no emotion. He was giving nothing away. The silence grew, stretching, filling up all the dark corners of the room. Finally he moved, blinked, something. Kate wasn't sure exactly how or why, but the stillness was broken, and then he spoke very distinctly.

"I didn't send you a package. If you're aware that the bomber used my return address on Friday, then you must also be aware of the implications of its use on any package you received. I suggest you discuss this with the police, Ms. August. And now if you'll excuse me," he said.

He was dismissing her. *Inviting* her to go to the police. Trying to make a bigger fool of her than he'd already made. Except they were both aware that Jack didn't send red confetti. Jack sent bombs. Explosives and shrapnel. Enough to kill. This son of a bitch was denying responsibility for what had happened today, talking to her as Lew had earlier, in the same soothing adult-to-hysterical-child tone.

"You're really something, you know. A real piece of work," she said, suddenly as angry as she'd been in the office. "I told you the truth about yourself, and you couldn't take it. The great Thorne Barrington couldn't face the fact that he's gone into hiding, so you had to have your revenge."

"Ms. August," he interrupted, but she went on, speaking over whatever he intended to say. Because it didn't matter what he wanted to say. She didn't want to hear it.

"Apparently there's no one around to tell you the truth. I did, and you couldn't deal with it. I let a little light into all this darkness, and you didn't like the man who was revealed. But that's not my fault, Judge Barrington. I didn't make you a coward who stopped living three years ago. Jack did that. So why don't you send *Jack* a package and leave me the hell alone.''

She saw and heard the depth of the breath he took before he answered her, but his face still revealed nothing.

"If you're finished, Elliot will show you out, but I strongly suggest you follow my advice."

He was angry. His features might not have changed, but his voice had. There was nothing like a blue-blooded Southern accent for expressing anger. She'd gotten to him all right. Since that had been her intent, she should be feeling a whole lot better than she was. Instead, she was disgusted with herself, ashamed of what she'd just said, and that made her mad at herself. What he'd done had been unforgivable, and so he deserved to hear everything she'd said if only because it *was* the truth.

"I'll follow yours if you follow mine," Kate said. "You called me a vampire, but *I'm* not the one who's afraid of the light. As a matter of fact, I think we ought to let a little more light in on this situation. The real kind. A little daylight into your mausoleum."

While she was talking, she walked around the velvet sofa to one of the long windows to the left of the fireplace. She jerked the bottom of the shade and released it, allowing it to fly up. She moved to the next one and sent it whirring to the top. She was a little shocked at how exhilarated she felt with the noise they made and with the flood of sunlight that invaded the room.

She moved behind Thorne Barrington, between his still figure and the fireplace, to the windows on the other side. She threw those shades upward with the same angry satisfaction. It was as bright now inside the room as it had been on the heat-parched street outside.

When she turned back to face the man who had so infuriated her, she realized that Barrington hadn't moved. Despite the noise, he hadn't turned around to watch what she was doing. Apparently he intended to make no response to her childishness, but the muscles in his broad shoulders and his back were rigid beneath the dark knit shirt.

Somehow she wasn't quite satisfied with that. Not enough reaction, she supposed. She walked back to where she had stood before, back to face the man who had sent her the package this morning.

"I guess I was mistaken," she said, her tone revealing contempt. The black eyes were slightly narrowed, but they met hers unflinchingly. "All this light, and you still didn't melt. Maybe you're not a vampire after all."

Barrington said nothing, his face set and controlled. Obviously, he didn't intend to give her the satisfaction of a reaction, and now that her tantrum was over, she realized how childish she must have appeared, throwing up the shades of his windows and shouting at him about how he should live his life.

She had already headed toward the sliding doors when they opened unexpectedly. Elliot entered, silver tray, tall glasses of tea with fresh mint leaves garnishing the tops, linen napkins, the works. *The best of the South,* she thought, cynically. *Real Southern hospitality.*

"I don't think I'll be able to stay for the tea, but thank you anyway, Elliot," she said, brushing by him. She just needed to be out of this room, out of Thorne Barrington's house.

She heard the butler's agitated exclamation behind her and the sound of breaking glass. She wondered if Barrington had thrown something, and knew that if he had, that would at least be some indication that she had gotten under his skin, threatened that iron control.

By that time she had reached the glass-paneled front door, but she turned back before she stepped through it, guilt and regret crowding her throat. What she had said had been unforgivably cruel, and in saying it, she had been both loud and rude, the only crimes a woman could be found guilty of in the South. She knew by the changes in the quality of light filtering through to the foyer that Elliot or Barrington was in the process of pulling down the shades she'd raised, returning the house to its eternal darkness. *Hiding.*

Three years hadn't changed this situation, and her cruelty certainly wouldn't. She shook her head, ridiculing herself for thinking she could change anything here. A piece of the red confetti he'd sent her fluttered to lie on the hardwood floor. She left it there and walked outside into the sunshine.

Chapter Four

By the time Kate had driven home, whatever adrenaline rush had carried her through the confrontation with Barrington was fading. She wanted only to crawl back into the bed she had not had time to make and pull the covers over her head.

She had begun the process of extracting her keys from the bottom of her purse before she reached the door to her apartment, shuffling through the junk she had shoved into the black leather bag for safekeeping. When she found them, she looked up to insert the key into the lock and realized the door wasn't closed. There was an inch of space between it and the frame, and despite her hurry this morning, she knew she hadn't left it that way.

The terror that mushroomed in her stomach was almost as strong as her reaction to the fake bomb had been. Was it possible that whoever had sent the package was waiting inside? *Not* Barrington. Was it possible that the package had *not* been the sick prank she had accused him of, but something else? Someone else. Someone really dangerous.

But if someone *were* lying in wait in her apartment, she forced herself to reason, he wouldn't have left the door open. That would be a dead giveaway of his presence, unless he was trying to do exactly what he had just accomplished—still trying to frighten her. *And if that is the pur-*

pose, then damn it, he certainly is succeeding, she thought, pushing the door open enough to see into her small living room. At what the widening doorway revealed, relief washed over her.

Byron Kahler was sitting on her couch, thumbing through one of the magazines she'd arranged on the coffee table. He had looked up when she pushed the door inward, hazel eyes assessing, but he didn't say anything.

"If I were Judge Barrington, I'd have you arrested for breaking and entering," she said. She walked into the apartment and put her purse down on the table to the left of the door.

"I picked up a few tricks of the trade through the years," Kahler said.

"And it seemed like a good idea to use them on my door?" She was relieved it was Kahler sitting on her couch, but a little surprised that he'd jimmied her lock to get in.

"I guess I owe you an apology," he said.

"I'll settle for an explanation."

"When I got to your office, Garrison told me you'd gone home. He was concerned about you."

"He sent you to check on me?"

"We have to talk about what happened anyway. Officially talk. I rang the bell, and when there was no answer…"

"You just broke in."

"I was afraid you might have—I don't know—gone off the deep end a little. When I couldn't get you to the door, I decided it might be wise to investigate. I even thought that whoever had sent the package might have tried something else."

She hesitated, weighing her feelings about the invasion of her privacy against the idea that he'd cared enough about her to come personally. "Thanks," she said finally, almost grudgingly.

"You're welcome," Kahler said, "and you need a better lock. All it took was a credit card and a few seconds."

"I'll keep that in mind."

She walked across the room and sat down on the love seat facing the couch. His eyes followed her, and knowing that questions were inevitable, given it was his job to ask them, she took a deep breath, trying to gather her control. When she thought she had found enough composure to talk, she looked up. The detective's usually penetrating gaze had softened, resting on her features with something that looked like compassion.

"You want to tell me your version of what happened?" he suggested. It took her a second to realize he meant what had happened at her office and not what she had done at Barrington's mansion. There was no way he could know about that. Not yet.

"There's not that much to tell. Trey brought the package in with the other mail. Plain brown paper wrappings. It was tied with string and had Barrington's return address. I thought it was a gift, maybe even some kind of apology for Friday night."

Kahler also couldn't know about the judge's appearance at the precinct house, but she decided not to get into all her reasons for opening the package, not unless he asked. "When I opened the box, it blew up in my face. It was filled with red confetti that went everywhere, all over the damn office."

"We don't think it was Jack, Kate, if that'll make you feel any better. I sent the package to the lab. We won't have the results for a couple of days, but I can tell you that in no way did it resemble what Jack sends. It worked through compressed air, just enough force to blow the lid and scatter the confetti."

He was reassuring her, she realized, trying to make her feel less afraid. Only he wasn't making her feel any better.

He was only reinforcing the conclusion she'd already reached.

"I *did* have enough presence of mind to realize that Jack doesn't fool around with confetti, Kahler. The only thing my package had in common with the others was they all blew up." She paused, again fighting her anger against the man who had sent the package. "And that son of a bitch knows exactly how it feels," she added. "That's the one thing I can't get over. He knows, better than anyone, how I felt this morning."

"You think it was *Barrington?*" Kahler asked, his voice expressing his surprise.

"Who else could it have been? He had motive—to get back at me for what I'd said to him, for coming into his house. The timing seems a little too coincidental *not* to implicate him. Who else would get his jollies scaring me spitless?"

"Nothing I know about Barrington would lead me to believe that he would do something like that."

"Nothing you know?" she repeated, letting her sarcasm show. "Like the fact that he never leaves his house, not even to attend his father's funeral. That he lives in the dark like some kind of—" She stopped abruptly, remembering all she had said to the man they were discussing. *Like some kind of vampire.* She remembered, too, Barrington sitting alone in the darkened room, the faint music floating out into the night like smoke. "Like some kind of creep," she finished instead. "Face it, Kahler. *He's* the one who's gone off the deep end." Her tone was bitter, but Kahler wouldn't understand. He didn't know about the folder with the pictures of the man she'd admired so long.

"Look, I know you're angry at Barrington for having you hauled off the other night, but there are…explanations for some of those things," Kahler said, his voice reasonable.

"He just sits there in the dark. What kind of explanation

is there for that? What kind of explanation for the crap he pulled with the package? What *kind* of explanation?'' she demanded angrily.

''We don't know he sent the package, Kate.''

She laughed, a small, tight derision of sound. ''Right,'' she agreed sarcastically. ''*You* may not know. If not His Honor, then who? Who else *could* it be?''

''Someone who doesn't like your writing style? Hell, maybe somebody thinks you misused a semicolon,'' Kahler suggested. The hazel eyes were carefully controlled, but his tone had lightened. ''There are a lot of crazies out there, August.''

He was certainly right about that, Kate thought. Several of the letters she'd received about the series had contained graphic illustrations of bomb blasts, dismemberments and the like—crudely drawn but effective. As a matter of course, she had pitched them into the round file, but now she wondered if she should have saved them, turned them over to whoever in the police department was in charge of checking out the crazies.

''Lucky for us,'' Kahler went on, ''not all of them want to kill people. Some of them just like sending stuff through the mail. Dead rats or birds. Voodoo dolls complete with pins. All kinds of crap. Maybe even red confetti. This wasn't Jack, but that doesn't mean it has to be Barrington.''

''Why send it to me?'' she asked. ''Seriously.''

''Maybe someone's been following the series. Maybe they didn't like what you wrote. Who knows what sets people off.''

''You admire him, don't you?'' she asked. His eyes widened slightly at the comment, and she realized that her thoughts had outpaced the conversation. ''Barrington,'' she explained.

''What makes you think I *admire* Barrington?''

''You tell me to leave him alone. That he's been through hell. You reject the obvious about the package—that Barrington was the crazy who sent it. You even defend the way he lives.''

"I'm not defending him, and you seem to have forgotten who we're talking about. Barrington doesn't need me to defend him. He's got all the marbles. If he wants defending, he can afford to hire the best. That's something you might want to remember before you start accusing him of this morning's prank. That accusation would probably be grounds for some kind of suit.''

"So you're telling me to ignore what happened today?''

"I'm telling you not to go off half-cocked. At least wait until the lab results come back. They might tell us something.''

"And they might not," she said. She knew that the materials used in Jack's packages had been frustratingly unrevealing.

One corner of Kahler's mouth quirked, acknowledging that possibility. "It depends on how much the sender knows about how mail bombers are caught. They'll at least let us see whether we're dealing with an amateur. Until that time, I don't think you're in any real danger, Kate." He smiled, and she thought how rare an occurrence that was. "Not if you get yourself a new lock. A dead bolt. A good heavy one.''

Kahler stood up, putting the magazine he'd been holding down on the coffee table between them. "Don't worry," he offered. "The last time I checked the statistics, nobody had ever been killed by confetti.''

She laughed, feeling better for his sardonic reassurance. It *had* helped to have Kahler here. She was even willing to forgive him for letting himself in. His eyes held a moment, and she found his rough masculinity more appealing than it had ever been before. He was a good friend, and he'd shown up at a time when she'd really needed one.

She walked him to the door. There was a brief, awkward moment when they reached it. It felt a little like saying good-night after a first date, unsure what the next move should be and who should make it.

"Thanks," she said, trying to put an end to the awkwardness.

"I'll let you know what the lab finds out," he said.

She nodded, and he turned to go. "What kind of explanation?" she asked. The words had slipped out, not even in her consciousness before they were on her lips.

"What?" Kahler asked.

"You said there were explanations for some of the things Barrington does. I just wondered what you meant."

"Off the record?" he asked.

"Yeah," she agreed. "Just between you and me." She felt free to accept his condition. This wasn't information she wanted for the series. It was personal. What could possibly explain the change in Barrington from the assured, charismatic man in those pictures into the cold recluse she had met today?

"If you use any of this, August, if any of it ever gets into print…" Kahler paused.

"Off the record," she said. "I swear. I just need to understand why."

Again the hazel eyes studied her face, trying to read, maybe, the reason she needed to know. Feeling the intensity of that assessment, her own eyes dropped momentarily, and she forced them back up to meet his.

"Personal?" he asked.

She hesitated, and finally she nodded. The muscles around Kahler's mouth tightened, and then, with an effort she could see, he deliberately wiped the sudden tension from his face.

"Since the bombing, Barrington has suffered from migraines."

"Migraines?" Kate repeated. "Headaches? What does that have to do with—"

"Apparently they're…extremely severe, and they're triggered by exposure to light."

"Light?" she echoed, remembering the satisfying whir of the rising shades, the sudden blaze of summer sunshine she'd sent into the darkened parlor.

"I don't understand all the mechanics," Kahler went on, shrugging his shoulders. "From what I was told, they're probably not related to his eye injuries, but to head trauma. Maybe damaged nerves or scar tissue. Maybe the speed at which his pupils react to sudden light. Maybe they're even psychogenic. Nobody seemed willing to pin down a definitive cause, but nobody would deny the kind of trauma Barrington suffered could cause all sorts of problems. The headaches began as soon as the bandages came off, and they haven't lessened in severity."

"How severe?"

"The usual treatment for headaches as intense as the ones Barrington has is an injection of something powerful enough to knock the sufferer out until the migraine's over. That's what they did for the judge while he was in the hospital."

"How long do they last?"

"For some people migraines can last several days. Given his situation, it makes some sense out of Barrington's decision not to expose himself to that risk."

"Why didn't you tell me about this?" Kate asked. "We talked about Barrington. Why the hell didn't you tell me?" Damn Kahler and his reticence.

"The information came from a friend, somebody at the hospital where the judge was treated after the bombing. Not Barrington's physician, but somebody who knew about the case and owed me a favor. None of this is for public consumption, August. I told you. The guy's been through enough."

"I just wish you'd told me," she said again, regret tightening her throat, regret for things she'd said and done that she certainly couldn't share with Kahler.

"I only told you now because you seemed convinced he'd sent the package, that the way he lives makes him more suspect. I wanted you to understand that there are some valid reasons for Barrington's seclusion. Maybe the headaches aren't reason enough for everything, but they help to explain the way he lives."

She nodded.

"What's the fascination, August?" he asked. His voice had changed. No longer a clinical assessment, but deeper, more intimate. *Personal.*

"I don't even understand it myself. It's just there. It's been there from the beginning."

"I guess all that money would be appealing. I can't speak for Barrington's supposed sex appeal," he said. "I never saw any of that." His lips had moved into a slight smile, but there was no matching amusement in his voice. "You know he may no longer even look the way he once did."

She almost denied that Barrington had changed—physically changed. She almost revealed that she'd seen him much more clearly since that first night when she'd acted on impulse and entered his darkened house.

"I know," she said. "For some reason, he just…interests me. Maybe it's seeing the effect Jack had on the one man who survived, and it's not the money, Kahler, no matter what you think. I can't explain what I feel. I know it's unprofessional. More than that, it's a little…weird," she admitted. "I know all that. I almost asked Lew to take me off the story because of it, but…I just can't seem to leave it alone."

"I think you ought to back off. For a lot of reasons. Let the series die a natural death. Maybe that's what the package this morning was intended to do—to tell you to back off."

"Is that what you really think, Kahler? Is that a professional assessment?"

Again the hazel gaze held hers. "Personal," he said. "I don't want you hurt, Kate."

She smiled at him. "Trust me, I don't want to be hurt. That crap this morning made me very aware of how easy it is to get someone if you really want to. All you need is an address. I found out I'm not nearly as brave as I thought I was."

"Good," Kahler said, his tone ordinary again. "A little less brave is a lot safer. Get a dead bolt, August, and think about the other—about dropping the series."

"I will," she promised.

He stepped through the door, pulling it closed behind him. The apartment seemed suddenly very empty. She walked back into the living room where they'd been sitting. She stopped before the table beside the couch. She hesitated, trying to resist, but finally she opened the drawer and looked down at the folder containing the pictures of Thorne Barrington.

She put her hand down on top of the file, but she didn't take it out. Instead she stood, touching it, the tips of her fingers whitened against the manila surface, remembering the cruelly exposing slashes of sunlight and the stillness of the man who had never turned to face the windows she'd uncovered.

"You okay?" Lew asked the next day. He pitched his question low enough that their conversation would remain private.

She glanced up from the words on her screen. "Better than yesterday. Thanks for sending Kahler. Talking to him helped."

"I don't think I can accept responsibility for that," Lew said, smiling at her. "He seemed worried about you. I think he just wanted to see for himself you were all right. He didn't seem to think your package had anything to do with Jack."

"I know. He promised to let me know what the lab finds."

"Kahler also thought it might be a good idea if you back off the series. You want me to get someone else to do the feature on the guy in Tucson, or you want to just let it stand with the articles you've done? It's your story, Kate. It has been from the beginning, so it's your decision."

"You think Kahler's right? About the package not being from Jack?"

"He gathered up the remains, and he's seen all the others."

"He told me everything was different. The mechanics. Everything. But the return address was the same on this one and the Tucson bomb, and that information hadn't been released. How could someone know about that?"

Lew shrugged. "There are always leaks. Any information gets out, if enough people know about it. Maybe not to the general public, but out just the same. The fact that Barrington's address was on the Tucson bomb would be interesting to anyone with Atlanta connections."

"I thought he'd sent it," Kate said.

"I guess that's natural, considering that you've been working on the bombings, but Kahler said—"

"Not Jack," she corrected. "Barrington. I thought Barrington had sent it."

"Judge Barrington?" Lew said, the disbelief in his voice reminding Kate of Barrington's reputation.

"I know. Kahler thought it was ridiculous, too. It's just that we have some…background." She glanced up in time to catch the surprise in Lew's brown eyes.

"I didn't know you knew Barrington," he said.

"We've met," she hedged. It was the truth, but it didn't explain why those meetings would make her suspect him. She wished that she hadn't started this. "I just keep coming back to Thorne Barrington as the sender, despite what everyone else seems to believe about him.''

"Why do you think Barrington would do something like that?''

"We had a run-in. I tried to talk to him about the bombings. I've always thought he was the key to understanding Jack's motives. There's got to be some significance to the fact that he was the first victim. But the judge made it pretty clear he didn't want to talk.''

"Knowing you, I'd bet you didn't accept his refusal.''

"Eventually. I didn't have a choice. But now I wonder if trying to talk to him made him angry enough that—''

"It wasn't Barrington,'' Lew interrupted with conviction. "There's no way someone like Thorne Barrington is going to pull a stunt like that. It's no secret he hates the press, and with reason, but still, I can't see him putting together the package you got yesterday. It's totally out of character.''

"Maybe your character changes when someone tries to blow you up,'' Kate suggested. She realized suddenly that Lew would be the perfect person to verify what Kahler had told her. "Lew, you've lived here all your life. You move in some of the same circles as the judge, know the same people. What did you hear about Barrington's injuries?''

"Information for the series?'' Lew asked.

"Not really. I just need to know. Kahler told me there was some trauma to his head. Brain damage can…change people. Personality changes. One of Kahler's sources mentioned the judge suffers from migraines, possibly psychogenic in nature.''

"Psychogenic?'' Lew questioned.

"I looked it up. It means having an emotional cause.''

"Like having a bomb go off in your hands, maybe?'' Lew asked, smiling. "That kind of emotional cause?''

Kate knew he was right. Even if the migraines were emotional in origin, that didn't mean Barrington had turned into the kind of crazy Kahler had talked about.

"I'll ask around," Lew surprised her by saying. "I know a few people who were close to Barrington at the time. They may not talk to me, but I'll see what I can find out."

"Thanks," Kate said.

"What about the series?"

"I'm not ready to give it up. Not yet. If it's possible, I'd really like to go to Tucson. I want to talk to Draper's widow. Personally, one-on-one. There's a connection between all these people, Lew. I know it in my gut. We just haven't found it yet. Somehow Draper and the others, Thornedyke Barrington included, are all connected. I don't care what the cops think, Jack's not working at random. And I think it's significant that the interval between victims has shortened. For some reason, suddenly Jack's in a hurry. Maybe we're closer than we think. Maybe the Feds have something. Or maybe he just wants it to be over. Maybe he wants to finish it."

"And nobody knows how many more people are on his list."

"We know there's at least one more name on that list," Kate said. Lew shook his head, puzzled by her comment. "One more name," she repeated. "The name at the top. The name he started with three years ago. Thornedyke Barrington."

HE OPENED HIS EYES slowly in the dimness of the massive bedroom. Even the slight movement of his lids hurt. Not the ice-pick-in-the-brain agony of the headaches, but the dull soreness in every muscle that they always left behind. He knew from experience that the effort of turning his head on the pillow would be a vivid reminder of the residual effects. He swallowed carefully, his mouth dry from the drug Elliot had administered.

He closed his eyes again. The dim, curtain-shrouded light that seeped in from the windows should not be enough to set off another attack, but it was sometimes hard to judge what was enough. Of course, with the sudden flood of summer sunlight yesterday, there had been no doubt. Because he had refused to stand there with his eyes closed while she shouted at him, he had known exactly what he faced from the moment Kate August had released that first shade. He had been too stubborn—or too stupid—to leave.

He opened his eyes again, raising the damaged right hand in an unthinking gesture, automatically protecting himself from even the faint light the draperies allowed into this sanctuary.

Vampire, he thought again, repeating the word that haunted him. *A damn vampire.* He usually had more success keeping the bitterness at bay, but remembering the troubling dreams he'd had about Kate August, he knew why that was now so hard.

KATE SPENT most of Thursday's flight to Tucson worrying about the letter she'd mailed before she left Atlanta. It had taken her most of the previous evening to write, despite the fact that she'd spent all day thinking about what she wanted to say.

Not exactly *wanted* to say, she admitted. She had written a couple of letters of apology at the beginning of her career when she had overstepped her own ethical boundaries. Because doing that had been extremely painful, she had let nothing like those incidents happen in the years since.

At least not until she'd rushed into Judge Barrington's home and thrown up the shades with the same kind of hysterical indignation that had propelled the temperance ladies to chop up bars with axes. Despite the fact that she was genuinely sorry if she had triggered one of the migraines Kahler had described and despite the fact that she was a writer by profession, it had been a very difficult letter to compose. And it had been harder to drop it into a mail slot and let it go.

That's what she had to do, she thought. Let it all go—

the guilt, the remorse *and* her fascination with Barrington. That was really what had gotten her into the situation in the first place. As soon as she got back to Atlanta, she intended to throw the folder and the pictures she'd collected into the trash. No more obsession with Thorne Barrington.

Chapter Five

Using Kahler's name and copies of the articles that had appeared in the series as her foot in the door, Kate had wrangled Jackie Draper's address and an introduction by phone from the Tucson Police Department. Although Hall Draper's widow had sounded a little confused about why she was being asked to talk to a reporter from an Atlanta paper, she agreed to the interview.

Mrs. Draper's eyes looked as if she hadn't slept since her husband's death, and Kate felt guilty about putting her through this. The comments the judge had made about her job crept into her head as she opened her notebook.

"I don't really understand what you want me to tell you, Ms. August. You said you were trying to help the authorities find a connection between the victims?"

"I don't believe Jack sends his packages at random. I think there's some link between the people the bomber targets, and if we can discover what that link is…"

"Then the police can catch him," Jackie Draper finished.

"Hopefully," Kate agreed, smiling at her.

"What kinds of things do you need to know?"

"Anything you're willing to tell me, really. The kind of man your husband was. His family. His background. Where he grew up. College. Career. Why don't you just talk, and

I'll listen. Then I can ask you anything I've thought of that you might not have covered. How does that sound?''

"Okay," Jackie Draper said.

Her eyes had already lost their focus, moving back into memories that might even provide some kind of comfort. Permission to go back to happier times. Kate found herself hoping that if what she was doing didn't help, at least it wouldn't make the grieving harder.

The soft voice went on a long time. The shadows lengthened, and the narrow strips of light that filtered between the closed slats of the blinds slowly inched across the carpet. She had begun with Hall Draper's childhood, spent in a tiny coal-mining community in Pennsylvania. It had apparently been a life of almost endless deprivation, never enough money, food or warmth.

"I think that's why he ended up here," Jackie said, a brief smile touching her lips. "He finally felt warm. You don't forget the things you do without in childhood. Or the way that doing without made you feel. You may not ever tell anybody, but you're always careful to see that your own children—"

Her voice broke, the emotion that comment had evoked seeming to catch her unaware. "I just can't imagine what Trent's going to do without him. They were so close," she whispered. "Hall's own father wasn't much. Not like we think of daddies nowadays. Maybe he was just a different generation, but remembering his own childhood, Hall always bent over backwards to make sure Trent knew how much he loved him. He was a good man, Ms. August. I don't understand why someone would do this. It doesn't make any sense. Why Hall? That's what I can't understand."

"Nobody can, Mrs. Draper. None of them really seemed to deserve what happened."

"But you think the killer *chose* them?"

"I do. I'm sorry if that…" Kate paused.

"It's all right," Jackie Draper said. "If he did do that, I want him caught. Especially if he thought Hall deserved what happened to him. If he did it out of hatred or revenge."

"Can you think of anyone who disliked your husband, Mrs. Draper?"

"Enough to kill him?" Jackie asked, shaking her head. "Hall didn't have an enemy in the world. I know that's hard to believe, but he really was a good man. He did a lot of *pro bono* work. I used to tell him we were going to starve to death while he was defending somebody who didn't have a cent. He'd tell me that people who had money would always go to someone else, and that I should be grateful poor people needed lawyers, too. I think they reminded him of the people he grew up with."

Mrs. Draper smiled slightly. Remembering. It had probably really been an issue, her chiding him for his willingness to help those who needed legal advice, but couldn't afford to pay for it.

"I wish I could take back all those things I said. All the times I fussed on him for doing what he thought was right. I just wish I could tell him—" Her soft voice stopped again, and the tears that she had mastered until now flooded the shadowed eyes. "I'm sorry," she whispered, wiping the moisture away with the tips of her fingers. Embarrassed to cry before a stranger.

"It's all right," Kate said. "I understand."

"If that's all you want to know..." Hall Draper's widow said, letting the suggestion trail.

"One more question, and then I'll leave you alone, I promise. I'm so grateful you were willing to talk to me."

Jackie Draper nodded, still trying to remove the traces of forbidden tears.

"Was there anything in your husband's life he felt he...shouldn't have done, maybe?" Kate asked. All these people, all Jack's victims seemed so ordinary, but Kate had

thought for a long time there must have been something
that made them targets for a madman. Jackie Draper's eyes
expressed her puzzlement, and Kate tried to clarify. "Something he shouldn't have gotten mixed up in? Or something
he regretted later. I don't really know—"

"Hall wasn't ever mixed up in anything that wasn't good
and decent, Ms. August."

Kate nodded, knowing she couldn't probe any deeper.
For some reason she felt exactly like the kind of vampire
Barrington had accused her of being. *Feeding off other peo-
ple's pain.*

"Thank you so much for seeing me, Mrs. Draper," she
said, standing up. "I hope some good comes out of the
information you've given me."

Hall Draper's widow nodded, standing also. Kate stuck
her notebook and pen back into the leather handbag. She
held out her hand, and Jackie Draper put hers into it. Kate
was surprised at how fragile it felt. She looked stronger than
the frail delicacy of that hand. Unless you looked into her
eyes, she thought. Kate had already turned toward the door
when the woman spoke.

"There was...one thing," Jackie Draper said, her voice
so quiet Kate had to strain to catch the words. "These
days..." She hesitated again, her shoulders hunching
slightly. "It doesn't seem like much today, but Hall was
always sorry. There wasn't anything he could have done
about it. He was just a kid, but he was sorry. Especially
after we had Trent, after he found out how much...it means
to have a child."

Kate held her breath, unwilling to slow the whispered
words.

"The girl was just...trash. I know that sounds harsh, but
she was. Hall never even knew for sure if it was his baby.
She said it was, but she was..." Again, the slender shoulders moved upward. "Even Hall knew it could have been
anybody's baby. He was sixteen. She was maybe a couple

of years younger. But the thing was…it *could* have been his baby, you know. It was possible. Hall admitted that. He told me about it. Years later. After Trent was born.''

The story died, and still Kate waited. The woman's eyes were focused again on the past, reliving the years that had moved so quickly, fluttering by with a sameness that always made you believe they would continue that way forever.

''What happened to the baby?'' Kate asked, her careful question pitched as low as the halting narrative had been.

The dark eyes came back, focused briefly on her face, and then turned away to contemplate the glowing lines of late afternoon light seeping between the slats of the mini-blinds. ''She had an abortion. That's all I know. That's all Hall knew. The family moved away after that, and he never saw her again.'' Her voice faded, and Kate thought it was the end of whatever she intended to tell her. Until she added, ''*That's* the one thing my husband regretted in his life, Ms. August. That poor lost baby.''

''They'll find the guy who did it,'' Kate said. ''I promise.''

Jackie Draper nodded, and her eyes returned to the windows.

KATE FOUND A MESSAGE from Kahler when she got back to her motel room. Apparently he had learned from Lew that Kate was coming out to interview Mrs. Draper. She sat down on the edge of the queen-size bed and dialed the local number he'd left.

''Kahler.'' The deep voice was pleasant, familiar, a welcome touch of home, despite the slight accent.

''August,'' she countered, smiling.

''Don't try to be cute,'' he said, his voice relaxing into something less official.

''What?'' she teased. ''You don't think I'm cute? I'm hurt.''

There was no answer for a few seconds. Kahler wasn't

usually slow with a comeback, and again there was something odd about the brief silence.

"I think you're cute," he said.

That had almost sounded sincere. Devoid of sarcasm.

"Thanks. I think you're cute, too—like a cobra or some other predator. So spill your guts. Tell me what you've found out since you've been here?"

"Meet me for dinner," he suggested.

"I don't know if my expense account will stretch that far. Unless you're game for McDonald's," she said, relieved they seemed to be back on a more normal footing.

"I'm inviting you."

"You get a raise?" she asked. "I thought cops were like reporters—in the business just for the sheer love of it all."

"I can afford to buy you dinner, August. You got a car?"

"Want me to pick you up?" she asked.

"No, I have a couple of things to finish up. Meet me at a place called Ellington's. Thirty minutes."

THE RESTAURANT was more upscale than the ones where they had eaten together in Atlanta. Kate briefly wished she had taken time to change her clothes and then shrugged away her concern. They didn't have the kind of relationship where you worried about how you looked. She had already been seated, looking over the restaurant's offerings when Kahler arrived. She glanced up when the hostess brought him to the table. He looked tired.

"Hard day?" she asked.

His eyes flicked up from their contemplation of the dinner selections. "A real bitch of a day."

"You go to Draper's office?"

He nodded, his gaze again deliberately focused on the menu.

Obviously, he didn't want to talk about the bombing. She couldn't blame him. She wished she had never gone to Austin. It had taken her weeks to get that scene out of her head.

Even now the images would reappear suddenly, out of no-where, catching her unaware, no less vivid for the time she had put between.

She looked back down at the menu, although she had already decided what she was going to order. Kahler had asked her to meet him, which meant he didn't intend to stonewall. She'd just have to let him work his way around to talking in his own time.

"The salmon looks good," she offered.

"I don't think you ever get used to it," Kahler said. His voice was low, just above the background buzz of conversation. He hadn't looked up, eyes still directed at the menu. "You think you're ready for it, that you've developed some—I don't know—some kind of barrier between yourself and the reality of it."

She let the noises of the restaurant drift between them a few seconds. "I talked to Draper's widow today," she said, closing her menu and laying it beside her plate. When she looked up, the hazel eyes were focused on her face. Waiting.

"It seems the worst thing Hall Draper ever did was *maybe* knock some girl up when he was a kid. Apparently that possibility bothered him for the rest of his life."

"His wife tell you that?"

"That and about everything else that ever happened to him," she said. Despite her attempt, somehow she couldn't be objective or cynical about Hall Draper. Something about his wife's hesitant memories had touched a chord, too deeply felt to be glib about. So she told Kahler the truth.

"He was a good man who had worked hard to get where he was. He did a lot of charity cases. She regretted fussing on him about those." She paused, remembering the pain in those shadowed eyes. "He didn't deserve to be blown up."

Kahler's gaze shifted, seeming to focus on the people that were being seated a few tables away. "What makes you think the rest of them did?"

She shook her head. Kahler was right. Nothing they had uncovered about any of the victims seemed to warrant the horror of what had happened to them.

"Some of them just seemed less real to me. Draper was raised in some little coal-mining town. He pulled himself up by hard work and his own force of character. Then the American dream gets blown to smithereens by some maniac who doesn't even have the guts to do it personally. Murder by long distance."

"Sounds like you've got the lead paragraph of your story."

There had been nothing reproachful in Kahler's tone, but for some reason the comment hurt. It had sounded too much like Barrington's crack. As if she were only interested in these people for the increase in circulation their stories provided.

"Believe it or not, I hadn't even thought about writing the story. I'm not quite the vampire Barrington accused me of being."

"Look, I'm sorry. Maybe getting together tonight wasn't such a good idea. Seeing the scene always makes me edgy. I always feel like there must be more that we could be doing. Only I never know what. Nothing we do seems to work with this guy."

"It's not your fault. Let's forget Jack tonight. Let's talk about something besides murder and mayhem for a change."

"I'm a cop, August. A homicide cop. I'm not sure I *know* anything else. I'm not good at social stuff, and other than Jack, you and I don't seem to have a lot in common."

"I'm not complaining. We can talk about the weather. Baseball. I don't care. I'm just glad I'm not eating room service alone. You don't have to be entertaining."

He laughed, the sound pleasant and unfamiliar. Kahler didn't laugh nearly often enough, she thought, smiling at him.

HE WALKED HER to her rental car after the meal. "How long are you staying?" Kahler asked, as he unlocked the door and then handed her the keys.

"A few days. I guess I need to see what else I can turn up on Draper. His widow's not exactly an unbiased source. I'll stay until I think Lew's gotten his money's worth out of the trip. How about you?"

"I'm going back tomorrow."

"I'll call you when I get back to Atlanta," she said.

Kahler nodded. Suddenly, the tension that had been between them at her apartment door was back. He had bought her dinner. Maybe he thought that meant he was entitled to a good-night kiss.

"Thanks for dinner," she said.

"Thank *you*. I needed the company."

"Me, too," she admitted.

The silence after that admission lasted too long, and she found herself looking for something to say. "I thought I might go to Draper's hometown," she offered. It was an idea that had been growing since she'd left Hall Draper's neat suburban house. She'd try it out on Kahler before she approached Lew.

"What for?" Kahler asked. They were still standing, the opened door between them.

"I don't know. Just to poke around. To see if anyone remembers anything about the story Mrs. Draper told me. See if I can find any trace of that girl."

"You think she's the bomber, August? Revenge for a pregnancy that happened years ago?" Kahler asked. Obviously, he wasn't impressed with the lead. Lew probably would be underwhelmed also, especially when he thought about costs.

"I don't think she's the bomber. I just don't have anything else to try. Dead end. Just like it's been all along with Jack. Just a lot of dead ends."

"I hope that wasn't supposed to be a pun," Kahler said.

"That's not funny."

"It wasn't meant to be. A lot of dead ends. Dead people."

"Who apparently didn't deserve to be dead. What kind of person does something like that?"

A strictly rhetorical question. There was no answer, and they both were aware of it. A group of diners leaving the restaurant passed within a few feet, glancing at them curiously.

Kahler waited until the party had moved on before he asked, "You remember a guy named Wilford Mays?"

"Mays?" Kate repeated, trying to place the name. She knew she had heard it, but she couldn't think in what context. "It doesn't really ring a bell," she said.

"School bombing back in the sixties? Two little boys who had gone back inside to get a forgotten book were killed."

Kate nodded her head, remembering hearing the story, but not details. The bombing was something that had happened more than thirty years ago, during the height of opposition to school integration in Georgia.

"Mays was probably the guy responsible, but he was never convicted," Kahler went on. "One of the men who had supposedly been in on the planning got religion in his old age. He tried to implicate Mays, but his own credibility was questionable and his memory faulty after all those years. The state could never put together a case they thought would convince a jury. They did eventually haul Mays into court on some charge that had resulted from a search of his house—possessing an illegal firearm, a short-barrelled shotgun, very minor stuff compared to the murders they wanted to stick him for. I don't remember everything, but the judge who heard the case put him away for as long as he could."

"And?" Kate said, waiting for the punch line.

"The judge on that case, the illegal weapons charge or whatever it was, was Thorne Barrington."

"Then surely somebody has checked Mays out before now."

"Whoever ran the dockets of Barrington's old cases saw only a firearms charge. Since there was no connection to bombs, no alarm went off."

"So how did you come up with Mays?"

"You keep telling me these killings are related, so I went back over those cases myself. For some reason, the name triggered something. I pulled the informant's information and then the original police reports on the school bombing. The MO, the materials, everything is different, totally different, so logic says there's probably no connection. But Mays is someone who at one time may have killed at long distance, and Barrington came in contact with him."

"*And* put him away," Kate said.

"Barrington sentenced him to the max, but with time off for good behavior, Mays served less than a year."

"You think Mays is Jack?"

"Not based on things we usually use to tie cases together. Nothing Mays did was like what Jack does, but still it's hard to deny the significance—another bomber with ties to Barrington."

"Does Mays fit the FBI profile of the Tripper? A brilliant loner? Product of a dysfunctional family? Probably abused?"

"Jack's fooled us on everything else. Why wouldn't he be able to screw us on the profile?"

"Is Mays that smart? Smart enough to get away with mail bombs? That's a hell of a lot different from setting off dynamite in an empty building—a supposedly empty building."

"No way to know," Kahler acknowledged, shrugging. "He left school in the sixth grade. He's uneducated, but that doesn't mean he doesn't have enough intelligence to—"

"To keep everyone in the dark for three years?" she interrupted. "About where he gets his materials? How he gets the packages through the mail undetected? That smart? You don't really believe that, Kahler. You're grasping at straws."

"Straws are all I've got, August," he said, quick anger at her sarcasm coloring his voice. "I'm trying to catch a killer who's been blowing people up for three years."

"I know," she said softly, genuinely sorry for her ridicule.

"It just seemed too coincidental that Barrington had dealt with Mays. Another bomber," he said again.

She knew that was really all he had. Mays had possibly set off one bomb, a crime for which he'd never even been charged, so maybe he was implicated in the more recent series. They both knew what a stretch that was—even given the Barrington link.

"You really think there's some connection?"

"I thought I'd talk to Barrington about him. Maybe visit Mays. Talk to the guys who investigated the school bombing."

"If any of them are still alive," she reminded him.

His mouth tightened, and his eyes moved to focus on the darkness beyond the boundaries of the parking lot. His face reflected his frustration. That must be something he had fought for the last three years. Finally, he looked back at her, a smile lifting the tight line of his lips only fractionally. "Call me when you get back to Atlanta. And thanks," he said.

"For what?" she asked. "You paid for dinner."

"For listening."

"Thanks for talking. As always, thanks for being willing to talk to me. I'll call you."

She got into the car and closed the door. Kahler waited

while she fastened her seat belt and started the engine. Before she put the car into gear, she lifted her hand to wave to him. He touched the top of the car with his fingers, almost like a benediction, and then turned, walking off into the shadows between the scattered pools of light.

THE PHONE WAS RINGING when Kate unlocked the door of her apartment in Atlanta the following Tuesday night. Despite her hurry to catch the call, she closed the door behind her and took a moment to slip the chain into place. She hadn't had time before she left town to do what Kahler had advised her to do—to install a good dead bolt. *Tomorrow,* she promised herself, setting her suitcase down and grabbing the phone.

"Hello," she said, her voice a little breathless. Probably Lew. No one else knew she was coming back tonight.

"Ms. August?" She had never heard this particular voice over the phone, but in spite of the electronic distortion, she recognized the caller immediately.

"Yes," she answered. All the possible explanations for a phone call from Thorne Barrington ran through her head.

"Did you take my advice, Ms. August?" he asked.

She could think of nothing he had said to her that might qualify as advice. "Advice?" she echoed.

"Did you tell the police about the package you received?"

Belatedly, she remembered that he *had* urged her to do that.

"Yes, I did, Judge Barrington." For some reason she seemed unable to manage anything beyond monosyllables. This was the last thing she had expected, given the situation between them.

"To whom did you speak, Ms. August?"

She hesitated briefly, wondering if she would be giving away her relationship with Kahler if she told the truth. However, it was well known in Atlanta that he was the detective in charge of the case relating to Jack. Barrington had enough contacts that he could easily check the veracity of whatever she told him. The last thing she needed was to be caught in a lie.

"I spoke to a Detective Kahler."

"What did he tell you?" Barrington asked.

She was beginning to wonder at his obvious interest in her package when the realization came that he was the one man in Atlanta who would be avidly interested in anything that might figure in the eventual apprehension of the bomber.

"He believes the package I received wasn't related to the Tripper bombings."

"On what grounds?"

"Everything was different. The packaging. The triggering device. Everything."

"Except my address," Barrington reminded her.

"Yes," she acknowledged.

"No matter what you believe, I didn't send that package."

She wondered how she should respond to that. Finally, she realized that she had already acknowledged his denial—before she ever left Atlanta.

"Did you get my letter, Judge Barrington?"

"Yes."

"I'm truly sorry for...what happened." Her voice was hesitant, lacking its usual confidence. Apologizing was something that didn't come easy to Kate August. She always hated having to admit that she'd made a fool of herself, and she knew that in this case she had done it with a vengeance. "I'm sorry for the way I acted and for accusing you of sending the package."

"Then you no longer believe I had anything to do with it."

"No. And I regret that I jumped to that conclusion. It just seemed...coincidental. Given our previous encounter."

"Then we're left with a real problem, Ms. August."

It seemed there were still a lot of problems, but she couldn't think of one she and Barrington shared. After a few seconds of silence, he went on.

"If you've accepted my denial and if Detective Kahler believes the package had nothing to do with Jack, then who sent it? And more importantly, why?"

The pertinent question. One for which she had no answer. Unless… Why not ask Barrington about what Kahler had suggested? During the days since the detective had mentioned the school bombing, she had thought a lot about the possibility that Mays was involved in this. The more she had thought about it, the more she had wondered what the odds were on two bombers being connected to Barrington. That *did* seem too coincidental.

"Do you remember a man named Wilford Mays, Judge Barrington? He came before you on an unrelated charge, but it's possible—"

"I remember Mays," he interrupted. "Where did you come up with his name?"

"Someone told me he was suspected of being the school bomber in the sixties. I know he was never convicted on that, but isn't it possible that he might have some involvement in this case?"

"Mays was still in prison when the bombings began."

Kahler hadn't told her that. Maybe he didn't even know. Or maybe Barrington was wrong. Kahler had said Mays had gotten time off for good behavior, so perhaps he had been out when the bombings began. She considered the judge's choice of words—impersonal and distanced, considering that the bombings had begun with the package sent to Thorne Barrington.

"But not for the others?" she asked. "It's likely he didn't act alone on the school bombing. Maybe he has an accomplice."

"That's not the usual pattern with mail bombers," he

said. There was a thread of interest in the denial. He was at least considering what she had said.

"Nothing about Jack's been *usual* from the start, and Mays is bright." There was a silence. She waited one heartbeat. Two. "Isn't he?" she prodded. Fishing now. Hoping he'd talk to her.

"I'd say he's cunning," Barrington said. "Shrewd rather than smart."

Her lips tilted. "I'd like to talk to you about what you remember about his case."

"I'm sorry, Ms. August, but considering our previous—"

"This time I'll ring the bell," she offered, allowing a trace of self-directed mockery into her voice. "And I promise to leave the shades alone," she added.

When the silence stretched again, she knew she had gone too far. Damn her smart mouth. This wasn't Kahler, and it wasn't the time for sarcasm. There was nothing funny about what she'd done to Thorne Barrington.

"I interviewed Hall Draper's widow," she interjected into the suddenly frigid silence. She offered the change of subject to make him forget what she'd just said. "I'd like to run the things she told me about her husband by you."

"Why?"

"To see if anything sounds familiar. I still believe there's a link between all the victims." *Wrong word,* she thought immediately. He was certainly a victim, but she shouldn't have called him that. At least he was still alive.

"What kind of link?"

"I don't have a clue," she admitted truthfully. "Something pretty obscure or somebody would already have picked up on it. I just thought I could tell you what Jackie Draper told me and see if any of it meant anything to you."

She waited, realizing that he hadn't said no, so he must be considering it. She closed her eyes, praying, wondering if she could possibly get lucky enough to have him agree to meet her. Despite all the ways she had screwed up, was it possible that he was even thinking about talking to her about this case?

"You'd have to come here, Ms. August."

She bit her lip to keep her gasp of elation from slipping out. Barrington was going to do it. Meet with her. Talk about Mays. Listen to Jackie Draper's story. All of it. And he wondered if she minded having to come to his house.

"Of course," she said. "That's no problem." She was pleased with how calm she sounded.

"Tomorrow?"

"The sooner the better."

"Four o'clock."

"You think Elliot will let me in?" she asked. Teasing again. Automatic. Only, what in the hell she was doing teasing Barrington, especially about her last visit?

"Try ringing the bell," he suggested, and then the connection was broken. There had been some nuance of amusement in his voice, and she realized she was smiling as she put her phone back on its stand. She couldn't believe he'd agreed.

"Yes!" she said softly, her voice full of triumph.

She glanced down at the small table on which the phone rested. Not even attempting to fight the urge this time, she opened the drawer and then realized it was empty. The folder containing Thorne Barrington's pictures was gone. It took a moment for the reality of that to hit her.

Although the drawer wasn't deep, she pulled it out further, running her fingers to the very back. There was no manila folder. She tried to think of the last time she had opened the drawer, tried to remember if she had taken the Barrington file out and had then forgotten to put it back. But despite the fact that she lived alone, the pictures were a forbidden pleasure. She knew she would never have left them out.

Still trying to remember what she could possibly have

done with the folder, she switched off the lights in the living room, at the same time turning on the light in the short hallway that led to the bedroom and bath. She walked down the hall, unbuttoning her blouse as she went, becoming aware again for the first time since she'd heard the phone ringing of how exhausted she was.

By the time she reached the bedroom, the blouse was off and she held it loosely folded in her hands. Too tired to find a hanger, she laid the garment across the top of the bedroom chair. She stepped out of her low-heeled pumps as her fingers found the button on the waistband of her skirt. She unzipped it and let it fall, stooping to pick it up and throw it across the chair on top of the folded blouse. She continued to undress, piling her slip, bra and hose on the other garments. She'd straighten up in the morning. That was one advantage of living alone—no one else would see the clutter.

She took a cream-colored sleeveless gown out of her drawer and slipped it on, enjoying the fall of soft cotton over her body. She thought briefly about how good it felt to be home and how wonderful sleeping in her own bed was going to be.

She stacked the sham-covered pillows on the floor beside the chair that held her clothes and then removed the comforter, putting it on top of the pillows. She walked back to the bed, reaching under her pillow to find the top edge of the sheet, pulling it and the lightweight blanket down at the same time.

It took her a moment to realize what was in the bed, lying red and somehow obscene against the smooth white fabric of the bottom sheet. Her hand was still gripping the top sheet and blanket, but it was trembling now. Very slowly she drew them downward, exposing the vivid spill of glittering confetti. The same red confetti that had showered her office the day she'd received the package.

In her mind, unwanted, without logic or reason, out of nowhere a phrase echoed, just as obscene and just as terrifying.

Jack's back.

Chapter Six

She opened the door, leaving the chain in place until she could be sure it was Kahler. He was more casually dressed than she'd ever seen him, but she'd gotten him out of bed to answer her almost hysterical phone call. He had told her he'd be right over and had ordered her not to touch anything—to stay out of the bedroom and wait until he got there.

She released the chain, opened the door, and then surprised herself by stepping into Kahler's arms. They closed around her, almost automatically, despite the leather case he held in his right hand. She hadn't even thought about her action, about what effect it might have on their relationship. She had simply been so glad to see him, so relieved not to be in the apartment alone.

"You're all right," he said, his mouth moving against her hair. She could feel the warmth, and she took a deep breath. The first real breath she'd gotten since she'd pulled back the covers to reveal the prankster's calling card.

"He was here," she said.

The words were almost a whisper. She still felt sick. She had been since she'd realized all the implications of what she had found. She had read that people whose houses were burglarized felt like this—invaded, violated. She shivered, despite the heat of Kahler's body still holding her. She found herself wondering if she'd ever really feel safe again.

This was her home, and whoever had sent the package to her office had been here. He had opened drawers, touched her personal possessions. Maybe run his fingers over the soft cotton of the gown she had put on tonight— a hundred years ago—when she had been so glad to be back to the familiar pleasures of home.

"He was here, Kahler. In my *apartment*," she said. She wondered if Kahler would understand or if he was too inured by the years he'd dealt with real violations. Suddenly embarrassed, she removed her body from the embrace she had sought.

"He's not here now, Kate. You're all right. That's all that's important right now."

She nodded, knowing he was right.

"Where's the bedroom?" he asked, and despite the situation, she felt her mouth react to the question, the corners lifting.

"What? No foreplay?" she asked, trying to pretend she wasn't devastated by this, trying to again be what she had always thought herself—a strong woman, able to joke about the sometimes dangerous or disturbing elements of her job.

Kahler wasn't buying the act. His eyes held hers a moment, and then, still unsmiling, he broke the contact, glancing around the apartment. He moved to the doorway of the hall which led to the bedroom and bath. She trailed him reluctantly.

He walked into the bedroom and stopped, looking at the spread of confetti, the metallic surfaces of the scattered pieces catching the reflections from the overhead light. From this angle, the metal bits looked exactly like the ones that had fallen onto the carpet that day. Like freshly spilled drops of blood.

Kate stood in the doorway, watching Kahler make his

careful observations. He hadn't touched anything, and he had moved around the room as little as possible.

"The bed was made?" he asked.

"Yes."

"Notice anything different about the way it was made?"

"I wasn't looking for anything different, but... I don't think there was anything—"

"Anything missing?" he interrupted.

Just my collection of Barrington's pictures, she thought. *My fantasy. My secret life.* Somehow she couldn't imagine confessing that loss, that particular violation, to Kahler. There was nothing the intruder could learn about the case from the folder he'd taken. Nothing beyond the fact that she was hung up on looking at pre-Jack photographs of Thorne Barrington, she thought, mocking her own obsession.

"No," she lied. "At least nothing I know of."

"I'll dust a few of the likeliest areas for prints, although truthfully I'll be surprised if we find any. Thanks to the tube, everybody knows enough to wear latex gloves. Unless you want to wait for the lab boys to come out and do it tomorrow?"

He turned to look at her, his eyes carefully impersonal now, although they had touched quickly over the smooth skin exposed by the low neck of her gown before they had lifted to her face.

"No," she said. "You do it. If you will. I just want to clean that up. Just get it out of my bed."

"Give me another set of sheets, and I'll take care of it."

"I don't want you to have to—"

"I'd like to take this set in. Test them for any physical evidence. We might get lucky. While I'm at it, I'll put the clean sheets on the bed."

She nodded again, grateful for the offer, however he wanted to justify it. When she brought sheets back into the room, Kahler had already begun dusting for prints.

"You can put them on the foot of the bed," he instructed.

She deposited the small stack and then looked around the room. "Sorry about the mess," she said, gesturing toward the chair where she'd piled her clothes and the bedding on the floor.

Kahler glanced up from what he was doing, and he smiled at her for the first time. "I grew up in a three-room house with my mother and sister. You don't have to apologize for the feminine clutter, August. It just makes me feel at home."

She returned his smile, wondering what Kahler had been like as a boy, what his early life had been, before he'd joined the military. He had told her almost nothing beyond the fact that he couldn't imagine having grown up surrounded by luxury as Thorne Barrington had, that he had not been born with a silver spoon in his mouth. And, of course, neither had she.

"You don't have to stay," Kahler added.

Kate realized suddenly that she didn't want to. She wanted out of this room, away from the violation. Kahler seemed to be very perceptive tonight where her feelings were concerned.

"Thanks," she said, and she turned and left him alone.

IT TOOK KAHLER maybe twenty minutes to finish. Kate sat on the couch in the living room while she waited, images of someone rummaging through her belongings invading her mind. Occasionally she thought about the missing pictures, wondering why he would have taken those. It didn't make sense. Unless...

Resolutely, she banished that thought. Barrington wouldn't want his own pictures. No one had believed her idea that the judge was involved with the package that had been sent to her office. Both Kahler and Lew had discounted that scenario. It was somehow even more far-fetched to imagine a respected jurist breaking into her apartment to throw confetti between her sheets.

She hadn't told Kahler that Barrington had called her or that she had an appointment with him tomorrow, and she didn't intend to. She had already confessed that she wasn't completely unbiased when it came to the judge. It was all too complicated to explain, especially with everything else that was going on.

"All done," Kahler said. "You want me to stay a while?"

He was standing in the doorway of the hall. She had the sudden, inexplicable feeling that he might have been there a few minutes, silently watching her.

"I'm not quite that big a coward," she denied.

"Sometimes having company helps," Kahler suggested.

"It's just the thought that he was here." She had said that before, but somehow it was the one thing she couldn't get past. He had been in her home. He had touched her things, had run his hands over the sheets of her bed. Violation. She shivered.

"Put the chain on. And get that lock tomorrow. Then if he wants in again, he'll have to break the door down. You just made it easy for him, Kate."

"I know," she admitted. "Who do you think could have—"

"Whoever sent the package. We've already played this game. I don't have any answers for you. We'll let the lab see if they can find anything. There's nothing more I can do tonight."

"Thanks for coming," she said. She stood up, aware for the first time of the sheerness of her gown. Not that Kahler had revealed he'd noticed.

"I don't like this, August. I don't like the way it feels. Usually creeps who pull stunts like this are harmless. But occasionally…"

"Occasionally, they do more than terrorize," she finished for him. She was very well aware of the dangers of stalkers.

"You be careful," Kahler ordered. "You're smart. Don't take any chances. And forget the series. Let it drop. It's not worth the risk. Not for some stupid story." His voice was suddenly passionate. No longer the detached professional. Apparently, this felt personal to Kahler also.

"It's my job, Kahler. If I run at the first sign of trouble, at the first indication that someone doesn't like what I write, then I'm not much of a reporter."

"Maybe they'll put that in your obituary. She was a hell of a reporter, but she didn't have sense enough to know when to leave it alone."

"If you're trying to scare me, I want you to know that you're doing a hell of a fine job." Her voice was tight with anger. He was supposed to be comforting, protecting her from this maniac, and instead he was just making it worse.

"Good," he said. "Get the lock, August. First thing tomorrow. Be late for work if you have to. Remember what they say." His voice was just as hard as hers, his eyes challenging.

"What do they say, Kahler? I know you're dying to tell me."

"Better late than never," he said. He stalked across the room and opened the door, every motion indicating anger.

She watched him, her eyes glazed with sudden moisture. She hated it, but it always happened. She always cried when she got mad. Kahler was supposed to be her friend. He wasn't supposed to tell her it was too dangerous to keep doing her job. That wasn't what she wanted to hear from Detective Byron Kahler.

"By the way," he said, turning just before he stepped through the opened door. She blinked, determined not to let him have the satisfaction of seeing her cry, but still his features were slightly blurred. "To me, August, foreplay won't consist of putting confetti between your sheets."

He closed the door behind him, the noise sharp in the confines of the small room. She opened her mouth slightly, almost the comical dropped jaw of the sitcoms, and then realized she had nothing to say. Even if she had been able to think of a comeback, he had timed it so it was far too late to deliver it.

THE HEAT WAS SHIMMERING off the pavement again. The members of the construction crew across the street were at least pretending to work, but somehow all the jobs they had found to do today were in the shade. Kate didn't blame them. The bank clock she'd passed on her way to the Barrington mansion had read 102, and it was probably ten degrees higher than that in the exposed upper stories of the dilapidated house they were renovating.

She followed the judge's instructions, ringing the bell. Her lips curved as she remembered the comment on which he'd ended their conversation last night. She had thought a lot about his tone. There was no doubt it had contained amusement. It was the first time in her encounters with Barrington that she had been allowed a glimpse of the man reflected in those old photos.

Her smile faded when she remembered the fate of the pictures. She had also thought long and hard about taking Kahler's advice, but she could no more have cancelled this appointment today than she could have confessed to the detective what she had confirmed during the sleepless hours of last night—that the only thing missing from her apartment was her secret collection of Thorne Barrington's pictures.

"Miss August." The old man had arrived, his trembling hands already beginning to deal with the gate.

"Hello, Elliot," she answered, smiling at him. She knew the butler would not have forgiven her for what she had done the last time he'd let her in. Not given the degree of affection that had been in his voice for his beloved "Mr. Thorne."

"Judge Barrington is waiting in the parlor," Elliot said, pulling the gate inward. "If you'll follow me." She could tell from his tone there would be no protective umbrella today and no iced tea. She had definitely not been forgiven.

He said nothing else to her as he led the way up the now familiar walkway and through the glass-paneled front door. The crystal tears of the chandelier in the foyer proclaimed their entrance as they had the first night she'd come to this house. She had expected Elliot to announce her, but instead he disappeared into the darkness behind the central staircase, leaving her alone in the artificial twilight.

This was what she had wanted—an interview with Thorne Barrington, so she didn't know why she was hesitating. Her palms were clammy, and it had nothing to do with the humidity. Unconsciously, she straightened her shoulders, and taking a deep breath, she pushed aside the sliding wooden door to reveal the formal parlor, exactly as it had been before.

Its dimness was a contrast even to the unlighted hall. Enough light seeped in from the porch-shaded glass door there to offer some illumination, but Kate had to pause on the threshold of the parlor to allow her eyes to adjust to its lack of light.

"Ms. August." The deep voice came from the shadows on the opposite side of the fireplace, the spot where he had been sitting on the first night she'd come here. Gradually, his figure began to take shape, emerging again from the surrounding darkness. And again he was standing—the perfect gentleman.

"Judge Barrington," she acknowledged his greeting, walking toward him with her hand outstretched. Properly brought up Southern men never extended their hands unless a lady offered hers first. Business women down here knew the rule—a rule that hadn't changed as far as the old-money crowd, a group to which Barrington certainly belonged, was concerned.

His voice stopped her before she had halved the distance between them. "I no longer shake hands, Ms. August. Please forgive me." There was no inflection in the statement, no embarrassment, and despite the way it had been phrased, no apology. Simply a statement of fact.

There must have been injuries to his hands, she realized, remembering what Lew had said. Something about how it would change your character to have a bomb blow up in your hands. She hadn't picked up on the significance of that. The comment had undoubtedly stemmed from some bit of gossip her editor had heard.

Her gaze dropped to Barrington's hands, to verify that was the reason for the curt dismissal of her attempted handshake. His arms were at his sides, the big hands almost touching the faded denim of well-worn jeans. She could see no details other than the seemingly normal shape of the thumbs and the profile of the rest, palms relaxed, curving slightly inward.

Belatedly aware of the rudeness of what she was doing, she forced her eyes up. His were focused calmly on her face, waiting, his expression absolutely unrevealing. She allowed her own hand to drop to her side. Like an idiot, she had continued to hold it out, even after his comment. All her encounters with this man seemed destined to be mired in embarrassment.

"I'm sorry," she said. "I didn't know."

"Since you're not at fault, I see no need for you to apologize. Would you like to sit down?"

"Thank you," Kate said, finding that another chair had been conveniently situated directly across from the shadowed one the judge had chosen. She sat down in it, putting her bag on the floor and fumbling in it for her notebook and a pen, attempting to hide her nervousness. She was aware when Barrington sat down, still moving as gracefully as the athlete he once had been.

"You said on the phone that you'd learned some things about the Draper bombing which you wanted to discuss with me," he said.

That really wasn't what she had meant to suggest when she'd talked to him. She didn't know what might be significant about the minutiae of Hall Draper's very ordinary life. She had just hoped something would trigger a response from the judge.

"I don't know that I've *learned* anything. Not anything relevant. I just talked to Draper's widow. I thought if I read you some of the things she told me, you might make a connection."

"Did you see some connection, Ms. August?"

She smiled, thinking how far removed from the privileged life-style of the Barrington millions Hall Draper had been. How different his growing up. His career.

"You and Draper seem light-years apart to me, but..." She paused, trying to think what she wanted to say, and he waited patiently through the hesitation. "But there must be something. Somewhere in your lives—*something* in your lives—must connect. It's the only way to make sense out of all this."

"You're still trying to make sense out of what he does?"

"You think he strikes at random?" she asked. This was what she had come for. To finally talk to Thorne Barrington. To get his take on the whole insane situation.

"No," he said simply.

"Then..." Again she hesitated.

"I think he chooses his victims," Barrington went on. "But despite the three years I've spent thinking about who might hate me enough to..." The break was brief, but there was a tinge of emotion that had not been allowed before. "...want to kill me, I'm no closer to an answer than I was then."

"What about Mays?" Kate asked. "Did he hate you enough?"

"He hated us all. With all the mad-dog rabidness you'd expect from a man who would blow up a school because a black child had been allowed to enter it. But he didn't seem to single me out particularly. I was just part of the establishment that had been trying to destroy his mind-set, his way of life, for the past thirty years. He seemed to despise the fellow conspirator who had gone to the authorities far more than those who were attempting to impose a long-overdue justice for what he'd done."

"But that informant didn't receive a bomb through the mail."

"No," Barrington confirmed.

"Do you think Mays was responsible for the school bombing?"

"Yes," Barrington said, with a conviction she could hear.

"No doubt in your mind?"

"No."

"And that's why you gave him the maximum sentence?"

From out of the shadows came a brief whisper of laughter. Unamused. Self-mocking. "The maximum? A year. Less than a year out of his seventy to pay for the deaths of two children."

"That was all you could do." Surprisingly, Kate found herself wanting to comfort that bitterness.

There was no answer from the man in the shadows.

"But you don't believe he's Jack?" she asked when he seemed disinclined to pursue the justice, or injustice, of Mays's sentence.

"Based on everything I know, he doesn't fit. It bothered me enough—the fact that I'd had personal contact with another bomber—that I *did* mention Mays to the police. Apparently, they've never found a connection."

"Who did you tell about Mays?" Kate asked, wondering why that information had never been conveyed to Kahler.

"I really don't know. At first..." The deep voice hesitated, and Kate recognized some trace of emotion, but again the pause was brief and whatever she had heard was gone when he continued. "At first there was only an endless confusion of voices. I never learned to separate them. Thank God, that was a skill I wasn't forced to acquire."

Thank God whatever damage there had been to his eyes hadn't been permanent, Kate realized. That had certainly sounded heartfelt and for the first time she thought about what blindness would have meant to the man Barrington had been. But at least he wouldn't have been a prisoner in his own home. Maybe what *had* happened had somehow been worse than the loss of his sight.

"And later on? Did you tell Kahler about Mays?"

"I don't remember mentioning the school bombing to Detective Kahler. I suppose I assumed that whoever I had told at first had investigated Mays and that the possibility of his involvement had come to nothing. There's never been any mention of him in anything that's been written about the mail bombings."

She wondered suddenly if that meant Barrington had read her stuff. He had been familiar with her name, so even with his disdain for the media, he had still followed the investigation.

"There's been nothing in *my* series, because I just heard Mays's name last week," she said.

"Who mentioned him to you?"

"A good reporter always protects her sources, Judge Barrington," she said, smiling. "Or pretty soon she doesn't have any," she explained the pragmatism behind that particular ethic.

"Thorne," he said.

"I beg your pardon."

"I was simply suggesting that you might use my given name."

"Of course," Kate said, her voice almost as breathless as when she'd realized whom she was talking to on the phone. "If that's what you prefer," she added.

"May I call you Kate?"

"Of course."

"Why do I feel that I've just made you extremely uncomfortable?" Barrington asked. The amusement was clearly back, touching the deep baritone with intimacy.

This was the way his voice must have sounded before, Kate thought, back when those beautiful debutantes had hung on his every word, their eyes drinking in the perfection of feature that had not changed. He was still as handsome, hiding here in the shadowed existence that he had chosen or had been forced to choose. The sexual magnetism was still there. With the dark, honeyed warmth of his tone she had felt its power move through her body, sensual and inviting.

"Thorne," she repeated obediently. She had never even called him that in her imagination.

"I know it sounds like one of those names Hollywood dreamed up—Rip or Rock or Cord. I *do* realize how ridiculous it is, but given the options available to her, I confess that I'm grateful my mother had the good sense to settle on Thorne."

Harlan Thornedyke Barrington, Kate thought—and then she laughed. He was right. By far the lesser of the possible evils. His laughter joined hers, and when she became aware of the sound, she was again unprepared for how intimate it was. He was just a man, she reminded herself. With her fascination, she knew that she truly had made him larger than life.

Just a man. Just like Kahler. Just like any of the other guys she had been involved with through the years. *Been involved with?* she repeated mentally, incredulous at what she had just thought. *Slow down,* she reminded herself. Just because she was here, finally talking to Barrington did not—definitely did not—mean they were involved.

"I thought I'd try talking to Mays," she said, attempting to get back on track, back to the reason she was here. This might be the only chance she would ever have to discuss these things with Barrington. She couldn't afford to blow it.

"My advice is to stay as far away from Mays as you can."

"You think he's still dangerous."

"The school bombing isn't the only crime Mays was involved in. The informant mentioned a lynching, and there were other things. Nothing Mays could be tied to legally, but he was a man filled with hate and more than willing to act on his feelings."

"Surely after all this time—" Kate began.

"A rattler's not any less dangerous because he's old. He's just bigger and meaner. More full of venom."

It was a Southernism. Something her grandmother might have said, and like all truisms, it was probably a very accurate opinion where a snake like Wilford Mays was concerned.

"Stay away from Mays," he warned. "Chances are he has nothing to do with the current bombings. The police would surely have investigated that possibility."

Only, Kate knew, that wasn't the case. No one, despite Thorne Barrington's initial request, had ever checked out Mays. She had even discouraged Kahler when he'd suggested an investigation of the alleged school bomber.

"Why don't you tell me the things Draper's widow told you," Barrington said. "It's possible there may be something there. At least, I think that's more likely to result in something useful than pursuing a seventy-year-old bigot."

Kate glanced down at her notebook and realized that in the dimness of the room she could barely make out her notes, a confusing mixture of real shorthand and her own personal variety. She could hardly ask Barrington to turn on the lights, and he was so accustomed to this omnipresent darkness that he apparently didn't realize there was a problem with what he'd just proposed.

Her eyes still lowered to the barely discernible words she had scrawled across the ruled paper, she realized there was only one thing to do. She would have to recount from memory what Jackie Draper had told her.

Kate took a deep breath, trying to think where to start. As she began to talk, however, she found that the events of Hall Draper's life—so ordinary as to be unremarkable—had made an indelible impression. She wasn't aware of the passage of time, eventually as lost in the narrative as she had been when she had listened to it in that sun-striped room in Tucson.

"And finally, when I asked her if her husband had ever been mixed up in anything...unsavory, she could only think of one thing, almost an afterthought. It was about a girl who had gotten pregnant at fourteen with what *might* have been Hall Draper's child. She had an abortion, either because she was forced to by her family or because that's what she wanted. Not what Draper had wanted maybe, but he had felt he was too young to have much effect on that decision. Mrs. Draper said that's the one thing in his life he regretted. That poor lost baby."

The words drifted away into the silence. The room was darker now, she realized. The man who had listened without comment to the story of Hall Draper's life was almost completely enveloped in the shadows that had deepened with the approach of twilight. Suddenly she was embarrassed for having taken up his afternoon on what was apparently an exercise in futility.

"Nothing in that story meant anything to you," she said. It wasn't even a question. Barrington had asked for no repetitions, had not commented on or questioned any of what she'd related.

"Perhaps not. Not in the way you'd hoped." The deep voice was almost disembodied, simply coming out of the darkness. "But obviously, it meant something to you."

She hadn't intended to reveal how moved she had been by the images of the Drapers' private lives, by the decency of Hall Draper, the grief of his widow.

"It just seemed to me that whatever mistake he made—at whatever point in his life—the way he had lived the rest of it should have made up for it. It should have been enough."

"But it wasn't," Thorne said softly.

"No," she whispered. "He died, and there doesn't seem to be a reason for his death. Not in anything she told me."

"Or for any of the others?" he asked.

She shook her head, and then wondered if he could see her, given the darkness. "No," she whispered.

"Perhaps you won't understand this, but knowing you feel that way helps."

"Knowing…?"

"That none of *them* deserved what happened."

"And that means that you didn't deserve it either," she said, suddenly understanding.

"I've spent three years wondering what I did. Maybe the answer is, I did nothing."

"But like Hall Draper—like all of us, I suppose—there are things in your life you aren't proud of."

"Like all of us," he acknowledged.

"What do *you* regret, Judge Barrington?"

It was the question any good reporter would have asked, but she was curious on another level. What did a man, highly respected for his integrity, his dedication to duty, a man who had lived the kind of life Thorne Barrington had, have to regret?

"Perhaps I'll tell you that the next time we talk," he said

softly. "Now, if you'll excuse me, I'm afraid I have another appointment." It was certainly a lie, graceful and polite, but still a lie.

"Of course," she said, pushing the unused notebook back into her purse. "I appreciate your agreeing to see me. Thank you for your time."

"A commodity of which I seem to have an unlimited supply."

"Does that mean I can come back?" she asked, deliberately injecting the teasing note. "When I have other questions?"

"As long as our conversations remain simply that," he surprised her by agreeing. "I'm not interested in having my name or my comments appear in your paper. I can assure you that…my situation attracted all the attention I ever desire in this lifetime. If you want my input, then like your other sources, I expect our relationship to remain completely confidential."

"Of course," Kate agreed. *Our relationship.* He meant professional, of course, but for some reason the words had echoed more strongly than the rest of the warning. "I never intended to make any part of our conversation public."

"Thank you," Thorne said. "Shall I ring for Elliot or do you think you can find your way out?" There was a pause before he added, his voice touched with humor, "Again."

His timing had been impeccable, and she paid tribute by laughing. "Thank you, but I believe I can manage."

She stood up, gathering up her bag, and began to cross to the sliding doors. Before she reached them, she remembered the retriever. "Where's your dog?" she asked.

"Elliot's fastened him in one of the rooms upstairs. He was afraid he'd frighten you." The amusement was still there, pleasantly intriguing in the deep voice. "For some reason, Elliot is under the impression that the retriever's a guard dog."

"Then I'm glad you've got a fence," she said.

She let herself out of the parlor, but she stopped in the wide foyer, looking up the stairs where Elliot and the puppy were waiting for her to leave. Then they would once again become a part of the limited world of the man they obviously adored. The man who had, for some reason, allowed her to enter this very private domain. Who had indicated he would allow it again, providing she, too, guarded the privacy which he seemed to value above anything else—even, it seemed, above human companionship.

HE LISTENED to the closing of the front door and the faint noise made by the crystals of his grandmother's Waterford chandelier. When those sounds had faded, he sat alone in the shadows, the house again completely silent.

It had been far too pleasant to sit and listen to her voice, to listen as she told the story of Hall Draper's life. It had been obvious that she had been deeply moved by her encounter with Draper's widow. The emotion had been there, enriching the quiet narrative. Clearly, she admired the kind of man Draper had been. Perhaps as she might have admired the man Thorne Barrington had once been, the kind of man he knew he was no longer.

She was a reporter working on a story. That was why she had come here. Nothing else. *I'm not news,* he had told her the first night, but even then he had known that he was, and that despite the passage of time, he probably always would be. He understood exactly why Kate August wanted to talk to him. What he didn't understand was why, given the situation, he had agreed.

Chapter Seven

Kate had spent another nearly sleepless night. She had not even entered the bedroom this time, having learned during the dawn hours of the night before the futility of trying to sleep there. She had instead pulled out spare bedding and made a nest on the couch, but sleep again eluded her. It might have had something to do with the fact that she couldn't bear to turn off the lamp and plunge the apartment into darkness. Or it might have been because of the voices that kept invading her mind.

The soft warmth of Barrington's amused baritone. Kahler's, slightly accented, in the darkness of the restaurant parking lot in Tucson, telling her about another bomber. Jackie Draper's whispering tribute to her husband—a good man.

The lack of sleep was beginning to show, she thought, putting on her makeup the next morning. The small bathroom light clearly illuminated the shadows under her eyes, and in them was the same frustration she had heard in Kahler's voice.

This had all gone on too long. Too many people had died, and she knew in her heart that there was a connection between them. Figuring out what that link might be was the key to stopping Jack. Dangerous or not, she knew that she could not give up the story. She didn't bother to deny, to herself at least, that there were a couple of personal aspects to the puzzle that she wasn't ready to step away from. Especially not now.

It had only taken her a couple of hours after she arrived at her desk to locate Wilford Mays. He was still living in the same house where he had been born. He was even listed in the local telephone directory. However reprehensible the rest of the world felt his actions to be, Mays had felt no need to hide from them.

She hadn't called to make an appointment. She had simply left a message for Lew and then driven out to the small rural community. It was only as she drove up the unpaved road the locals had told her led to Mays's house that she allowed herself to admit this might not be a good idea.

The sprawling farmhouse-style board-and-batten sat under the spread of an oak that was at least a couple of hundred years old. The house itself had probably been built in the early years of the century. There was a profusion of multi-colored impatiens and petunias trailing from baskets hanging between the square white columns of a porch that ran the length of the house.

As she walked up the liriope-bordered sidewalk, Kate could see that someone was sitting in the old-fashioned porch swing. The woman, whom Kate guessed to be Mays's wife, had stretched her small, rounded body to its full height in an attempt to identify the driver of the car that had pulled into her yard.

"Hello," Kate called, as she climbed the wooden steps. She knew that despite the xenophobia of city dwellers, she was not likely to be unwelcome here, even if she were uninvited. "Miz Mays?" she questioned, using, without any conscious decision, the old Southern form of address she had been taught as a child.

"I'm Velma Mays," the woman answered, stopping the gentle sway of the swing with one foot. Mrs. Mays stood up, holding the blue-and-white-speckled colander into which she'd been snapping beans. Her print dress had been carefully ironed, the starched cotton appearing as fresh as it must have when she'd put it on this morning. There wasn't a strand of iron-gray hair out of place, the curls so tightly permed that they didn't look capable of escaping from the style they'd been tortured into.

Her face was relatively unlined for her age, smoothly white. Kate's grandmother had this nearly flawless complexion—fed by the constant humidity and vigilantly protected from the damaging rays of the sun. It was the mark of gentility in their generation, a Southern legacy of climate and convention.

"Ms. Mays, my name is Kathrine August," Kate said, smiling. She didn't offer her hand. It was perhaps acceptable in the city for women to shake hands, but it was not the custom in rural Georgia. "I'm a reporter for an Atlanta newspaper, and I'd like to talk to your husband, if he has time."

The curve of Velma Mays's mouth, a small Cupid's bow, widened. Her blue eyes sparkled behind the wire-frame bifocals. "Time?" she questioned, poking fun at Kate's politeness with her friendly smile. "Wilford Mays's got nothing *but* time, and that man surely likes talking, especially to somebody as pretty as you. Just as pretty as a picture. You from Atlanta originally?"

They were about to play an old Southern game called *Who Are You Kin To*. Kate was as familiar with its rules as her hostess. "Tupelo," she said readily.

"I don't believe I know any Augusts," Velma said, raising her chin to get a better view of Kate through the half-moons at the bottom of her glasses, as if trying to judge her genealogy by an examination of her features. "Who's your mother, dear?"

"She was a Montgomery. Her daddy was Boyd Montgomery, but he was raised on the coast. Near Savannah."

"Montgomery," Velma said, crinkling her forehead in

an attempt to place the family. "There's a big family of Montgomerys lives near Dalton. Wilford had some business with a man there named Herbert. Any kin to your granddaddy?"

"I don't think so," Kate said truthfully. She knew it didn't really matter if they made a connection. It was the attempt that was important.

"Well, no matter. I'm sure your family's real proud of you. A reporter, you say. Why, when I was growing up, we'd never have thought about a woman being a reporter."

Kate smiled again, feeling no reply was necessary. Apparently none was expected because Velma continued.

"Why don't you sit down, Miss August, while I take these beans in and then find Wilford for you. He won't have gone far. There isn't far to go out here," she said with a laugh. "And I'll bring you some tea while you're waiting. This weather is just awful. I don't know how you people in the city stand all that concrete. It just seems to magnify the heat."

Kate sat down obediently in one of the white wicker rockers that flanked a matching table. All the furniture was lined up in a row, backs against the front of the house, facing outward for the best view of the passing traffic on the narrow road.

"I'll be right back," Velma promised. She bustled by to disappear through the screen door. Kate had caught the faintest whiff of rose water as she passed, pleasantly reminiscent.

Despite what Barrington had told her about Wilford Mays, despite the trepidation she'd felt in coming out here alone, the visit so far seemed as pleasant as an afternoon spent on her grandmother's wisteria-shaded veranda in Mississippi. After a few minutes, Velma Mays pushed open the screen with her elbow to carry out a glass of tea, the clinking movement of ice inviting. She put it down on the table by Kate and handed her the small paper napkin she carried.

"Now you just sit here and try to keep cool while I locate Wilford," she said. She walked to the side of the porch and, putting her hand on the column, she stepped down the three low steps, and then disappeared around the corner of the house.

Kate picked up the glass and sipped. The tea was sweetened, of course, and flavored with something that she couldn't identify. The taste was tantalizingly familiar, but elusive. She took a larger swallow, rolling the coldness over her tongue.

"Grape juice," Wilford Mays said. He was standing on the bare patch that Velma's small feet had made through the years, trampling the grass as she had stepped off those low steps, always in the same exact spot, the repetition demanded by the placement of her steadying hand on the porch column.

"Of course," Kate said. "I couldn't quite figure it out."

"Velma's mother always put grape juice in her ice tea."

"It's wonderful," Kate said, preparing to stand.

"Don't bother to get up. Velma said you wanted to talk to me. Something about a paper in Atlanta."

"I'm Kathrine August—" Kate began only to be interrupted.

"You're doing that series on the bomber," he said. "The one they're calling Jack the Tripper."

Kate felt a tug of unease that he had so readily recognized her name. He was watching her reaction, his eyes penetrating in a way his wife's had not been. He was as spare as Velma was rounded, dressed in overalls over a plaid shirt, both as meticulously starched and ironed as his wife's housedress.

"That's right," she said, offering the same smile that had created a matching friendliness in Mrs. Mays. His eyes remained cold, and the thin lips never moved. He ascended the steps and folded his length into the swing his wife had vacated.

"I don't have nothing to do with those," he said. There was no rancor in his denial. Only a statement of fact.

Kate was surprised. She had been prepared for coyness, a denial of his reputation even, but not this open disclaimer of responsibility for the current murders. She needed to be careful of what she said, she reminded herself. Mays was no fool. Barrington had characterized him as both shrewd and cunning.

"That *is* why you're here, ain't it?" he asked.

"Not really," Kate lied. "I wanted to talk to you about Judge Thornedyke Barrington."

"I read your piece. You seem to think mighty highly of that conniving bastard. Talked about him like he's some kind of hero. He's got you just as hoodwinked as the rest of 'em."

"Hoodwinked?" she repeated.

"All that mess you wrote about his fine record, his *integrity*." His inflection of the word was an insult. "That's all it is, Miss August. A bunch of mess. He railroaded me, and if he'd do it to me, then you can be sure he done it to a heap of others. I'm surprised somebody ain't tried to blow up that crooked son of a bitch before now."

"Why would Judge Barrington want to railroad you, Mr. Mays?"

"'Cause he was in cahoots with the cops. In their pockets. They spit, and he had to jump. He needed to make a name for hisself. His daddy had a career in politics all laid out for his boy, and then ole Jack come along and ruined it." He laughed, the sound without humor, bitter and vindictive.

"And you've always blamed Judge Barrington for your conviction," she suggested.

"You trying to get me to say I got a motive for blowing the bastard sky-high? You got a microphone hid somewhere? That's been tried, only I wasn't born yesterday."

"I just thought, since you feel so strongly, that you might

like to comment on Judge Barrington's character, to provide a different slant. Something I could include in the series as a contrast to the view of him we offered our readers before."

"You ain't interested in my views. You're just interested in making a case against me for being the one trying to blow him up. Only you ain't quite figured out why all them other people got blowed up, too. Why do you think I'd do those, Miss August? What's your explanation for all those other people dying?"

"All I know is, from what you've told me, that you aren't an admirer of Thorne Barrington."

"I ain't told you nothing," he said. There was no discernible change of expression and his voice had not changed, but suddenly malice toward her was in his eyes. "And I don't *intend* to tell you nothing. You or no other reporter."

"Did the authorities ever come out to talk to you about the bombings, Mr. Mays?"

His lips moved, deepening the creases age had carved into the lean cheeks, but his cold eyes didn't change. "Somebody come all right. Scared Velma to death. She thought they was fixing to put me away again on some other trumped-up charge, 'cause I keep fertilizer in the barn, maybe, and folks been known to make bombs out of that. Took me more'n a week to calm her down."

"And you still deny that you had any part in the school bombing?" she asked. That wasn't what he'd been charged with, but she wanted to see how he responded to the suggestion.

"Somebody told you I did that?" he said, a pretended disgust at the ridiculousness of that accusation in his tone. "Do I look like a man that would want to blow up a school or want to kill some poor little children? Do I strike you as that kind of man?"

His eyes were openly mocking now, the questions sarcastic, and Kate felt a shiver of apprehension. Barrington had been right. A venomous old snake. Still dangerous, still deadly.

"I'll let you in on a secret, Miss August. One you might do well to remember. A bomber's a special kind of man 'cause he ain't real particular about who gets blowed up by what he does. He can't afford to be particular. Anybody could have opened those packages. A secretary. Anybody. Or they could have gone off by accident 'fore they ever reached the person they was intended for. A man who sends bombs just don't care. You understand what I'm telling you? He don't *care* who gets blowed up in the process of getting what he wants. A bomber's got to have that kind of mind. You remember that. He purely don't care."

"Even if it's children who get blown up?" Kate asked, forcing her eyes to hold his.

"You ain't old enough to remember how it used to be down here, are you?"

"No," she agreed softly. There was some shadow of the irrational in his eyes and clearly now there was hatred, gray and cold as winter. "I don't remember. I'm just glad, despite the efforts of people like you, it's not *that* way any longer."

"You get off my property, girl," he said, his voice as low as hers had been. "Don't you ever come near us again. I don't like you, and I sure don't like that piece of trash paper you write for. Now you get out of here before I regret lettin' you."

She stood up, frightened, despite her determination not to be, by the bizarre transformation. Mays was openly menacing now, no longer bothering to hide his hostility.

"You ready for some more tea, dear?" Velma asked, coming out of the screen door with a cut-glass pitcher in her hand. "Oh, surely you're not thinking about leaving," she protested in dismay when she saw Kate was standing.

"You just got here. And you haven't even touched your tea."

"Now, Mother," Wilford said, the polite veneer again in place before his wife. "Miss August has a long drive ahead of her, and she knows her business better than you. Besides, she don't *like* your tea." There was a deliberate cruelty about the comment, considering the effort Velma had made to be kind.

"Oh, I'm so sorry, dear. I should have asked. I can fix you another. Fix it any way you like."

"The tea's delicious, Ms. Mays, but your husband's right. I do have a long drive, and I better get started."

"I hope Wilford told you what you wanted to know. Since you came so far to talk," Velma said, smiling at her.

Kate stepped off the porch onto the front steps. She could still feel his eyes focused on her, cold as a snake, although she didn't look at him again. "Mr. Mays has been very helpful. Thank you, ma'am, for your hospitality."

"You come again, dear. We're always glad to have company."

IT WAS AFTER FOUR before she got back to the office. She had spent the drive into Atlanta thinking about what Mays had told her. Every time she remembered the madness in his eyes, she shivered, but she was really no closer to knowing whether or not he had had anything to do with the current bombings.

She still was left with the possibility of three different bombers, and no way to know if there was a connection between them. Obviously, she had been targeted because of the series—obvious unless she was willing to believe that Thorne Barrington had sent the confetti-filled package because she had entered his house uninvited. If he had, then he had also been the person who had broken into her apartment while she was out of town and put the matching confetti in her bed.

But if that were true, why would he agree to meet with her—despite his well-known hatred of the media? And what did Wilford Mays have to do with the Tripper bombings? There was no doubt he hated Barrington enough to do almost anything, but as he had reminded her, there would also have to be a link between him and the other victims. Logic told her there couldn't be three bombers, but she couldn't decide where the incidents overlapped.

She stopped by Lew's office on her way to the newsroom. He was working, on the phone, top shirt button undone and his tie loosened, but he motioned her in. She sat on the other side of the cluttered desk and listened to him handle whatever problem had arisen with his usual efficiency. He hung up, jotted a final note on his desk calendar and then looked up to smile at her.

"Change your mind?" he asked. In contrast to the gray hatred in Wilford Mays's, Lew's brown eyes were full of understanding. He thought she had come to beg off the series.

"No, but I probably should," she admitted. "I just spent the afternoon with Wilford Mays. Remember him?"

"Mays?" Lew repeated, questioning, but his memory was better than hers had been. "The school bomber?"

"*Alleged* bomber," she corrected, smiling.

"You think he has some connection to what's going on now?"

"Not if you consider only method, but the interesting thing is that Barrington was the judge who finally put him away. On some lesser charge, of course, but he burned him with as much time as he could. Barrington's convinced Mays did the school bombing. Mays, as you can imagine, hates Barrington's guts."

"So what does that mean as far as the Tripper bombings are concerned?" Lew asked carefully.

"Damned if I know," Kate said, shrugging, feeling the frustration of not knowing as strongly as she had on the way back into the city. "But it's *got* to mean something. Doesn't it?"

Lew said nothing for a moment, thinking about whether it did or not, she guessed, trying as she had been to fit the pieces of the triangular-shaped puzzle together. Only, Lew was probably not considering the confetti bomber as part of the equation.

"Even if that's a motive for sending a bomb to the judge, why would Mays hit the others?" he finally queried.

"He asked me that—why would he want to kill those other people. I didn't have an answer. I still don't. But that's a hell of a coincidence. Barrington and Mays."

"How many cases was Barrington involved in through the years, on and off the bench? Is it such a stretch to imagine that one of them might involve another bomber? Have you talked to Kahler about this?"

"He's the one who mentioned Mays. Barrington says he told the police about Mays from the first, but somehow the word never got back to Kahler. He just picked up the connection on his own, going back over the cases Barrington had handled one more time."

"But he thinks there's some connection?" Lew asked.

"Kahler's like the rest of us, grasping at any possibility."

"What did you think about Mays?"

"That he's one scary old man. You believe at first he's this harmless old coot, and then all of a sudden, you see something in his eyes. I think he's capable of almost anything. He certainly hates Barrington, but that doesn't mean he had a reason to kill the other people Jack targeted. To be fair, it's been a long time since Mays was even rumored to be involved in anything violent—thirty or thirty-five years."

"Any current association with the hate groups?" Lew asked. He had picked up the pen he'd been jotting notes with and doodled along the edge of his crowded appointment calendar.

"I don't know. You think I should try to find out?"

"Let me ask around, talk to Kahler about running the membership lists, and I'll let you know. Maybe we ought to do exactly what Kahler did."

"Which is?"

"Go back over everything we have one more time. Re-read it all. Try to see if anything reaches out and grabs us."

"I don't have to reread it. I know it all by heart. I swear, Lew, there's nothing else there. And I'm still left with the confetti bomber. I don't even know if that's connected to the others."

"A one-time shot. Some kook thought it'd be cute to send the person writing about the bombings a fake bomb. It probably has *no* connection. Kahler said everything was different."

"There was confetti in my bed when I got back from Tucson."

It took a split second for the impact of that to be reflected in his eyes, and another few while he sorted through the implications. "In your *bed?*" he repeated. His voice was still calm and restrained, but his eyebrows had arched, his forehead wrinkling upward into the receding hairline.

"It was worse, somehow, than the other. I felt violated. Invaded. He was in my home."

"That's it, Kate. No more. This has gotten beyond crack-pots sending letters. It's too damned dangerous."

"I had a new lock put in. Kahler says my lack of security was just an invitation to trouble."

"At least that should take Barrington out of the picture for you. There's no way he would have anything to do with that."

"Given the fact that he never leaves home," she agreed. "At least not in the daylight. Counts Dracula and Barring-ton."

Lew laughed. "Don't you think you're letting your imag-ination run away with you? Are you picturing Barrington as some kind of night crawler? A monster who only comes out after dark? Come on, Kate. Think about the reality of the man we're talking about. Even given your theory about head injury, you know that's a stretch.''

"That reminds me. What have you found out about Barrington's injuries? You said you'd check around.''

"Yeah, I know. I haven't found out much of anything yet, but I'll try again,'' he promised, making a note. "I want you to understand that I'm not doing this because I think the judge had anything to do with your harassment. That's way off base, Kate. Way out in left field.''

She nodded, relieved that Lew was as adamant in his denial as he had been before. She didn't want to believe Barrington was capable of doing the things that had been done to terrorize her. It didn't fit with any of her impressions of the judge, either before or after she had met him. Unlike Wilford Mays, her sense of Thorne Barrington was free of menace, and she acknowledged to herself that she really wanted it to stay that way.

THE GATE WAS CLOSED, standing guardian again against the invasion of the outside world. She turned off the engine and sat in the darkness, looking at the wrought iron patterns and thinking about what Mays had told her.

Had Barrington allowed the state to frame the old man because he needed the goodwill of the political establishment? A different picture from the one that had formed in her mind and from the one Barrington had painted when they'd discussed the case. It was obvious that the old man believed he'd been done wrong. The ring of that conviction had been in every word. And insanity behind his cold eyes, she reminded herself.

Because she didn't want to go home, dreading again having to walk into a place she knew had been touched by a different kind of insanity, she opened the car door and then after a moment stepped outside. The heat was less intense since the sun had gone down, but the humidity was still as oppressive. As she stepped up onto the sidewalk in front of the Barrington house, she lifted her hair up off the back of her neck. She should have put it up, she thought. Or maybe she should just get it cut. She was getting too old to wear it this long. Everyone said—

A hand touched her arm and she gasped, turning around with both fists raised defensively. At some point before she completed the blow her terrified brain had ordered, she recognized the man standing behind her. Her right hand almost connected with the side of his jaw anyway, her flash of recognition not quick enough to override the motion she had begun. Thankfully his reflexes were faster than hers. Thorne Barrington caught her arm, holding it high between them, holding tightly enough to prevent another blow.

"God, I'm sorry," she whispered. "I thought—"

Her gaze had fallen to where his right hand was wrapped around her wrist. At least what was left of his hand, she realized. The thumb and the first two fingers seemed to be intact, heavily scarred as was the back of the hand, but at least they were still there—unlike the other two that should have been and were not. Her shocked eyes moved to his face to watch all the muscles tighten, his mouth firming to a slit and his eyes narrowing. His hand unclenched suddenly, freeing her wrist.

"Sorry," he said.

She knew what he was apologizing for. For touching her with that mutilated hand. He had told her he no longer shook hands and this was, of course, the reason. She could imagine the polite, veiled reactions that damage might provoke, especially if one was aware of the way in which he had been injured.

The dark eyes were still stubbornly holding hers, but there was something different in their midnight depths. Not a coldness like Mays's, but still, something.

"What are you doing out here?" he asked, without making any reference to his damaged hand. "Were you coming to see me?"

"I came..." she began and then wondered what in the world she could tell him. "Because I couldn't stand to go home," she finished, a truth she had certainly not intended to share.

"What's wrong?"

"The bastard put his damn confetti in my bed. It was there when I got home from Tucson. I just couldn't face walking in there again tonight. I know how stupid that is, but I couldn't make myself go home. I was just driving around, putting off the inevitable, and somehow...I ended up here."

He was still looking at her with that focused intensity. "You don't have to go home. Not until you're ready. Come inside," he said. "We can talk. Have you eaten? Elliot's probably got something stashed away."

It was an invitation she had no right to expect, and for some reason, her throat tightened with its unexpected kindness. *Come inside*, her subconscious echoed, recognizing how unusual this situation was. Thorne Barrington was standing beside her on the sidewalk outside his house.

"What are *you* doing out here?" she blurted out her unthinking question.

"Out with the *normal* people?" he mocked her surprise, the amusement she had heard before suddenly back in his voice.

"Considering the folks I've been around lately, I'm not so sure about the normal part," she said smiling. "You seem far more normal to me than the people I've been dealing with."

"At least I promise not to put confetti in your bed," Thorne said, and suddenly she remembered Kahler's comment about foreplay. She took a breath, fighting the images the word had produced in her head and knew that despite everything, her obsession with him was still there.

Her eyes fell, determined not to let him see the effect he had on her. When she raised them again, he was smiling at her. Just the smallest lift of that very sensuous mouth. She felt her own lips move, answering. "I'll count on that," she said.

He turned back to the darkness behind him and whistled, the sound low and pleasant. It was apparently as compelling to the dog that bounded out of the shadows along the fence he had been investigating. Kate bent to welcome the cold-nosed greeting, and then watched the retriever return to dance around his master as if they had been separated for days instead of the few minutes Barrington's attention had been directed to her.

"This is why I'm outside," Barrington explained, allowing the dog's unrestrained welcome without the least trace of annoyance. He caressed the silken ears with his damaged hand, and when Kate realized she was watching that movement, she deliberately pulled her eyes away. "Elliot's gone to visit his sister. She had a stroke a few days ago."

"So you had to walk the dog."

There was a small silence before he said, his hand still touching the puppy's head, "Despite the fact that you believe I'm in hiding."

"I had no right to say that to you, Judge Barrington. I wish—"

"Thorne," he corrected. "I thought we'd settled that."

She didn't repeat the name this time, still hesitant to believe that he wanted to be on a first-name basis with her.

"Why is that so difficult for you?" he asked.

"Since I started working on this story, in my head you've always been Judge Barrington. Someone who was not quite…real, I guess."

"Not real?" Again his tone was openly amused.

"Someone I had read about. I wanted to interview you before I did the profile, but you had an unlisted number, and you didn't answer my written request. You just seemed…unapproachable. Unknowable. Always at a distance.''

"Do I still seem unapproachable?" he asked.

"No," she said.

"Would you *like* to come inside, Kate?" he asked again. Patiently. "At least it would offer a respite from having to face your apartment."

"I'd like that," she said, managing a smile, although incredibly her mouth had gone dry, her stomach nervously fluttering. She didn't know why he affected her this way. She could only hope her fascination wasn't obvious.

"So would I," he said. The line of his mouth was controlled, no answering smile, but again there was something in the dark eyes that she had not seen there before.

If this had been any man other than Thorne Barrington, she would have had no doubt about what was in his eyes, but he was so far removed from the world she inhabited that she wasn't quite ready to assign to him its normal masculine attributes.

He was being kind because she had told him she was afraid. That's all it was. She shouldn't imagine there was anything else involved in his invitation, she reminded herself. Despite that very sound advice, her heartbeat had accelerated slightly because what she thought she had seen in the depths of Barrington's eyes had been a very different invitation, one not motivated by kindness or decency. Very compelling to someone who had spent a major part of the last four months daydreaming about him, she admitted, and when he turned to unlock the gate, like the puppy, she followed him inside without question.

Chapter Eight

"Would you like something to drink?" he asked. The retriever had bounded ahead, disappearing into the darkness behind the staircase, but they had stopped in the shadowed foyer.

"I thought you mentioned something about food," she reminded him, smiling.

"You haven't eaten?"

"That was something else I didn't want to do alone in my apartment. I thought about grabbing a bite somewhere, but…"

She paused, because she didn't really know how to explain why she hadn't. She had tried to phone Kahler at work, only to be told he was out. She hadn't left a message, because she didn't know where she was going to be. Not at her apartment. Maybe at some restaurant. Indecisive, she had simply told the policeman who had taken her call that she'd try again later.

She hesitated over confessing to Barrington that while she had daydreamed about him the last four months, Detective Kahler had been her only dinner partner. It sounded as if her relationship with Kahler was more personal than it really was.

"I know," Thorne said. "I always hated eating out alone." His left palm rested lightly against the small of her back, directing her toward the dark into which the dog had disappeared. "There's something about the way people look at you, as if they're wondering why you don't have a friend to join you."

"Or if you're a woman, they decide there's something wrong with you because you couldn't get a date."

She must have hesitated as the passage behind the stairs narrowed to a small hallway, so black she couldn't see three feet in front of her face. The pressure of the guiding hand increased minutely and then disappeared.

"Sorry," he said. "I forget how dark this must seem."

The explanation faded as Thorne stepped around her to lead the way. The white knit shirt he was wearing made following him easy, even through the shadowed hallway. The kitchen was better, illuminated by the filtered glow of the streetlights outside.

"I can make you a sandwich. And there's peach cobbler left from dinner."

"I'll settle for the cobbler. If it's not too much trouble," she added.

"You're sure?"

"Just the pie. I have a sweet tooth."

"Confessions of the damned. Me, too. That's why Elliot plans dessert before anything else."

As he talked, he opened the refrigerator and took out a casserole. Kate wondered why the action seemed vaguely wrong, and then she realized there had been no automatic flash of light when he opened the refrigerator. He closed the door and set the dish on the counter.

"You want it heated?" he asked.

"Not really. When I was a kid I used to eat the leftover cobbler cold. I'd stand in front of the refrigerator, grab a couple of spoonfuls straight out of the bowl, and gobble them down. My mother would have died if she'd caught me."

He laughed. Like Kahler's, his laugh was deep and pleasant, nice to listen to. She watched as he dipped two generous portions into bowls and then opened a drawer to supply them with spoons. The damage to his right hand didn't seem to have caused any loss of dexterity. He had learned to compensate for the missing fingers, and here in his familiar darkness, it seemed he had also forgotten to be self-conscious about them.

He carried the bowls to the small round table set in a windowed bay. He pulled one of the chairs out for her and then seated her. He sat down across from her, unconsciously licking the thick juices of the cobbler off his thumb. The dark eyes looked up to discover she was watching him.

He grinned. Not distant. Not unapproachable.

"My mother would have killed me, too," he said.

She laughed, and then embarrassed to have been caught staring at him, she concentrated on the cobbler and not on Thorne Barrington. The pie was cold and delicious, the peaches sweet and the thickened juices congealed under the sugar-glazed crust.

"This is wonderful," she said after a few mouthfuls. "My compliments to the chef."

"I'll tell Elliot you enjoyed it."

"You don't have a cook?"

"Elliot's the only staff I have. We have a cleaning service that comes in once a week, but Elliot cooks. He's wasted on just me, I'm afraid. His talents were appreciated in my mother's day when there was a lot of entertaining."

"Then he hasn't always been your butler?" she asked, taking another bite of Elliot's cobbler.

"He started in service here when my great-grandfather was alive and worked his way up. Or, as he explains it, he simply outlived everyone else. Becoming my butler was the only way he'd consider letting me pay him half of what he's worth to me. Elliot's standards of being in service are rigidly pre-war."

There was something archaic about his speech patterns,

she thought. She had noticed it before. Maybe it was simply the rarefied social atmosphere he had grown up in. Maybe they all talked this way. It wasn't that she didn't like the way he talked. It was just a little more formal than she was used to, a little out of her league, as she and Kahler had decided. She hadn't even been sure which war Thorne meant. Someone accustomed to those who were "in service" would probably have known what the phrase implied, but her family had never had a butler or a cook, other of course, than her mother.

"The first time I saw Elliot," she said, "I thought he looked like something out of those thirties comedies, Carole Lombard's butler maybe."

There was a small silence, strained, and belatedly she realized she had reminded him of the day she had met Elliot. The day she'd come to accuse Thorne Barrington of sending her the confetti package. The day she'd decided to let a little light into his darkness. "That day," she said, remembering. "Did throwing up the shades cause—"

She cut off the question. The migraines were something he didn't talk about. He had never publicly discussed his injuries. He was a very private man, and just because he had relaxed that vigilance with her tonight didn't give her the right to probe.

Embarrassed, she looked down into the cobbler. She pushed her spoon through a piece of the crust, breaking it into two pieces, the thick, pink-tinged juice seeping up between them.

"Obviously…" he began, and she looked up when he hesitated. "Obviously, you now know some things about me that you didn't know when you came here that day. I find myself curious as to how you know them."

A good reporter protects her sources, she had told him before, but that excuse wouldn't suffice any longer. He had invited her into his home out of kindness, because she had admitted that going into her apartment gave her the willies. He deserved an explanation rather than a brush-off.

"Detective Kahler told me some of them," she said.

"Kahler?" He sounded surprised by the revelation, and given the detective's normal reticence, she understood why.

"And my editor knows some people who...know you." That certainly was vague enough.

"Lew Garrison?" he questioned.

She nodded, pushing her spoon into the cobbler again.

"I see," he said.

When she glanced up, his face had tightened, the line of his mouth again straight and uncompromising. Probably the way he'd looked at the about-to-be-condemned standing before his bench.

"It's not really the way it sounds," she offered. "I just thought I needed to understand what had happened to you."

"I'm always surprised when people I know are willing to talk about me. It's disappointing that friends would share that kind of personal information."

"At first, I believed you'd sent me the package, and I thought that...it was weird that you live the way you do. Lew and Kahler both defended you, gave me some background, some reasons for..."

"The fact that I *hide* in the darkness," he finished for her. His eyes were steady on her face.

"Yes," she said. It was only what she had already said to him. Why bother to deny it? There was another silence. She realized that he had stopped eating a long time ago, his cobbler almost untouched.

"As a matter of fact, a friend of mine called today," he said. "He wanted to warn me that someone had been asking questions about the bombing, specifically about my injuries. He seemed to think it involved an upcoming news story. He suggested I might want to take some kind of legal action to stop it. To stop the invasion of privacy. I'm not a public figure, Kate. I haven't surrendered my right to privacy."

That must have been Lew, she thought, following through on the request she'd made. An entirely personal request for information, now that she was sure Thorne Barrington hadn't been involved with the package she'd received.

"*That's* why you invited me to come in tonight," she said, realizing the truth. "To issue a warning. *Not* because I told you I was afraid to go home." She had wanted him to be some kind of knight in shining armor, so she had made him into one. She had made a fool of herself. Surely she was smarter than this, she thought in disgust.

"Did you have anything to do with that inquiry?" he asked.

She considered lying to him. Denying that she had been the one who had set it in motion. If she didn't deny it, she knew she'd never see him again. But, she reminded herself, what did it matter? Tonight hadn't been what she had thought. Just because she was obsessed with him didn't mean...

"Kate?" he said.

"Yes, I did."

He said nothing in response, although she met his eyes, had made hers make contact until his fell. He was still holding the spoon with his right hand. He put it back into the bowl and pushed it away from him. She could see the depth of the breath he took before he spoke.

"I see," he said. "I suppose I shouldn't be surprised. You *did* try to warn me."

She shook her head, wondering what he meant. She couldn't remembering trying to do anything of the kind.

"If you'll forgive me, Ms. August, I think that it might be wise if we call it a night," he said. Despite what he believed, he wouldn't be rude to her. It wasn't in his nature or in his training.

"It's not what you think," she said and watched the subtle realignment of his mouth. Cynicism this time and not humor.

"I believe that's what you told me the first time," he said.

She remembered then the conversation he was referring to. The parking lot outside the police station. Her confession.

"I could have lied to you. Both times."

"Why didn't you?"

"Because you'd have found out sooner or later."

"And that mattered to you?"

"Yes."

"Because you thought I'd eventually give in and give you a story? Something about my life after Jack? About the bombing itself? How I felt?"

Now she should lie, she thought, hide her real motivation behind what he believed, the easy out his contempt of her profession provided. "No," she said instead.

He didn't probe, but she knew he was still looking at her. She could feel his gaze. She couldn't confess the real reason she had always told him the truth, the real hope behind the things she'd done. Not if he hadn't figured it out on his own, if he didn't feel whatever this was between them.

Between them, hell, she ridiculed. What was between *them* was all in her head. Since she'd collected his pictures. Since she'd done the profile. It had all been just in her head.

She pushed her chair away from the table suddenly and stood up. She had been guilty of doing all the things he hated. She had pried into his private life, had even asked Lew to question his friends. It didn't make any difference that she was really trying to help Kahler catch a madman. If she couldn't convince herself that was the reason for her interest in Thorne Barrington, how could she think she might convince him?

"Thanks for the cobbler," she said. "And for the company," she added, almost bitter that this had all turned out to be something very different from what she had been imagining when he'd invited her in.

She crossed the room and entered the small, dark hallway. Barrington moved fast for a big man. And silently. He caught her before she had emerged into the part of the foyer under the grand staircase. This time he didn't release the grip he had taken on her arm, not even after he had pulled her around to face him and her eyes had fastened again on the damaged hand holding her wrist with such strength.

"Was that *all* it was?" he demanded. "Just for some damn story? Is that what all this is about?"

She struggled, but he refused to let her go.

"Answer me, damn it," he ordered. Although his features were hidden by the shadowed darkness, the black eyes glittered, hard and demanding.

"No," she whispered.

He was close enough that she could smell him. Closer than in the big car the first night. The scent of his body more intimate here in the shadows. Still pleasant. Warm. Male.

"Then what?" he said. "If not for a story, then why the hell do you keep coming here?"

"Please let me go," she said. "You're hurting my arm."

It was a lie, but the hot moisture had begun to burn behind her eyes. She didn't want him to see her cry, and she couldn't tell him the truth. *I'm here because I've fantasized about being with you like this, held close against your body in the darkness.* That was the truth, but not one she could confess. Too humiliating. Too bizarre.

He released her. She had known he would. He was too much a prisoner of his upbringing to do anything else. She didn't move, held motionless by her obsession as she had been from the first. She could see nothing of his expression. There was no clue in his darkness to tell her what she should do.

Leave, her brain ordered suddenly. *Get out.* The instinct to flee was primitive, but very strong.

Obeying it blindly, she began to turn. His left hand, the one that had survived the attempt on his life virtually un-scathed, was suddenly pressed, palm flattened, against the wall beside her, his outstretched arm a barrier to prevent her escape.

She hesitated, unsure again. His hand left the wall and moved to the back of her neck, slipping under the fall of her hair. She didn't react, couldn't have moved away from him had her life depended on it. His fingers slowly threaded upward through the long strands and then spread out against her scalp, cupping the back of her head. The lobe of her ear rested in the V formed between the spreading fingers and the caress of his thumb, which had begun to move back and forth over her cheekbone.

Her eyes closed, her breath sighing out in a small unin-tended whisper of sound. At her response, his hand shifted, drifting forward so that his fingers trailed over her jawline and the sensitive skin beneath it. His thumb teased along her lips, which opened, without her volition, to allow her tongue to touch him. He used his thumb to force her mouth open more widely, pulling downward against her bottom lip, the moisture on his skin cool against her own as his thumb skimmed down her chin to lift her face for his kiss.

His mouth tasted of peaches. Sweet. So sweet. Just as she had imagined. Through the long months. Imagining this so long. His tongue found hers, demanding response. Touch and retreat. Savoring the warmth of his mouth, finally where it belonged. Over hers.

He was exactly the right height, tall enough that she found her body straining upward, made small and somehow more fragile, more feminine by his size. She liked how that made her feel, but she had always known it would feel this way. This rightness.

The kiss wasn't long. He broke the connection, leaning

back slightly as if to read her expression, and she wondered suddenly if his vision were more acute than hers in the darkness. Because this was the way he lived. Surrounded by darkness.

"Not just for a story," he said softly. His voice was deep and intimate, not colored with amusement and not cynical. An acknowledgment of all that had been in her response.

"I told you the truth," she said. "It wasn't for the series. That wasn't why I was asking questions."

He stepped back, half a step farther away, but she felt exposed by the distance between them, by what she had confessed. There was always vulnerability in admitting how you felt. It was inherent in caring for someone and probably necessary, but so risky. The possibility always existed that the other person wasn't interested or wasn't affected in the same way.

"Now what?" she whispered. Get it over with. Find out if she had been as foolish as she felt right now.

The pause was too long. He didn't touch her, and he didn't answer her question. She felt the elation of the kiss begin to fade, and humiliation grow to replace it, rising hotly into her chest and then upward to fill her throat.

She had thrown herself at him. Her mother used to warn her about doing that when she was a teenager, madly in love with her latest crush. *Just don't throw yourself at him, honey.* The words taunted from her memory.

"I don't know," he said, but finally his left hand came up to find her upper arm, thumb smoothing over her bare skin, exposed by the sleeveless silk blouse she was wearing. "I don't know," he said again.

She thought she heard pain in the whisper. "Okay," she said. "It's okay. You don't have to know. As long as you understand that…it isn't the series. I'm not working on a story about you."

"It's been a long time," he said.

The silence that had preceded his comment was not as

strained as before because he was still touching her, but then he didn't go on, didn't finish whatever thought he had had. *Since he'd kissed someone?* she wondered. *Felt this way? Made love?*

"Since?" she prodded softly.

He laughed, a breath of sound.

"Since I kissed a woman. Or wanted to."

"Then I guess I should be flattered."

"Probably not," he said. He had moved closer to her again. She could feel the breath of that comment against her forehead.

"Why not?"

His lips touched where his breath had, almost as lightly.

"This used to all come so easily," he said instead of answering.

"Gettin' women?" she teased, her own laughter soft, buried against the warmth of his throat.

"Knowing what to do. What to say."

"You don't know?"

"My life…" he began. When he stopped, she waited through the pause. "Everything's a lot more complicated than it used to be," he finished finally.

"It doesn't have to be. Complicated."

"Given my…situation, it probably does," he said.

"It wasn't tonight. We sat at the table together. We ate. We talked. It seemed pretty simple to me. Uncomplicated."

"Normal," he said, his tone mocking.

"You're not some kind of…" The phrases Lew had used were suddenly in her head. *Night crawler. Monster.* And then her own. *Vampire.*

"Recluse?" he offered, and her brain relaxed, relieved he hadn't known what she had been thinking. "Yes, I am, Kate. That's exactly what I am."

"By choice," she argued.

"Not really."

"It doesn't matter," she said.

For the first time she took the initiative, moving against him, putting her hands on the wide shoulders. Raising her face for his kiss. Inviting it now.

There was time to wonder what she would do if he didn't respond before his mouth closed over hers. Deeper now, more intense. They both knew now that this was what the other wanted, too, and there was freedom in knowing that. No one was going to have to pull away in embarrassment.

His arms closed around her, and he held her, pressing his body into hers. She realized, a little surprised by the discovery, that he was already strongly aroused. Her back was against the wall of the hallway, his hands possessive over her bottom, pulling her upward into the hard evidence of how much he desired her. It was all happening a little faster than she had expected. She had known how she felt, but he had given her no clue before tonight that he found her attractive. Obviously, he did. At least—sexually attractive.

For some reason she was disconcerted by that idea. Maybe it made no sense, but faced with the unexpected reality that this man was flesh and blood, and not the fantasy she had created, she was suddenly unsure. Her hands flattened against his chest, exerting their own pressure. He released her immediately, again stepping backward into the shadows.

"Maybe you better go," he suggested.

"While the going's good?" she asked, still breathless.

There was again the whisper of his laughter. "It might be easier."

"Easier?"

He took a deep breath, the broad shoulders in the white shirt lifting, visible in the darkness. "Cold showers. Think about something else. All that good advice."

"Do those work?"

"Not with you," he said softly, and her throat closed, hard and tight. "Sometimes I'll wake up in the middle of the night wanting you. Thinking about you being there with me. Where the darkness doesn't matter. Where it's an ally, a friend.''

He had left her with nothing to say. She had thought she was the one taking the risk in confessing how she felt, but what she had done had been not nearly so brave as that.

"Thank you for telling me that," she said.

"I thought it was already rather obvious," he said, and again self-amusement underlay the words. "Pretty damn difficult to hide. Women have all the advantage when it comes to that."

"I guess we do," she agreed.

"When can I see you again?" he asked.

She almost said: Anytime. It was what she wanted to say, but somehow she was still a little guarded. His was a confession to be examined. When she was alone. Just to see if it was as promising as it had sounded when he'd made it.

"You could call me," she said instead.

"I will," he promised.

His left hand was touching her hair. She knew suddenly that if she didn't get out of here pretty soon, she was going to end up…just where he'd said he wanted her. In his bed.

"I really need to go," she said, forcing her voice to remain steady. His fingers were touching her earlobe now.

"I know," he said.

"Thank you for inviting me in."

He put his mouth over hers, enclosing the last word, caressing it with his tongue. More demanding this time. Wanting her. She knew now that he wanted her. She pushed away again, knowing how close she was to giving in to him, giving in to her own obsession. She walked toward the rise of the steps, black against the light filtering around them from the beveled glass door. When she opened it, the crystal tears moved, a small cascade of notes falling into the silence. Then she closed the door behind her, stepping out into the heat of the summer night.

HE STOOD in the shadowed darkness of the hallway, listening. There was no place in his life for the emotions that had flared between them tonight. He had told Kate August the truth—about that, at least. It had been a long time, and it all seemed too complicated now. Too hard to explain. Or too hard to justify.

He knew she was destroying the world he had created—the safe world into which he had retreated. She had accused him of hiding in the darkness and had forced him to contemplate exactly what he was hiding from.

He closed his eyes, but he could still smell her perfume, the scent caught in the shadows that surrounded him and had surrounded him so long. He was no longer sure which was more powerful—the darkness that protected him or what he felt for the woman who had touched him, who had wanted to touch him, despite what he was.

He put both hands flat on the wall before him. The left was as finely made, as strong and powerful as it had ever been. The other was as scarred and damaged as he knew himself to be. His lips twisted with the irony that he had believed—even briefly—that a woman like Kate August might really want to enter his darkness.

Vampire, he thought again, and the mutilated hand curled into a misshapen fist.

KATE DIDN'T go straight home. Not because she was afraid. She just wanted to savor what had happened, to think about what it might mean. Her professional concerns had taken a back seat to events that might have begun as a result of her work but were, as she had suggested to Kahler, very personal.

It was almost eleven when she pulled into the parking lot of her apartment house. Although it was well lighted, the lot was deserted at this hour on a weeknight. She sat in the car a moment, looking around the expanse of concrete and the low plantings around the building. For some reason she hesitated to get out of the car and walk the short distance to the entry door. This was a good neighborhood, which was why she had chosen it, but since the invasion of her home, nothing had felt the same.

Angry with herself for letting the confetti bastard make her lose her courage, she opened the door and stepped out, pressing the automatic lock. She started across the browning strip of heat-dried grass that separated the lot from the entryway.

With every step she took, the feeling she'd had in the car grew. The silence surrounding her felt wrong. Eerie. Like someone was watching her. Eyes following her passage. Only a few more feet. A few—

"Hey!"

Her blood froze. Congealed and stopped, clogging her veins with ice. She whirled around and found Kahler walking toward her. Her relieved gasp was audible.

"What the *hell*, Kahler! You scared me to death. What the hell do you think you're doing?" She was overreacting, but given that he was very well aware of what had happened in her apartment two nights ago, it seemed that he'd have more sense than to sneak up behind her. At least he hadn't touched her. Not like Barrington had earlier. She *would* have had a heart attack.

"Waiting for you. I was worried that you hadn't come home," he said.

His eyes were studying her face. She knew she looked like hell. It had been a long day, and she'd had almost no sleep for the last two nights. "Well, thanks, I guess, but you just came closer to doing me in than anything else that's happened lately."

"Working late?" he asked.

She hesitated. She supposed she could classify the visit to Barrington as work. It wasn't, of course, but he was a legitimate part of the bombing story. "Yeah," she said. "And I'm really tired. Since the home visit of our prankster, I haven't been sleeping too well. I've just been putting off coming back. Dreading finding something worse in my bed.''

"You got the lock," he reminded her.

"I know. Maybe he can pick locks. Who knows?''

"Want me to walk in with you? Check the place out?''

It was a nice offer. He was a nice man, and she truly appreciated his concern. Concerned enough to sit in a dark parking lot waiting to make sure she got home all right.

"How long have you been here?" she asked.

"Sergeant Arnold said you'd called. You didn't leave a message, so I thought maybe it was…personal.'' The hesitation had been revealing. Kahler had given her enough clues in the last couple of weeks to know that he wanted their relationship to be personal. Only, after what had happened tonight—

"Give me your key,'' he said, holding out his hand. "I'll take a look around, and then you'll feel better. Sleep deprivation plays hell with your nerves.''

"To say nothing of your looks,'' she suggested, smiling.

"There's nothing wrong with the way you look, August. Even sleep-deprived.''

She wasn't sure how to respond to that. His eyes were still on her face. She put her key into the outstretched palm and said simply, "Thanks, Kahler. There's nothing wrong with the way you look, either.'' She wasn't sure if that was supposed to be comfort for the fact that she knew he felt differently about her than she did about him. It was a pretty lame remark even if concern had been her motivation.

He put his left arm around her and turned her in the direction she'd been headed when he had stopped her. His hand squeezed her shoulder slightly, and he said, "Come on. You'll feel better inside.''

Probably not, she thought, remembering the last two nights, but she obeyed. She really didn't have a choice, unless she wanted to ask him if she could go home with him. Or unless she wanted to go back to Thorne Barrington's dark mansion, to curl up in his arms, safe and sound from night terrors, maybe, but very vulnerable to a lot of other kinds of danger.

KAHLER EXAMINED the apartment with a casual efficiency. She checked her answering machine while he walked back to the bedroom. There were two messages. She glanced toward the hall leading to the back and decided to play them while Kahler was doing his thing.

After the familiar machine noises came the recording of the slightly accented voice of the man in her bedroom. *"Kahler. They said you called. Give me a ring as soon as you get home."* Short and to the point, she thought, smiling.

The second message was from Lew. It was longer and far more intriguing. *"I did what we talked about, Kate. And I found something that might be... I don't know. Maybe important. Maybe nothing. Just call me. I'll be at the office for a while. I need to run this by you."*

The second call had come in at 7:40 p.m. Sometime while she'd been driving through the twilight streets of a subdivision trying to decide whether to go home or to eat out alone. More than an hour before she had ended up at Barrington's mansion.

"That sounded important," Kahler said from the doorway.

She nodded. Lew rarely called her at home. It was part of his unspoken code of management. "I better call him."

"It's pretty late," he said.

"I'll call his office. If he's not there, I won't bother him at home. Whatever he wants can surely wait until morning."

She had already picked up the phone and begun punching in Lew's private number at the paper. She let it ring maybe fifteen times, but no one picked up. She put the phone back in its cradle and looked up to find Kahler watching her.

"He must have gone home," she offered.

"I guess I'll do the same," he said, moving toward the door.

"Thanks for coming in with me. And for waiting for me."

"You weren't at the paper?" he asked.

She had told him she was working late, but if she thought Lew had been at the office when he tried to get in touch with her, then it was obvious she hadn't been.

"I had an interview," she said.

"They must work the night shift," Kahler suggested. He had stopped at the door, hazel eyes assessing.

She shook her head, knowing he was too smart for her to lie to. Especially a lie as stupid as that one.

"Whoever you were interviewing," he explained, pretending to believe she was puzzled by the comment.

"I went to see Barrington," she said.

"Pretty late for a social call. Or maybe the…interview lasted a while."

"I drove out to see Mays today. I wanted to touch base with the judge about what he told me."

"What did Mays say?"

"Pretty much what you'd expect. That he has nothing to do with Jack. That the state and Barrington framed him on the firearms charge. That Barrington's an SOB who put him away in order to advance his political career."

"Sounds like he gave you an earful."

"Of hate. He's still spewing it out. Barrington's a favorite target."

"You think he's Jack?" Kahler asked.

"What does it matter what I think? Do *you* think he's Jack?"

"Give me a gut reaction," he suggested.

She took a breath, trying to decide what she thought, remembering the cold gray eyes. But it didn't feel right.

Gut reaction. "No," she said. "I don't know why, but I don't."

Kahler nodded.

"Are you still going to talk to him?" she asked.

"Eventually. I *do* have a couple of other cases I'm working on. I haven't had time to get around to Mays yet, but I will. It's too big a coincidence to ignore."

"Is he right about Barrington? About going along with a frame? You read the transcript."

"I didn't have time. But what if Barrington *did* do what Mays said? What's so wrong about putting a killer away, however you can, for as long as you can?"

"The same thing that's wrong with cops planting evidence. With federal labs skewing test results to favor the prosecution. You know what's wrong with it."

"The idea of the judge screwing the old man—metaphorically, of course—" Kahler said, an edge of sarcasm in his voice, "doesn't sit too well, does it?"

"It just doesn't fit with what I believed about him."

"Maybe you better reexamine some of your beliefs," he suggested. "And in the meantime, come put the chain on the door. Things will look better in the morning. They always do."

He closed the door behind him. Kate waited a moment, listening to his footsteps fade. She crossed the small living room to slip the chain into place. When she turned around, the apartment looked cold and empty. It was home, but it sure didn't feel very welcoming.

She didn't want to go into the bedroom the prankster had invaded, but the idea of spending another night trying to sleep on her couch wasn't appealing. She hated it, but there wasn't any need to try to deny how she felt, at least not to herself.

Her eyes found the phone and her mind replayed the message Lew had left. She glanced again at her watch. Maybe she should try Lew at home. He'd certainly understand her need to know just what he thought he'd found out about the case that had baffled everybody for the last three years. Lew would certainly understand—even if she woke him up to ask.

She looked up Lew's home phone number in her address book and again listened to the phone, counting the rings before the answering machine picked up. She put the receiver back in its cradle without leaving a message. If Lew wasn't at home, that meant he must still be at the paper, maybe just not in his office. Looking at microfilm, maybe. Reading the articles the local papers had done on the Barrington bombing. Trying to decide if the ''might be nothing'' thing he'd discovered might be something instead. And if he were still at the paper...

Without giving herself time to decide it was a bad idea, Kate picked up her purse, scrambling through the junk to find the car keys she had dropped inside. It might be a wasted trip, but at least it would burn a few more minutes of the night—a few minutes' reprieve from trying to sleep in the contaminated apartment.

Chapter Nine

Lew wasn't at the paper. They told her that he'd left around eight, which didn't make a lot of sense, given the contents of the message on her machine. Lew had definitely indicated he would be working for a while, and then he'd left the office less than half an hour later.

She even went upstairs to see if he might have put a note on her desk to explain where he was going. He must have known that the enigmatic message on her machine would set her wondering. There was, however, nothing on the surface of her desk except the same mess that had been there when she'd left the office this afternoon. And the door to Lew's office was locked.

It took her about ten seconds after she got back into her car to make the choice between going back to her apartment or heading to Lew's house.

As she drove, she fought the useless speculations about what Lew might have discovered. She tried to remember his exact wording and wished she'd saved the message so that if this journey turned out to be a wild-goose chase, she could at least play back the tape when she got home. *I did what I promised... Or I did what we talked about...* She wasn't positive how Lew's opening sentence had been phrased.

But she did know that he had told her he'd check out

Mays's possible association with any of the current hate groups and that he would contact people who knew Barrington and make some inquiries about his injuries. Based on what Thorne had told her, she knew that Lew had done exactly what he'd promised as far as pursuing information about the judge's injuries was concerned, so if he'd found out something that might be important...

Her mind retreated from that conclusion. She didn't want to believe that Lew had learned anything that might have made him change his mind about Barrington's involvement in the confetti package or in invading her apartment to leave that distinctive message between the sheets of the bed she slept in every night.

Into her head drifted Thorne's confession. *Sometimes I'll wake up in the middle of the night wanting you. Thinking about you being there with me.* Was it possible that because he was sexually attracted to her he had...

Again, she forced the rejection of the thought that seemed disloyal, somehow, after what had happened between them tonight. *Between them,* she thought, remembering her earlier fears. Despite her worries over how whatever Lew wanted to tell her might reflect on the man she had admitted she was obsessed with, she liked the sound of that. The reality of it. *Between them.*

There were lights on inside Lew's house. He must have had some errands to run between leaving the paper and coming home. Maybe he had talked to someone else between the time he'd put the message on her machine and the time he'd left the office. That would help explain why he wasn't there when he'd clearly indicated he planned to be around a while.

She opened the car door and stepped out onto the brick driveway. She had been here before. Lew had hosted a few employee Christmas parties before his wife's death from ovarian cancer almost four years ago. To everyone's surprise, Lew had chosen to keep this house in the suburbs rather than moving into a town house or an apartment, smaller and more convenient for a man living alone. It must get lonely at times, she thought, rattling around in this big empty place alone. Lew didn't talk about his private life, and she didn't ask. She considered him a friend, but they didn't have that kind of relationship.

She rang the bell and heard the distant melodious chime. The street behind her was as quiet and peaceful as you'd expect from a neighborhood with houses in this price range. Very far removed from the crime and violence that plagued the hearts of major cities. Out here in this pricey neighborhood the inhabitants could imagine themselves safe from that particular taint of society's ills.

There was no response to the bell. She hesitated, wondering if she could be mistaken about the meaning of the lights. Maybe Lew simply left a few burning downstairs as a safety precaution. She was going to feel like an idiot if he showed up in his pajamas and robe, awakened by her repeated demands at his door. Even as the image formed, she pressed the ivory-colored button again and listened to the interior chime once more.

Her hand dropped to touch the elaborate brass handle of the door and without her conscious direction, her thumb pressed the release. The latch moved downward and the door opened. A sense of unease twisted in her stomach. Not the slight worry about embarrassing herself she had felt before, standing outside ringing her boss's doorbell at eleven-thirty on a weeknight. This was much stronger, much more compelling. Doors were supposed to be locked at night. That was the twentieth-century reality, even in the old, exclusive neighborhood where this house stood.

The foyer the opened door revealed was dark, but there was light filtering in from somewhere beyond the hall. The white-and-pink marble squares of the foyer floor reflected the shadowed illumination from the house's interior, softly gleaming in the dimness, inviting in their timeless beauty.

She opened the door a little wider, leaning into the entrance hall without actually stepping inside.

"Lew," she called, pitching her voice into the waiting stillness. There was no answer, so she called again, more loudly this time, her voice echoing slightly, bouncing off the cold expanse of the marble. Unanswered. The feeling that something was wrong was growing, fear, as it had in the parking lot tonight, mushrooming with sick certainty inside her body. What was she so afraid of? she wondered. Why the hell was she making such a big deal of this?

Because she was spooked, and she had been for a couple of days. Because of the confetti and maybe because she had talked to Mays today, had seen the cold hatred in his eyes. The craziness. All of this was crazy. She ought to get out of here. Lew would be at the office in the morning. She could talk to him then, and he'd never have to know she'd come to his house tonight. This was as stupid as walking into Barrington's mansion that night because the gate had been open. *I don't know why he didn't shoot you,* Kahler had said. That was the normal twentieth century response to someone entering your house at night. What she was doing was dangerous. Stupid and dangerous.

Except, her rational mind reminded, there *had* been something wrong at Barrington's. Her instincts then had been right on the money, and something wasn't right tonight. Despite the urge to cut and run, she knew that something was very wrong here.

Steeling herself, she stepped inside the foyer, but she left the door open behind her. She tried to remember the layout of the house from the parties she had attended here. That had been several years ago, and the house then had echoed with noise and color, filled with Christmas smells. Candles and holly and perfume. Spiced cider. While she stood uncertainly in the darkened foyer, the pleasant memories swirled inside her head.

"Lew?" she called again, questioning the silent darkness. There was still no answer, so she walked across the marble squares, her footsteps echoing as hollowly as her voice had. She remembered the layout as she walked, the pieces of memory floating into her head. Spacious living room to her right. Dark. The dining room where Lew's wife had arranged the buffets during those Christmas parties was on her left. She kept walking, past the stairs that rose beyond the double doorway to the living room. They were nothing like the curving staircase at Thorne's house. Only the darkness at the top was the same.

The room at the end of the entrance hall was lighter. The den or great room or whatever people were calling it now. But the light she had seen from the first was coming from the kitchen. She headed across the den to the left, remembering white, glass-fronted cabinets, and a lot of hanging brass. It had been a nice blend, new and old elements, clean and open.

It, too, was deserted, looking ordinary and functional in the cold fluorescent light of the above-the-sink fixture. Nothing scary here. The wide windows that surrounded the breakfast table were uncurtained to let in the morning sun. The neatly landscaped backyard and the subdued underwater lights of the pool they looked out on were beautiful in the moonlight.

She turned around, looking back across the kitchen, back the way she had come. Nothing was wrong, her brain reassured. *Gut reaction?* Kahler had asked. And her gut reaction right now was that something here was very definitely wrong.

Lew's office, she remembered. He had been very proud of his new computer system the night of the last party. A relatively recent convert to the wonders of technology, at least home technology, he had dragged anyone willing to be dragged back to the office to examine the equipment, delighted to show it off.

The study was on the other side of the den. She walked

back to the doorway of the kitchen and looked across the shadowed den. The door to Lew's office, almost directly across from where she was standing, was closed. There was a thread of light under the bottom, just visible between the mahogany and the thick pale peach of the den carpet. As she started across the room, the phrase from childhood games of hide-and-seek intruded. Getting warmer. Much nearer to whatever was going on, she thought, when she was standing before the door. "Lew?" she called. There was no answer. She waited a moment before she repeated the word. She raised her hand and tapped against the solid wood as she spoke. "Lew?"

Then, as it had at the entry door, her hand made its own decision, reaching downward to touch the knob, which turned easily under her fingers. She pushed the door open, her eyes seeking the big antique desk that dominated the opposite end of the room. The light she had seen under the door had come from its green-shaded lamp.

The reason Lew hadn't responded to her repeated calls was apparent. Behind the spread of equipment, she could make out his body slumped forward, his head pillowed on his right arm that was resting on the top of the computer system's printer.

Working too late, she thought, smiling in sudden compassion. And no one to miss him upstairs. She debated leaving him, but given his cramped position among the electronic peripherals on the crowded surface of the desk, she knew he'd pay the price tomorrow. A sore neck. A short temper. Some price.

"Lew," she said again, relief making her voice stronger. She took a farther step into the room and then stopped. All the images from the devastation in Austin burst into her head. This was a different devastation, but even in the play of light and shadow, there was no doubt, now that she was this close. Lew Garrison wasn't asleep. There could be no doubt about that either, given the fact that the back of his head...

Retching, she turned away, stumbled across the small office and out into the den. She had enough presence of mind to realize she had to get out of the study. Not just because of the horror it contained, the splatter of blood on the wall behind the desk, the smell hot and strong and distinctive as no other smell, but because whatever she touched would be contaminated.

Crime scene. The familiar words were in her head, their importance fighting her natural inclinations to go to Lew, to make sure of what she already knew. And fighting also that other inclination. The one that screamed at her to run, as far and as fast as she could manage. To get the hell out of this house.

She stopped in the middle of the expanse of expensive peach carpeting and made herself take a couple of calming breaths. Her head swam sickeningly when she closed her eyes, so she opened them and held them open by sheer will to look for a phone.

She knew she couldn't go back into Lew's office, even if that was the most likely place to find a telephone. She couldn't go upstairs, into the unknown darkness where, perhaps, whoever had killed Lew was hiding. How could she be sure the killer had left? she thought, the panic building again.

She fought it down, knowing that what she *had* to do was call the cops. No one had known she was coming here. It had been impulse. Lew's murderer wasn't waiting for her. He was long gone. Her rational mind knew that. She was reacting like a child and not like an adult. Not thinking, just feeling. But when she began to move again, it was toward the light, toward the pleasant openness of the white kitchen.

Thank God there was a phone on the wall. She dialed 911, trying to remember Lew's exact street address before the operator picked up. She had looked it up in her address book before she'd gotten on the interstate, so the numbers were still in her head, despite the fact that she'd left her purse in the car.

She had to repeat her story a couple of times, and then she did exactly what she had been told to do. Despite all her instincts screaming at her to get out of the house, she stood in the kitchen, waiting for the patrol car they had promised was on the way. But she never took her eyes off the doorway.

IT WAS PROBABLY half an hour after the first police car had arrived that Kahler got there. She had told the cops she believed Lew's death had something to do with Jack and had urged them to call Detective Kahler. The men she had talked to were so calm, accustomed to dealing with violence and its aftermath. Once she would have claimed that after her years on the paper, she was pretty acclimated to man's inhumanity to man, but Austin had taught her better. And tonight.

They had sent her out onto the patio that surrounded the pool. One of the cops had stayed with her, taking notes on what she told him and then probably staying just to keep her company. Eventually, with her repeated assertions that she was fine—just as false as those she'd made the day in the office when the fake bomb had gone off in her lap— he'd gone back inside.

Through the glass of the patio doors, she had watched Kahler arrive and disappear with the forensics people into the study. She was still watching when he came out and posed his questions to the cop who'd taken her story. The cop pointed to the backyard, and Kahler looked up, his eyes meeting hers through the glass.

She watched him cross the den and open the patio door beside the fireplace and walk over to stand in front of her. He didn't say anything for a moment, and then, as she had once before, she moved into his arms, which opened automatically to enclose her.

Kahler held her tight, safe and protected. "What the hell made you decide to come over here tonight, August?" he asked.

She could feel the words rumble through his chest, his breath stirring against her hair. She knew she should step away, formulate some kind of answer, quit hiding, but it was physically impossible to move. All her reserves of strength had been sapped by the realization that Lew was dead, so she answered with her cheek still resting against the starched blue oxford cloth that covered Kahler's shoulder.

"The message he left on my machine. I couldn't get it out of my head—the thought that finally Lew might have found something. I knew I wasn't going to be able to sleep, so I went back to the paper. Lew had left about eight, but that didn't make any sense to me. So, I decided to come over here on the chance he might still be awake." She shivered, remembering her initial reaction to the body.

"Why did you come in?" Kahler asked, his lips against her hair. His hand was making comforting circles over the tightness in her shoulders. Relaxing a little of the tension and the fear.

"There was a light. I thought..." She paused, trying to recreate exactly what she had thought. "I rang the bell and no one answered, and then I opened the door. It wasn't locked, Kahler, and I knew it should have been. I looked around, and when I remembered Lew's study, I went back there."

"It's all right," he said, apparently feeling the shuddering force of the breath she took. "Everything's okay. I'm here. Nothing's going to happen to you, Kate. I won't let anything happen to you."

An official promise maybe, but his tone had not been very official, she thought. Definitely not. She was infinitely grateful for his personal attention, grateful for his kindness, and especially grateful for that assurance.

"Did you touch anything?" he asked.

"The phone in the kitchen. The front door. The door to the study. I can't remember touching anything else."

"Good girl," he said, his voice warm, complimenting.

"I went about halfway into the study. I thought he was just asleep. Then I went in far enough to see…"

"It's all right," Kahler said again. His voice was still calm, soothing her obvious distress.

"Whatever he found out," she said, leaning back from his embrace far enough to see his face, "it was enough to get him killed, Kahler. Something pretty damned important."

He nodded, agreeing with her, still comforting.

"Was there anything on the desk that would give you a clue to whatever…?" she began and saw the quick, denying movement of his head.

"We don't know yet. We have to wait for the lab boys to finish, let the coroner remove the body, before we can look for anything like that."

"Oh, dear God," she said softly, finally feeling the tears begin to slip out past her control. She raised her head, looking upward into the night sky, biting her lips to keep from letting it all pour out. *The body.* Maybe to Kahler, long inured to this, Lew was just "the body," but to her he had been a friend. Someone who had died perhaps because he had asked the questions she had wanted him to ask. *Her* questions had gotten him killed.

Kahler pulled her against him, his hand on the back of her head, pushing her face into his shoulder. He was only a little taller than she, and she buried her head and let the tears come. The words he whispered while she cried weren't official either, but right now she needed what he was giving her, needed to feel the strength of his arms holding her. Very human comfort.

Eventually she cried it all out, her mind drained by the shock of what had happened. The ugly sobs lessened, and she had presence of mind enough to think what a female thing crying like this had been. Someone who broke down into hysterical tears wasn't exactly the image she had always had of herself, certainly not the one she wanted to portray to the world. She pushed away from him to wipe her nose, and then using the back on her hand, she tried to rub away the evidence of her tears.

Kahler pulled out a handkerchief and began to clean the mascara off her cheeks. He worked gently, with steady concentration, and she found herself really looking at his face for the first time. Thinking about him as a man, and not a cop.

Not the flashy good looks Thorne Barrington had, maybe, but a nice face. Strong. She especially liked the lines around his eyes. He looked up from the mess she'd made of her makeup to find her eyes on him, and he smiled at her.

"Thanks," she said, embarrassed to have cried and to have been caught studying his face, maybe her own revealing what she'd been thinking.

"My pleasure," he said, and the corners of his mouth lifted again, the small creases around his eyes moving. "Let's get out of here," he suggested.

She was a little surprised that he wanted to leave, would be willing to walk away from the scene. Somehow she had thought Kahler was as obsessed with this case as she. "Now?" she asked.

"I need to get you home," he said.

The small sound of protest she made in response to that idea was automatic. Her apartment was the last place she wanted to be. Trying to deal with Lew's death, with her guilt over her role in it, and remembering that damn confetti in her bed. She knew that she'd be wondering all night how it all was related.

"My place?" Kahler suggested.

Ordinarily, she'd never have agreed. It was a bad idea, considering what she believed about Kahler's feelings, but right now it felt like an answer to prayer, so she nodded.

"Please," she said.

"Let me tell them inside. I'll be right back. We won't go through the house. I'll take you around. Wait right here."

She was more than willing to follow his instructions. More than willing to let Kahler make the decisions. More than willing to let him take care of her. And she realized that it felt pretty good to *have* someone take care of her for a change.

KAHLER FIXED HER the bourbon and Coke she had asked for, a taste left over from college, and seated her on his oversized sofa while he disappeared into the back of the apartment to make a couple of phone calls. She imagined they were related to Lew's death and that he knew she didn't need to hear them right now.

She sat on the couch, shoes off, feet up, sipping the sweet, smoky darkness of his good bourbon, and let her eyes wander around the room. It was masculine, dark colors, massive, comfortable furniture. There were some nice prints on the walls, well-framed and well-placed, and a lot of books. There was only one photograph, a small, maybe five-by-seven-inch print in a wooden frame. Because she was curious, she got up to look at it, fighting the lethargy of the bourbon and the emotional trauma.

It was a photograph of a pre-adolescent Kahler, the strong features distinctive, even given the difference of more than a couple of decades, and a pretty little girl, maybe three years old. She had the same hair as Kahler. Same shape eyes, but darker than his, more chocolate than hazel. He had told her he grew up with his mother and sister. Obviously, this was the sister. She hadn't realized the difference in their ages. She was still holding the framed photograph in her hand when Kahler came back into the room. She turned to smile at him, and his eyes flicked to the picture she held and then back to hers.

"Is this your sister?" she asked.

He nodded.

"I didn't realize there was so much difference in your ages."

"Nine years," he said. He walked to the counter where the bottle of bourbon stood and poured two fingers into the bottom of a kitchen glass. He leaned against the counter, watching her as she set the photograph back in the spot it had occupied on the small desk. He was rolling the bourbon around on his tongue, obviously more a connoisseur of good whiskey than she. He had probably thought the concoction she was drinking a sacrilege.

She went back to the couch and put her feet back up. *Making myself right at home,* she thought, taking a sip of her drink.

"You want to talk about this or wait a while?" Kahler asked.

"About Lew?"

"You can come down to the office if you'd rather. I just thought it might be easier for you if..."

"If I just told you."

"Whatever you want to do, Kate. There's no hurry. You can just sit here and get soused, if you feel like it."

"That won't make it go away."

"You're right about that," he acknowledged.

He took the last of his bourbon into his mouth and set his glass down on the counter. He walked across to take the chair opposite the couch she'd adopted. Despite their closeness earlier tonight, she appreciated the distance. Appreciated his recognition that this wasn't the time or the place for moving in on her. She didn't need that kind of pressure right now.

"Let's get it over with," she said finally. "I'd rather talk to you than someone else."

"Then start with the message on the machine. Garrison said, 'I did what we talked about.' What did he mean?"

"I couldn't even remember what he'd said. I tried to think, but I couldn't remember, and I'd already erased the message."

"What had you talked about?"

About Thorne Barrington, she thought. *About Lew asking questions about his injuries, talking to his friends.* That was something she knew Lew had done, but telling Kahler that was going to be hard. It made it sound as if Thorne must be involved in Lew's death, and she didn't believe that. Besides, Barrington hadn't been the only thing they'd discussed.

"I'd just gotten back from Mays's house. I went to tell Lew where I'd been because he'd been out of the office when I left. I wanted to run what Mays had said by him, to get his reaction."

She hesitated, trying to remember exactly what had been said. It was the kind of conversation she and Lew had had a hundred times. She couldn't have known, of course, how important what had been said might prove to be. Or that it would be the last conversation she'd ever have with him. She cleared that thought from her mind and concentrated on remembering.

"We talked about Mays. I told him what Mays thought of Barrington."

"Did you tell him you didn't feel Mays was Jack?"

She shook her head. She hadn't made that decision until Kahler's question had forced her to, after she'd talked to Lew.

"He asked me if Mays had any association with any of the hate groups," she said, remembering. "I didn't know, so Lew said he'd ask around, talk to you about that. Did he call you?"

Kahler shook his head.

"He probably didn't have time to get around to it," she suggested. She racked her brain trying to think what else had been said. Now was the time to tell Kahler that Lew *had* had time to do the other thing she knew they'd talked about. He *had* made inquiries about Barrington's injuries. It felt so wrong to tell the police that, but just because she knew Thorne had nothing to do with Lew's death didn't mean she could withhold evidence.

"Lew told me he'd check on the possibility..." She paused, realizing how awful her idea would sound in this context. It hadn't sounded so brutal when she'd believed Thorne might have had something to do with the confetti bomb, but now, with Lew's murder, it sounded...incriminating. "About the possibility that Barrington had some brain damage. From the bomb. If it could make him do things that were...out of character."

"Brain damage?" Kahler repeated, his tone disbelieving.

"Sometimes after a head injury, people do things they would normally never think about doing," she argued. It sounded a lot dumber now than it had the first time she'd proposed it.

"Like blowing people up?" Kahler asked sarcastically.

"No, of course not. I didn't think even then that Barrington was blowing people up. I *never* thought Barrington was Jack, Kahler, but I *did* think for a while he'd sent me the confetti. You knew that. It was just weird enough..." Again she paused, feeling disloyal.

"What did Garrison think about your idea?"

"That it was way off base. Like you, he never thought Barrington was involved with any of this. Other than being the first victim. We talked about that, too. Maybe not the last time I talked to Lew, but sometime. That Barrington was one name we knew was still on Jack's list."

"You think he's going to try for Barrington again?"

"Before he's through," she said, nodding. "We just don't have any idea when that will be."

Kahler didn't comment. There was really nothing to say, but she suddenly realized the possibility Jack wasn't through was a lot scarier than it had been when she and Lew had talked about it. Before she had gotten to know Thorne. Before they had…

She turned her thoughts away from the shadowed hallway in Barrington's mansion. What had occurred there seemed to have taken place a long time ago instead of only a few hours. Too much had happened in between. With Lew's death, the reality of Thorne Barrington's danger had been graphically reinforced.

"Who was Lew supposed to ask about the injury?" Kahler interrupted that sudden realization.

She looked up, wondering how long she'd been thinking about Barrington instead of what she was supposed to be doing. "I don't know. He just said they had some mutual acquaintances. He didn't mention names."

"So we'll probably never know if he got around to asking."

Now, her brain ordered. *Tell him now.*

"He asked *somebody,*" she said, feeling sick.

"How do you know?"

"Judge Barrington told me. At his house tonight."

"How could he know?"

"The friend called him. Told him someone was asking questions for a news story. He thought Barrington might want to fight the invasion of privacy with some sort of legal action."

"And Barrington was willing to talk to you after that?"

Kahler had been the one who had told her how much the judge hated the press. No wonder he was skeptical.

"I think he wanted to pick my brain. Maybe warn me to back off any story about him."

"He thought you were the one making inquiries?"

"I think he knew it was Lew, but he also knew this had always been my story. That whatever Lew was asking was for me."

"Was he angry?"

Before or after he kissed me? Before he confessed that he wanted me in his bed? Or maybe, she thought, maybe he had been just setting her up—a willing and ready source of information. Maybe he believed that coming on to her was the way to get her to drop the story. Suddenly, nothing that had happened tonight seemed to mean what she had thought it meant.

"Kate?" Kahler prodded.

"About like you'd expect. He doesn't like publicity."

She looked down at the drink she still held. The ice had melted. She took a sip, trying to banish the doubts from her mind. *Not what she had thought it was* wouldn't leave her head, circling along with all the other memories of this night.

"Did Barrington kick you out?" Kahler asked.

"No," she denied. *He kissed me. He told me he wanted me in his bed, had thought about having me there. About making love to me.* "No, nothing like that," she said aloud.

"What time did you talk to him?"

"I got there…maybe 8:45. Maybe closer to nine. I don't know exactly."

"Barrington was home when you arrived?"

"Yes," she agreed, and then she realized why he'd asked, the significance of that question. "You don't think—" she began and hesitated while she thought about what that meant. "Kahler, you can't believe Barrington had anything to do with Lew? Because of what *I* said?"

"This is my job, August. Asking questions. It's your job to answer them. Your duty as a good citizen." There was an edge of cynicism in his voice that hadn't been there before.

"What time did Lew die?" she asked.

"We won't know until we get the coroner's report."

"When will that be?"

"A few days."

"Barrington had nothing to do with this," she said, trying to let him hear her certainty.

"Given the fact that he never leaves the house, that should be easy enough to prove," Kahler agreed.

But he had, Kate realized. He had been outside the house when she arrived tonight. Because Elliot had been away. Thorne's explanation had been logical, of course, but—

"Is Barrington a suspect?" she asked.

He didn't answer her immediately, but it didn't matter because she already knew.

"Because of what I told you," she said, despairing. "God, you're so wrong. Don't make a fool of yourself, Kahler. Because you're wrong, and as you reminded me, Barrington's got all the marbles, all the high-powered attorneys."

His eyes studied her face for a moment.

"Just like he always has," Kahler said simply.

Chapter Ten

She spent the night on Kahler's big couch. She even managed to sleep a few hours. After bringing sheets and a light blanket and showing her the bathroom, Kahler had disappeared into his bedroom, and he hadn't come out again. Kate appreciated the privacy as much as she did the comfort of knowing he was there, that she wasn't alone.

When dawn arrived, throwing its weak light into the room, she was ready, welcoming permission not to have to lie there any longer, letting the events of the previous night tumble through her head. She walked barefoot across the beige carpet to push the linen-weave draperies back from the center of the window.

She looked down again at the photograph of Kahler and his sister. She wondered what kind of brother he'd been. Protective, maybe. He had treated her that way last night, like a brother. There had been no embarrassment and no discomfort about spending the night here. Just a safe place to stay.

She picked up the picture, turning it into the fragile morning light, examining both subjects. Kahler, before the reality of what he did for a living made all those intriguing lines she'd noticed last night. Young. Innocent. Like the little girl with her dark, trusting eyes. She had probably worshipped the boy he had been, looking up to him from the far distance of nine years.

Kate smiled, carrying the frame back to the coffee table and again taking her place on the big couch. She pulled the blanket up over her feet and legs, the air-conditioning a little too efficient, especially this time of day.

"Good morning," Kahler said from the doorway that led to the hall. He was already dressed for work, another starched blue oxford cloth shirt, gun and shoulder holster in place. He walked into the kitchen to begin making coffee. "You get any sleep?"

"More than I expected," Kate said. "Thanks for letting me stay. I really don't think I could have gone home last night."

"That couch is available anytime. Just say the word."

"Don't offer unless you mean it. After all that's happened, I might take you up on it too often."

"I don't think you're in any danger, Kate. If I did—"

"How can you say that?" she interrupted. "Lew's dead because of something he found out about Jack. And everyone knows this is my story. What makes you think whoever killed Lew won't think I also know whatever he had found?"

"Because no one was watching your apartment last night. No one was following you. It was Garrison the killer was interested in, because he let the wrong person know that he'd discovered something dangerous."

"I'm the one who went to see Mays."

"I don't think Mays has anything to do with it."

"He's crazy, Kahler. Crazy enough to do anything. You didn't see his eyes."

"If Mays was going to take out after someone, who would it be? Think, Kate. Who does Mays blame for his troubles?"

"Barrington. The authorities."

"*Not* Lew Garrison."

"Maybe Lew found out that Mays *is* involved in one of the hate groups. Maybe he asked that question to someone besides you, asked the wrong person, just like you said. Lew had sources all over this city. This is his city, and after all these years, he knows the people who know where all the bodies are buried."

"I'll check it out," Kahler said, but there was no conviction in the promise, obviously made only to pacify her.

"You think it was some *other* question he asked that precipitated what happened to him last night." She knew what he thought. He had already made that clear.

"I'll check that out, too."

"You're the one who told me what an upstanding citizen Barrington was. You and Lew. Why are you now—"

"Because Lew's dead. Apparently he wasn't as good a judge of character as he thought. He confided in somebody or tried to investigate something he should have left to the police. Playing cop will get you in trouble every time. That's something you better remember, August. You let me ask the hard questions."

She nodded. There wasn't much else to say. Something Lew had said or done had gotten him killed, and she didn't want to be next. Kahler was only trying to protect her. Her eyes moved back to the little girl in the photograph. Big brother.

"Did she ever get mad at you for trying to boss her around?" she asked, indicating with her hand the picture she'd moved.

"Probably," he said, hazel eyes studying the photograph as if he hadn't looked at it in a long time.

"Your folks still alive, Kahler?"

He shook his head. "Yours?"

"Yeah, both of them. Same little town. Nothing ever changes with them. And I hope it won't," she added.

"Then you're lucky."

"I know. So what was growing up like for the two of you?"

"Ordinary. Small town."

"Me, too."

"I don't remember my father. He wasn't around long enough to make an impression. My stepfather just disappeared one day. Mom kept telling us he was coming home soon. Jenny may have believed her, but I knew better. It was no great loss. He hadn't been much while he was around."

Kahler was leaning against the bar as he had last night, sipping orange juice this time. Relaxed. Discussing what was just another part of the reality of his life, something he had apparently accepted a long time ago.

"Your mom raised you alone, you and your sister?"

"With the help of a succession of…boyfriends." There was an underlying harshness in his pronunciation of the word. It would have been hard for an adolescent boy to accept another man in his mother's life, no matter what the circumstances were. "We were always pretty much on our own. I guess my mother did the best she could, given…the circumstances."

His voice faded, and she watched him lift the glass to swallow the remainder of the liquid it held.

"What does your sister do? She's not a cop?"

"No, not a cop," he said. Kate waited through the pause. His eyes, almost as dark now as the little girl's, were again on the photograph. "Jenny died. Almost eight years ago."

"God, Kahler, I'm sorry. I never dreamed… She must have been very young."

There was no response.

"What happened?" she asked softly.

He glanced up, not at her, but at the light coming from the opening she'd created when she'd pushed the curtain aside.

"An accident. A drunk driver," he said dispassionately, but the emotion was there. Hidden, as always, with Kahler.

"I'm sorry. That must have been really rough."

"It happened a long time ago. You learn to deal."

She nodded.

"You want to take me to work, or you want me to call somebody?" he asked, the memories deliberately cleared from his voice. He had driven her car last night, allowing her time to sit in the darkness and deal with what had happened at Lew's. *You learn to deal,* Kahler had said. And she would.

"No, I'll drive you. I need to get back to my place and change clothes."

"You going in to the paper?"

"Yeah," she said, and she was surprised by how reluctant she was to do that. "It's what they pay me this enormous salary to do. I want to look around in Lew's office. It was locked last night. I thought he might have left whatever he was working on in there. There could be something that might give me a clue as to what direction he was pursuing."

"I'm not sure that's a good idea," Kahler said. "Why don't you let someone from the department take a look? The less involved you are with whatever Lew Garrison found the better."

"How can the police know what was new, what Lew discovered only yesterday? I know everything that's in those files, Kahler. If Lew jotted down notes or made a stray comment in the margin, it might tell me what he was thinking. No one else knows what was already there. No one else can recognize what's been added."

"Given the time frame, Garrison probably didn't have time to make notes. I wouldn't get my hopes up. I've got a feeling he found what he found and then, probably without thinking too much about what he was doing, he mentioned it to the wrong person. Maybe he was trying to feel them out and it backfired.''

"Lew wasn't stupid.''

"I don't mean to suggest that. But he's dead, and my guess is that whatever he was talking about on your answering machine is the cause.''

She nodded again. It was the obvious conclusion.

"If you find something in the files, Kate, don't act on it. That's not your job. Come to me. I'll pursue whatever it is, and unlike Garrison, I'll bring along some backup. I don't want you ending up like your boss.''

"Okay, big brother,'' she agreed, smiling at him. "I can assure you I don't want to end up…'' She paused, the image of the room last night suddenly too vivid in her memory. "I promise, Kahler, not to make a move without you.''

SHE HAD DROPPED Kahler off and driven home in the early-morning traffic, changing lanes and making her exit automatically, her mind still involved with everything that had happened in the last twenty-four hours. It was almost too much to assimilate. Her brain worried at each separate event like a terrier working over a well-chewed slipper, trying to fit them together until, at the end of each train of thought, logic asserted itself to reiterate that they didn't fit. Nothing tied together. At least, not in any way she wanted it to.

Her apartment looked ordinary in the light of day. She wondered why it didn't look this way—safe and nonthreatening—when darkness fell. She threw her suit coat over the back of the sofa and began unbuttoning the silk blouse.

She wanted to get out of her clothes, send them out to the cleaners as soon as possible. She wanted to take a hot shower and wash her hair. As if by doing those things she could cleanse the horror of what she had found at Lew's house from her mind.

She punched the play button on the answering machine by habit, not even looking at the display. She knew that she'd almost certainly erased both Kahler's and Lew's messages, automatically destroyed them, since there had been no phone numbers left with either. That was the usual deciding factor.

She was right. The voice that filled the room was not the accented one of the man whose couch she'd slept on last night. Its timbre was as deep, but it was homegrown, the cadence so familiar it didn't even qualify in her mind as having an accent.

"I just wanted to say good-night," the recording of Thorne Barrington's voice said. "Call me when you get in." And then he gave his number, which she knew was unlisted.

Her hand hesitated over the erase button, and instead, she hit rewind and listened again. The same tone as in the darkened hallway. Soft and intimate. Deliberately, this time she punched the erase button and listened to the machine destroy the message.

SHE WAS MORE than an hour late. It didn't matter, of course, because when she got to the paper the police were already at work. Clusters of people stood around in stricken silence. Obviously news of Lew's death had filtered out.

She put her purse down on her desk and stood a moment watching the shapes move behind the frosted glass walls of Lew's office. Through the opened door, she caught glimpses of Kahler's familiar figure, muscularly compact back and shoulders filling the starched blue shirt or his dark head bent over Lew's desk. She even overheard the occasional comment, his voice directing the operation with unthinking authority.

She wasn't surprised that Kahler had come to oversee this search himself. He believed that whatever Lew had found had gotten him killed. As Kate did. She only had to be patient and eventually Kahler would tell her if he discovered anything.

"You okay?" one of the feature editors asked. She was standing almost at Kate's elbow, her eyes filled with concern.

Kate hadn't even been aware when the woman had approached her desk. "I guess," she said, questioning in her own mind if she'd ever be okay again.

"Someone said that...you found him."

Kate nodded. The tightness was back in her throat, and she began to wonder if coming in today had been a good idea. Being here. Exposed. Surrounded by the curious, their eyes all searching for some response, some reaction, a display of emotion.

Why don't you tell our viewers, Ms. August, how it felt to find your editor with the back of his head blown away, his brains splattered against the wall behind him?

"Excuse me," Kate said, managing what was almost a smile. She moved past the sympathetic face of her coworker to stand outside the opened door of Lew's office. She found that she had put her hands again on their opposite shoulders, smoothing her clammy palms down the short, silk-knit sleeves of the summer sweater set she'd pulled blindly from her closet this morning.

Maybe if she appeared to be watching the police do their job, no one would ask questions or demand that she recount what had happened last night. *The public's right to know,* she thought bitterly. Only not now. Not yet. Please, just not today.

"Did you find anything?" she asked when Kahler came out, pitching her voice low enough that the onlookers couldn't overhear. The hazel eyes assessed her face, so she smiled at him. He shook his head, a single tight movement and then he moved past her, carrying the trailing team of men with him.

The contents of the familiar office were clearly visible from where she stood, the papers on Lew's desk straight and more orderly than she'd ever seen them—Kahler's imposed order, not Lew's comforting disorder.

She wondered again who Lew had talked to yesterday. A friend of Barrington's—that was all she knew for certain. Suddenly the remembrance of Lew jotting something on his desk calendar as they talked was in her head. The image of his pen moving quickly across the already crowded whiteness. She hadn't told Kahler that. Maybe...

She glanced toward the newsroom doorway, but there was no sign of the cops. With their departure, most of the staff had made some pretense of getting back to business as usual. Someone would step in to organize, to direct the operation of the paper as Lew had for so many years. Maybe soon. They might even take over the office, clear out Lew's things. There would be no reason not to. The police were apparently through here.

She stepped inside Lew's office and pulled the door closed behind her. She waited a moment, feeling guilty, expecting to be challenged. She had no right to be here. Except this had always been her story, and Lew Garrison had been her friend.

When nothing happened, no protest concerning the invasion, she walked across the room to Lew's desk. There were too many memories here, and she felt her eyes burn, suddenly and unexpectedly. She fought the emotion by pushing Kahler's neatly stacked pile of documents off the calendar desk pad. She ran her finger down the right-hand side of the page, the place where Lew had been jotting notes as they'd talked. There were names and numbers written there, appointments, reminders as innocuous as "laundry 2:00." Nothing about Barrington. Nothing that seemed to relate to their conversation yesterday.

"Damn," she said under her breath. Just to be sure, she ran her finger across this week's block of days. Maybe Lew had written whatever he'd written on the appropriate day. Yesterday had been Wednesday the tenth. Only it wasn't.

It was the thirteenth. Wednesday, the thirteenth. It took a moment for the significance to hit her. She looked up and found that the calendar page she was examining so closely wasn't for July, but for March. Last March. Which meant someone had removed—she stopped and counted backward—four months' worth of pages. She took all the pages out of the pad and rifled quickly through them, just to make sure that the missing months hadn't been shifted to the back during the police search. They weren't there.

Kahler must have taken them. But he'd said they'd found nothing, so why take the calendar pages. Unless it hadn't been Kahler. Unless someone else had taken them. Someone who had reason to fear whatever Lew had jotted on their margins. She took a deep breath, trying to think. Either Kahler had lied to her, or he hadn't noticed the pages were missing.

Kahler would have noticed, she thought. He was bright and he was thorough, which meant he'd taken them. There had to be a reason for that. Something he didn't want her to see because he was afraid if she did, she'd pursue it, despite his warning.

Because it related to Barrington? Because she'd all but admitted to him how she felt about the judge, not exactly unbiased? *Call me,* Thorne had said on the tape. And before that, *When can I see you again?*

To find out what she knew? To find out if Lew had told her whatever had gotten him killed? Kahler said no one had been waiting for her at her apartment last night and no one had followed her. Was it possible that the person involved hadn't had to follow her because…because she had already gone to his house? Because he already knew that she wasn't aware of whatever Lew Garrison had discovered?

But Thorne hadn't even asked her any questions. They hadn't talked about anything dealing with the case—other than Lew's phone call. Was Barrington astute enough to know from the little she'd said that she hadn't been aware that Lew had made that call? That she certainly didn't know to whom it had been made?

She tried to reconstruct their conversation, the exact words, but it was no use. The words she remembered, the phrases that echoed in her head, burned into her memory, all concerned something else. Something very different.

Sometimes I'll wake up in the middle of the night wanting you. Thinking about you being there with me.

She had done her duty. She had told Kahler about Lew's phone call to Barrington's friend. That didn't mean she had to believe Barrington had something to do with Lew's death. The man who had held her, who had kissed her last night, who had confessed how he felt, had *not* just returned from killing Lew Garrison. She had always trusted her instincts, and there had been nothing there last night except what he had openly confessed to—incredibly, the same obsession she'd felt for weeks.

Someone tapped on the frosted glass upper half of the door, and Kate watched it swing open before she could formulate a reply. The editor who had spoken to her before stuck her head into the opening.

"Kate?" she said. "I thought you must be in here. I looked everywhere else."

"What is it?" Kate asked.

"Judge Barrington's on the phone. Line one. I thought you'd want to take it. Since it's Barrington," she added.

"Thanks," Kate said. She had felt a brief flutter of unease at the comment, and then she realized all the woman could know about Barrington was that he'd been Jack's first victim. She would assume the call had something to do with the story. No one could suspect that her connection to him was far more personal. She waited until the editor closed the door behind her, and then she took a deep breath, and she picked up the phone.

"Kate August," she said.

"Kate?"

With the sound of her name, all the doubts she had had about Thorne Barrington's possible involvement in what had happened to Lew last night—doubts she hadn't even acknowledged—seemed to slip out of her head.

"Are you all right?" he asked.

"You've heard?"

"On the news. They said you found the body. Are you okay?"

For some reason his concern caused the moisture to sting behind her lids again, but she fought it.

"Not really. It was... To be honest, it was just as awful as Austin." She realized that he might not know what she meant, so she added, explaining to a man who certainly needed no explanation of the horror Jack wrought, "I went to Austin. I thought I wanted to see... I had thought, if I was going to be working on the story, I needed to understand—"

He interrupted. "Kate," he said softly. Only her name, his voice, again rich with concern, caressing her agitation. And then, "Don't. Don't think about it."

She took another breath, trying to obey. She knew that wasn't what she needed to talk to him about. Not today, anyway. Maybe sometime they might talk about that, but today...

"I told Kahler about Lew's call," she said.

There was a small silence. Maybe he was trying to put that together with what she had said before, but he was as smart as she had always been told he was.

"His call to my friend?"

"Lew left a message on my machine last night. Something about doing what we'd talked about. Asking around about you was one of the things we'd discussed. Kahler heard the message. Lew's call to your friend must have been one of the last things he did." An explanation for why she'd told Kahler.

"Of course," he said simply.

"The police will probably want to talk to you, Thorne. I'm sorry, but I didn't know how to—"

"There's nothing to apologize for. A man's dead. As far as the police are concerned anything he did might be important." There was a silence, and then he added what she hadn't asked for. "His name is Greg Sandifer. We've been friends since elementary school. He's a doctor. Not mine, but...the fact that he is a doctor is probably one of the reasons Garrison called him."

She didn't say anything. She knew why he was telling her this. Not to pass on to Kahler, but for her own information. To satisfy her own need to know what his friend had told Lew. To put to rest the doubts that he must have realized had crept, certainly unwanted, into her head since she'd found Lew's body. For her information—personal and not professional.

"You didn't have to tell me that," she said.

"Call him," he said. "Tell him I said to talk to you. Ask him anything you want about his conversation with Garrison." He began to reel off a number, and her hand automatically found a pen, adding the seven digits to the crowded calendar page on Lew's desk. "That's his private number. The fact that you have that number should be introduction enough."

"I don't—" she began, not really certain what she needed to tell him.

"Call him," he ordered, interrupting, and then the connection was broken.

She stood a moment with the phone in her hand, the dial tone annoying. Finally she put the receiver back on the cradle and looked down on the number Barrington had given her. He was right. She did need to know exactly what had been said to Lew Garrison. She needed to know for her own information. *Personal.*

DESPITE THE FACT that Thorne had given her Dr. Sandifer's private number, she still had some problems getting through. He refused to speak to her at first. She had thought it only fair to give her name and the paper's name, and he had refused to take the call. She had then used Barrington's name and the reminder that she had been given Sandifer's private number. The masculine voice that finally replaced the smooth politeness of his secretary's was brusque.

"I told Lew Garrison everything I have to say to you people. If Thorne *did* give you this number—"

"Lew's dead," Kate said, breaking into his indignation.

"Dead?" Sandifer repeated, as if it were a word he'd never heard before.

"He was murdered last night. Apparently your conversation was one of the last he had. The police will almost certainly want to talk to you to confirm exactly what was said. Because Lew was working on my story, asking questions I'd suggested, I'd like to know what you told him. Judge Barrington gave me your name and number and said to tell you to talk to me."

"Why? Why would Thorne want me to talk to you?" he asked. The voice that had been full of anger and then shock was ripe now with suspicion. It was certainly a legitimate question. Kate wasn't sure she had a legitimate answer.

"For personal reasons," she admitted finally.

Sandifer said nothing for a moment. He was so quiet she could hear background noises from his end of the line, voices, faint and indistinct.

"Are you trying to tell me…" he began, and then he stopped. Apparently the thought of Thorne Barrington being involved with a reporter was simply beyond his comprehension. "You and Thorne are…" Again, he paused, and despite the situation, at the obvious disbelief in his tone Kate's mouth moved, almost a smile.

"Involved," she affirmed. The word had been in her mind and it had simply come out. Why not? It was true, given last night.

"Peg said you're a reporter."

"That's right," Kate said.

"Look, in spite of what you claim, I can't tell you anything about Thorne. I don't talk to the press about my friends."

"You talked to Lew," she reminded him.

"That's exactly what I told Garrison."

"That you wouldn't talk about Barrington?"

"That's right."

"Nothing else?"

Sandifer didn't say anything for a moment, and then he sighed, deeply enough to be audible.

"He came up with some crap about Thorne's migraines being emotional."

"Psychogenic," she said.

"As a matter of fact, that's the exact word he used."

"We had a mutual source," Kate acknowledged.

"But the way Lew said it, he made it sound as if it equated with crazy. That's not what the term means, Ms. August."

"Are they?" she asked.

"I wasn't Thorne's doctor."

"But?" Kate asked softly, because the qualifier had been in his tone.

"In my opinion, they're not."

"In your opinion? Or based on something you know? Something you've heard."

Again there was silence. "I don't discuss my friends with reporters," he said finally.

"But that *is* what you told Lew yesterday. Nothing else?"

"Our conversation was very brief. I was ticked off that Lew would even ask, that he thought I'd supply any information about a friend's medical condition. Even if I *had* any information. I've known Lew a long time, and frankly I was surprised he'd call me and ask that. I thought it was out of character. I remember telling him to leave Barrington alone. I called him a couple of less than complimentary epithets, and I hung up. Then I called Thorne and told him what had happened. I was angry at Lew, but I didn't kill him if that's what y'all are thinking. If you and the cops are trying to make some kind of case out of me calling Lew a couple of names—"

"No one thinks anything like that," she reassured him, smiling slightly. "You're not under suspicion, Dr. Sandifer. That's not why I'm calling you. It's not why the police will call. They'll just want to know if you told Lew anything…" She hesitated, searching for the right word. "Incriminating."

"Incriminating? About me?"

"No," Kate said.

"About Thorne?"

"Yes."

"They think *Thorne* had something to do with Garrison's death?" The question was derisive. Apparently, Greg Sandifer was just what he'd claimed to be, a friend of Barrington's.

"I think it's more a matter of checking out all the possibilities. They know Garrison called you concerning Judge Barrington's injuries, and they know someone killed him shortly after your conversation. They'll just be trying to determine if the two are in any way related."

"I can tell you that they're not. Not in *any* way," Dr. Sandifer said. "If that's all, Ms. August?"

"You can call Judge Barrington. He really did give me your number."

"You can be assured that I will," he said succinctly, and then the connection was broken.

Kate put Lew's phone back in the cradle and stood a moment looking down at it. She hadn't handled that conversation very professionally, but at least she knew that the friend of Barrington's Lew had called hadn't told him anything that might have gotten him killed. Apparently Dr. Sandifer had given her editor no real information at all about Barrington's injuries. She took a deep breath and realized only then how tense she had been. Now she could relax, knowing that the doubts that had begun to circle in her head like vultures were groundless.

She would have to call Kahler and give him Dr. Sandifer's name. Barrington would, of course, but she needed to confess to the detective that she had made her own call. Kahler would probably chew her out, but the relief she felt as a result of Sandifer's comments would make his lecture a lot more bearable.

She took another careful survey of the materials on Lew's desk, but Kahler had apparently told the truth about that. With the exception of the missing pages from the calendar, nothing else here seemed to relate to Jack. The material she had collected through the months she'd been involved in the story was in the file drawer of her desk—with the exception of the pictures of Barrington that had been taken from her apartment. That was something else she needed to confess to Kahler. Since he now knew something of what she felt about Thorne, that confession would finally be possible. She could pretend that she had just discovered the photographs were missing.

She walked out of Lew's office and closed the door behind her. She was a little surprised that Kahler hadn't ordered the office locked, but maybe their search had been thorough enough that he was convinced there was nothing else to be learned from Lew's papers. Or maybe Kahler, bless his heart, had left it open so that she would have the opportunity to do exactly what she had just done—to take her own look around.

She sat down in her chair and opened the bottom left-hand drawer of her desk. It was immediately apparent that something was wrong. Half the file folders were lying face down in the front of the drawer, the rest propped drunkenly against them.

She hesitated a moment, trying to decide what was going on. Finally, she picked up the fallen folders and pushed them to the back of the drawer, all upright again. She began to thumb through the tabs on top, but she knew what was missing. The thick collection of her materials relating to the Tripper bombings was gone, just like the newspaper pictures she'd taken home. She wouldn't be able to do what she'd told Kahler she'd do, read through all the material to see if there was anything—

Suddenly she remembered. That was the other thing she and Lew had talked about. She had told Lew that Kahler had found the Mays connection by reading back through the dockets of Barrington's cases, and then Lew had said something about maybe that's what they ought to do. *Read back through everything to see if there was anything they'd overlooked.*

She had been so smug that day, bragging about knowing every detail included in the material. But maybe she'd been wrong. Maybe Lew had done exactly what he'd suggested they should do—read back through all the files. Maybe he'd taken them into his office, sat down at his desk, the material she'd collected spread out before him, and gone over it all with a fine-toothed comb.

She pushed her chair back and walked to Lew's office. Instead of putting the files back in her drawer where he'd gotten them, maybe he'd simply stuck them in his own file cabinet, in a hurry because he'd found whatever he'd found. But first, she prayed, he'd marked whatever it was, underlined it, made a notation. *Something* that would let her follow the path—

She stopped, suddenly remembering where that path had led, the darkened study in the silent house, Lew's lifeless body slumped over his desk and behind him— She jerked her mind away from the image, and she knew she had to remember what Kahler had told her. *Don't play cop.*

She moved to the tall, five-drawer cabinet and pulled out the first drawer. She had no idea about Lew's filing system and the drawers were unlabeled, so she began to methodically go through the folders. Lew's careful lettering on the tabs, the printing small and very precise, was so familiar that she had to blink to clear her vision.

She worked her way through the files, even the two drawers that held material clearly not related to any ongoing stories. Her folders on the bombings were not here. And, she had realized sometime during her search, neither was the material the stringers were sending in from the cities where the murders had taken place. Lew had been collecting those for her for the segment dealing with the official hunt for the bomber. Everything they had collected about Jack had disappeared.

She closed the bottom drawer and stood up, aware of how long she'd been searching by the cramping ache in her legs. Either Lew had taken everything with him when he'd left the office last night or someone else had at some point cleaned out the files. If Lew had taken the material, it was probably at his home. Maybe lying on that blood-soaked desk. But of course, whoever had killed Lew would not have left those folders there if he had been aware of them, and he must have been if they had indeed contained whatever information Lew had indicated he'd discovered.

She knew that she couldn't put off calling Kahler much longer. There were too many things she needed to tell him, things that might help him find Lew's killer. Or help him find Jack. One and the same? That seemed obvious unless you considered the roles of the confetti prankster and Mays. None of them fitted together, but that wasn't, thank goodness, her job. She was going to take Kahler's advice very seriously. She didn't intend to play cop. She didn't intend to end up—

She forced her mind away again from what had happened to Lew and left his office, pulling the door closed behind her.

Chapter Eleven

It was after lunch before Kahler returned her call. She had spent the morning rereading the articles she had done on the bombings. Those were, of course, still available. It was all the material that had provided the sources for these very condensed versions that was missing.

"August? I had a message to call you," Kahler said when she picked up the phone. "Something wrong?"

"I'm just the bearer of bad news now?" she asked, smiling at the concern in his voice.

"I didn't mean that. I know how hard last night was. Finding Garrison. I was worried about you."

"I know," she said. She did know how he felt about her. He hadn't made much of a secret of his feelings lately, and she appreciated his automatic concern. "I'm grateful, but I didn't call just to listen to your voice, Kahler, as pleasant as it is."

Somehow that came out wrong. Personal. She didn't know why it was so hard to find the bantering tone their conversations had always had. Maybe because too much had happened, because the violence they were dealing with was now very up close and personal. No longer murder at long distance.

"You found something," Kahler said. His voice was controlled, the tone tight and almost flat.

She hated to have to disappoint him, so she gave him the little bit of information she did have. "The friend of Barrington's was Dr. Greg Sandifer. He didn't tell Lew anything, refused even to talk about the judge's injuries. He called Lew a couple of names and hung up. Then he called to warn Barrington that the paper was asking questions." There was a small silence, and Kate pictured Kahler jotting down the information. "I have his private number if you want it," she added.

"You called him," Kahler said. It was not a question.

"Barrington told me to."

Silence again, and then he asked, "What did you tell Barrington, Kate?"

"Tell him?" she asked, puzzled by his tone. "*He* called me. He'd heard about Lew. When I mentioned that I'd told you about Lew's call to his friend, he gave me Sandifer's number. I didn't 'tell' him anything, Kahler. What's that supposed to mean?"

"He asked you to pass Sandifer's number on to the police?"

There was an edge to the question. Sarcasm? Anger? She wasn't sure what she was hearing, but it was clear Kahler didn't like the idea that she'd talked to Sandifer. Or maybe...the idea that she had talked to Barrington? Personal? she wondered. If so, maybe it was time that she made it clear exactly how personal her relationship with Thorne Barrington had become.

"I don't think that's why he gave me the number," she said. "I think he knew that...I had some questions of my own about what Sandifer had told Lew. Some personal questions that I needed to have answered. I'm just passing on the information to you because I thought you'd want to talk to Sandifer yourself. In your case, talk to him professionally, of course."

None of that had come out as she'd intended. It had sounded abrupt, as if she thought it was none of Kahler's business why Barrington had given her the number. That hadn't been what she'd intended to convey, but she could tell by the coldness in the detective's tone that that was indeed how she had come across.

"Then thank you for the information. Anything else?"

"Don't," she protested softly.

He made no response for a long heartbeat, but he didn't pretend not to understand. "How did you expect me to react?" he asked. The coldness was gone, but his voice was not the same, not what it had always been before.

"I don't know," she said. "I don't know what to say, Kahler. I'm sorry," she added.

"Yeah," he responded. Flat, dispassionate. "Me, too."

"I can't help what I feel. You should understand that," she added, and then knew that was the wrong thing to say. She wasn't sure there *was* a right thing in this situation.

"Would it make any difference if I told you that I don't think being involved with Barrington is a good idea?" he asked.

"I don't think it would. Not now."

"For professional reasons, Kate. Not personal."

"Because?" she asked.

"Gut reaction," he said.

"That's not an explanation."

"It's all I've got."

"Well, thanks for the advice, but I don't think that's enough. Not anymore."

"You sleeping with him?" The tone of his question was bitter, and given what she knew about his feelings, she supposed it should not have been unexpected, but it was. Totally out of character. Totally hurtful.

"What the hell, Kahler? What gives you the right—"

"Eight people are dead. Is that enough *right?*"

It stopped her outrage as he had certainly known it would.

"What's that supposed to mean? That Barrington's involved in those deaths? Is that what you're trying to suggest?"

"I'm trying to remind you that eight people are already dead. I don't want you to be another victim."

"Of *Barrington?*" she mocked, angry now. No matter how he felt, it didn't give him the right to make unfounded accusations. "You might want to remember that Judge Barrington was one of Jack's victims. Or are you suggesting that he sent *himself* a bomb? Tried to blow himself up? Is that your professional opinion, Detective Kahler? Because if so, I have to tell you—"

"Maybe he had an accident. Did you ever think about that?"

"Never once," she said in disbelief. "But then I'm not blind with jealousy. You have some proof that's what happened? Because if not, I'd like to remind you of *who* you're accusing. Now, if you have some legitimate reason for telling me not to see Thorne Barrington, then spit it out. Otherwise I just might think your motives in issuing that warning are not as pure as you'd like me to believe."

"You think whatever the hell you want to, August. I'm just offering advice. Stay away from Barrington. You don't know what you're dealing with."

"But as always, I'm sure you're dying to tell me."

"My best advice," he repeated and hung up.

Kate sat stunned for a moment, still holding the phone, angry enough to slam it down, but since Kahler had beat her to the punch, she resisted the urge.

She hadn't told Kahler about the missing files or about the calendar pages, she realized suddenly. That had really been the reason she'd called, and instead she'd been given a lecture—not exactly the one she'd anticipated. *Stay away from Barrington,* he'd said, but he hadn't be able to come up with any reasons. Personal. Almost certainly personal.

She lowered her head, resting her forehead against her joined fingers, elbows propped tiredly on her desk. Now there was no one to talk to. Not Lew. And not Kahler. No one to offer comfort and support. Except...there was, of course.

Sometimes I'll wake up in the middle of the night wanting you. Thinking about you being there with me. Where the darkness doesn't matter. Without giving herself time to decide it might be a bad idea, she picked up her purse. Suddenly she knew exactly where she wanted to be.

WHEN ELLIOT CAME to the gate, he didn't wait for her to ask to see the judge. He unfastened the inside lock and pulled the heavy wrought iron inward. "Miss August," he said politely. "Is Mr. Thorne expecting you?"

"He should be," she said, smiling at the old man.

"If you'll come this way. You don't have to be frightened," he added, and Kate spent a second attempting to figure that out.

"Frightened?" she asked.

"Of the dog," he explained. "I always fasten him upstairs when I hear the bell."

"Thank you, Elliot, but I'm not afraid of the dog. What's his name, by the way?"

They were almost to the front steps, Kate again matching her longer stride to the slow one of the old man.

"Prince Charles Edward Stuart," he said. "They're Scots, you know."

For a moment Kate couldn't think who "they" might be.

"Retrievers," Elliot explained. "They originated in Scotland."

"I didn't know that," she said.

The old man opened the front door, and its movement sent the crystal tears into their small ballet. "Mr. Thorne persists in calling him Charlie," Elliot said, disapproval in his voice.

"And you prefer?" Kate asked.

"Something with a bit more dignity."

"Prince," she guessed.

"Oh, dear me, no." He looked horrified at the thought, and Kate found herself smiling again. "Stuart," he announced solemnly. "I think it's very fitting for such a fine animal. Royal, you know," he added as if that settled the entire issue.

Kate smiled at his obvious love for the dog. He was such a nice old man. She suddenly remembered what Thorne had told her. "By the way, Elliot, I was so sorry to hear about your sister. I hope she's improving."

"Oh, she's doing very well, thank you. Much better than expected. She may even be released from the hospital today."

"That's wonderful," Kate said. There was a small silence, the exchange too personal perhaps for Elliot's idea of his role.

"Mr. Thorne is in the parlor. Shall I announce you?"

"I believe—if he won't mind—I'd rather just go in."

"I can assure you he won't mind," Elliot said simply.

Kate smiled at him again and pushed open the sliding door. Thorne was standing, both hands resting on the mantel of the white marble fireplace, looking down into the empty grate. He turned his head at the small noise made by the door. In the ever-present dimness, Kate couldn't read what was in the dark eyes, but they watched her as she crossed the room. When she was almost to the fireplace, he straightened, removing his hands from the mantel and turning to face her.

"I didn't really need to talk to your friend," she said.

"I called Kahler and told him what I had told you," Thorne said. "I gave him Greg's name and number."

"Apparently, Dr. Sandifer didn't give Lew any information. That should certainly prove…"

She hesitated, reluctant to put exactly what it should prove into words.

"That I had nothing to do with Garrison's death?"

"I never thought you did," Kate said.

The midnight eyes held hers, assessing, and finally he nodded. "And Kahler?" he asked. "What does he believe?"

"I don't presume to speak for Kahler."

"Don't you, Kate? Somehow I've gotten the impression that you two are…close."

"Close?" she repeated carefully, wondering what he'd been told and who had told him.

"Close enough that some time last night he was in your apartment, listening as you replayed your messages."

She had told him that, she realized, not thinking about what interpretation he might put on Kahler's presence.

"I tried to call you last night, Kate. Several times. I even left a message. Did you get in too late to return my call?"

Kate didn't say anything. She couldn't think of anything to tell him but the truth, and she knew how that would sound.

"You didn't spend the night at home," he said, statement and not question.

"No," she agreed.

He turned his head, looking down again into the shadowed recess of the fireplace.

"I told you my apartment gives me the creeps. Because of the confetti, the idea that someone had been inside, in my bedroom. Then last night… After finding Lew, I knew I couldn't go back there."

He turned his head toward her again, his gaze tracing over the line of her mouth and then almost reluctantly lifting to meet her eyes. "You could have come here," he said.

She knew that was true. She had known it last night, but for some reason, she had chosen not to. "I didn't think coming here was a good idea. After we…" She paused, trying to decide what to call what had been between them.

"After I kissed you," he said into her hesitation. "Told

you that I've thought about you for days. Did that make you afraid to come back here?''

"Not afraid. Not because of that. It just seemed it would be...rushing things.''

His eyes held hers a long moment. "I see,'' he said finally.

"I came today,'' she reminded him.

He touched her then. He put the tips of his fingers on her cheek, and she turned her head to press her lips into his palm, because she had realized that she wanted his touch, wanted it very badly. His right hand came up to smooth around her shoulder, urging her body closer to the solid strength of his. She raised her face, watching, almost mesmerized, as his head lowered, his mouth moving inexorably toward hers, which opened in response. Anticipating.

The impact of his kiss was as powerful as it had been last night. His tongue moving against hers with familiarity now. With sure expertise. And with emotion. It didn't last long, and then he raised his head to look down into her eyes, his own still dark, almost fathomless. The beautiful line of his mouth curved. The perfect features were enhanced by his smile, and her own lips moved in answer.

You don't know what you're dealing with echoed suddenly in her head, and to banish Kahler's voice, she stretched on tiptoe, her body straining to Thorne's. His arms enclosed her, his size again making her feel fragile, in need of protection. That wasn't a feeling she would ever have imagined could be as pleasurable as she was finding it to be. Fragile and feminine weren't adjectives that she had sought as descriptors of herself, but that was how Thorne made her feel, and she was a little surprised to find how much she enjoyed that feeling.

She was also surprised that their embrace was having the same immediate effect on him that their kiss last night had had. His body was already hardened with desire, and he wasn't embarrassed to let her become aware of that. For some reason, today she wasn't uncomfortable with the realization of how he felt. She raised her hand to touch the back of his head, her fingers splaying through the thick, black hair. It curled around them, seeming to welcome their caress. It had been so long, he'd told her last night. *So long.*

He drew her closer, pressing his body into hers. She could feel his breathing change, the small, telltale increase in his heart rate. His hands cupped under her hips, pulling her into his arousal, holding her to him. His mouth turned, deepening the kiss. Wanting her. Making it obvious that he wanted her.

Her breathing shortened, tremulous, anxious, feeling the force of desire move through her own body. Surging upward. Hot and powerful and almost new, like nothing she had felt before. Stronger. Deeper.

Perhaps he became aware of her response, her loss of control imminent. For some reason he eased his big body away from her, the distance between them slight, but suddenly far too wide, the space unwanted and invasive. Involuntarily she moved toward him, seeking again the pleasant heat of his body. His hands found her shoulders, and he held her. His denial was gentle, but there was no doubt that he was holding her away from him.

She opened her eyes to find him watching her. Whatever emotion had been briefly revealed in his face shifted before she could name it, altered subtly as she watched, realigning itself into something more familiar, safer.

"It's all right," she comforted. Maybe he thought he was rushing her. Because of what she'd said about last night. Maybe he didn't realize how she felt about him. Maybe he still thought that Kahler—

"Don't tempt me, Kate," he said. He didn't smile, but she had already been aware of his desire. There was no doubt that she was doing exactly that.

"Why?" she asked, smiling at him.

"Because becoming...involved with me probably isn't a good idea," he said.

"*Becoming* involved?" she repeated, letting him hear the emphasis.

"Becoming intimate," he said simply.

Old-fashioned, she thought. The wording was uniquely Barrington. *Becoming intimate.* She couldn't think of a nicer way to express it, even if the phrase was archaic. Intimate. An intimate relationship.

"I think I like the sound of that," she offered.

He made another small movement. Away from her again. His hands exerted a quick pressure, a small squeeze, against her shoulders, and then he released her.

"What's wrong?" she asked.

"I had a lot of time to think last night. While I was waiting for you to return my call."

"Look," she said, knowing this was too important for misunderstanding. Such a stupid misunderstanding. "It was nothing. I was in shock from finding Lew. Kahler offered me his couch for the night, and I accepted. It didn't mean anything."

"It's not that," he said quickly. And then nothing else.

She shook her head, feeling some of last night's anxiety resurface. If not the fact that she'd spent the night at Kahler's apartment, then what? What was wrong? "Then what is it?" she asked.

"I realized you'd been right about a lot of things."

"What kinds of things? I don't understand."

"The things you told me. About myself."

"Thorne," she said, her tone full of regret. She shook her head slowly, knowing how far she had come toward understanding. "When I said those things—" she began.

"You were far more objective than you are now," he suggested. For the first time since he'd touched her, he smiled at her. "Far more apt to tell me the truth."

"I thought you'd sent me a bomb. How objective is

that?'' she argued. "I wanted to hurt you. I had no idea of the reasons…"

When she hesitated, he turned back to face the marble fireplace. Unthinkingly he put his hands again over the edge of the mantel. The marred right one was nearer, and she found her eyes drawn again to the scars, the mutilation. Marked forever by what had happened.

Suddenly she remembered, against her will, what Kahler had suggested. *Jealous,* she thought, *and striking out blindly. We all do it.* Kahler wasn't exempt from human emotion. He'd apologize the next time she saw him, and until then she certainly didn't have to give any credence to his jealous speculations.

"I didn't understand all that had happened to you," she said.

He turned his head to look at her again, dark eyes examining her features, slowly, as if imprinting them on his memory.

"I realized last night that I *have* been hiding," he said.

She felt her throat tighten, and she swallowed, fighting the emotion. Something constricted in her chest, hating his humiliation, hating that he felt compelled to make that confession to her. She wasn't surprised, given what she knew about the caliber of the man standing before her. She had never heard anything derogatory said about Thorne Barrington by anyone in Atlanta. Only recognition of his abilities. His integrity. This was a manifestation of that same integrity. He was being brutally honest with her. Honest about himself.

"I think you had cause," she said quietly.

"To be a coward?" he asked. There was derision in his voice. Mockery. All self-directed.

"You're not a coward."

He turned back to the fireplace. There was a long silence, and she didn't break it. She had said the truth. What she felt. Even if he had hidden, that didn't make him a coward.

"You have an image of yourself. Everyone does," he went on. "A perception. And for most of us, that perception *is* who we are. What we *think* we are." His voice stopped, but she knew from the tenseness of the muscles in those broad shoulders that this wasn't all. Not complete. "I think that's what I hate most about what happened. He destroyed my perception of who I am."

"You're not a coward," she said again. "Sane people don't put themselves into situations where they can be hurt or injured. If light causes pain, you avoid it. The burned child avoids the flame. That's called self-preservation. It's called sanity."

He turned to look at her again. Once more assessing.

"You have headaches," she said. "No one would choose to do anything that might trigger a migraine. Especially a severe one."

"Are you quoting Kahler?" he asked.

"He told me about the migraines," she admitted.

"Because they couldn't pinpoint the physical cause of my headaches, couldn't stop them, they suggested I see a psychiatrist." There was no inflection she could read in the statement. No longer hiding.

"Did you?"

He laughed, the sound short and bitter.

"I *knew* the headaches were the result of the injuries. They just couldn't find out what was wrong, so therefore I must be at fault. I was furious that they suggested it."

"So you never went."

"Maybe I was just afraid of what he might discover."

"I'm not sure I blame you. I never had much desire to have all my neuroses exposed to the light of day."

The silence stretched, expanded, became uncomfortable long before he broke it, his tone less emotional than it had been before. "I have migraines," he said, speaking as if she didn't know, finally explaining. "Triggered by light, especially a bright or unexpected light. A camera flash, even something as small as a refrigerator bulb in a darkened room.''

"The photographer," she realized suddenly. "After the bombing. Is that…?''

"That was the first. Luckily, I was still in the hospital. I didn't even understand what was happening. I thought something had exploded in my head, some damage from the bomb they hadn't found.''

"But that wasn't the only one?" she asked.

"No, but you're right. The burned child learns very quickly to avoid the flame.''

"And there's nothing they can do for them?''

"Injections. Something to knock me out. I'm still aware of the pain on some level. I lose a couple of days of my life. And even afterwards…there are residual effects. So I…avoid the cause. I live in the darkness.''

"There's nothing wrong with that. I told you. Self-preservation. Sanity.''

He said nothing, still leaning forward against his hands which gripped the mantel.

"I thought," she said finally, "when I left work today, when I decided to come here… I thought about what you said. About being here where the darkness doesn't matter. It doesn't matter, Thorne. I want to be here.''

He turned to look at her. She remembered that he had made his confession last night. Braver then than she had been. It was only fair that she tell him now how she felt, how she had felt for so long. "I've wanted to be here far longer than you can possibly imagine.''

"Will you come back tonight?" he asked, still watching her face. "Stay here with me? If the darkness really doesn't matter," he added.

Seeing what was in his eyes, she smiled at him, and then she nodded.

SHE WENT BACK to her apartment. She still wanted the long soaking bath she had needed this morning when she had made do with a quick shower and shampoo. Before she went back to Thorne's tonight, she intended to soak out some of the tension of the past few days. Not her grief over Lew and probably not her fear. That had become an almost constant anxiety. But maybe she could do something about her nervousness over her stalker, the confetti bandit. The tensions of her argument with Kahler. His accusations. She'd climb into the tub and try to banish all of those from her mind. Then she'd dress and go back to Thorne's.

She wasn't sure if he had simply been offering a refuge or if he intended something different. A seduction, maybe, she found herself thinking as she undressed in her small bathroom. She thought she'd probably like whatever old-fashioned ideas about seduction Thorne Barrington had. Maybe even like pretending that he needed to seduce her, that she wasn't coming to him already seduced—by his voice, his pictures, by his reputation even. By every experience she had had with the man himself. At last, reality and not fantasy.

She had just been stepping out of the tub, unconscious of how long she had spent there, thinking about tonight, again anticipating, when she heard the doorbell. She picked up her watch that she'd placed on the tile counter and found that it was after seven.

Kahler, she thought. *Coming to apologize. To back off the stupid things he'd said out of jealousy.*

She pulled on her white terry robe and leaned over, letting her long hair fall forward. She wrapped a towel, turban-like, around her wet head. She thought briefly that Kahler had never seen her like this. No makeup. Wet hair wrapped in a towel. Then she acknowledged that she really didn't care. Somewhere inside she was disappointed in Kahler, that he'd let his personal feelings enter into his investigation of a murder case.

"Who is it?" she asked automatically as she approached

the door. She looked through the peephole and saw her neighbor from across the hall.

"It's me. Carol Simmons."

Kate released the chain and opened the door slightly.

"Sorry," her neighbor said. "I got you out of the shower."

"It's okay."

"I just wanted to give you this," Carol said, holding a blue-and-white Ty-Vek envelope toward the opening in the door. "It wouldn't fit into the mail slot, and when I came out to get my mail, I told the postman I'd take it and give it to you when you got home. Only, with the noise the kids were making, I guess I missed hearing you come in."

Kate opened the door wide enough to accept the bulky envelope, glancing automatically at the address block. Her name and address and the sender... The sender had been Lew Garrison.

The envelope wasn't the folder thing the post office had—not the letter-size cardboard mailer. This one was big. Big enough to hold... Files, she realized suddenly. Big enough to hold all the Tripper files. She forced her eyes up from Lew's careful lettering, just as neat and precise as it had been on the tabs she'd examined today, to meet her neighbor's.

"The postman gave it to you?" she asked carefully.

"Uh-huh," Carol said, a brief puzzlement in her green eyes.

"The regular postman?"

Carol shrugged. "Yeah. I mean I don't know if he delivers our mail every day, but I've seen him before."

"The real postman?" Kate said.

Carol laughed. "The honest-to-God, real-life postman," she said, still smiling. "What's wrong with you?"

"Paranoia, I guess," Kate said, knowing she was making a fool of herself. "I've been working on the bomber thing. Jack the Tripper."

"Oh, God, Kate, and you're afraid this might be…" Instinctively, Carol stepped back a couple of feet and with that automatic reaction, Kate realized how silly she was being.

"That was just paranoia. It's from my boss. I recognize his handwriting. My…hesitation was just a momentary insanity," she explained.

"You better call the cops," Carol said. "Don't you open that thing without having the cops check it out. That guy blows people up."

"I know," Kate said, "but I promise this isn't from Jack. It's from Lew Garrison. He's my editor."

She held out the envelope to allow Carol to see the return address, but as the package approached her, Kate's neighbor moved another step back, toward the safety of her own door.

"But I thought…" Carol began and then hesitated. "I thought he was dead."

"He is. He must have sent this…" *Before he was killed.* A message or a warning. From beyond the grave. Kate shivered and then realized how melodramatic those words were. Lew Garrison would certainly have red-lined that phrase had she been dumb enough to use it in a story. Despite the fact that he was gone, she smiled. *Lew's not stupid,* she had assured Kahler, and apparently she'd been right. If this was what she thought it might be…

"Thanks, Carol," she said, in a hurry now to get back inside and open the envelope.

"You call the police, Kate. You hear me? You call the cops. Don't you open that thing. Anybody could have sent that. Just because it's got somebody's name on the front—"

"Thanks," Kate said, closing the door on the last part of that warning. She turned and walked across the room and laid the package on the coffee table, on top of the magazines Kahler had been reading that day as he'd waited for her to come home.

She briefly considered doing exactly what Carol had suggested: picking up the phone and putting in a call for Kahler. Only... Too much had happened between them. Too many things had been said. She felt as if she'd forfeited her right to ask for Kahler's help.

Besides, she thought, sitting down on the couch in front of the blue and white envelope, this was Lew's handwriting. She'd certainly seen enough of that today that there was no doubt. She didn't want to wait for the cops. She wanted to know what was in the package Lew had mailed, apparently shortly before he'd been killed. Truly a message from beyond the grave, and at that thought she shivered again, even as she reached for the opening of the envelope.

Chapter Twelve

Despite Kate's surety that Lew's hand had addressed the package, she examined by touch what it held as fully as she could through the thin, tough skin of the envelope. She could feel the thicker manila of the folders and even the sheaf of papers each held. She briefly considered whether there could be explosives concealed in the center of one of the files, but in handling the package when she'd taken it from Carol, it had been obvious that it contained only flexible materials.

She looked again at the address. Everything was correct. It wasn't marked Private or Personal. If it had been, that would have been a clue that it might contain a bomb, intended exclusively for the hands of one person. There was nothing suspicious—no lumps or bulges, no wires, no stains on the outside—none of the signs you were supposed to look for in a mail bomb. And without a doubt, the handwriting was Lew's, by far the strongest argument for its safety.

She didn't realize she'd been holding her breath until she had carefully peeled the last section of the adhesive flap away from the envelope. She knew better than to try to pull the contents out, so she got up and walked around to the end of the coffee table.

She stood as far away from the opening of the envelope

as she could and stretched out her right hand to lift one corner of the bottom. The image of Thorne Barrington's right hand was suddenly in her head, and she hesitated again. *Coward,* she mocked herself, trying to gather her faltering courage, *you know this is from Lew. Just do it!*

She turned her face away, closing her eyes, and dumped whatever the package contained onto the table. The mass of material slid out without resistance. When she opened her eyes, only a stack of manila folders lay on the surface of her coffee table, looking totally innocent. She took a deep breath, feeling foolish and relieved and very lucky all at the same time.

What the hell did you think you were doing, August? Kahler would say. *You got a death wish?* She didn't, of course, especially after seeing the room in Austin, after finding Lew.

She remembered to take another breath, finally feeling her heart rate begin to steady. This had probably been the dumbest thing she'd ever done, but she had *known* the package was from Lew. Thankfully, she'd been right. *Stupid risk,* her subconscious screamed, *no matter who you thought it was from.*

She laid the empty envelope on the table beside the folders and realized only then that she had handled it without gloves, maybe destroying whatever evidence it contained. But, of course, so had Carol and the postman and the dozens of people who had processed the package on its way to her. Her fingerprints were already all over the files—as were Lew's. Especially if he had really done what he'd said they should do, if he had really again examined everything they contained.

If he had, it was obvious he'd found something—something that had gotten him killed—but not before he'd sent the files on to her. Maybe on his way to meet his killer? She didn't know, and it didn't make much sense to speculate on what had happened that night. What was important was that Lew had sent these to her, and whatever he'd found that had gotten him killed, almost certainly lay within these files.

Unconsciously, she pulled the damp towel off her head, letting her the hair fall around her face and shoulders. Impatiently she pushed it back, finger-combing the damp strands out of her eyes and away from her face with both hands.

There was enough material here that it would take her hours to go through it all. Unless, she thought suddenly, Lew had stuck a note in one of the folders, or marked something in one of the files, something that would direct her search.

She sat down on the couch and opened the first folder in the stack. A file for a victim profile. She quickly fanned through the pages, but there seemed to be nothing there. No note, nothing that didn't belong. She opened the second folder in the stack, doing the same thing. She continued the process through all of them, carefully restacking the folders she'd searched upside down in the order they'd been in when they'd arrived.

There appeared to be nothing in any of the folders except what she had put into them originally. In her cursory search, she hadn't seen any notations, no circles or stars. Only her files and the ones Lew had begun collecting from the stringers in the scattered cities where the bombings had taken place. She supposed she had looked at those at some time in the past, maybe when they'd come in, but she couldn't really remember too much about them because she hadn't written that article yet.

Interviews with the hunters, Lew had called these files. Profiles of the men who were desperately looking for Jack because he'd killed someone in their jurisdiction, someone who was supposed to be under their protection. Murder had been done on their watch, and they were still looking for the murderer. She laid the final folder on top and then lifted the entire stack, turning it over so that the files were again in the order in which they'd arrived.

Whatever message Lew had intended to send her, he hadn't made it easy. Maybe he hadn't had time. Maybe— She'd probably never know, she realized. It was useless to speculate. Only Lew and the killer knew what the situation had been last night.

She picked up the stack of folders and carried them to her kitchen table. Because the terry robe was damp and becoming uncomfortable in the air-conditioning, she took a moment to go back into her bedroom to slip out of it and into a pair of shorts and a T-shirt before she sat down in one of the kitchen chairs. She ran her fingers again through her drying hair, securing the curling tendrils behind her ears, and then, opening the first folder, she began to read.

SHE JUMPED when the phone rang, sharp and unexpected in the hours-long silence. She lifted her head from where it rested, propped on her hand, and the ache in her stiffened neck was a reminder of how long she'd sat in this same position, carefully reading through her own material. She thought about letting the machine pick up, and then she realized the caller might be Kahler. She felt a moment of guilt because she knew she should have called him hours ago, when the package had first arrived. She stood up and moved across the room on legs that were also stiff, catching the phone on its fourth ring.

"Hello," she said, anticipating the accented voice of the detective. After all, she'd been expecting him to call all afternoon to apologize for the things he'd said.

"Kate?" Barrington said.

It took a second to make the shift in her thinking. With the arrival of the package, she had forgotten the arrangement she and Thorne had made this afternoon. She glanced at the kitchen clock and realized with shock that it was almost eleven.

"Are you all right?" he asked.

"I forgot about you," she said truthfully, an answer to the question he hadn't asked, and it was not until the lack of response stretched that she realized how that would sound.

"I see," he said finally, his tone carefully neutral.

"No," she said. "No, you don't. Something's happened."

"What's wrong?" he asked.

She was grateful for the immediate concern, as welcome as Kahler's had always been.

"Kate?"

"I got a package from Lew."

"Don't touch it," he ordered harshly.

He was certainly qualified to give that advice. Thorne would think she was as stupid for opening the envelope as Kahler would.

"I've already opened it. It wasn't a bomb."

"Thank God." Barrington's deep voice breathed the words. "What the hell, Kate—"

"It's the files. *That* was the other thing Lew said he would do that afternoon. The last time I talked to him. I didn't remember until today. He said we needed to read back through the files because that's how Kahler had found Mays."

"Did he read them?"

"I couldn't be sure. I looked for them today at the paper, but everything was gone. Then tonight, when I got home, my neighbor brought over this package. It was the missing files. Lew had sent them to me."

"And you've read them?"

"Not all of them."

"Have you called Kahler?"

"Not yet. I thought you might be..." She paused, remembering what she believed about her relationship with the detective. "When the phone rang, I thought it might be Kahler. I was going to tell him."

"Come over here, Kate. Right now. Get the hell out of that apartment. I don't want you there alone."

"I know I told you I get the willies here, but I don't—"

"Something in those files may have gotten Lew Garrison killed, Kate. Don't be a fool."

"I know, but when Kahler finds out I've got these, he'll pick them up and give them to someone else to read. He wants me to back off, to play it safe. But no one else will be able to recognize what's important. I *know* there's something here. Why else would Lew have sent the files if he didn't think they'd tell me something? I'll be all right. No one knows I have them. I just need to finish reading them. I have to. This is my job."

"The public's right to know," he said bitterly.

"The public's right not to be dead."

Again there was long silence across the line, and then she heard the depth of the breath he took before he spoke. "I can't stand the thought that you might be in danger."

She waited, knowing what was going through his mind, the horror of the memories he lived with. *Make the offer,* she urged him silently. *Come over here and stay with me while I do my job, a job we both know I have to finish.* There was only silence until she broke it.

"I could bring them with me," she offered. "You could look at them. Maybe someone who hasn't seen everything a dozen times might spot whatever it was Lew found. Maybe I'm too close to all this. And I haven't changed my mind. I really don't want to sleep here tonight. The invitation still open?"

"Of course," he said. She could hear relief in his voice. "Bring everything with you. We'll look at them together."

"Could you..." she hesitated, hating to let him know that his reminder of the dangers posed by whatever was in these files had struck home. Too many people dead, she had acknowledged, and she really didn't want to be next. "Would you meet me at the gate?"

"How long will it take you to get here?" Thorne asked, as if he didn't even think it was a strange request.

"Ten minutes," she guessed. Traffic certainly wouldn't be a problem at this time of night.

"I'll be at the gate," he promised.

HE WASN'T. The gate was unlocked, standing slightly open when she arrived. She pulled her Mazda along the curb and sat a moment in the car, trying to decide what to do. Was it possible that something had happened to him in the short space of time since she'd listened to the comforting assurance of his promise?

That sudden fear propelled her into action. She opened the door and ran around the front of the Mazda and across the sidewalk that bordered the fence. She touched the gate, pushing the narrow opening wide enough to allow her to slip through and onto the grounds. "Thorne?" she called.

There was no answer from the surrounding darkness. She hesitated briefly before she pulled the gate shut behind her, feeling infinitely better when the iron lock slipped into its niche with a metallic clang. She was safely inside the urban fortress the Barringtons had built against the encroaching violence of the twentieth century. The only question was: Where was Thorne? She ran up the steps to the porch, but she hadn't had time to cross its narrow expanse to the glass-paneled front door, when she heard her name from the shadows behind her.

"Kate."

She looked back and saw Thorne standing outside his own security fence, a restraining hand on the collar of the retriever. The puppy stood beside him, panting, his tongue lolling out of his friendly dog-grin, looking up trustingly at his owner, whose tall frame was bent sideways in order to maintain his hold.

Running back down the steps, Kate hurried down the sidewalk and then spent a seemingly endless minute struggling with the gate's release. "I thought something had happened to you," she said breathlessly when it finally yielded.

Thorne laughed, the sound deep and warm, totally relaxed. The prosaic explanation for his absence was also comforting.

"I made the mistake of letting Charlie come out of the house with me. When I unlocked the gate, he thought we were going for a run. He pushed through before I could grab him. I couldn't let him roam around loose. He hasn't figured out that cars are dangerous. I thought we could get back before you arrived. I left the gate unlocked," he explained, "in case we didn't."

By that time he was inside, pulling the gate inward again, and she listened once more to the satisfyingly secure clang of its mechanism engage. The dog's greeting was cold-nosed and enthusiastic, and she found herself smiling, forgetting briefly what had sent her hurrying through the darkness to this man.

"I'm glad you're here," Thorne said. He drew her against his side, his body big and solid and protective. He touched his lips to the top of her hair. "You smell good," he said.

She remembered that she had washed her hair, allowing it to dry naturally, a process that she knew would have resulted in a mass of uncontrollable curls. "That's good," she said, "'cause I probably look like hell."

He laughed.

"Do you think we could go inside?" she suggested. "Despite your fence, I still feel a little exposed out here."

"Of course," he said. He put his arm around her shoulder, pulling her to him again, and they walked together to the porch where the dog was patiently waiting, his gaze fixed on the closed door, anticipating being allowed back into the familiar domain as much as she was now. The house seemed welcoming, in spite of its ever-present darkness.

Thorne slipped his long fingers into the front pocket of his jeans, his hand flattened to fit into the skin-tight material, and fished out the key.

"Where's Elliot?" she asked. Maybe the old man was already asleep, and Thorne didn't want to disturb him.

"I suggested he spend the night at his sister's. She was released from the hospital today. I thought you might be more comfortable if...we were alone," he offered.

He was right, she realized. For some reason, she *would* have been embarrassed for Elliot to know she had come here to spend the night with Thorne, and she was grateful again for his consideration of feelings she hadn't even anticipated that she might have. But he had. Kindness or old-fashioned good manners? Either way, it was especially welcoming.

Thorne fitted the key he'd retrieved into the lock and then turned the handle. When the door swung inward, the soft cascade of glass notes shimmered into the silent hallway as the draft of night air touched the crystals of the chandelier.

The retriever padded like a golden shadow across the foyer, his nails ticking softly on the parquet, disappearing again into the darkness behind the staircase. Heading to the kitchen and his dishes, Kate thought, in need of a long drink of water after his unexpected midnight run.

Like the Southern gentleman he had been raised to be, Thorne allowed her to precede him into the dim foyer, and then he pulled the door closed behind them. "Have I told you how glad I am that you're here?" he asked.

"Despite the fact that I'm about four hours late?"

"Apparently you had a good reason. Where are the files you wanted me to look at?"

"Damn. I left them in the car. When you weren't at the gate..." She hesitated, again hating to admit how paranoid all this was making her. Thorne's warning that even possessing the files was dangerous had somehow made the threat seem more real. What she was doing was not an exercise in intellect, but a search for a killer.

"Did you think *I'd* forgotten *you?*" he asked. There was a trace of self-directed amusement in the question, and she knew he was remembering the confession she'd made over the phone.

"I thought something had happened to you," she admitted.

"To me? Why would you think that?"

If he hadn't realized, as she had told Lew, that his was one name they knew was still on Jack's list, she wouldn't be the one to suggest it to him. Thorne Barrington had had enough to deal with during the last three years. Her idea that Jack would try again wasn't something that would help in this situation.

"Just an indication of how shook up I am, I guess. You'd said you'd be there and when you weren't..." She shrugged, letting him put his own interpretation on that fear. Fear for him. A very real fear, she believed, whether he had confronted it yet or not.

"I'll go back out and get them," he offered.

Suddenly, she didn't want him out there, out in the darkness. "We could leave it until tomorrow," she surprised herself by suggesting. "There's not much left to read. I had read all the victim profiles."

"Everything?" he prodded softly. "Every word?"

"Except yours," she admitted. She had laid the thick folder to the side when she'd come to it. She already knew everything it contained. There were no secrets there. It had seemed far more important to examine the others. "I'd already read it a dozen times before, and I *knew* you weren't involved."

"I appreciate the vote of confidence," he said. There was a hint of amusement in his tone, and she knew he had recognized the significance of that confession. She had read his file a dozen times before because of her fascination with him.

"I had read a couple of the files on the investigators, and then you called. I swear I didn't see anything I hadn't read a hundred times before. I can't imagine what Lew found."

"It's always possible that it wasn't something in those files. It's possible that Garrison uncovered something else."

That was a possibility, of course. Lew had promised yesterday to pursue other things. Mays's connections with the current hate groups. Thorne's injuries. She had been the one who had asked for that, a long time ago, before she had come to know the man standing beside her. But of course, those scenarios wouldn't explain why Lew had mailed her the files.

"We could start fresh in the morning," Thorne's voice broke into her thoughts. "Maybe when you're less tired..." He let the suggestion trail.

"I just want it over. I just want to find whoever killed Lew. Whoever—" Whoever had sent the bombs. Like the one that had arrived here three years ago and had forever changed Thorne Barrington's life. "Just over," she finished.

"I know, but I think you've probably dealt with enough during the last couple of days. You don't have to figure it all out tonight."

"You have another suggestion?" she asked, smiling at him.

"Let it go," he said. "Don't think about it. About what's happened. About the files. Don't think about anything. Not tonight. Just let me hold you while you sleep."

Don't tempt me, he'd said, and now he was tempting her. A very tempting offer. To forget about it all. Finally to feel safe again.

"I'd like that," she said simply, the absolute truth. "I'd really like that."

THEY CLIMBED the dark stairs together, Thorne's arm still comfortingly around her shoulder. The bedroom he led her to was huge, with furniture massive enough to fill its soaring dimensions. The draperies had been pushed back from the expanse of windows, so that the moonlight filtered into the room through the leaves of the trees that lined the street outside. Even in the moon-touched dimness it was obvious that the room's decor was masculine.

"This is your room?" she asked.

"The phone's here. I thought—"

"That wasn't a complaint. Only a question."

She took a breath, acknowledging the inherent awkwardness in their situation. Like the first kiss, neither of them could be sure what the other was feeling.

"It's all right," Thorne said. "I meant what I said. You need to sleep tonight—far more than you need anything else."

"What about the other?" she asked, smiling at him. She was relieved that he seemed able to read her so well.

The dark head tilted, questioning, and a faint crease formed between the winged brows. "The other?" he repeated.

"To hold me while I sleep. Is that offer still good?"

"I can't think of anything that would give me more pleasure than to hold you," he said softly.

She couldn't resist, despite the quiet romanticism of that. "Not...anything?" she teased, lips tilting.

"I'm trying to be a gentleman, Kate, but I have to warn you that you're pushing your luck."

She laughed. Despite everything that had happened in the last few days, despite the horror and fear, something relaxed inside.

"Come to bed," he invited.

He held out his hand, like a courtier from another age, and she laid hers in it. He led her to the wide bed and sat down on the edge, still holding her fingers. He looked up from them, his gaze moving over her features, and then he smiled.

"I like your hair like that, soft and loose, as fine as a child's."

In spite of what he had promised, the deep voice was seductive. Suddenly, she knew that she wanted his fingers entangled in her hair, touching it. Touching her. Finally, touching her.

Drawn by that image, she moved closer to him. He opened his legs, creating a space between them for her to stand in, welcoming her body between the strength of his thighs. Freeing her fingers from his, she laid her palms on the wide expanse of his shoulders. His hands found her waist, and with their movement against her body, she could feel the play of muscle under her palms.

She looked down into his face, the features masculine and strong, yet perfectly aligned, perfectly formed. She had thought about Thorne Barrington for months, but being with him was different from anything she had imagined. Because *he* was different from the man he should have been. Despite the fact that he must have grown up accustomed to the adoration of the opposite sex, there was none of the sexual arrogance often found in men who were this attractive.

His hands had slipped under her T-shirt, their slight roughness pleasant against her skin. The big fingers skimmed slowly upward, over the small, regular protrusions of her ribs. He wasn't smiling now, and again she could see the starkness of desire etched in the spare planes of his face.

He wanted her, and she was fascinated that he did. Fascinated by the idea that someone like Thorne Barrington could be attracted to her. Fascinated by him. By his touch. There was no resistance in her mind to what he was doing. She wanted him to touch her, had wanted it for a long time, far longer than she had ever admitted, even to herself.

Finally his hands found the full, unrestrained softness of

her breasts, cupping under their weight, holding her, still gentle, carefully controlled. She heard the depth of the breath he took. Trying to maintain that control. "Kate," he whispered.

"I know," she said. This was not what he had intended—not what he'd promised—but it was what they both wanted.

His thumbs swept across the sensitive swell of her breasts, across nipples hardened with her own desire, taut with the promise of his caress. And then back. No demand. Only need. A need she shared.

She moved closer, putting one knee on the bed beside his narrow hips—leaning against him, letting him support her—and then the other knee on the other side, so that she was kneeling above him now.

His hands shifted under her shirt. Behind her now. Holding her. Pulling her to him, to be locked against the wall of his chest. She eased down into his lap, put her head against his shoulder, and was held in his arms like a child. His size seemed to give her permission to feel fragile, permission to be vulnerable, and she no longer needed to fear that vulnerability. He was certainly strong enough to protect her.

His hands slid over her spine, moving under the thin shirt, soothing out tension and fear. "It's all right," he promised. "Everything will be all right."

She eased her body away from his, only far enough to look into his eyes. This was inevitable. Their relationship had been building to this for days, weeks. Months, she acknowledged. Long months when she had only looked at his pictures, had dreamed about him.

"Make love to me," she whispered. She hadn't intended to ask him that. She had hoped that he, too, would be aware of the inevitability of this, but she was afraid that he might have meant to do exactly what he had promised. She knew now that to be held was not what she wanted from him tonight. Not *all* she wanted.

His hands had stilled. He held her, unmoving, apparently trying to read what was revealed in her features.

"Please," she added.

"Are you sure, Kate?"

"I don't think I've ever been as sure of anything in my life," she admitted. "I want you to make love to me."

Something shifted in the taut lines of his face. It was not a smile, but a softening, a relaxation of tension, perhaps. Relief that the restraint he had promised was not what she needed from him? Relief that she, too, needed something else? Something very different from the control he had been seeking.

"I want to see you," he said. Already his hands were tangled in the loose fall of her shirt, helping her ease it off over her head. The curling tendrils of her hair were caught up briefly in the fabric, and when the shirt was off, they fell back against her neck and shoulders in a mass of shampoo-fragranced confusion. Unthinkingly, she raised her hands, running her fingers through the disordered strands, pushing them up and away from her face.

"Don't move," he ordered softly.

Surprised by the tone of the command, which she had instinctively obeyed, her eyes sought his. He wasn't looking at her face. His gaze was instead on her breasts, thrown into prominence by her raised arms, their small peaks thrusting upward as if seeking...

She knew exactly what they were seeking as she watched his lips lower to touch against one and then the other. She held her breath, feeling his against her skin, warm and damp and feathering over the too-sensitive flesh she had exposed for his touch. Because she had wanted him to touch her there. Had wanted him for such a long time.

His mouth fastened over one nipple. His tongue mimicked the motion his thumbs had begun, slowly across and then back. She could feel her skin tightening in response and wondered what that movement felt like against his tongue, wondered if he could know what he was doing to her.

Her breath caught, a small half sob of sound, like a child fighting the onslaught of tears, struggling now for her own control. Her hands deserted the wild profusion of her curls. She lowered her head over his dark one, which was still bent to allow his mouth its torturing contact with her body. She put her lips against his hair and then turned her face so that its silken caress was under her cheek. Her breath shivered out in small, audible gasps. His mouth was suckling, pulling and releasing in a pulsing rhythm, slow and strong. Too strong. Too demanding. The pulse was echoing somewhere in her body. Low in her belly. Demanding. Aching. The sweet, age-old ache of desire.

"Please," she whispered again, her mouth moving against the coal-black softness of his hair.

His lips hesitated, the rhythm he had created broken. In the silence between them, she was aware again of the slightly sobbing quality of the breath she drew into lungs hungry for air. Had she forgotten to breathe as he touched her? Or did her body need more air, like a furnace that demanded oxygen for the fire he had ignited?

When he didn't move, his stillness too prolonged, she put her hand over the back of his downturned head, cupping the smooth roundness of his skull and then moving down the strong column of his neck.

Suddenly, he fell back against the mattress, carrying her with him, her body lying on top of his. With the change in position she was very aware of how much he wanted her. The evidence of his desire was blatant through the thin material of his worn jeans, straining upward into the soft cotton knit of her shorts. So little between them. But she wanted nothing between. Nothing between the hair-roughened skin of his chest and her bare breasts. Nothing between the small convexity of her belly and the ridged muscles of his. Nothing between...

His mouth found hers. It was open, waiting for him. His tongue invaded. Seeking. Demanding. His hands were against her back. Despite the damage Jack had inflicted, they drifted again with sensuous grace over the slender, contoured planes of her body. Touching her shoulder blades, covered by skin that shivered into his caress. Along the ridge of her spine. Big hands slipping into the waistband of her shorts to curl over her bare bottom.

She could feel his breathing beginning to deepen, his hips straining upward into hers as his hands pushed her body downward. Their mouths released, and his slid, opened, across her cheek, a pulling sensation, dragging against her flushed skin. His lips touched the dampness of the curling tendrils that gathered at her temple and then moved to her ear. She turned her head, accommodating, seeking whatever intimacy his touch suggested he wanted. The warmth of his breath first, softly stirring against the outer fold of the sensitive channel. His tongue moving inside. Caressing. Tantalizing. Hot and wet.

He breathed her name again, so close, speaking it into the small, ivory cavern of her ear. She allowed her knees to slide away from him, lowering herself, millimeter by millimeter, her desire fusing now with his. She could feel the heat of his body through the barrier of their clothing. No barriers, she thought again. No barriers of any kind. Not tonight.

She was more aware of his breath, slipping out in small aching gasps almost over her ear. The other sound was subliminal. She would have ignored it, not unheard but unacknowledged, had she not felt the sudden stillness of his body beneath the bonelessness their lovemaking had reduced hers to.

She felt the change and wondered, and then into her head came the belated recognition of the sound she, too, had recognized. The same sound that had echoed into the darkness of the mansion each time she had come here—the small, crystal teardrops of the glass chandelier touching together in the draft created by the opening front door.

Chapter Thirteen

"What the hell?" Thorne said. His voice was almost sound-less, a breath, but with the shocked whisper there could be no doubt that he had heard and recognized the same noise that had finally penetrated her desire-drugged brain.

She sat up, pushing away from him. Suddenly she was aware that she was half-naked and cold. Cold with her sep-aration from the solid warmth of his body. Cold with fear.

Thorne still lay motionless on the bed, the pale fabric of the coverlet he was lying against a frame for his darkness. Dark hair and shirt, black eyes holding hers. She knew that he was listening. Both of them listening, without breathing. Listening in the eerie silence of the old house whose night sounds he would be infinitely familiar with.

There was nothing else. No other ghost of noise drifted, almost but not quite soundlessly, upward to the second floor.

"Elliot?" she whispered.

Against the ivory of the counterpane the dark head moved once, a negation, but that movement seemed to free Thorne from whatever spell had held them motionless. His body began to lift, and she scrambled off the bed to stand beside it on legs that trembled. Thorne touched a button on the speaker phone, and she finally remembered to take a breath. The cops had arrived quickly enough the night he called them to pick her up. The first night she had come here. So long ago.

Then, suddenly, Thorne's long fingers were turning the phone. "Son of a bitch," he said, the words again only a breath, the comment made to himself and not to her. At what was in his voice, her stomach roiled, moving upward toward her throat from the cold, hard knot of fear that had begun to grow within it.

He picked up the receiver then and put it to his ear, but given the silence that surrounded them, she already knew. There was no dial tone. There was no longer any connection between the mansion and the outside world.

"The line's been cut," he confirmed, and the coldness in her stomach shifted and reformed, enlarged and blossomed, threatening to engulf her.

He pushed her shirt into her hands, which were trembling so much it was hard to put it on. Before she had the crumpled material completely in place over her body, Thorne had grasped her arm, drawing her away from the bed and toward the shadows of the hallway. She resisted, knowing that the danger they faced was below. Surely they were safer here in the upstairs darkness.

"We can't go down there," she protested, still whispering.

"There's someone inside. We have to get out."

Thorne pulled her out into the hall, not toward the curving central stairs they had climbed together, but deeper into the dark bowels of the vast house. They hurried, moving almost noiselessly over the carpeted hall, passing closed doors. The farther they got from the streetlights, the darker the interior of the mansion became. She ran into him when he began to slow.

"Stairs," Thorne warned, the command almost silent. He released her arm, placing her hand on the smooth wood of the stair railing. She heard him move in front of her, and she knew she had no choice but to follow him.

The kitchen was lighter, more open, as it had been the night they had sat at the table and talked. Thorne didn't give her time to enjoy the openness, a welcome contrast to the claustrophobic narrowness of the walls on either side of the steep stairs they had just descended. He pulled her across the room. Awakened from some puppy dream, startled and confused, Charlie barked once, the sound echoing, too revealing. The shock of the unexpected noise paralyzed her, like a thief discovered in the act. By that time Thorne had the door open. He turned back to grab her hand, drawing her out into the now-safer blackness of the urban night.

He led the way unerringly through the small grounds that surrounded the mansion. Behind them, she could hear the echoing frenzy of Charlie's barking increase. Then the sounds faded as they rounded the front corner of the house. The gate was open again and beyond it stood her car.

"I have a phone," she gasped, the words ragged from lack of breath. It was only after she had spoken that she realized how ridiculous that comment was. They didn't need a phone. In her earlier panic that something might have happened to Thorne, she had not only left the folders in the car but also her keys. All they had to do was to reach the Mazda, get in and drive away.

She led the way to the sidewalk, but it was Thorne who moved automatically to the driver's side. She stood by the passenger door, breath sobbing, from physical effort now and not desire, waiting for him to release the lock that would let her in. Looking down into the car, she realized with shock that the folders she had piled on the passenger seat were no longer there. But when Thorne's fist pounded once on the roof of the car, his expletive soft but expressive, she became aware that they had a more immediate problem than the disappearance of those files.

"Locked," he said.

Suddenly the lights came on in the mansion behind her. She glanced back at the house through the bars of the surrounding fence. The chandelier in the foyer, which she had never seen lighted before, was blazing out into the dark stillness.

"Come on. Across the street," Thorne ordered.

She turned back in time to see him sprint toward the darkened hulk of the mansion that was being renovated. She followed, rounding the front of the Mazda as the porch light came on behind her.

Thorne seemed to melt into the shadows of the ruined house that loomed out of the darkness before her. She had always thought his vision must be more acute than normal because of the way he lived, and now she realized that their very lives might depend on his ability to negotiate in the blackened interior of the silent, ghostly ruin.

He was waiting for her beside the opening where the front door had once been. His damaged hand closed around her wrist, and despite the fact that she had known instinctively that he wouldn't leave her behind, she jumped with the shock of that unexpected contact.

"Upstairs," he breathed, his mouth pressed against her ear.

From the street came the sound of footsteps, unmistakable in the surrounding night. Thorne drew her into the foyer. She wondered briefly about the safety of climbing the stairs that loomed before them, about the safety of walking on the upper floors, but she had seen the workmen there. And would she and Thorne be safer to stay below? To wait for whoever was following them, for whoever was working, fairly successfully now, to keep the sound of his pursuit hidden?

Her tennis shoes made no noise on the wooden risers, and surprisingly, for such a big man, Thorne moved almost as silently, guiding her again with unhesitating certitude into the darkness at the top. She could barely see, following him blindly, forced to trust his superior night vision.

She thought once that she heard someone moving behind

them, but the fire-damaged beams of the structure might have produced that sensation. Just as they might be revealing their progress, she acknowledged ruefully. Thorne guided her around workmen's paraphernalia, leading her ever toward the back of the house.

They climbed another set of dark, narrow stairs, up to the third floor now. The hallway they ran down was becoming brighter, and when she looked up, she realized why. The door it led toward had, like most of the outer doors, been removed, and the passage ended in a view of the night sky beyond the sagging banister of what must have been the back stairs of the mansion.

As she watched, a figure moved up those stairs into the dim illumination provided by the backdrop of moon-touched sky—a man, silhouetted suddenly within the framework of the missing door.

A flash of light exploded out of that darkness. She flinched before its brightness even as she realized the powerful beam wasn't directed at her. Its intensity had pinned the man moving ahead of her down the hall. Thorne's hand raised in automatic response, trying to protect himself from the glare.

"Kate?"

She identified the speaker immediately, although she could see nothing beyond the glare of the flashlight. *Kahler,* she realized. *My God, it was Kahler.* And the police? Even as she thought it, she realized there had been no sirens, no arriving patrol cars. Only Kahler.

"Are you all right?" Kahler asked, shifting the light slightly to include her figure within its illumination. "He hasn't hurt you, has he?"

"I'm all right," she said automatically. Why would he think Thorne would hurt her?

"You don't have to be afraid, Kate. Everything's under control," Kahler went on, his voice reassuring.

"What the hell's going on?" Barrington's voice, as

coldly furious as the night she had first walked into his house. "What were you doing in my house?"

I picked up a few tricks of the trade, Kahler had said the day she had found him inside her apartment, and she realized Thorne was right. It had to have been Kahler who had entered while they were upstairs. There was no one else. At Barrington's question, the flashlight had been refocused, its powerful light again directed at Thorne's face.

"It's over," Kahler said, his voice as cold as Barrington's. "Finally, you're going to pay for what you did."

"I don't know what you're talking about," Thorne said. He had lowered his head, his hand still shielding his eyes. "Get that damned light out of my face," he ordered.

"You couldn't leave Kate alone. Maybe because of your hatred of the media, but whatever you intended tonight is not going to happen. You're not going to hurt her."

"I don't know what you're talking about. Kate came here because—" Thorne's voice stopped suddenly, whatever he intended to say deliberately cut off, and she wondered why. Because he had realized that Kahler was jealous? That telling him why she had come tonight would only make him more angry?

"Because you tricked her into trusting you," Kahler said. "Because she believed what everyone else believed about you. Because she doesn't know what you really are."

"And you do?" Barrington asked. His tone had changed, anger overlain by a rigid control and by an emotion she couldn't read.

"I know *exactly* what you are. A murderer. A fine, highly respected, sanctimonious murderer."

"Kahler," Kate said, a protest. She could sense the unraveling fury in his voice, and thankfully, with her interruption, the beam of light came back to her.

"What are you doing here, Kate?" he asked. "Didn't you get my message?"

"What message?" she asked.

"About the lab results. The results on the physical evidence from Garrison's office and from the sheets I took off your bed. The hair and fiber samples."

He said it as if it should mean something to her, but it didn't. In all that had happened, she had even forgotten about the sheets he had taken from her apartment that night. The realization that he seemed to be implicating Thorne Barrington in that break-in and in Lew's murder began to filter into her head.

"What's that supposed to mean?" she asked.

"They're consistent. I told you. On the message. I couldn't figure out why you'd come here tonight..." He paused, and then the voice she had always thought so pleasant continued. "They match the DNA."

"What DNA? What the hell are you talking about?"

"Barrington's. From the bombing. They match Barrington's DNA."

"That's a lie," Thorne said softly, almost as if he were speaking only to her. "There was no DNA profile done. There was no reason for that to be done."

"Are you saying that Thorne put the confetti in my bed?" she asked. Her lips felt numb, unwilling to form the question.

"*And* killed Garrison," Kahler agreed. "There's enough physical evidence to tie him to both. I told you all this. You didn't get my message?"

"No," she said. The cold knot was back. Was it possible that what Kahler was saying was true? She had gone straight into the bathroom when she'd gotten home today, too eager to get out of her clothes, too eager to return to Thorne, and then Lew's package arrived. She had never bothered to check her messages.

"If you really believe what you're saying," Barrington said, his voice still controlled, still enforcing a calmness she knew he couldn't feel, "then I would like to call my attorney."

"You can call from the precinct," Kahler said dismissingly. "Kate, come down the hall toward me. Don't try to touch her, Barrington. I'm not likely to miss at this range."

"He said there was no DNA profile done," Kate said. "There was no reason for one."

"We were suspicious from the start," Kahler said. "Despite the old man's explanation about destroying the wrappings from the package, none of the rest of it made any sense. It always seemed strange that the judge would be opening his mail in the basement, but given Barrington's reputation—"

"That's a lie, Kate," Barrington said, speaking over the detective's explanation, his voice still low, directed only to her. "That's not how it happened. You know that."

But she didn't. She couldn't remember anything in the files about the location of the explosion, perhaps because of the press blackout Barrington himself had imposed or because the police had tried to protect his privacy.

Again Kahler's voice came from the darkness behind the light, almost an echo of her thoughts. "We were suspicious, just not enough. We were too willing to believe what he said because of who and what he was supposed to be."

She wished she could see Kahler's face. He had told her none of this before, despite the times they'd talked about the case, about Barrington. Something here didn't ring true.

"Are you telling me that the police have suspected all along that the first bomb *didn't* originate outside Barrington's house?"

Kahler *had* suggested that, but only recently. *Maybe he had an accident. Did you ever think about that?* And she hadn't. She had been so certain that Kahler's warning had been born of his jealousy. Certain because she had already been caught up in her own fantasy about Barrington? A fantasy that had become so real that it had interfered with her judgment?

Standing in the darkness of the narrow hallway, she was

no longer sure of anything. Her instincts about Thorne Barrington had been completely free of threat. She had trusted him, and now...now she didn't know who to trust.

"You're alone?" she asked. That wasn't right. No cop went into an unknown situation without backup. Kahler was too good a cop not to follow the rules.

"My backup hasn't arrived," he said.

"Then you *have* called someone? They're on the way?"

"Of course."

But with the word "call" she remembered that the phone lines from the house had been cut. The police didn't cut lines. Kahler shouldn't have done that, even if he were acting alone, even if he'd been worried about her safety. And why would he take the folders from her car? Unless...

Oh, dear God, she thought, the realization producing a roller coaster of sensation in her stomach. Because there was, of course, a folder in that stack about Byron Kahler, one of the hunters, his name neatly labeled in Lew's script. A folder she had never read, had never seen before. But maybe Lew had. *Oh, dear God,* she thought, *Lew had.*

Kahler had come to take care of the unfinished business he had begun three years ago, and the knowledge that she was in Thorne Barrington's house had not been a deterrent to his plans.

"I got a package tonight, Kahler," she said softly. "It came through the mail."

"Kate."

That was Thorne, trying to warn her. He had already figured it out. That's why he had stopped before, why he hadn't told Kahler the reason she had come to his house. Now he was trying to warn her not to mention the folders, but he didn't know what she knew. Kahler had already discovered she had the files. He had taken them out of her car, and he must be aware of whatever damaging information was in the one with his name on it.

Obviously Lew had given himself away. Somehow he'd

revealed whatever he'd found, perhaps unthinkingly, maybe in a phone conversation to the detective, jotting those habitual notes of his on the desk calendar as they talked. Then, belatedly realizing that what he had said might be dangerous, Lew had thrown the files into one of the big Priority Mail envelopes, conveniently on hand in the newsroom, and addressed it to her—the only person he could be certain would understand the significance of what he'd found.

Had he then rushed to the seeming safety of his suburban home, trying to decide if he should act on whatever he'd found? *Maybe important. Maybe nothing,* his voice echoed in her memory.

Oh, God, Lew, I wish you'd been right. I wish it had been nothing. She knew that she was not mistaken. It all fit. Even the profile the FBI had done so long ago matched what she knew about Byron Kahler. A loner. Product of a dysfunctional family. Very smart, meticulous about details. It all fit. As a bonus, he had an insider's knowledge of how the game was played.

And if Kahler *were* Jack, he wouldn't let her go. He couldn't afford to. He knew she had seen the files. He had removed them from her car. What he couldn't know was that she hadn't finished reading them. And he would never believe that, she realized. It had been so against her character not to read them all. She hadn't, but only because of Barrington's invitation, only because of what she had heard in his voice.

"A package?" Kahler said finally. Although the thoughts had been tumbling through her mind at lightning speed, she knew the pause before his response had been fractionally too long.

"Don't," Barrington said again. He didn't know that the files had been taken out of her car. He was still trying to protect her, as he had been when he'd requested to be allowed to call his lawyer. He didn't realize, as she now did, that Kahler *had* to kill them both. Thorne still thought she could be saved, but she knew better. Kahler wouldn't leave a witness to whatever was going to happen tonight. No witnesses at all.

A bomber don't care who gets blowed up in the process of getting what he wants. He purely don't care. Wilford Mays's voice was in her head, cold and full of hate.

Kahler had given her Mays's name, she remembered suddenly. When she had mentioned she might go to Hall Draper's hometown, he had thrown out the information about Mays's long-ago contact with Barrington to stop her. When she had indicated that she might try to find the girl Jackie Draper had told her about, Kahler had sent her off in another direction, pursuing a thirty-year-old case against another bomber. A wild-goose chase—to direct her away from whatever connection Draper had with Kahler. Through the girl? she wondered. Through the girl Hall Draper had gotten pregnant so many years ago? The image of a dark-haired child in an old black-and-white photograph flashed into her mind.

With that realization, she must have made some sound, some movement, because Barrington said again, questioning, "Kate?"

He couldn't see her, of course. He stood with his head lowered, both hands raised now against the intensity of the light Kahler kept focused on his face. She knew that what Kahler was doing was deliberate. The migraine had probably already begun. Thorne was trying to protect her, even as he was fighting the maelstrom of pain pounding sickeningly in his skull, and suddenly she *knew* who to trust. No longer any doubt in her mind.

"What kind of package?" Kahler asked.

"The files," she said. "All the Tripper files. Lew mailed them to me before he died." She took a step closer to them both.

"You've been through them?" It was said without inflection, but despite his effort, the tone was subtly wrong, more obviously wrong perhaps because she *couldn't* see his face. There was only the voice she had admired speaking from the darkness.

"I didn't have time," she said. She needed to be closer. Whatever happened, she could do them no good so far away from the gun. She had to keep up the pretense. Keep him talking until she could get closer. "I brought the folders with me. That's why I came here tonight. I thought Barrington might be able to see something I hadn't seen. I'd been through them a hundred times. I thought he might see something, and instead…"

"It's all right," Kahler said. "It's over, Kate. You're safe. Move past him."

Was he only trying to get her to move so they would be closer together, a more certain target in the darkness, or was it possible that he had believed what she'd said?

"They're in the car," she added. "I'll get them before we leave. We'll take them with us to the station." She took another step, near enough now that she could have reached out and touched Thorne.

"I don't think there's anything there," Kahler said. "If there were, someone would have found it by now." It was the same lie he had told her from the beginning.

"You're probably right. You don't think that's why he killed Lew? Because of something Lew found in the files?" she asked. She took another step, turning her body so that she could slip between the wall and the shoulder of the man who stood unmoving beside her, hands still shielding his eyes.

"He killed Lew because Garrison discovered what he really is. Maybe one of Barrington's friends revealed something about his medical condition. Maybe the brain damage you suspected. *Something* unhinged him and turned him into what he is."

"A murderer," she said. Another step. Past Thorne now.

Nearer to Kahler. "Why would he kill all those people?"
she asked. "Why would anybody kill all those people?"

"I've told you from the first I don't have any idea why
he's done the things he's done. That's for someone else to
figure out. All I know is I've got evidence tying Barrington
to two crime scenes, one of them a homicide."

"You're going to take him in."

"As soon as help arrives. Then I'll take you home and
all of this will be over."

"I guess you must be right," she said softly. She was
almost to Kahler, able to see him clearly now that she was
past the intensity of the beam. He looked just the same. The
flashlight and the gun were remarkably steady, professionally held. *And why not?* she thought bitterly. He was a
professional, with years of training at his command. A real
insider. That was why he had been able to get away with
it so long.

"I can't help but believe he must have had a reason.
Something set him off," she went on, playing for time,
trying to create an opportunity. Hoping for any opportunity.
"Why did Barrington *start* building bombs? Why do people
set out to kill other people?"

"You've always thought there had to be a connection,"
Kahler said, a hint of mockery in the deep voice.

"Yes," she acknowledged.

He smiled, the small intriguing lines around his eyes
moving, the top of his face shadowed and the lower high-
lighted by the light he held, still focused at Thorne Barrington.

"Was it because of Jenny?" Kate asked. Her voice was
very low, but she was close to him now. So close. "Was
Jenny the girl Hall Draper got pregnant?"

"Jenny?" Thorne said, his voice coming from behind
her. She didn't turn at his comment, still watching Kahler,
still waiting for a chance. And then Barrington said, not a
question this time, but a realization. "Jenny Carpenter. My

God, Jenny Carpenter.'' There were so many emotions trapped in the soft shock. Recognition. Remembrance. Regret?

"I'm surprised you even remember her," Kahler said. "She was just a nobody. One of the hundreds of nobodies you dealt with through the years."

"I never thought she was nobody," Thorne said.

"A cheap hooker. An addict. Of course you did. Did you even care what happened to her? Did you even know?"

"I knew."

"What happened?" Kate asked. She could not prevent the question. *The public's right to know* brushed through her consciousness, but *she* needed to know. *She* needed to understand what had set all this off.

"He put her in a cell, and she hanged herself."

The words were brutal, as cold and as horrible as the imagery they evoked.

"To him, she was scum," Kahler went on. "So he put her away, locked her up. Just to get her off the streets of the city his family practically owned. It didn't matter that someone had loved her. That she had once been someone's child, someone's—"

The sentence was broken, the pain it had revealed silenced, but in the darkness, Kate spoke the words he had left unspoken.

"Someone's sister," she finished for him, her voice almost as agonized as his.

"The bastards destroyed her. They *all* destroyed her."

"All those people had something to do with Jenny?" she asked. This was the heart of the mystery, the soul of the evil he'd perpetrated. A girl too young to die. A child in a black-and-white photograph. Innocent.

"They brought her to that cell. They all played a part in her destruction, so I found them. I hunted them down. All the steps on her journey to that place. It took me years, but

I didn't care. I needed to understand what had happened. They all were guilty. They all killed Jenny.''

"So you killed them," she said softly.

"Do you pity them, Kate? They used her. They corrupted her. From Hall Draper's teenage rutting to that bastard's sanctimonious judicial murder, they all were to blame for her death. First they taught her to use her body, a way to earn affection. That was one of my mother's many boyfriends.'' The word was bitter, still hating, still vindictive. "Jenny's father had deserted her. She just wanted someone to love her. That's all she wanted, and he used that need. They all used her.''

"How did you find them?" she asked, so close to him now she could have reached out and put her hand on the gun. *Just keep him talking,* she thought. *Try to think of something to do.*

"The diaries," he said, a thread of amusement, gentle with memory, in his tone. "She'd kept them. I had given her the first one. She was maybe six or seven. A birthday present, one of those little plastic things girls used to buy at the five-and-dime. Hers were always pink. Even the last one was pink.''

Kate could hear the memories in his voice. It had changed, the accent of his youth stronger now. He was lost in the past, a time when he had been the whole world to a little girl. When he had bought her a birthday present, a simple thing she had cherished, maybe because she had so little else.

"When she was dead, they sent all those diaries to my mother. I found them when she died. Those pitiful childish books were what Jenny had kept through the years, and everything I needed to know was there. The boyfriend. Draper. The college boy who gave her her first hit. The people who pushed her down when she tried to straighten out her life. People who fired her from jobs, put her back on the streets because she wasn't strong enough to leave the stuff alone. She wasn't strong like you, Kate, but she didn't give up. She didn't stop trying to make something of her life, trying to straighten herself out…''

His voice stopped, controlling emotion that had crept in. Not regret. Not even love, Kate thought. Hate? The need for revenge had occupied Byron Kahler for so many years, long, patient years of seeking those he believed had led Jenny to a cell, to a cold and lonely dying. She was sorry for the lost child Jenny Carpenter had been, but surely that was not reason enough…

''He has to pay for his part, and then, finally, it's over,'' Kahler finished.

Did he really believe that? Was he so twisted by hate and his need for revenge that he thought this insanity made sense?

''And me, Kahler? What about me?'' she whispered the unwanted thought aloud. She hadn't been mistaken about what he felt for her. She knew that he cared. Even as she was falling in love with Thorne Barrington, she had known that Kahler loved her. She had been sorry it was not a feeling she could ever return, that he was not the man she loved, but now she understood why.

''You were so strong. I admired that. Jenny was…''

Kate watched him swallow emotion, the movement of the muscles in his throat visible even in the shadowed darkness.

''You were so different. So determined to find the answer. I tried to keep you safe, Kate. I tried to warn you.''

''That's what the confetti was—a warning?'' she asked. ''And then you sent me after Mays to take me away from the connection between Draper and Jenny.''

''I didn't want you to be the one to figure it out. After I met you…I just wanted it to be over. I couldn't stop. Not until it was done. Until the debt was paid. You understand that. But when I met you, I wanted it to be over.''

''That's why the timetable changed. Because of me?''

she whispered. Hall Draper had died three months early because of her. Because of Kahler's growing feelings for her. *Just get it done.* The need to make everybody dead, so he had broken his own rigid schedule. He had gone against the pattern.

"I deserved something," Kahler said. "After all this time. Something for me. Was I wrong to want that, Kate? To want you?"

His gaze shifted for the first time from its competent, professional focus on Barrington. It moved to search her face. *Seeking acceptance of what he had done?* she wondered briefly before she realized he had given her the opening she needed.

She threw herself at the hand holding the revolver, hoping that if nothing else she might disrupt his aim enough to give Thorne a chance to run, to disappear into the darkness of the narrow hall behind him—if he were still capable of running. Instead of the gun, it was the flashlight that fell. It bounced across the bare wooden boards of the hallway, and then began to roll, its light spiraling in revolving patterns along the wall.

Kahler grabbed her around the waist with the arm that had been occupied with holding the light. In the sudden darkness of the hall she could hear Thorne running. *Toward* them, she had time to realize. Toward them and not away as she had intended. He was reacting to the chance she had tried to give him by charging Kahler, again trying to protect her. Not trying to avoid Kahler's gun or the bullet, a bullet fired by a professional—calmly, coolly and accurately. Even in the darkness, the hallway was so narrow there was little chance Kahler would miss such a big target.

And of course, he hadn't. She knew that from the noise Thorne's body made as it fell against the wall and then heavily onto the wooden floor. With the realization that Barrington had been shot, she began to struggle again, fighting against Kahler's hold, writhing fiercely to free herself.

Kahler took a step backwards, trying to control her, but she twisted her body from side to side, hating him. Needing to get to Thorne. A primitive urge to protect. She wasn't intellectually aware of all that was fueling her desperation to get away from the arms that held her. Arms that she didn't want around her. Arms she had never wanted there.

"Stop it, Kate," Kahler ordered, but it had no effect on the frenzy that possessed her. She dug her heels in, pushing backwards, turning and twisting in his hold. He moved again, dragging her arching body with him, fighting to control her. "It's all right," he said. "It's all over."

Insane, she thought. *He really is insane. Beneath all that cold control is only madness.*

The sound was subliminal. Like the crystal teardrops. Something she had heard before. Somewhere. Sometime. But she couldn't place it.

Not Barrington, she had time to realize with despair as the shadow launched itself out of the darkness at their struggling bodies, clearly outlined against the night sky behind them. The retriever hit with all the momentum of his sixty-five pounds. Big enough and strong enough to push them through the doorway and out onto the top of the wooden stairs.

She was aware that Kahler's arm released her as they fell backward, the three of them falling together, her body sandwiched between the man and the muscled, silken frame of the dog.

The sound of splintering wood seemed to register on her consciousness simultaneously with the force of Kahler's palm against her back. He shoved hard, throwing her body toward the doorway, back toward the hallway where Thorne Barrington lay, and away from the rotten banister.

Unbalanced, hampered by the frightened dog who was struggling to find his own footing, Kate fell—forward and not back—to lie stunned over the threshold of the doorway. Kahler made no sound as he continued to fall, the impact of their bodies having shattered the railing behind him. But the noise as he struck the tiled roof of the portico three stories below was like nothing she had ever heard—dull and leaden and somehow, she knew, very final.

Kate lay a moment where she had fallen, her mind struggling to accept the fact she was still alive. The retriever had made it to his feet, apparently unhurt. He stood beside her now, whining, his cold nose examining her out-flung arm before he turned to disappear into the darkness of the hallway from which he had appeared like a miracle. Elliot's watchdog.

Charlie's bark, sharp and loud, came from the darkness down the hall. He was trying to arouse his master. Kate got to her knees, and then, using the frame of the doorway she had been thrown into, finally to her feet. She staggered, knees shaking, toward the light of Kahler's flashlight. It had all happened so quickly that the big, black handle was still rolling, moving slightly back and forth in an ever-decreasing arc, over the smooth wooden floor.

She picked it up and, more in control now, she ran down the hall toward Thorne's sprawled body. She pushed the dog out of her way and knelt beside the man. She put her hand against the side of his neck and felt the reassuring pulse of blood through the carotid artery. *Alive. Thank God, he was still alive.*

The bullet had struck his temple, and the wound was bleeding. Like all head wounds, it was bleeding a lot. There was a frighteningly large pool of blood already under his head, and she knew that she had to get help. Call 911. Call somebody. Find a phone. She stood up, and the dog looked up at her, trusting eyes following her movements.

"Stay with him," she said. "I'll be right back. I have to get help." He whined and then barked once, the noise echoing loudly in the narrow passage. "It's okay," she said, touching the retriever's head. "Everything's all right. He'll be all right."

She was reassuring a dog, she realized, when she should be getting help. Shock? Was that what was wrong with her? Was that why she was still standing here in the ruined house, trembling, fighting sobs that were pushing upward from her chest. What the hell was wrong with her?

"Stay with him," she whispered the command past the knot in her throat, and then she ran into the darkness to find someone who would help.

Chapter Fourteen

The media circus of the next four weeks was far worse than Kate could ever have imagined, and this time, of course she was in the center ring. The local news crews had arrived almost as soon as the police that night, camera lights providing graphic illumination for the work of the paramedics.

She had said too much in her panicked call for help. She should never had mentioned the Tripper bombings, never have said Thorne Barrington's name, too well-known to go unnoticed by those who avidly listened to the scanners. *The public's right to know,* she had to remind herself, but the phrase echoed in her heart with bitterness now.

News of Jack the Tripper's death had spread like the proverbial wildfire, attracting national attention. Of course, it had been a national story all along. Kahler's victims had been scattered across the country, connected only by the thread of the drifting, aimless life of a young prostitute, a life which had ended one night, virtually unnoticed, in a Georgia jail cell.

What had Jenny Carpenter been doing in Atlanta? Kate often wondered. Had she come here to find her brother? Had Kahler known she was in his city? Was that what had precipitated Jenny's tragic suicide—the fear that Kahler might find out what she'd become? Or the fear that she might embarrass the brother who, despite incredible odds, seemed to have transcended their tragic, broken beginnings?

The authorities were still studying the diaries they had found during their search of Kahler's apartment, but they had discovered no bomb-making paraphernalia there. The speculation was that the bombs had been put together elsewhere, somewhere safe and private—a small, lock-it-and-take-the-key storage building maybe, the necessary equipment concealed in strongboxes. All Kahler would need would be a folding table and chair, easily stored in the same building, maybe in another city, hundreds of miles away from the public life Detective Byron Kahler had lived.

Despite the publicity, no one had come forward claiming to have knowledge about such a rental. Just as no one had ever claimed to have seen him mail the packages through the years. He had been too smart for that. None of those accidental sightings, no bystander's intuition, would have brought Kahler down.

After Kate had told her story—at least half a dozen times, it seemed to her—the police had asked her to read through Lew's neatly labeled folder containing the material the paper had collected on Byron Kahler. They wanted to know what Garrison had found that had gotten him killed. Despite her feelings about all that had happened, Kate was surprised to find that she, too, still needed an answer to that question.

What she found in the folder wasn't even an interview, not like the other "hunter" files she had read the night she'd received the envelope. Kahler's file contained only two sheets of paper. One of them was a polite letter from the public information officer of the Atlanta PD, which explained that, due to the press of official business, Detective Kahler was forced to deny the request for an interview at this time.

But the helpful officer had supplied what small bit of information she could—something she obviously had not

cleared with Kahler. She had sent the newspaper a photo-
copy of Kahler's employment application. Despite the detective's refusal to do an interview, the department had attempted to cooperate with Lew's request, to provide some
background on the person who was carrying out the official
investigation of the Atlanta bombing. Knowing Kahler,
Kate suspected that this single sheet of paper was all the
personal information the department had.

Kate scanned the lines of the form that had been neatly
filled in more than fourteen years before, the ink faded, but
Kahler's printing almost as meticulous as Lew's. Her eyes
moved down the page to next of kin, and what she found
was a little surprising. No name had been entered in the
space.

She almost turned the form over without reading anything else on the front, but somehow a word caught her
eye. Pennsylvania. It had almost jumped off the page at her,
and then she looked at the town printed before it in Kahler's
distinctive hand. Falls Bend. Place of birth. Falls Bend,
Pennsylvania.

She knew immediately where she'd heard that name—
during Jackie Draper's whispered narrative, but she also
knew she had never transcribed her notes from that interview. She hadn't had time. Too much had happened and
that task had been forgotten. So how would Lew have made
the connection?

The cop to whom Kate made her request looked skeptical, but eventually he brought what she had asked for. She
was right. None of the news releases in the file on Hall
Draper mentioned his birthplace. Community activities in
Tucson. Boy Scouts. Little League. Church. Nothing about
his childhood, about where he had grown up, the tiny coal-
mining community where he had known a girl named Jenny
Carpenter, but probably, Kate realized, given the difference
in their ages, not her older brother.

Hall Draper's death would have posed the greatest risk for Kahler, of course. There was always the possibility, however remote, that someone might make that connection. In remaining as reticent about his background as he had always been, Kahler had, before he'd ever embarked on his quest for revenge, unwittingly done everything that could be done to prevent any link to that past. And he had saved for last the two people who were connected to Falls Bend. One had been the old man in Austin, who, given his age, must have been his mother's boyfriend that Kahler had told her about, the one who had taught Jenny the dark lessons that had haunted her life. He might have had only a tenuous link to the town, a transient in all probability.

And the last victim, the strongest link to Kahler's past, would have been Hall Draper. Lew couldn't have known the name of the town where both Kahler and Draper had been born, she finally concluded. The name wasn't anywhere in the Draper file. Only in her notes. Had Lew put it together on the very remote link provided by the state of Pennsylvania?

Maybe important. Maybe nothing. Lew wasn't stupid. He would never have let it slip to Kahler if he'd discovered he and Draper were from the same town, but maybe, just maybe, he'd mentioned Falls Bend, or mentioned that he'd been given Kahler's application form.

Maybe Kahler had heard something in Lew's voice. Maybe the thought that Kahler and Draper might have known each other had struck Lew in the middle of that conversation. He certainly had had access to the information that they had been born in the same state. She herself had told him about Draper. Would that have been enough to make an old journalist like Lew Garrison suspicious? Maybe, she thought. Maybe just enough.

No one would ever know exactly what had happened, but Lew had said or done something that had made Kahler afraid it was about to come unraveled. Maybe Kahler had realized if Lew had the application form, and if he were curious enough to check on the name of the town where Draper had been born, it was all over.

Then, after he had killed Lew, he had come to Kate's apartment to wait for her because, she had finally realized, he had to find out if Garrison had told her what he had discovered. While he was there, she had played Lew's message in his hearing—and in doing so, she had saved her own life.

Finally, only Thorne Barrington stood in the way of having it finished. *I wanted it to be over,* Kahler had told her. Because he had loved her. In his twisted, insane way he had paid that debt, too, when he had pushed her away from the splintering railing. There was no doubt in Kate's mind that had been deliberate, the last act of the man who had been Byron Kahler. And Jack the Tripper. In his insanity, he had collected Jenny's debt, but he had also paid his own. He had given Kate her life.

Experts all over the country were explaining what had made Byron Kahler tick, examining every detail of the painful past he had seemingly escaped, laying out all its dirty secrets for public scrutiny. All the things Kahler had hidden through the years—the grinding poverty, his stepfather's abuse, his mother's addictions—were now the property of a detail-hungry media.

The public's right to know.

Kate realized she had again been sitting, simply staring at her computer screen. Despite the managing editor's repeated requests that she write the conclusion for her series, she was probably the only journalist in the country who had not written one word on the death of Jack the Tripper. Interest would eventually have to fade, she thought, and maybe she wouldn't be forced to write the ending of the story she had lived. She had found that she had nothing to say about Kahler, nothing that could satisfactorily explain what had happened to the man who had at one time, she truly believed, been a good cop.

She took a deep breath and expelled it loudly enough to cause a couple of heads to turn, a couple of quick glances in her direction. No one asked what was wrong, probably because they already knew. It seemed that everything about her life was now public knowledge. There had been heated speculation—more than speculation in the tabloids—about the relationship between Kate August and the two men at the center of the Tripper bombings.

She had to admit that all the elements were there for a great story, begging to be sensationalized: the reclusive millionaire, the poor-boy-made-good cop who had gone so desperately wrong, and the woman between them. "The Eternal Triangle" one tabloid headline screamed. The grain of truth, Kate supposed, hidden in the mass of chaff that had been written about the case, about Kahler's death, and about Judge Barrington's injury.

She had waited through the hours of surgery that night and had breathed a prayer of thanksgiving when she had been told that he'd survived the operation, but that his prognosis was guarded. Whatever the hell that meant. The police, who had waited patiently for her statement, would wait no longer, and when she had returned to the hospital, it was to find that the same impenetrable security that had been imposed at the time of the first bombing was again in place.

She had been denied admittance to Barrington's hospital room—she and every other reporter. Nothing she had said or done in the intervening weeks had made any difference to that wall of silence. For some reason Greg Sandifer blamed her for what had happened—or at least for the media attention. He had made that clear in the one conversation they'd had. Kate had gotten news about Thorne's condition just like the rest of the world, through carefully phrased statements given by the hospital spokesman, always to the effect that "the judge was progressing as well as could be expected, given the seriousness of his injury."

There was no one living at the mansion, she knew. The gate was locked, and no one had answered the bell on any of her visits. She had no idea what had happened to Elliot or to Charlie. Even the unlisted telephone number had been disconnected. Greg Sandifer, with the help of Barton Phillips and his firm, had succeeded in keeping the press at bay, but what they hadn't taken into account was that their efforts had simply made the media more rabid to find out exactly what they were trying to hide.

She hadn't talked to the press, and she didn't intend to. Not about her relationship to Thorne Barrington. What had been her relationship, she amended. That wasn't and never would be public property. In the statement the paper had released on her behalf, she had told the truth, that Barrington had been shot trying to disarm Kahler, trying to save her life. That had only added fuel to the frenzy, the press turning Barrington into some kind of romantic figure: heroic, tragically wounded, and inaccessible.

She thought about how much he would hate that image, and she smiled. But the inaccessible part was certainly accurate. She found herself wondering, as she had a thousand times, if that were his choice. Or if that decision had been made for him because he was no longer capable of making his own decisions.

She closed her eyes, fighting emotion, fighting fear. When she finally reopened them, she had again found control, a control she had demanded of herself through these long weeks. But she might as well admit that she was wasting her time here. She wasn't working, and she didn't see much point in pretending.

She opened her bottom drawer, took out the black leather purse, and, offering no explanations, walked out of the newsroom. Maybe another day she could do this—satisfy the public's right to know. Maybe some day, but not today.

SHE HAD SPENT a long time soaking in water into which she'd thrown a handful of Shalimar-scented bath crystals, leaving behind in the small bathroom a cloud of fragrant steam when she'd finished. She put on shorts and a tank top and walked barefoot into the kitchen to try to think about something for dinner.

Eating had moved very low on her list of priorities, and it was beginning to show. She had probably lost six or seven pounds, and she was disgusted. Being too upset to eat was about as neurotic as you could get, and she was determined to put an end to that ridiculous behavior. It was time to get on with her life. Especially since she had been left no other choice.

She opened the refrigerator, automatically inventorying its contents. Eggs. A container of milk she wasn't real sure about. A small, hardening block of cheese. Some assorted condiments and a jar of pickles. An omelet or a cheese sandwich? she debated, fighting the urge to close the door and forget it.

The sound of the doorbell shouldn't have been unexpected. It had certainly happened often enough before. The police had put someone outside her complex for a few days after Kahler's death to keep the media in control. When the paper had released her statement, the press had been told that was all she intended to say. After that, the number of reporters awaiting her departures and arrivals had eventually begun to dwindle, but despite the passage of time they hadn't entirely given up. Even tonight she had walked by a couple, ignoring their questions and the microphone thrust at her face.

She knew she should just ignore the bell, too, but when it rang again, she felt her frustration boil over. *Damn it, weren't they ever going to let it go?* The flare of adrenaline sent her storming across the dark living room to slip the chain off and throw open the door.

"Look," she began, "I've told you guys—"

The man standing outside her door was literally the last person she expected to see there, his presence here a scenario she had never imagined in any of her fantasies.

"Hello, Kate," Thorne Barrington said.

Her heart jolted painfully, and she had to think about taking the next breath, the action no longer involuntary. Her eyes examined every detail of his appearance: dark glasses, a navy polo and worn jeans, the raven's-wing blackness of his hair, worn much shorter than she had ever seen it, short enough that it didn't quite hide the reddened line over his temple. The newer scar obscured the small white one she had noticed there before.

"What are you doing here?" she said. It wasn't what she wanted to say, but it was the logical question. *What are you doing showing up on my doorstep after putting me through absolute hell?*

"I thought we needed to talk."

"Talk?" she repeated carefully.

"Do you think I could come in? There are a couple of reporters outside, and I don't imagine it would do either of us any good if—"

"Okay," she interrupted, knowing he was right. The bidding would be sky-high for any picture of the two of them together.

When he was inside, she closed the door and led the way across the room to the facing sofa and love seat. She was aware that he took a look around the dark apartment before he sat down. She wondered with a touch of amusement if he were comparing her place to his. She sat down opposite him, the coffee table and the expanse of her small Oriental rug between them.

Neither of them said anything for a moment, the atmosphere growing uncomfortable. Whatever connection had existed between them had obviously disappeared. She found herself wishing he'd take off the glasses, so at least she could see his eyes. And then she remembered why he couldn't.

"Do you want me to cut off the kitchen light?" she asked.

He glanced toward the lighted kitchen and then back to her, shaking his head.

"It's all right," he said, dismissing her concern.

She didn't have the right to ask any of the questions she wanted to ask, and apparently he wasn't ready to reveal whatever it was that he had come here to talk about. The hope that he wanted to do more than talk was beginning to fade in the strain.

"Are you okay?" she asked. For an encore, she mocked herself mentally, she could ask him about the weather.

He looked up from the contemplation of his hands, the dark lenses a barrier to whatever he was thinking.

"I'm fine. Even Greg turned me loose."

She nodded again.

"I found out some things that I think you ought to know. About Kahler," he added. "And Jenny."

She wasn't sure she wanted to know any more. What she already knew had circled endlessly through her head night after night. Especially Hall Draper's death.

If Kahler hadn't fallen in love with her, if she had let him know at once that it wasn't going to happen for them, would Draper be alive today? Would someone have caught the Tripper before it was time for him to hit again? Was there any way she could have known how screwed up Kahler was? She was a reporter. Where were her instincts? She had always been so sure—

"He came to see her," Barrington said, breaking into the

questions that had tormented her since the night he'd been shot.

"What?"

"Jenny. That night. Before she hanged herself. Kahler came to the jail. He signed the visitor's log."

"But he said..." She hesitated, trying to think exactly what he *had* said. He had given the impression that he hadn't known about Jenny's death until he'd found the diaries. And instead... She wasn't sure exactly what the instead was. "What does that mean? That he got the diaries then?"

"No. That part was apparently true. They *were* sent to his mother. Jenny's mother. Maybe he did find them later."

"But he knew about Jenny's death."

"He must have. It happened between the time he left and the next cell check. Since he was the last visitor, he would have been questioned."

"He came to visit her and when he left, she hanged herself?"

"Within minutes of his departure."

"But why? Why would she..."

Thorne didn't answer. The dark lenses were again focused downward toward his hands.

"What in the world could he have said to her?" Kate asked. The question was very soft, rhetorical, because she knew they would never know the answer.

"Whatever it was," Thorne said, "it was something she couldn't live with."

"*He* caused her death. Whatever he said that night. And he *knew* that. All those years, he knew it."

"But he couldn't accept that guilt."

"So eventually he decided that other people had to be to blame. You and all the others. He set out to get revenge for something *he* had done. God, he really *was* crazy," she said. "So damn crazy. She killed herself because of whatever he said to her that night, but he couldn't admit it. So everyone else had to be made to pay for Jenny's death.''

He nodded.

''Does knowing that make it any easier?'' she asked, remembering what he'd told her.

When he looked up, she realized he hadn't understood.

''To know that you had done nothing to deserve what he did to you? Is it any easier to know that?''

''I put her in that cell, Kate. Just like he said.''

''That was your job. You were supposed to do that.''

''Maybe. But maybe there might have been something…'' He shook his head, the movement small and contained. Again he let the silence stretch before he broke it. ''It was a sweep. Teenage hookers. Most of them runaways. Jenny Carpenter was picked up with the rest. She looked about sixteen, but she wasn't, of course, and she had a previous conviction. For possession.'' He took a breath, deep enough that the movement was visible in the dimness. ''So instead of sending another kid home to her family, I sent her to jail. I knew she wouldn't be able to make bail…''

His words faded again and the silence was back. A different silence now. Full of cold and darkness, the lonely silence of a cell. The silence that must have remained after the words of her brother had stopped echoing through the darkness.

''There was something about her…'' Thorne said softly. ''Something in her eyes. Lost. Alone. She was the most alone person I'd ever met.''

''It wasn't your fault,'' Kate whispered.

''You asked me once if there was anything about my life that I regretted.''

Like Hall Draper, and like Kahler, Thorne, too, had been haunted by Jenny Carpenter.

''It wasn't your fault,'' she said again.

"But he was right. We all played a part. He was right at least about that."

"No," she denied. "Not even about that."

His mouth moved, the muscles tightening briefly, and then he nodded. "Thank you," he said.

She was aware that the ghost of the dark-haired child who had been Jenny Carpenter had not been laid to rest, but she didn't know what else to tell him.

They were quiet again for a long time until finally he said, "I kept thinking that you might…"

He let the sentence fade, and he looked back down at his hands. He held them both palm upward in his lap, the right one on top. She knew that mutilated hand would always be a reminder of how one man's insanity had forever changed his life.

"That I might what?"

"I thought you might come to the hospital," he said. He was looking at her now, but she couldn't read his expression because of the glasses.

"I *came* to the hospital," she said. "How the hell can you think I wouldn't come? They wouldn't let me in. Your friend Sandifer. All of them."

"I never knew you'd come, Kate."

"I was just another blood-sucking vampire of a reporter. They made it pretty obvious I wasn't welcome, so eventually I quit beating my head against that brick wall."

"I'm sorry," he said.

"Yeah. Me, too. It would have been nice to know whether you were…" She stopped because she couldn't say out loud the horrors she had imagined, all the things she had known could result from a head injury. "Whether you were all right."

"I'm all right."

"Okay," she said.

Why was this so hard? The last thing she remembered

saying to Thorne Barrington was to beg him to make love to her, and now they couldn't even carry on a conversation.

"I guess I'd better go," he said finally. "I just wanted to tell you about Jenny. I thought it might make you feel better about Kahler's death."

He stood up, and she was aware again of how big he was. She stood also and followed him to the door. He had simply come to tell her about Jenny. It seemed there was nothing left of whatever had been between them before. Violence and death were barriers too hard to overcome, and all those deaths, especially Jenny's, and even Byron Kahler's, lay between them now.

They stood together by the door, as awkward as she and Kahler had once been. She didn't want to open it. Despite the strain, despite the awkwardness that seemed to be all that was left, she was reluctant to let him leave.

"Thanks for coming," she said.

"What are you crying for?" He raised his hand and brushed the tear off her cheek with the pad of his thumb. "There's nothing to cry about."

She hadn't even realized she'd been crying. Embarrassed, she rubbed at the place he'd touched with her fingertips.

"Why the hell didn't you call me? You could have let me know you were okay."

That had slipped out, just like the tears, past her control. She hated crying women. About as much as she figured he'd hate a nagging one. He had given her no right to question what he did. They had made no commitment. Except it had felt as if they had. A whole lot of commitment.

"For a while..." He began and then he hesitated. "I wasn't in any condition to make my own decisions. I didn't understand why you weren't there. I knew I wanted you there."

"I tried," she said.

He smiled at her tone. "Greg probably did what he

thought was best. He read your press release. Maybe he thought…'' Again he hesitated.

"That I shouldn't have told them anything? That I had only made it worse?"

"Maybe."

She shook her head, knowing that wasn't true. The security Sandifer had imposed around Thorne Barrington had ensured that the press would come after her. Her statement had been necessary, and she knew it. He should have known it. That was the way things were done.

"The fact that none of you guys would talk to them made it worse. I was the only one left. They would never have given up without something."

"I'm sorry you had to go through that," he said.

"And later? You could have called me later."

Why didn't she just tell him everything? she thought in disgust. Go ahead and confess the sleepless nights she'd spent worrying about him, her inability to work, the tears. Lay it all out there for him to smile at the next time he thought about her and her stupid obsession.

"There were some things I was learning to deal with," he said.

"What kind of things?" she asked, a small flutter of fear in her stomach.

"I haven't had another migraine. Not since that night."

She waited a moment, trying to think what that meant, what his tone meant. "And that's bad?" she asked, shaking her head. "You sound like that's bad."

He smiled at her, and his hand lifted to brush away another tear. "It probably means that they were right, that the headaches were…" He stopped and she could hear the breath he drew.

"Emotional," she said, finally understanding what he was thinking.

He nodded again.

"Do you think I care?" she asked. "Even if that were true, do you think I would care?"

"I think *I* would."

"Okay," she said. "*You* care. I don't. I'm glad they're gone."

He didn't say anything, and she reached up to put her fingers against the slash of the scar. He didn't avoid her touch.

"Maybe this had something to do with the headaches going away. Maybe it...rearranged whatever had been damaged before."

He laughed, and she smiled at the sound.

"It's a reasonable explanation to me," she said. "Are you telling me no one else thinks so?"

"Greg said it's possible."

"But you decided not to believe him because..."

He shook his head, the glasses again a barrier to reading his eyes. It didn't matter because she knew, of course, what he was thinking. He had already told her—that even the possibility that the bombing had affected him psychologically somehow made him something less than he had thought he was.

She *knew* the kind of person he was—the kind who would run toward a madman pointing a gun at him because she was in danger. And she didn't understand why the other would even matter.

"Is this some macho kind of crap?" she asked. "You get a bomb that blows off half your hand and damages your eyes and cracks your skull, and you think it's *not* supposed to make any kind of impact on your life?"

"Kate," he said.

"Is that what you think? You been reading your own press? You think you're a hero, Barrington? Is that what this is? You think you're different from the rest of us?"

"I don't think that—"

"That bastard put a little confetti in my bed, and I didn't sleep for a week. Does that make me a coward?"

"Of course not, but—"

"I think you're bright enough to figure this out. You're supposed to be so damn brilliant. Figure it out," she ordered.

"Kate."

"Don't 'Kate' me. Don't talk to me like I'm some kind of hysterical child. You don't have migraines anymore, and we should be celebrating, and instead we're standing here yelling at each other."

"I'm not yelling," he said.

"You go to hell, Thorne Barrington. You go back to that damn mausoleum where you holed up for three years and you hide in the dark. I don't give a damn if you do. If you think I give a damn, then you can just..."

"I wasn't hiding," he said.

"Yeah?" she said, derisively. "Except you can't have it both ways. And I don't care if you were. It doesn't matter. Why don't you understand that? I'm no bargain, Barrington. I'll probably not ever be able to hear a backfire without being scared spitless. Some nights I sleep with the lights on. Does that mean you don't want to sleep with me?"

"No," he said.

The single syllable took her breath. She didn't know how his voice could be so different, but whatever had been there the night Kahler had interrupted them was back.

"It doesn't?" she asked, her mouth suddenly dry.

"No."

"Then I guess that means you do."

"I told you a long time ago I want to make love to you." She nodded.

"Nothing's changed about the way I feel."

She nodded again. And then she said it out loud. "Nothing's changed about how I feel about you either."

She didn't make a conscious decision to step into his arms, but they closed around her when she did. Closed and held her tightly enough to put to rest any doubts she might have had about whether he wanted her there. It felt so good being held. So good to be safe. She hadn't known until she was here that this was the only thing that would truly ever make her feel safe again—being held in Thorne Barrington's arms.

SHE WISHED she had cut the lights off in her bedroom. It was so bright, stark as daylight—not like the welcoming, moon-touched darkness of his that night. It hadn't been difficult then to undress, to expose her body for him. He had asked her and she had wanted to.

She stopped at the foot of the bed and turned around to find him still standing in the doorway, leaning against the frame. As she watched, he reached up and removed the dark glasses. He folded them and held them in his hand. His eyes were as dark as she had remembered. His gaze intense. Waiting. Too polite maybe to make the first move. She smiled at that thought.

His head tilted, questioning the smile.

"If the headaches are gone, why did you wear those?" she asked.

"Hiding from the guys outside, I guess."

She nodded. "It must have worked."

"And maybe because I'm not convinced the other is over."

"Maybe we ought to cut off the lights," she suggested.

He didn't say anything for a moment. "I'd rather leave them on," he said finally. "If you don't mind, of course."

"It's a little scary making love for the first time with the lights on," she admitted.

"I've been in the dark a long time, Kate."

A long time since he'd made love to anyone? she wondered. He had implied that before.

"And I'm…a little beat up," he added. "A few nicks and craters."

She smiled at him. "That's okay. I've got a few nicks of my own. Not bomb scars, of course. Life scars, I guess."

"I'd be more than willing to kiss them and make them better," he said softly. Whether it was the depth of his voice or the accent, she didn't know, but that didn't sound nearly as dumb as it should have. It sounded…interesting. Romantic. Old-fashioned and so damned romantic. Just like Barrington.

"I think I'd like that," she invited.

So he straightened and stepped into her room.

Epilogue

It was dark now. Some time during the long night through which he'd made love to her, Thorne had cut off the low lamp beside the bed. She had a memory of his long arm reaching upward, plunging the room into sudden darkness. And that wasn't, of course, the only memory she had.

She knew him intimately now. How his hands felt, both of them, tantalizing against her body, examining contours that had never to her seemed worthy of such a prolonged exploration. She knew his mouth and his tongue, trailing moisture over her shivering skin, caressing every guarded, secret place from which he could coax sensation. She knew the texture of his skin, even the scars he had warned her about, old and fading into paleness against his darkness or hidden by the thick hair on his chest.

She had wondered that night how his body would feel against hers, dark, hair-roughened skin moving over the wanting smoothness of her breasts, her nipples hardening under the gliding touch of his. She *had* wondered, but now she knew.

She knew so much about him. His strength. And his gentleness. His patience, she remembered with wonder. Infinitely patient. Taking an eternity over everything. Never hurrying. Learning the subtle differences in her needs, her responses. Enjoying her. She had known that because he had *wanted* her to know it.

He had taken pains to let her know that he delighted in every trembling breath he forced her to take, every uncontrolled movement, every sigh, every gasping word she whispered against his throat or his shoulder as he had moved above her. Patient. Endlessly patient with her pleasure.

There was definitely something to be said for making love with a Southern gentleman. The old regional analogies stole into her consciousness. Slow as molasses, hot as a summer's day, and as enduring as the land. Thorne Barrington was every bit as good as he was cracked up to be, she thought, her lips lifting into a small smile against the smooth, brown skin of his shoulder.

One long leg lay sprawled across one of hers. She bent the knee of her other leg to run the arch of her foot up his calf, the hair coarse and pleasant under her instep, the muscle firm. He shifted, his body moving over hers as it had so many times last night.

She felt the rush of moisture, anticipating his entry, wanting the now familiar invasion. He slipped his palms under her thighs, lifting, positioning her, and more than willing to obey, she wrapped her legs around his narrow hips, and felt him push into the slick, wet heat of her body.

She gasped, surprised as she had been before that her body could be so ready for him, so wanting, and yet he could fill her so strongly that it seemed he threatened the walls of her soul, the limits of what she was, of what she could ever be. Full and so deep. Entering and retreating, and then moving deeper still, past inhibitions and hesitations. Pushing toward the center of her desire that seemed to expand even as he moved within her. It had been this way from the beginning. As it had been with no one else. Ever.

She belonged to him. She had known it since she had

seen the pictures. Obsessed with him. Obsessed now with this, with possessing him and being possessed.

His mouth was over hers, his tongue echoing the slow, deliberate movements of his body. Control. His was the control, and she was lost in it. He had given her permission to be lost in it. Making love to her. This was the reality of that oft-misused phrase—the reason it was new and different and so powerful. Thorne made love to her. And there were no demands except that she let him, that she accept what he wanted to give.

She could feel her body responding, lifting to meet his, to arch into the strength of each downward stroke, its power seeping into her body. Upward to make her heart pound and her breath a panting rhythm. Downward to tighten the muscles of her legs around his body, drawing him to her. Closer. Deeper. Always deeper and more powerful, moving within her. Forever. Endless. Until finally, after an eternity, she exploded, her frame rocking against him with the force of her release. She dug her nails into his back, unaware of what she was doing. On some level, she felt his skin moving against hers, wet and trembling, the heat of it burning against the sudden coldness of hers.

"Now," she said hoarsely. A request or permission. She didn't know, but she felt the response, hot and sudden within her arching body. She had wanted that. Together. Always together. As they were meant to be. As she had known from the first.

She lay exhausted in his arms. Somehow he had known that was important. To hold her. To keep her safe in the darkness. Once he had belonged to the darkness, and so long as she was with him there was nothing frightening about the night. Not any longer.

The sheets beneath her were damp and twisted. They should have been uncomfortable, but in the pleasant lethargy after his lovemaking, which left her body boneless and unmoving, there was only comfort and safety. Her breathing was beginning to even again, and her heart rate to slow.

He lifted away from her onto his elbows, dark eyes looking down at her face.

"I knew the first night you came to my house that I was going to make love to you," he said.

"Did you know it would be like this?" she asked.

"I knew I wanted it to be, but nothing has ever been like this."

"I thought—" she began and then realized that wasn't something she should say to him, even after the intimacies they'd just shared.

"What did you think?" he asked when she didn't continue. He leaned down to brush his lips against her throat, his breath warm over the film of perspiration that had captured floating tendrils of her hair to curl against her neck.

"That you couldn't possibly live up to your reputation," she admitted, smiling again. She was glad he wasn't looking at her.

His mouth paused in its drifting caress, and after a long moment he lifted his head again. "What is that supposed to mean?" he asked.

"That the debutantes of Atlanta must have been feeling very deprived for the last few years, bless their little diamond-encrusted hearts."

"Debutantes?" The crease she had noticed before was between the dark brows.

"I had a picture of you—" she began, and then she realized for the first time what had become of that picture and all the others.

"How could you have a picture of me?"

"From the paper's files," she said, not really thinking about what he had asked. Thinking about Kahler, about Kahler's hands searching through her things, finding the folder with those pictures. Violated, she thought again. He had violated her privacy, and so he had known all along how she felt about Thorne Barrington.

"Kate?" Thorne asked.

"I had a collection of pictures. Pictures from before...before the bomb. He took them," she whispered, feeling sick despite the fact that Kahler was dead and Thorne was holding her.

"Took them?" he repeated, and then suddenly he understood. "*Kahler* took them?"

She nodded. "He must have taken them when he put the confetti—" *Into the bed they were sharing.*

"Don't," he whispered, and his arms tightened around her. "It's over. There's nothing to be afraid of."

He held her, and eventually there was a relaxation of the tension that had been in her body. And then he asked, his deep voice touched with the amusement she liked to hear there, more cherished perhaps because it was rare and often unexpected. "Tell me about the debutantes."

She laughed, remembering how many times she had looked at that picture. Envying those women because they knew him and she hadn't. "They were all looking at you," she said. She lifted her hand and ran her thumb along the line of his bottom lip. "Like they could eat you up with a spoon."

"And?" He caught her thumb in his mouth, holding it.

"That was all. Just looking at you. I used to look at that picture and wonder what you were really like."

"Now you know," he said. He had released her thumb, but he turned his head to press a kiss into her open palm.

"Not anything like I thought you'd be," she said. She put her hand over his cheek, the stubble rough against the smoothness of her skin.

"Disappointed?" he asked.

"No," she said. She moved her head against the damp

sheets, side to side. "No," she said again, "I'm not disappointed."

"I just aim to please," he said softly. Another Southernism.

"Your aim's pretty good. Practice make you perfect?"

She regretted the question as soon as she asked it. She had no right. No rights at all where he was concerned. She had given herself to him freely, willingly, without any vows or commitments. That wasn't the way it was supposed to be, not the way she'd been raised, and now she knew why. It hurt too much to realize that he could go back to that life tomorrow. There was no reason now for him *not* to go back, she realized. Back to what he had been before.

He didn't say anything. There was a code about that, too. Gentlemen never discussed their conquests, no matter how numerous they were.

Deliberately she moved her gaze away from his. She focused on his mouth, as sensuous, she now knew, as it looked.

"Kate," he said, and she forced her eyes up.

"It's okay," she said. "I always knew that—"

"I love you. Don't you know that?"

She couldn't think of a single teasing answer. Men said that all the time. It didn't mean anything anymore. Just something they said. But still she took a breath, so hard it was almost a sob.

"How could you not know I love you?" he asked.

"Because you never told me. And then these last weeks, I didn't hear from you. How was I supposed—"

"You just know," he said. "You have to know. I love you, Kate August. Maybe I'm not much of a bargain, but—"

"I guess you haven't been reading your press. Or checking your bank balance," she said, smiling at him, beginning to believe him, maybe because she wanted to believe so much. Or because she recognized the doubt in his voice. It was one of the things she'd liked about him from the first—that he really didn't seem to know how attractive he was.

He didn't say anything, and she wondered if she had gone too far. "I didn't mean that. I don't care about that."

"I know," he said.

They were quiet for a while until then he said, "Tell me about the pictures."

She laughed. "I'll bet that's a real ego trip. To know I obsessed about you. Drooled over your pictures."

"Considering what I *thought* you thought about me."

"Now you know better."

"What exactly do I know?" he asked, the dark eyes smiling at her.

"That I love you. That I've loved you for a very long time, even before I knew you. That's why I came to find you."

"Into the darkness," he said softly.

She put her mouth against his, which turned, fitting over hers. Meant to fit. It seemed she had always known that.

Bless their little deprived hearts, she thought again, and then she smiled.

ACCIDENTAL BODYGUARD
Julie Miller

For my good buddy, Debra Webb.
A talented writer and a first-class friend.
I always enjoy our chats. I love bouncing ideas
off you, talking business, commiserating about
the trying times and celebrating the good ones.
Thanks for sharing your enthusiasm for books
and writing and life. I can hardly wait until the
next time we get to hang out together.

Prologue

No beast so fierce but knows some touch of pity.

—William Shakespeare
King Richard III

Faith Monroe slipped her key into the lock of her office door and halted as the reinforced steel barrier drifted open with barely a nudge.

What the heck? She glanced over each shoulder up and down the corridor. She was alone, right?

Seven in the morning wasn't all that early in her experience. The security guard at the front desk, Danny Novotny, had teased her about keeping farm girl hours, and beating everyone else to work. She was just interested in beating Saint Louis's rush hour traffic.

So who else was in here?

Her initial confusion became a cautious suspicion. Her boss might have worked through the night, but the 10:00 p.m. or 6:00 a.m. security check would have either locked him in or locked up after he'd gone. Logic, if not the unsettled feeling in her gut, told her something was wrong.

"Hello?" She pushed the door open the rest of the way. "Dr. Rutherford?"

The sterile glass-and-steel architecture of the Eclipse

Building had always seemed cold and uninviting to Faith. Its ultramodern design left her doubly chilled in the pall of silence that swallowed up the traces of her Ozark accent.

What was going on? Faith twisted her mouth into a frown and stepped inside. Eclipse Labs was a company that preached security at every staff meeting. An open door like this was cause for a reprimand in someone's file. Probably hers. Not an auspicious beginning to her fledgling career.

Even if it wasn't her fault. She didn't make mistakes like this.

She'd locked that door yesterday evening. "Dr. Rutherford? It's Faith. Are you okay?"

Sometimes she relished the quiet, like when she watched the peaceful sunrise over the river on her uncle's farm. But this was too quiet. The charged air filled her with the sense of something or someone holding its breath and waiting. Waiting for the chance to exhale and break the false calm. She hated that kind of watching, creeping silence, and all the monsters and villains and nightmares her imagination could fill it with.

Her skin shattered with goose bumps as her imagination tried to kick in. But she was stronger than that. She flipped on the light switch and looked around.

Everything looked normal. Her desk was tidy, the chair pushed in. Her lab coat hung over the back of the chair. But something wasn't right. Was something missing? Out of place?

The blinds had been pulled along the glass partition that divided her office from Chief Design Engineer William Rutherford's. But the door to his office stood wide-open, giving her a glimpse of indistinguishable shadows inside. Another open door. Faith's pulse quickened in her veins.

"Dr. Rutherford?" She hastened through the doorway, reaching for the lamp on his desk. The toe of her shoe collided with something hard and unyielding. "Ow!"

Too small to be one of the guest chairs. Feeling her way

around the obstacle, Faith leaned across the cluttered desk-top and switched on the lamp, flooding the room with light.

And plunging her into the middle of chaos.

"Dr. Rutherford? William!"

Her boss had been hired at the think tank for his brain, not his neatness. But as she spun around, stumbling over the broken humidor that had once sat atop his desk, crush-ing scattered papers beneath her feet, she knew this was more than an aging absentminded professor's mess.

Every desk drawer had been pulled out and tossed onto the floor. Every file cabinet had been jimmied open, their contents spilled around the room. His sketch table had been turned over. And his computer—her gaze swept the room once more—the hard drive tower was completely gone.

"William?" Faith hitched the long strap of her purse over her neck and shoulder, freeing her hands to climb over the debris toward the reinforced stainless steel door that led from the office into Rutherford's private lab. If anything had happened to that dear, sweet...

The earsplitting screech of metal colliding against metal shot through her eardrums. The sound ended in a muffled thud on the opposite side of the door. "Doctor!"

Faith snatched at the door handle, but the damn thing was locked. She pounded against it. "Dr. Rutherford, an-swer me."

Silence.

"Hell." With a fumbling sense of urgency, Faith tugged at her ID card which was around her neck. But the cord snagged on a button, then twisted in the collar of her blouse. Spurred on by the chainlike rattle of dragging metal from inside the lab, she gave up trying to free herself and leaned over and swiped the card through the automated lock that sealed the door. "Doctor?"

Why didn't he answer?

Faith shut off the panic that clouded her mind and tried

to recall the code numbers she needed to punch in. She hit the keypad. Four. Three. No.

A frustrated curse growled in her throat. She hit Clear and swiped the card again. "Three. Four. K. Zero—"

The latch clicked and the door swung open, shoving her back into the room. "Faith?"

"Dr. Rutherford. What's going—?" The portly, balding man staggered through the doorway and lunged for her. "Doctor?"

A flash of bright crimson blurred before her eyes as he hugged her and collapsed, dragging them both to the floor. "Faith—" His words came on a ragged, wheezing gasp. "Listen—"

A fit of coughing seized him, but it was a shallow, pitiful sound that told her he was barely able to breathe. She pulled herself up to a sitting position and cradled his head and shoulders in her lap. "Shh. Don't try to talk." She pulled her cell phone from her purse. "I'll call security."

"No—" With a startling burst of energy he snatched her wrist and jerked her hand down to his chest. "No..." He tried to catch a breath. "Don't trust...security."

A gooey, gel-like substance stuck to her skin as his fingers weakened and fell away. Faith gasped and struggled to take a breath of her own.

"Oh, God." The red stuff was blood. The front of his white lab coat was soaked in it. Her first aid skills dated back to her Girl Scout days, but she pushed aside his coat and the sticky front of his shirt to check his wound. "Don't talk."

"No, you must—"

"Shh." She urged him to conserve the energy that was quickly draining from his body. Her fingertips slid inside an oozing crevice that felt like raw meat. "Oh, God. William."

He'd been stabbed. Cut through the belly more than once. Faith felt her own blood rushing toward her feet, leaving her light-headed. She breathed in deeply, willing herself to stay calm and lucid. She looked down into the inventor's wan brown eyes and stroked his clammy forehead to reassure him. She gently pulled free of his token grip on her wrist and punched three numbers on her phone. "You need to let me call an ambulance."

His head bobbed from side to side. "Too late—" He squeezed her hand in a trembling fist and disconnected the call. "He's here."

"Who? Who's here?" Since help wasn't coming, she pressed her hand against the worst of the wounds and tried to staunch the bleeding herself. But he'd already lost so much blood. "Who did this to you?"

"Copperhead." He puffed out the word on a strangled breath.

"This is no snake bite."

"No—" Oh, damn, why couldn't she understand? The man was killing himself trying to communicate with her. With shaky, stiff-jointed fingers he pulled a white handkerchief from the pocket of his lab coat and pushed it into her palm. "Take—"

"What is it?" A souvenir of her three brief months as his assistant? She clutched it tight. "What should I—"

A crash of glass and metal exploded from the interior of the lab complex. Faith jumped in her skin. "Oh, God."

"Searching…won't find—"

The Eclipse Building was constructed in the shape of a wheel, and whoever had trashed this office was moving inward, toward the most securely designed rooms at the hub of the complex. But searching for what? The design for a newer, better toaster? Hardly worth stabbing a man. But she was too new to the design team to be privy to its innermost secrets. She could only shudder with fearful anticipation as the sounds of unimpeded destruction continued.

She stuffed the handkerchief into the front pocket of her navy slacks. "Doctor, what's going on?"

With a massive heave of determination, he snaked his bloody hand up around her neck and pulled her ear down to his mouth. He sputtered and wheezed against her temple. "Dar…n…Fry."

"What and fries?" She frowned and shook her head, not understanding his guttural whisper.

He grew heavy in her arms. She adjusted him in her lap, supporting his head and watching every nuance of his expression to help her comprehend his cryptic message. He took a breath and steeled his body for one last, life-draining effort. "Darien."

A name. She repeated it. "Darien."

"Frye."

"Frye."

"Say it." There was blood bubbling between his lips now. He was shaking in her arms. Faith sobbed a tearless breath at the new friend she was about to lose. "Say it."

"Darien Frye." Once she uttered the words, his head fell back into her lap and his eyes drifted shut, his entire body spent with the effort of speaking. He was fading. Dying. And she didn't know what to do to save him. "Should I give his name to the police? Is he someone I should call? Will he help?" She couldn't help but shake him, willing him to return to her. "William!"

A door slammed somewhere inside the heart of the lab. Faith glanced up, hearing the slam like an ominous portent deep inside. Then there were footsteps. Sure. Deliberate. Long strides coming ever faster. Coming closer. Coming for her.

"What should I do?"

William Rutherford, kind, fatherly figure that he was, blinked his eyes open. But he couldn't focus. Faith's own eyes steeped with tears and spilled over in hot trails down her cheeks. She tried to hug him, tried to comfort him, tried to shield him from the danger that was coming.

But he was nearly gone, bleeding to death in the circle

of her arms. He summoned the remnants of life left in his body to speak one last word before his eyes closed for the last time.

"Run."

Chapter One

Sixty-year-old men who couldn't match their socks or re-member the pencil tucked behind their ear didn't get mur-dered. They didn't bleed to death in her arms. They didn't warn her to run from the heavy, stalking footsteps of a predator who tore through the lab, knocking aside equip-ment, shattering glass, moving relentlessly closer to seize whatever he was searching for.

Whatever he was willing to kill for.

Faith drove several miles until she felt calm enough to pull off onto the side of the road and phone the police. The officer she spoke with was surprisingly sympathetic as he listened to her halting report of William Rutherford's mur-der.

No, she hadn't seen the actual stabbing. Yes, she believed the killer was still on the premises. No, she didn't know what the intruder was after. Yes, the inventor made her believe she, too, was in danger.

"He told me to get out of there," she sniffed, trying her stubborn best to keep the tears of grief and panic at bay. "He told me not to trust the security there."

"Did he suspect one of the guards?"

She shrugged, hoping she didn't sound as useless and helpless as she felt. "I don't know if he meant they hadn't done their job or if he thought they were responsible."

The officer's brief lecture about leaving the scene of a crime had been followed by *Are you safe?* and a promise to have some detectives meet her at her house to take a formal statement.

"I understand. I'll be there."

She tossed her cell phone onto the seat beside her and pulled into the traffic she'd risen so early to beat an hour ago. By the time she reached the quiet residential neighborhood where she lived, she was ready to trade all the possibilities of a stellar career as an engineer for the predictable, slow-paced lifestyle of her uncle's farm.

As she waited at a crosswalk for a pedestrian and her dog, Faith stared at her white-knuckle grip on the steering wheel and the sticky crevices between her fingers. The adrenaline in her system fizzled out and her stomach knotted inside.

A man was dead.

She had his blood all over her clothes and hands. Faith glanced up into the rearview mirror. Even her face, where she must have brushed aside a loose strand of golden hair, bore traces of her hellish morning.

"A shower," she promised the sallow reflection in the mirror. Her eyes had blanched to a dull olive color. Her next course of action would be a long, hot shower. Lots of scrubbing. Extra soap. With that much of a plan finally formulated, she drew her first normal breath since pushing open that unlocked door at work.

Faith pulled her car into the driveway of her boxy gray stone house and parked. Good. She'd beat the detectives here. She retrieved her keys and hurried toward the side door.

Letting herself in through the kitschy fifties-style kitchen, she tossed her purse and keys on the counter and headed straight for the fridge. She'd already unbuttoned her blouse before opening the door and pulling out a bottle of water. The chilly air hit the bare skin of her torso, waking her senses, reviving clear, rational thought. She tipped her head back and drained half of the icy liquid before even closing the refrigerator. The water cleansed her mouth and throat of the bitter taste of fear, and soothed the questions still churning in her stomach.

Half-dressed, with her mind and body finally relaxing their staunch guard against the gruesome events of that morning, she flicked the lid onto the counter and headed into the living room.

Into destruction.

"What…?" The bottle dropped from her hand. Its contents soaked, unheeded, into the carpet. She scanned the entire room, from the shattered Lladró figurines to the shredded cushions that had once been her couch and chairs. "How the…?"

A creeping sense of being watched, of someone knowing more about her than she herself knew, pricked wave after wave of goose bumps across her skin.

Just like Dr. Rutherford's lab and office, her home had been invaded.

But what did she own that was worth this much devastation?

And why did running still feel like the smartest move she could make?

"WAS ANYTHING TAKEN?"

Faith raked her fingers through her hair and caught the wavy strands in a fist at the back of her neck. None of this made any sense. "They went through my CD collection, but didn't touch the player. They dumped out my jewelry box, but left a diamond pendant and earrings that belonged to my mother." She released her hair and threw up her hands in frustration. "Things might be broken, but I think it's all still here."

She'd barely had time to throw on her robe over her slacks and bra before Detective Jermaine Collier knocked on her front door. She'd had no time to deal with the shock of the break-in, much less sort through what was left of her things.

"You've only been gone a couple of hours?" The tall, mahogany-skinned detective gave the appearance of laid-back charm with his tailored suit and easy smile. But there was something sharp, almost omniscient, in his dark, nearly black eyes. And though he didn't share his opinions with her, Faith got the idea the mind inside his shaved head was elsewhere, making observations she couldn't see, connecting pieces to a puzzle she couldn't even picture yet.

"That's right. I left for work about 6:40. I came back early...." She hugged her arms around her waist and shivered inside her robe despite the warm temperature of the early September day. "Because of my boss."

"William Rutherford?" She nodded as he checked off something in his little black notebook. "Eclipse Labs is where you found him dead?"

"I didn't *find* him dead." She squeezed her eyes shut, unable to stop the bombardment of horrific images. When the constriction in her throat eased enough to speak again, her eyes popped open to find the detective carefully studying her reaction. "He stumbled out of his research lab and collapsed into my arms. He died a couple minutes later."

"That's all his blood on you?"

The detective had already bagged her discarded blouse as evidence. Faith nodded, reliving Dr. Rutherford's death and inexplicable warnings over and over. "I tried to help, but it was too late. He wanted to talk. So I just held him."

Detective Collier's forehead creased in a sympathetic frown. "What did he say?"

One of the crime scene technicians indicated that the sofa had been cleared, and it was okay to sit. Faith chose to remain in the doorway of her untouched kitchen. "He told me to get out, not to trust anyone at the lab. One of the guards tried to stop me on the way out, but I ran." She hung her head and stared at the badge clipped to his belt. "I know I'm not supposed to."

"You didn't call the police until you left?"

"I tried to call for help right away. The intruder was still in the lab." She breathed in deeply, tucked her hair behind her ears and forced herself to look the detective in the eye. "But Dr. Rutherford said there wasn't time, that he wanted me to listen. I think he knew he couldn't last much longer."

Collier tapped his pad with his pen. "Listen to what?"

"A name."

His eyes narrowed to thin slits of midnight. "And the name?"

"He... This is hard for me." The detective's piercing scrutiny finally short-circuited through her nerves. An uncomfortable shiver rippled through her from head to toe. "Would it be okay if I changed? And at least washed my hands?" One of the technicians had already swabbed beneath her fingernails.

"How close were you and Dr. Rutherford?"

Closer than anyone else she knew in the city besides her former college roommate. "I've only been in Saint Louis since I graduated in May. William was sort of an adopted grandfather. I don't have much family. We ate lunch together every day." She smiled at the memory. "Otherwise, he'd forget. He'd work straight through the day and night if I didn't remind him to take a break from time to time."

"What was he working on?"

Faith shrugged, trying to think of all the brainstorms her boss had concocted or refined in the past months. "A solar-powered toaster. An airport luggage-scanning system."

"Any kind of weapon design?"

Something deadly from Dr. Rutherford? It'd be a stretch, but not impossible. She'd filed away reams of doodled ideas on everything from toys to communication satellites. If the mind could conceive it, chances were William Rutherford already had. Faith's pulse picked up its pace as that sense of foreboding she had temporarily quashed tried to reassert itself.

She didn't want to say too much before she knew the answer herself. "I'm just an assistant. I'm not privy to everything that goes on at the lab."

"It's my understanding Eclipse Labs has contracts with the metro police department as well as the area National Guard and Reserve units." The detective sure knew a lot about her employer for only a couple hours' work. Had he investigated them before?

"In the past I know he worked on a lightweight, bullet-proof flak jacket." But that equipment had already been implemented by the police department. It certainly wasn't an invention worth killing for.

"Nothing new?" Collier kept pressing for an answer he wanted. "Nothing that an illegal element—organized crime, terrorists—might want to get their hands on? A gun? A bomb?"

"No, I—" Was something missing from the lab? Faith was growing distinctly uncomfortable with this line of questioning. "Are you interviewing me about his murder, or the break-in here?"

Detective Collier strolled over to the stone hearth and nudged aside bits of a broken clock with his pen. "There are no signs of forced entry at either location. Both places have been searched, but not robbed." He turned and nailed her with an accusation. "I'm thinking there's a connection. And you're it."

"But how could he get from there to here so soon?" Faith pulled herself up to every bit of her five feet five inches she could muster. This interview had suddenly taken a disturbingly personal turn. Even she could hear the strident edge of defensiveness that pinched her voice. "The man he called Copperhead was still at the lab when I left."

"But you didn't see him."

"I heard him. He was trapped inside. I shut the steel door

and scrambled the locks. He must have heard me in the office. He was coming after me. I was defending myself."

"Really? Or were you covering up a crime?" He wasn't bothering with the friendly facade anymore.

"No."

"Yes, the lab was sealed. But we found no intruder inside." He slowly paced off the length of the room, all the while keeping his gaze fixed on her. "We did find two dead bodies, though."

"Two?"

"Dr. Rutherford and a security guard." He skimmed through the pages of his notepad until he found the name. "Daniel Novotny."

Danny? "But—" She squeezed her eyes shut and shook her head. How could that be? She'd just seen him. He'd grabbed her in the hallway when she'd run out of Rutherford's office. He'd had his gun drawn and was calling for backup. She opened her eyes and demanded her own answers. "Danny was okay when I left."

"Was he?" Jermaine Collier's inquisition took on a nasty innuendo. "He wasn't stabbed and bleeding when you departed?"

Another gruesome image to add to her memory bank. "No. I told him William was dead and that we had an intruder."

"But Dr. Rutherford told you not to trust anyone there."

"That's why I got out before calling the police."

Detective Collier snapped his notebook shut and tucked it inside his suit jacket, purposefully holding open the front of his coat to give her a good look at his gun. "Miss Monroe, I'd like you to come down to the station for some further questioning."

"I didn't do—" His unblinking stare warned her it wasn't a request. Had she woke up this morning in some alternate universe? What was going on? She was a witness. A victim. Not a suspect. This was all too crazy. Too far beyond her control. But a refusal would look even more incriminating. She needed a lawyer. She didn't even know one. "Can I at least change first?"

"Of course." He sounded almost kind, solicitous, but Faith saw the hawklike watchfulness in his eyes. "But I want those clothes as evidence."

Assuming the conversation was finished for now, she went back into the kitchen to gather her purse. She paused at the phone hanging on the wall above the counter. She really should call a lawyer. The police thought *she* had something to do with Dr. Rutherford's murder. That she had something to do with Danny's death as well. Besides the killer, was she the last person to see them both alive? This was all getting way out of hand.

With a quick glance over her shoulder to see Detective Collier consulting with one of the crime scene investigators, she opened the drawer with the phone book and picked up the receiver. She flipped open the yellow pages under A. "Attorney. Attorney," she muttered, trailing her index finger down the page.

It took a full second for the dead silence beside her ear to register.

"What are you doing?"

Startled, Faith dropped the receiver. By the time she fumbled it out of her hands, the tall, rangy detective was striding across the room. He wasn't smiling.

She'd been caught. If he wasn't already suspicious of her, the rush of heat flooding her pale cheeks would be a dead giveaway that she'd been up to something. She had a right to call a lawyer. But somehow, Jermaine Collier didn't look as if he saw things the same way.

"Who were you calling?" Was that a query or another accusation? When he bent down to pick up the receiver, Faith closed the phone book and slyly tucked it back inside its drawer. She jerked back when he reached across her to hang up the phone. "Well?"

Faith played dumb. No sense drawing attention to her suspicions about Collier. About the technicians in her living room. About this whole, screwed-up, sanity-robbing morning. She rattled off the first lie that came to her. "A friend of mine. We were supposed to have lunch. I was going to call and cancel. Unless you think I'll be done by noon?"

He scoffed as he straightened the front of his jacket. "You can call from the station."

No *done by noon,* huh?

Her phone line was dead. But then, she had a feeling he already knew that.

"Okay." She pointed past him to the doorway. "I'll just go change, then."

"Five minutes," he ordered. "Then we'll go. I'll drive you."

Of course, he would. No sense giving her any freedom. Any autonomy. Any sense of trust or security.

"Five minutes." She nodded her agreement, but was already thinking ahead. Dr. Rutherford's advice didn't end at the lab. She needed to get out of here and find someone who could help her.

But if she couldn't trust Eclipse security, and she couldn't trust the cops, where could she go?

With only five minutes to come up with a plan, Faith wasted little time in the bathroom, scrubbing her hands and splashing cool water on her face. In her bedroom, she stripped down to the skin and put on fresh underwear. But as she stuffed her soiled clothes into the paper sack the crime lab had given her, a corner of plain white cotton caught her eye.

Dr. Rutherford's handkerchief.

A sudden rush of fiery tears stung her eyes and burned in her sinuses. She pulled the wadded handkerchief from the pocket of her slacks and sank onto the foot of her bed. She cradled the unexpected treasure in her hands, lifted it to her nose and inhaled the old-fashioned spicy scent of the man himself.

Faith wept anew at the familiar, grandfatherly smell. One last gift. Folding it neatly into her palm, she laid the cotton square against her cheek. Soft as a soothing caress, it offered her the first bit of comfort she'd known since…

"What the heck?"

Something hard and round was pressing against her cheek. Something inside the handkerchief.

Sweet memories vanished in a heartbeat. Instinctively turning her back to the closed door, Faith stood and unfolded the handkerchief. Inside she found a shiny silver disk, no bigger than a dollar coin. One of Dr. Rutherford's mini computer disks.

Faith flipped it over and read the distinctive scrawl on the label on the other side. "NT-6. Prototype." She closed her fingers around the disk and frowned. "NT-6?" She couldn't recall any project with that code, and she transcribed all of his notes. Was NT-6 something independent he'd designed? Something more top secret than her clearance allowed her to work on?

Was the secret of NT-6 worth killing for?

"Oh, heaven." Faith clutched her fist to her chest and forced herself to breathe in and out before she fainted.

Dr. Rutherford had stuffed this into her hand and told her to run. Such a tiny little thing. Someone had gone through Rutherford's office looking for it. They'd gone through his lab. They'd gone through her house.

She glanced over her shoulder, knowing Collier and his men were waiting for her in her living room. Did he know she had this? Did he suspect? Was he trying to protect her until she gave the disk to this Darien Frye that Rutherford had mentioned? Or did Collier want whatever it contained for himself?

"Okay, girl. Think." She tapped her fist against her forehead, knowing her time was running out. Should she tell

Collier she had the disk? Would he think she'd killed Rutherford and Novotny to get it? She shook her head. Her boss
had told her to run because he knew she'd be in danger.
Collier didn't make her feel safe.

Never one to fuss with her appearance, Faith rewrapped
the disk in the handkerchief and pulled on a pair of jeans.
Socks and sneakers followed. She stuffed the disk into her
pocket and pulled a teal T-shirt over her head.

She couldn't go back for her jacket in the hall closet, so
she tied a matching sweater around her waist. Slipping her
purse strap around her neck and shoulder, she peeked out
the window. The backyard was clear.

Thank God her first renovation had been to replace the
noisy, sticky, rope-and-sash windows. With a final backward glance to make sure her escape went undetected, she
opened the window and raised the screen.

When her feet hit the soft dirt outside, she crouched behind the bare lilac bush and scanned her surroundings. Using her car would be out of the question. The CSI van had
parked in the driveway behind her. Adrenaline cleared her
mind, making the next few steps in her impromptu plan
clear. For the moment.

Her car would be too easy to trace, anyway. Stealth was
her best ally.

With Jermaine Collier still ordering his men about inside
her house, Faith slipped through the neighbor's backyard,
lost herself among the trees and hedgerows and made her
way to the nearest commuter bus stop.

"ARE YOU KIDDING? Oh, my God. This is like *The Fugi-
tive!*" Liza Shelton's brick-red curls bounced around her
shoulders as she popped up off her chair and joined Faith
on the couch.

Faith buzzed a weary sigh through her lips. There was
nothing fun or adventurous about her life spinning out of

control. "This isn't funny, Liza. I think I'm in serious trouble. Will you help?"

"Of course. You got it. This is like the coolest thing to happen to me since Kurt Johansen asked me out."

Without the luxury of time to think long and hard about her destination, Faith had ended up at her former college roommate's apartment near the Gateway Arch in downtown Saint Louis. Now she was wondering whether she'd been wise to put her friend in danger. Especially when she had a hard time keeping her facts straight. "Kurt Johansen was a bum. He stood you up."

"Details, schmee-tails. The campus heartthrob was almost mine." Liza waved her short red fingernails in the air, dismissing the conversation. "So your boss died. The guard died. And the cops think you killed them? That's wild."

If Liza added an *awesome* to the end of that sentence, Faith would have screamed. As it was, she schooled her patience and shared her plan, forgoing any mention of the disk or an unknown party's murderous interest in it. "I need to borrow your car. I want to get out of town and talk to someone I can trust, so I'm heading west toward Kansas City to meet my uncle up near Saint Jo." Liza's eyes started to glaze over, so Faith hurried to give her instructions. "In the meantime, I need you to call the FBI."

"The FBI. That is so cool."

Faith exhaled a steadying breath. She and Liza were both only twenty-four, but today she felt decades older than her friend. "There's a local office here in Saint Louis. The number's in the phone book."

Liza nodded. "Right. Call the FBI. Give them your name, mention you have information about Eclipse Labs and tell them you'll meet them at the Kansas City office."

Maybe her friend *had* been listening. "Exactly. You can use my car if you need transportation."

"Are you kidding?" Liza retrieved her purse and fished out the keys to her Ford Focus. "This will the perfect excuse to ask Gabe downstairs in 3A to give me a ride. I've been looking for an excuse to get to know him better.''

Faith traded key rings. ''Glad I could help.''

''So when are you leaving?''

''Right now.''

NEARLY FIVE HOURS later, Faith parked Liza's red car at a Kansas City convenience store and filled the tank with gas. It wouldn't hurt to refill her tank, too. She'd called ahead to her uncle's house on a farm outside of Saint Joseph, Missouri. There'd been no answer, so she'd left a message that she'd be paying a surprise visit. But that was still another hour away.

She carried an armload of drinks and snacks to the center of the store where the clerk was flipping through the channels of the TV hanging above his head. He rang up everything, added the gas and swiped the credit card Faith handed him.

The pudgy man's frown when he ran the card the first time didn't alarm her. The fact that he spoke to her after running it a second time did. He held the card up between his thumb and forefinger, finally giving her his full attention. ''Computer says it's been canceled.''

''What?'' She only used the card for gas and travel. And she made a point of paying off the balance every month. ''That's impossible. Run it again.''

Her indignant panic went unheeded. ''Won't do no good. The message says I should cut it up. I ain't saying you did it, but the card was probably stolen.''

Faith blinked away the shock that threatened to paralyze her. Did everyone think she was a criminal? ''It's not stolen.'' She pulled out her billfold, searching for her license to back up her claim. ''That's me.''

''Sorry, miss. I'll need cash.''

She watched helplessly as he pulled out a pair of scissors and snipped the card in two. But that wasn't what stopped her argument cold. She looked beyond him, above his head to the TV screen that had been tuned to a twenty-four-hour news channel.

A familiar photograph from her college yearbook caught her attention from the top right corner of the screen. Brick-red hair. A shade brighter than Faith had seen it just that morning. Liza Shelton. The reporter was standing in front of Liza's building, interviewing an official in a conservative gray suit.

"Agent Carmichael, what can you tell us about the body?" asked the reporter.

The man identified as Special Agent Rory Carmichael cleared his throat before answering. He recited the information with the cold diction of a heartless man. "Ms. Shelton was found by a neighbor who ID'ed her. Apparently, the victim interrupted a robbery in progress. She was cut up pretty badly according to the Saint Louis police. I haven't seen the body yet myself."

"Cut up?" Faith mouthed the words. Her eyes refused to blink. Liza, dead? Stabbed? She was going to faint.

"That's how it goes." The clerk had misinterpreted her question. "There ain't nothing I can do. You have to call the company yourself."

Glad for the distraction—any distraction—Faith tore her gaze from the image of her friend on the television and dug thirty dollars out of her wallet. If her credit cards had been canceled, handing over that precious cash would be risky. But she didn't want to draw any more attention to herself. She just wanted to get on the road, get to Uncle Wes's. Get someplace safe.

As she gathered her things and grabbed her change, the FBI agent's words seeped into her thoughts of escape. "The Bureau is involved because Ms. Shelton called this morning with a crime tip. I can't comment yet on whether the crimes are related."

"What the heck is on that disk, anyway?" she muttered to herself, wishing someone could give her answers.

"Miss?"

Another death, following hot on her trail. Another sense-less death. She stared at the clerk. Would this innocent man she'd spoken to wind up dead, too? *Run.* "Nothing. Thanks."

Faith spun out of the parking lot and onto the highway, circling north onto I-29. Her hunger was forgotten. Her thirst, forgotten. Her plan to meet with the FBI, turn over the disk and report everything she had seen and suspected— all forgotten. It was all she could do to drive. To stay one step ahead of the faceless killer who had turned her life into a waking nightmare.

But the rolling green hills of northwest Missouri, with its lush farms and tree-studded rivers, had always been a sooth-ing landmark to her. Symbols of home and safety, famil-iarity and comfort. By the time she'd traveled the long gravel road to her uncle's farm, she was beginning to hope. Beginning to think that with his sage advice and sheltering arms, she'd find a way to make sense of all this. She'd be strong enough to handle whatever she had to do in order to clear her name and track down a murderer.

As she pulled up to the two-story white house, however, a niggling of doubt filtered in to spoil the last vestiges of hope. The place was deserted. Her uncle's truck and her grandmother's car were gone. No farm dog ran out from the barn to greet her. There was nothing but the heat of the early September afternoon beating down to welcome her.

Faith climbed out of her car and headed for the front door. "Uncle Wes? Gran?"

They could be running errands. Gran might have a doc-tor's appointment. Wes could be catching pie and coffee at the downtown café. Faith didn't worry too much about the front door being unlocked. It was one of the peculiarities of country living so a farmer didn't have to carry his keys into the field, and a neighbor would always feel welcome. "Uncle Wes?"

But as she pushed open the door, her suspicions blossomed into full-blown fear. "Wes! Gran!"

She could barely hear her own voice over the pounding pulse inside her ears. Her grandmother's antique furniture, the portrait of her parents that had hung above the mantel, Uncle Wes's gun cabinet—all of it had been slashed. Broken.

Ransacked.

Picking through the memories by rote, feeling the violation of her childhood home—not through her fingertips, but rather through some detached sixth sense that kept her from going completely mad—Faith searched the house. Upstairs and down. The basement. The back porch. She didn't know whether to be relieved or terrified that she hadn't found her family.

"How can they do this?" She spoke to the remains of what had once been her grandmother's spotless kitchen. "How do they know?"

She prayed that her uncle and grandmother were all right, that they hadn't been here when the place had been searched. Where would the killer go next? Where else would he strike? What part of her life had he yet to touch and destroy?

For a moment, Faith was too frightened, too utterly alone to string together a coherent thought. She fingered the disk in her pocket. NT-6. A sentence of death and terror to anyone who knew her. Why? Dr. Rutherford. Danny. Liza. Wes and Gran?

"Why?"

There was no answer. Only a single word playing over and over inside her head.

Run.

Faith heeded the only idea that made any sense. She had to get away from everyone she knew, from every place she loved. She climbed back into Liza's car, ignored the map and drove away. She was too numb with shock and confusion to do anything more.

Day faded into night. Night became a blanket of stars. Moonlight gave way to a shadowy darkness.

And still she drove.

She covered the flatlands of Nebraska and wound her way steadily westward toward the craggy elevations of the Rocky Mountains. The last road sign she read was Elk Point, Wyoming. A tiny town of two thousand nestled at the base of the Grand Tetons.

Now, in that creeping darkness before dawn, it started to rain. A few noisy splotches on her windshield quickly became a downpour.

"Why not?" She tapped her foot on the brake. Her hoarse whisper encroached the powers that be. "It fits. Let the heavens open up. You've dumped everything else on me."

She was beyond tired, surviving on adrenaline and caffeine, mindlessly putting as much distance between her and hell as she could. She slowed the car as it wound back and forth across the rutted asphalt road she hoped would take her over the mountain. But even with the windshield wipers on max she couldn't see more than a few feet in front of her. She gripped the wheel in weary fists and squinted the fatigue from her eyes.

Leaning forward to judge the next curve, she focused on the curtain of rain and darkness. Lightning flashed, illuminating every tree and leaf and pothole for a split second. Faith jumped in her skin, but managed not to jerk the wheel. She stomped on the brakes to slow her speed to a blind crawl as she was swallowed up in the darkness that followed. Just as she remembered to exhale the fearful breath she held, thunder crashed down around her. This high in the mountains, it was a giant concussion of sound that shook the car and reverberated through her entire body.

This time, she did jerk. The car swerved toward the ditch, but she quickly steered it back into the center of the lane. "Bring it on, Mother Nature!"

She was laughing now, a crazy, taunting laugh that echoed through the car. "What else you got?" she foolishly challenged a world that had been less than kind in the past twenty-four hours.

In answer to her dare, the engine sputtered and a yellow light blinked on in the dashboard. "No." She slammed her fist against the wheel. "No!"

Her crazy laughter gave way to tears as the engine died. She let the car roll off onto the shoulder of the road and parked it. Out of gas. The stupid, stupid thing was out of gas.

So was she.

With nothing left in her, Faith folded her arms across the top of the steering wheel, laid her face in her hands and wept.

Time lost all meaning in her world of death and darkness and pouring rain. It might have been an hour, or only a few minutes before she became aware of the bright spotlight shining in through the back window of the car.

By the time she realized a car with spinning blue lights had pulled up behind her, someone rapped at her window. Faith's heart leaped into her throat. She clapped her hand over her mouth to stifle her startled yelp at the sight of the shapeless creature outside her window. She slid toward the passenger seat when he bent down and shined a flashlight in on her.

But someone stood at the other door, too. She was trapped.

"Oh, God, please help me," she whispered, truly fearing that divine intervention would be the only way she could be saved now.

"Ma'am?" A man's voice shouted through the glass. He

knocked on the window again. "Ma'am, I'm the sheriff of this county. Are you all right?"

Sheriff? Rational thought pinged through her brain like the targets of a pinball machine, trying to make sense of where she was and whom she was with.

"Hey, lady," the voice from the passenger side shouted. "Are you hurt?"

Would these two men know who she was? Had the make and plates on Liza's car been broadcast across some sort of national wire?

Faith cracked her window, turning her face away from the rain that splashed against her cheek. "I need to see your badge," she ordered. She pointed to the other man. "And I need him to move to your side of the car."

While the man on the passenger side cursed and mumbled something about pouring rain, the man at the driver's window pulled up his yellow rain slicker and let her read the badge and ID hanging from the chest pocket of his brown uniform shirt. "That's smart to be safe, ma'am. My name's Hamilton Prince." Now both men were standing at her window. "If there's something wrong with your car, we can drive you into town for the night and get it fixed in the morning."

Get in a car with two men she didn't know? A paunchy sheriff and... "Who's he?" she asked, nodding toward the grumbling man.

"Mel Prescott. Part-time deputy. He owns some land up this way."

Mr. Prescott apparently had had enough of doing the neighborly thing. "C'mon, Ham. If she doesn't want our help, let's get moving. I'm late enough getting home as it is."

"Cool your jets, Mel." Sheriff Prince's poncho caught on the polished brown handle of his gun. Faith's eyes widened, suddenly thrown back to yesterday morning at her home, when Detective Collier had let her get a good look at his weapon as a subtle means of intimidation. But maybe her tired brain was imagining it. The sheriff bent down far enough so she could see his face through the window. "Could I see your license and registration, ma'am?"

Faith tensed. "What for?"

He smiled. It was a gesture meant to be charming, but its overt friendliness alarmed her even more. Danny Novotny and Jermaine Collier had been friendly and polite moments before talking to her as if she were a criminal. "Standard procedure. I like to know who's in my county. And you still haven't told me your name."

Give him the opportunity to find out she was wanted for questioning regarding a string of murders? No way. "I'm okay, Sheriff. Honestly." She managed to dredge up a false smile of her own. "It was hard to see and I got tired, so I pulled off the side of the road to take a nap."

"You look like you've been crying."

Faith's fingers flew to her face. She did feel hot. And that puffy swelling around her eyes wasn't entirely due to fatigue. "I'm fine," she repeated.

"Ma'am, you don't want to be alone up here at night. Not on this part of the mountain."

"You think he knows we're here?" asked Mel, shifting nervously on his feet. Making Faith nervous. *He* who?

Sheriff Prince hooked his thumbs into his belt and straightened beyond her sight. "I'm sure that son of a gun knew we were here the moment we stopped. That freak's got cat eyes in his head. He's probably watching us right now."

Mel swore and stomped back toward the sheriff's car, kicking up mud and water with each step. "Then I'm out of here. If she doesn't want our help, let's go."

"Dammit, Mel." The sheriff followed his buddy back to the car. "I've got a job—"

"Hey, Ham, there's something on the scanner."

Feedback? Information on her?

Faith saw her chance. She had no intention of letting the sheriff run any kind of check on her until she knew it was safe to contact law enforcement. For all she knew, he'd already run the license plate and was reading that the car belonged to a dead woman. The scanner might list the car stolen. She had to get away. And since the car was temporarily out of commission...

With surprising coordination for a woman who'd been sitting for nearly twenty hours, she grabbed her purse and opened the door. The force of the rain soaked through to the skin almost immediately. She slipped on the slick asphalt, but scrambled to her feet and ducked around the front of the car to disappear into the shadows.

"Ham!"

"She's running!"

"Lady! Ah, nuts." A slew of swear words dogged her as she stumbled into the ditch, landing ankle-deep in a puddle of water.

"Stay away from me!" she yelled, climbing up the opposite side and plunging into the line of trees. Lightning charged the air again, skidding in an ionized shock wave across her cold, wet skin, showing her a glimpse of a path before throwing her into the darkness of the mountain storm once more.

As she tore through the thick stand of pines and aspen, she could hear footsteps following her. Two heavy-footed men in hot pursuit. The light from their flashlights danced across the trunks of the trees, playing tag with her, trying to catch her. Why chase after her if they meant her no harm?

Run.

"Dammit, lady!" Mel sounded totally pissed and almost—panicked. "Don't go up there. It isn't safe."

"Ma'am—please." The sheriff sounded more rational.

But Faith didn't stop. She ran. Uphill. Grabbing handholds on trees, blinking the water from her eyes. Breathing so deep and fast her lungs burned with the altitude. Thunder banged in the air, jerking her like a gunshot. She stumbled a step, but refused to fall. Refused to slow down. Refused to give up her freedom until she felt safe.

Run.

"Lady!" Mel swore.

"Watch yourself!"

Faith burst into a clearing. Her soggy shoes shifted around her feet as they hit gravel. A driveway. Lightning flashed. She looked up. A cabin. Shelter. A door to lock behind her.

Someone who *wasn't* the law inside.

She bolted up the steps to the long front porch. She pounded on the door with the flat of her hand. "Help! Help me!"

She glanced over her shoulder.

The men with the badges and flashlights and guns were coming. "Oh, God." She whirled around, her fist raised to pound again. "Help—"

The door swung open. Lightning splintered the sky, giving her one swift, shocking look at the Goliath who filled the doorway.

He towered over her, all muscle and bulk and golden skin above the unsnapped waist of his jeans. She tilted her head back, processing the afterimage of sharp, shadowed features. His unnerving, icy blue eyes seemed to hold and reflect the light. And a slash of scar across one eyebrow made the man look like the very devil himself.

Faith screamed.

Chapter Two

The woman at his door retreated. Fast. She'd roused him from a decent sleep, begged for help and now she was running away.

Typical.

Friendly first impressions had never been his strong suit. He didn't care. Let her leave.

But when she missed the top step in her rush to get away from him and plummeted toward the ground, Jonas Beck reached out. In one easy stride, he snatched her near the top of each flailing arm, picked her up and set her squarely down in the middle of his porch.

The instant she began to struggle he released her and backed off. He was years beyond feeling the sting of her repulsion. But he'd never outgrow the habit of learning all he could about the people around him. Whether she'd prove to be the enemy or not, it was the first rule of self-defense.

He could guess the woman wasn't a threat. With her wet clothes clinging to her like a second skin, there wasn't much about her he couldn't assess. She wasn't armed or wired. She didn't clutch her purse as if it held anything valuable or useful as a means of self-defense.

Her height hit him about midchest, putting her at five-five or so. And he'd held on long enough to learn that she had a healthy layer of meat on her bones. If she was lost, she hadn't been away from food and civilization for long.

And she didn't know him, not even by reputation, or else she would have known what to expect when she knocked on his door. She wasn't dressed for trekking through the wilderness. She was too young to have ever been a part of his old life, and she wasn't local.

Or else she'd have chosen the thunderstorm and the mountain over seeking shelter with him.

Let her go, he reasoned. Let her disappear back into the trees and the night from whence she came. The only reason he reached out to steady her now as she dashed down the rain-slick stairs was that he didn't want to mess with a lawsuit if she hurt herself while she was on his property.

"Don't touch me!" She swatted at his big hand like a pesky fly getting back at the horse. Jonas almost laughed. Almost. Genuine laughter hurt in ways he couldn't begin to describe.

He raised both hands in mock surrender and watched her tight, curvy butt as she ran across his driveway. Good riddance. People were nothing but trouble. And he'd had enough of that in his life.

Jonas heard the crack of wood and sensed the danger before the woman skidded to a halt halfway between him and the line of trees and brush. Two men dressed in wide-brimmed hats and yellow ponchos broke through the natural barrier. He recognized them as the sheriff and one of his fake deputies.

Like the beastly guard dog he'd once been trained to be, Jonas's hackles rose. As the chilling rain beat down on his naked shoulders and torso, a fever erupted inside him, shooting fiery trails of adrenaline to every defensive muscle and filling his senses with a hyperawareness that let him instantly assess their intent and the woman's charged reaction to them.

"Oh, God." Her cry was half confusion, half terror.

"Lady, get away from there." The sheriff's buddy and bootlicker, Mel Prescott, had his gun pulled from his holster. He used it instead of his finger to point at the woman and urge her to move. Jackass. "You come with me now."

Instinctively, Jonas patted his hip. He didn't waste the time or energy swearing at the discovery that he'd left his hunting knife strapped to his belt beside his bed. When he'd first sensed the disturbance outside, he'd simply swung out of bed and pulled on his jeans. He'd taken out armed men with his bare hands before, though. Mel Prescott wasn't a threat to him. But the woman...

"Put away your gun, Prescott." Jonas's voice rattled like thunder over the mountain.

The man who would be bully dared to look beyond the woman and briefly challenge Jonas. "This isn't personal, Beck. And it doesn't concern you."

But the woman, frightened of him though she might be, had chosen sides. She was scrambling backward toward the cabin—toward Jonas—as quickly as she had run away.

That made it personal.

As soon as she was in arm's reach, Jonas grabbed her and pushed her behind him on the stairs. "It takes both of you to handle this little thing?" he challenged the intruders.

"We're not trying to *handle* anything, Beck," insisted the sheriff, cautioning his partner to holster his weapon. "We want to help the lady. Her car broke down on White Horse Road. I know you don't cotton to trespassers, so we tried to stop her when she ran from us." He was trying to appease him with that overly friendly politician's voice. "'Course, folks don't usually run from the law unless they got something to hide."

Eight fingers brushed against the small of his back, jolting his sensitized body with an unexpected sexual awareness as the woman curled her fists into the waistband of his jeans. He felt her breath between his shoulder blades as she whispered her plea.

"I didn't do anything wrong. I just want them to leave me alone. Please." *Please?* When was the last time anyone asked him for a favor? He carried out orders. No one ever asked. "I just got scared. With the storm, and being lost. And I'm so tired. Don't let them take me. I'm not ready."

Not ready? What the hell did that mean? *Had* she broken the law?

"Please."

Somehow, that one soft word wiggled its way beneath his tough hide. He'd defended a lot of men and women in his former career. But not once had any one of them deigned to *ask* for his help. It was worth playing this out just for the perverse kick it gave him.

He backed up onto the porch, shielding the woman from the brunt of the rain as well as the cautious advance of Hamilton Prince. "How do you know she wasn't coming to see me, Sheriff?"

Jonas couldn't resist the dig. He'd never caused anyone down in Elk Point a moment's grief. Still, the rare times he ventured to town for supplies, folks walked a wide berth around him. They gossiped and embellished his shady history. Sheriff Prince was a big part of that. It didn't hurt Jonas to live up to his reputation as the reclusive beast of the mountain. Hell. He already had Mel Prescott shaking in his boots.

"No one ever comes to see you. Not on purpose." Prince moved slowly, his hands outstretched and petting the air as if he thought the symbolic gesture might actually placate his adversary. "She's got out-of-state plates, so I figured she didn't know what kind of trouble she was getting into."

"She's not in any trouble here, Sheriff."

"The car she's driving belongs to a dead woman. I'd like to ask her about that."

"I can explain," she whispered barely loud enough for Jonas to hear. "But I don't think he'd believe me. Don't turn me in. Please."

There was that damn word again. Jonas glanced over his shoulder. She was standing close enough that he should be feeling her body heat. But this woman was generating nothing but chill. And he didn't think it was entirely due to the wet, brisk weather.

Why wouldn't she want the sheriff to hear her explanation?

Didn't matter. Jonas hardened himself against the natural curiosity and caution most people might feel. The woman's story was of less interest to him than getting rid of Prince and his sidekick. The storm was lessening its intensity, but he tipped his face up to the steady rain, taking advantage of a last web of lightning burning itself out across the sky. The illumination would highlight the scar, and pick up the glow in what his stepmother had years ago called devil eyes.

He succeeded in scaring Mel Prescott back a step. "She's nothing but trouble, Ham. She can deal with Beck on her own. We warned her. Let's get out of here."

Wise choice. "I'll take care of her car," Jonas promised.

Clearly, Sheriff Prince wasn't comfortable with leaving her alone with him. Or did it have more to do with his own ego? It must stick in his craw to have a pretty young woman turn to Jonas Beck instead of *his* pompous ass for protection. "It's part of my job to help stranded tourists. And I hate to put you out when—"

"It's nice of you to be concerned about me. But I can manage."

The sheriff had more brains than he had guts. If he couldn't work his way around Jonas's defenses, he'd go after weaker prey. "Ma'am? You don't have to stay with him if you don't want to. I promise to take you to the motel in town, not jail. We can talk this all out in the morning."

Her hands trembled in their grasp, though with her half-hidden behind him, he couldn't tell whether she was shaking from fear or the cold or if she was just plain angry. Jonas didn't try to persuade her one way or the other. Ultimately, it would have to be her choice.

He knew the instant she released him. Typical. He'd put himself on the line for a handful of pretty words and she still saw him as the worse of two evils. When she stepped around him, Jonas moved aside. The breath he released was long and deep and riddled with the bitter truth he'd learned to accept long ago.

He could fight. He could track. He could protect. He could kill.

But he couldn't feel.

It was the only way he'd ever really been hurt in his life. And he refused to hurt again.

Let her go. He'd tried. He didn't care.

"I'm going to stay."

Jonas went still at the quiet yet firmly articulated words. Hell. The woman had spunk. Or she was a damn idiot. But she'd made her choice. It was a tiny little victory over a world that had no place for him. He'd never needed anyone's approval except that of the men he'd once worked for. The same men who'd called him to Washington last December and told him his services would no longer be needed. At forty years of age, he felt over the hill, and the skills he lived and breathed were out of fashion.

He sure as hell didn't need this washed-out spitfire's approval. But it did feel good to stick it to Hamilton Prince.

Jonas took a moment to make sure the sheriff understood that, too. He walked down the stairs to the woman's side and draped his arm around her shoulders, latching on to keep her from pulling away. She stiffened up tighter than the rain-soaked planks on his porch. But she didn't scream and he didn't release her. "You're right, Ham," he mocked. "I don't like trespassers."

He dropped the heavy hint and turned, pulling her along at his side up the steps and into his cabin.

"I expect to see her in town tomorrow, Beck," the sheriff called after him. "I'll come lookin' for her if I don't."

Jonas didn't dignify the veiled warning with a response. The conversation was over. As soon as he locked the door behind them, he let the woman pull free. She darted across the main room to the kitchen area, putting as much space between them as the great room would allow. That was all right. She'd got what she wanted. And, in a way, so had he. A few minutes' reprieve from his self-imposed prison. But a few minutes of interaction with the normal world was all he ever allowed himself. He stayed where he was, peering out the window until he was sure Prince and Prescott had gone for good.

When he turned back to look at her, she was rubbing her hands up and down her arms, pacing behind the kitchen table. If she put any more distance between them, she'd be out the back door. Jonas didn't mind the obvious snub. He could guess there was more than twice as much of him as there was of her. He was taller, bigger, and just as scary as he looked. If their positions were reversed, he'd be smart enough to keep his distance from the potential threat, too.

He supposed he should offer some kind of reassurance. But that didn't come naturally to him. He was more curious to know why a young woman would come tearing through the trees and beat on *his* door in the witching hours of the night. Running from the law, no less.

Once, he used to track down runners who'd skipped prison or jumped bail. Sometimes it had been his job to keep those very same criminals alive long enough to testify against a bigger threat. But despite her bedraggled appearance, this woman hadn't seen the inside of a jail cell. She was more likely a victim or a witness—or just plain paranoid. "What kind of trouble are you in?"

Her eyes rounded open, revealing twin orbs of deep, true green in the center of their puffy, bloodshot rims. "Trouble?"

She hugged herself tight around the waist, pushing the hard tips of her breasts up against the wet shirt and sweater she wore. His flesh tingled with an instant alertness at the unintentional display. But he ignored his body's base response to her generous figure. She was too young, he thought. A good fifteen years his junior. She was definitely a grown woman. Physically. But as far as life experience went...

"Trouble," he repeated. "You brought it to my doorstep, and I made it go away. For the time being. You'll take it with you when you leave. Is that clear?"

She was pretty, too. Nothing dramatic or striking. But even with mascara streaking down her pale cheeks he could tell her skin was flawless. Her coloring was fair. Her mouth was wide and full and just a shade crooked, giving her a natural, not plastic version of beauty.

He could also tell by her sudden shift in focus that she was about to lie. She gave it a good try, though, raking all ten fingers through the short, rain-darkened hair that hugged her head and nape. "I'm sorry to inconvenience you. But I'll admit it, I was stupid. Here I am, looking for the national parks, and I run out of gas. I would have walked back to town, but then the storm hit—"

"Try again."

Those big green eyes stared at him in shock for a moment, then glanced away as her cheeks flooded with rosy heat. Her heavy sigh bespoke fatigue more than embarrassment, but to her credit, she lifted her face and held his gaze. "Obviously, you weren't expecting to be thrown into the middle of anything tonight. I'd rather not talk about what's going on, but I do want to thank you for getting rid of Sheriff Hotshot."

Jonas nodded. She'd pegged Prince, all right. She could keep her secrets. Lord knew he guarded plenty of his own. He didn't want to work too hard to uncover the truth, anyway. Because that would mean getting involved. Rescuing a woman in distress when she came pounding on his door was one thing. But getting *involved* just wasn't an option for him.

"I promise to get out of your hair once my car's going again," she continued. "And I'll pay you back. I'm not sure when or how, but I will. If you'd just let me stay for the night—"

"Stay the night? You don't even know me."

"I know, but—"

"Maybe you should be more afraid of me than of whatever's chasing you."

She hesitated. Thinking of another lie? A way to ease the bruise she thought she was about to inflict on his ego? "I am afraid of you."

She hugged herself impossibly tighter and ran her blanched gaze from point to point across his shoulders and chest, as if just now calculating the imposing dimensions of his body. Her voice was soft, distant, when she spoke again. "But I'm out of money. I'm out of friends. And you're the first person who hasn't demanded anything of me today." Her crooked mouth eased into a timid smile. "Believe me, if you tried to be nice, I'd be out that door and running again."

She didn't want him to be nice?

Her honesty threw him for a moment and all he could do was stare at her until his eyes hurt. The monster pursuing her must be even more frightening than even he'd imagined. Old instincts simmered in his veins, and a desire to even the odds tried to take hold. He ignored it. "It wouldn't be right for you to stay here. Elk Point's a small town. Folks'll talk. Good money says Sheriff Prince is already spreading the word about the danger you're in, here with me."

She considered the import of his words. "Would you hurt me?"

"Shit." He scraped his palm across the crown of his hair. If he was some kind of rapist-murderer-slime, would she trust the honesty of his answer? Her naiveté bordered on foolhardiness. But he gave her the truth, anyway. "No."

"Are you a cop?"

Odd question. Not exactly. Not anymore. "No."

"Then I'd like to stay the night." Her forehead crinkled with desperation. "Please?"

"Stop saying that." He turned from her and paced off the length of the sitting area.

Jonas had no idea what he was going to do with the woman until morning hit in a few hours. It wasn't like he had a guest bedroom in his rustic sanctuary. He'd never had company here before. He'd never asked for any.

But he couldn't turn her out in the rain and the cold and the dark and the danger. He couldn't send her on her way when she didn't know where she was going. He couldn't let the sheriff get his hands on her. Not when she'd said *please.*

"Damn." He balled his hand into a massive fist and punched the air. His conscience was kicking in.

Or maybe there was something from his old life left in him that refused to die. A need to protect. A need to do something useful with the size and strength and face he'd been cursed with.

He'd smelled fear before. More than once in his hellish other life. And this woman reeked of it. Whatever had spooked her was far more intense than any intimidation Ham Prince and his gutless sidekick had conjured. She was dead on her feet, too. A sign that she'd been living with that fear for a lot longer than it had taken her to run up to his cabin from White Horse Road. Longer than she'd had time to get a good look at him and be justly afraid.

Some habits died hard.

Like wearing a crew cut and avoiding people.

And protecting a frightened little rabbit of a woman like… "What's your name?"

"Faith. Faith Monroe."

Ironic.

He'd lost his faith in the world a long time ago. If this was some kind of cosmic test, he wasn't interested in seeing whether or not he'd fail. "Jonas Beck."

"Thank you, Mr. Beck. I—"

No more nice words. She'd said she didn't want them. "For what's left of the night, you can sleep on the couch. I'll take care of your car once it's daylight and the rain lets up. Then you're out of here. Understood?"

"Yes—"

He strode past her to his bedroom, forgoing decent hospitality and ignoring the way she flinched when his elbow brushed her shoulder. He closed the door behind him, leaving her standing in his kitchen, drenched and alone.

He vaguely expected her to fade away into mousy acceptance of his unsociable behavior and his soul-deep need for privacy and peace. He expected her to curl up quietly and stay out of his way and stay off his conscience.

He didn't expect her to come knocking at his bedroom door.

When he pulled the door open, she was there. Right there. Close enough to touch. Close enough to smell. Close enough to see the black pupils of her eyes dilate with aroused emotions.

"What?" he grumbled, catching a whiff of the pine-tinged rain that saturated her clothes and hair.

She tilted her gaze but not her face, giving her wholesome features an innocently seductive expression. Jonas curled his hand into a fist at his side and channeled what tension he could there. He was noticing way too much about this woman.

But, of course, there was no mutual fascination revealed in her matter-of-fact question. "Do you have a blanket? I'm soaked to the skin. I can't afford to get sick right now, so I want to take off my clothes and let them dry."

Take off her clothes?

A naked woman?

Jonas's body lurched in response. He'd never had a woman invade his mountain sanctuary before. He never had much to do with anything sweet and innocent. He wasn't about to have someone soft and shapely—and naked!—running around his cabin.

There were some temptations a man just didn't have to endure.

Uh-uh. Not under his roof.

"Here." He pulled the blanket off his bed and snatched

a denim shirt from the closet. He tossed both at her. She caught them against her chest. "Go to sleep."

He heard her say "Thank you" as he shut the door on her. He was stalking toward his bed when he heard an even softer "Good night."

FAITH STRIPPED in the darkness of what she supposed was the living room, since it had a sofa and a rug. No coffee table, no bookshelf, no TV. At the back of the long front room was a table and a chair—one chair—next to a wood-burning stove, a fridge and a sink that passed for Jonas Beck's kitchen.

There wasn't a photo or painting on any wall, no plants of any type or condition in sight. The only indication that showed the cabin was actually lived in was the stack of library books on the floor beside the sofa—histories mostly—the Punic Wars, the Reformation of England, the Underground Railroad, a travel guide to Alaska and an autobiography about a woman who'd survived child abuse. Odd selections. But then her host was an odd man.

She hadn't been able to see around him to judge the decor of his bedroom, and find out if it looked any more welcoming. Even in the bathroom she'd discovered nothing but a single brown towel to soften the stark lines of cedar paneling and white tile.

In the harsh grandeur of the Teton Mountains, he lived a spartan existence. She could guess he wasn't a man who sought out or appreciated company. He spent time with books instead of people. His home and his temperament both attested to that.

And yet he'd helped her.

At first glance she'd been terrified when he opened his door. In the sudden flash of lightning she'd seen a movie monster come to life. A creature that was half man, half beast. The Terminator. Mr. Hyde. Frankenstein. All rolled into one.

But even a handsome man would have spooked her,

given her circumstances. She'd been running from men she
didn't trust. She'd lived in terror all day long. She'd imagined a portly sheriff and his good-ol'-boy deputy were monsters, too.

That horrible scar that bisected Jonas Beck's face wasn't
as long and savage as she'd first imagined. But it was un-
luckily placed, across the line of his brow and prominent
bridge of his nose, and up into his hairline. She wondered
what sort of injury he'd suffered to leave such a cruel mark.

And, Lord, he was big. Well over six feet tall, probably
closer to seven. He was built like those huge professional
wrestlers she saw on TV. And from what she could tell, his
bulk was all muscle.

Just to look at him, she imagined he'd led a harsh, difficult life. It told in the grim set of his mouth and the deep,
growly voice that boomed inside that grizzly-size chest. Everything about him was big and hard and harsh.

Except for those strangely fascinating eyes. They'd
seemed cold and soulless when she'd first glimpsed his
craggy face. But just now their glacial surface had melted
with an onslaught of emotion. Maybe it was only anger and
annoyance. But he felt things. Felt them deeply. Even if he
didn't want to.

And even if he didn't want to take her in, he had. So,
for whatever reason he had opened up his home, sparse and
uninviting as it was, she was grateful.

She slipped into the soft, faded denim shirt he'd given
her and buttoned it up to her neck. The tails hit her above
the knee, and she rolled the sleeves three times just to get
them past her fingertips. It was a vivid reminder of how
much bigger he was than she, how much stronger. More
man than she had ever seen before in real life. Miles and
miles of sculpted chest, sprinkled with earth-brown hair and
dotted with streaks of silvery snow just like the salt-and-
pepper hair that crowned his head. Jonas Beck was a force
of nature, like the storm or the mountain itself.

It seemed only fitting that a man like that should finally

come to her aid and—temporarily, at least—stop the madness that pursued her.

Faith draped her clothes over the shower rod in the bathroom, then settled onto the boxy, antique gold sofa. She pulled Dr. Rutherford's handkerchief from her purse and checked to be sure the disk was intact. Then she carefully rewrapped it, inhaling the fading reassurance of Dr. Rutherford's spicy scent.

There were tears in her eyes as she stretched out beneath the scratchy, government-issue wool blanket. But she was warm and she was dry. And she was too exhausted to decide whether or not she trusted her misanthropic host.

Faith slept. Deep and hard. Her dreams were filled with visions of faceless stalkers with hands that tore at her and snatched away her memories and hopes. She ran from huge, wicked knives that cut her unmercifully, that sliced out her heart. She ran and ran until her legs gave out. And then she was falling. Spinning helplessly out of control, down into the stormy rapids of a bloodred stream.

Before she crashed against the rocks, a giant, blue-eyed bear caught her in his jaws and pulled her free. His massive paws held back the flood of crimson as he carried her to shore.

But was he taking her to safety? Or was she a tender morsel about to be gobbled up?

WHAT THE HELL?

Was that coffee? Jonas pushed the pillow off his face and crinkled his nose, testing the air once more. The fragrant, homey scent reminded him of one of the earliest memories of his childhood. Before…

"Ah, hell." He shot up in bed, scratched at the stubbly beard growth on his jaw and neck, and cursed the morning. He knew enough about the harsh realities of life to hate them.

This was the worst time of day. A time when soldiers woke up to surprise attacks. A time when the creeps and cheats and villains of the night scuttled away to hide, lying in wait for the next sunset and their next innocent victim. Morning was an unsettling time when he never knew what to expect from the day. Peace or violence? Success or failure? Life or death?

For him it had never been about the mouthwatering smells of food cooking and coffee brewing. Not in his house.

He pushed aside the cotton sheet that pooled at the waistband of his black boxers and swung his feet to the icy wood floor. It might be the end of summer, but at this altitude, mornings were still downright cold.

He pulled on his jeans and scrounged through his dresser for a clean pair of socks. If he didn't have company, he'd have skipped the white T-shirt he shrugged over his arms and torso. He strapped on his watch. It was only 7:00 a.m. What was she doing out there, anyway? Humming? Singing?

He'd have to put a stop to that right now. His scruffy morning glower ought to do the trick.

She saw him as soon as he opened the door. "Good morning."

She was pouring herself some coffee at the stove. She set down the mug and started puttering around the kitchen area with an efficiency that hurt his sensibilities. Jonas could only take up space and stare. God, she was bright and cheery. Sunny in looks and disposition. The hair that had been too wet to identify in color or style last night now fell in soft tawny waves across her forehead, while golden wisps of it brushed the apples of her cheeks, the straight line of her jaw and the nape of her neck.

Could he feel any more beastly compared to her fresh, fair-haired beauty? He'd never had to deal with company in his home before, much less perky, pretty, female company.

"I made breakfast." When she pulled out the chair at the table and indicated he sit, he noticed she'd set a place with matching silverware and a folded paper towel for a napkin. What the hell was she trying to pull with this domestic crap? He'd taken her in, hadn't he? He'd promised to get her car running again. What more did she want from him?

Jonas slowly eased himself into the chair, keeping a guarded eye on his houseguest. She still wore the shirt he'd loaned her last night. The sleeves were rolled up to her elbows and the tails were tied at her waist, revealing a stretch of smooth skin and the indentation of her belly button as she reached for the oven mitts on top of the fridge.

The chair legs scraped across the floor as he angled himself away from her Suzy-Homemaker-goes-to-camp impersonation. He shouldn't notice things like that about her. And he refused to acknowledge his vivid response to a little female flesh. His brain and mood might be frustrated, but his body wasn't too used up to resist the sexual call of an attractive woman. And that was wrong. It was pointless. She'd leave. No. He'd send her away. He had to.

Faith Monroe just didn't seem to have grasped that concept yet.

Jonas glared while she carried the plate to the stove and filled it. Then she poured him a mug of coffee and brought everything over to the table. "It took me a while to figure out how to fire up the woodstove. But then I realized it's a lot like the one my grandma had near Carthage. That's in southwest Missouri. Down in the Ozarks. That was before she moved in with Uncle Wes and me up near Saint Jo. That was after my folks died. Car crash. Uncle Wes and Gran raised me."

He watched her lips move, baffled by how she could have so much energy and make so much noise this early in the morning. "Do you always talk this much?"

His broody silence finally registered. That soft, crooked mouth snapped shut and the sunshine faded from her face. She paused a good foot from the table, forcing herself to lean forward at an awkward angle to set the mug down.

Then she quickly backed away to the sink, as if realizing too late that she'd climbed right into the cage with the hungry bear. "I wanted to thank you for helping me last night. I didn't have anywhere else to turn."

"You could have turned to the sheriff. Most folks would have."

"Sheriff Prince doesn't strike me as the kind of man who would listen to a different opinion once he makes up his mind about someone."

"He's not."

Curious. Last night she'd said Prince wouldn't let her explain her side of the story. He wondered what that story was and what was so unbelievable about it? Had she done something that made her afraid of being caught? Or had it been done to her? How long had she been running from the law?

And how desperate did a woman have to be before she decided *he* was the safest option?

"I'm sorry that I made myself at home." She turned her back on him, running soap and water in the sink and setting the skillet in to soak. "I know you said you wanted to fix my car and send me on my way. I didn't realize you meant at first light. I'm sorry for delaying you."

"Quit apologizing."

"You've done nothing but help me. I'm taking advantage—"

"Shut up."

A beat of silence passed.

"Excuse me?" Her spine stiffened before she turned, and there was reckless hell to pay brimming in her eyes. "I know I'm an inconvenience, Mr. Beck, but there's no call to be rude."

"I wasn't—" Jonas squeezed his hands into fists and shook them beneath the table. He didn't know which ticked him off quicker—that insulting, poor-me string of apologies, or her apparent ability to function in both perky and self-righteous modes so early in the morning. "I know that wasn't polite. But you said you didn't want nice, so I was just being myself.'' He breathed in deeply, collecting himself, digging up what he could remember of civil behavior. ''I don't know what you have to deal with, lady, and a lot of me doesn't care. I just…I need quiet in the morning.''

''Okay.'' Her face squinched into a cautious, contrite expression. ''Do you take milk or sugar in your coffee?''

He glared.

''Sorry. No talking.'' She pantomimed zipping her mouth shut, but it didn't work. ''I'll just leave you to eat your breakfast and go back out on the porch. You had a beautiful sunrise this morning.''

This woman was full of surprises. ''You were up to see the sunrise?''

Her gaze drifted to some place far away. ''I didn't sleep all that well. I have a lot on my mind.''

Welcome to the club.

But Jonas didn't comment out loud. He picked up his fork and debated as to where to start tackling the mound of food she'd piled onto his plate.

Obeying his request for silence, she dried her hands, picked up her coffee and headed toward the front door. His alert eye couldn't help but notice how the baggy sea of his shirt tied above her waist emphasized the hug of her jeans across her firm, round backside. But the peace and the view were too good to last. At the door she turned, her expression sheepishly apologetic. ''I ate two eggs and two slices of bacon and a piece of toast.''

Jonas shrugged. ''Why do I care?''

''So you know how much I've borrowed from you.'' She pulled a small notebook from the shirt's pocket and snapped it in the air. ''I've written everything down. This is my second cup of coffee, too.''

''You wrote all that down?''

''Of course.'' She stuffed the notebook back into the shirt. ''So I'll know how much to pay you back. I'm strapped for cash right now, but as soon as everything is resolved, I'll—"

"I'm not broke. You can eat my food."

"That's not the point. I was raised to be responsible."

"I'll bet you were."

He'd been raised to... Hell. Even though she'd dropped that clue about losing her parents, she probably came from a wholesome, sane, *Leave-It-To-Beaver* childhood. He came from the system. He'd been raised to survive. As an adult he'd been trained to ensure that others survived. If she had the least inkling about the men and women he'd put in prison or *eliminated* to keep those who protected his country honest, she'd bolt out of here just as fast as she'd run up his mountain in the first place.

If his shocking appearance and beastly mood didn't scare her away, the truth certainly would. He'd noticed her enough to make him edgy with a sexual hunger. He'd noticed her enough to be curious about her story. He'd noticed her enough to regret being such a grouchy son of a bitch in the mornings.

And none of that was good.

Fix her car and send her on her way.

He decided he wasn't going to give a damn about Faith Monroe and her fears. He wasn't going to get riled up over her sassy sense of fair play. And he definitely wasn't going to care about how an innocent like her was going to survive in the world once she left his mountain.

"We'll settle up later," he offered, saying what she needed to hear in order to get what he wanted. "Now, go on and give me some peace."

Once she closed the door behind her, he pulled the chair up to the table to eat. He pushed the first forkful into his mouth and stopped short. Damn. This was good. It was just eggs and bacon and toast, but she'd done something with the eggs and—ah hell—he didn't want to like this. He didn't want any special treatment or for her to feel beholden to him or have any reason to stay one minute longer than she had to.

Jonas wolfed down the breakfast a shade too fast to really enjoy the savory tastes, then hit the bathroom for a shave and finished dressing. He was going to fix Faith Monroe's car and get her out of here.

Whatever her trouble was, it couldn't be worse than his.

"Faith?" It felt odd to say a woman's name on his tongue. But when he walked out onto the porch, he found it empty. Her coffee mug sat on the railing in front of the porch swing, which was swaying gently back and forth in the morning breeze. Damn. How long had she been gone? His internal radar was on the fritz. That was another reason he needed to get rid of the distraction of having a woman around. "Faith?"

When the hell had she disappeared? Had she gone of her own free will?

The wilderness was a minefield of dangers for a greenhorn like her. It was too late in the morning for the big predators to be out hunting. Though a wolf or black bear wouldn't follow the usual rules if they were hungry. And the grazers were armed with horns and antlers and hooves. Elk. Mountain sheep. Hell, even a skittish mule deer could be a threat if she startled it.

And if she'd gone off into the forest with an animal of the two-legged kind...

Years of training cast aside disruptive thoughts and put his senses on full alert. He tuned his hearing to the slightest of sounds, scanned the clearing for any sign of a struggle. His black Humvee sports utility vehicle was still parked out front, so she hadn't stolen his car and run off on her own. Had she gone on a stroll to check out the scenery? Bingo. He squinted his focus to verify his suspicion and descended the steps two at a time. He jogged toward the flattened grass at the edge of the gravel drive and found a trail of feminine-size footprints.

She'd gone to her car. Instead of following the drive

down to White Horse Road and around the curve, she'd tried to retrace the shortcut she'd taken last night in the dark. Jonas muttered an annoyed curse and plunged into the brush after her. The steep terrain was muddy and slick. Forget the wildlife. If she lost her balance, she could hit a tree or a rock. She'd be damn lucky if she didn't break her neck before she reached the bottom.

"Damn fool woman."

This was how she repaid his help? Getting herself lost? Forcing him to get his boots muddy?

"Stop!" Her hoarse shout cut through the crisp morning air.

Jonas froze, every sense fine-tuned to his surroundings. But was that panic or pain or outright fear he heard in her voice?

"Stop it!"

A cry for help. Protective instincts that were as much a part of him as the blood flowing through his veins sparked to life. He unsheathed the bowie knife that hung at his side and charged down the hill to find her.

Chapter Three

Faith darted up the road, futilely giving chase to the unmarked white tow truck until the taillights of her car—or, more accurately, Liza's little red car—disappeared around the bend behind a thick carpet of aspen and lodgepole pines. She slowed to a walk, taking several more steps along the crumbling asphalt shoulder.

"Come back." Her last cry was muted with shock. The creep had stolen her car.

Surrendering to the truck's power and the road's incline, she finally stopped. The man in the tan coveralls and hooded sweatshirt had completely ignored her shouts. He'd taken off as soon as she spotted him through the trees. Why? Who was he? Had the police or the FBI—or Copperhead—found her? Had the man who'd murdered her boss and old school friend tracked her across three states to abandon her to the elements on this godforsaken stretch of highway?

Changing directions, she hurried back down the road toward town, trying to stay one step ahead of her panic. Whom did she call now? Sheriff Prince? Darien Frye? There had to be a way to track down the name Dr. Rutherford had given her. But how could she report the theft without drawing more attention to herself? And if the man was legit, why wasn't he towing the car down to Elk Point?

Did he plan to ransack the car as well, searching for the disk and the key to NT-6—whatever that might be?

Faith breathed deeply, in and out, her nostrils flaring. The same fight or flight tension that had propelled her out of Eclipse Labs and forced her to sneak out of her own home surged through her veins once more. A couple hours of sleep and one amazing sunrise were to be the only reprieve allowed her.

She was still on the run.

Faith patted the soft bulge of the well-wrapped disk in her pocket. She was still being pursued.

She slowed her pace to a deliberate walk and scanned her surroundings. The road cut a narrow swath between the trees and rocky landscape, leaving a stalking killer plenty of places to hide. Maybe he was here. Right now. Watching her. Waiting for her to walk into his trap. Waiting with his knife to gut her the way he had William Rutherford and Danny Novotny…and Liza Shelton.

Copperhead. A venomous snake all too common around the Ozark lakes and mountains where she'd spent her childhood. A deadly expert in camouflage, lying unseen along a dirt path or hidden among the roots of a tree, waiting to strike its unsuspecting prey.

It was an apt nickname, fitting the deadly stealth of the man who pursued her. Who terrified her. Who had taken over her life in the span of one very long day.

Then she heard him. The same invisible menace who'd trashed his way through William Rutherford's lab thundered down the mountain behind her. The truck driver? Was he Copperhead? Had he parked the truck out of sight and come back to seal her fate?

Faith looked over her shoulder and saw a glint of silver shining in the dappled light among the trees. She instinctively retreated from the encroaching danger—a distorted shadow that descended the tree-studded incline at surprising speed, darting this way and that around obstacles in its path, moving relentlessly closer.

The silver flashed in the light again, its reflection lasting long enough for a weapon to take shape and dimension. A knife.

Copperhead.

"No—"

Faith stumbled backward, righted herself, then took off at a dead run down the center of the road. Her legs pumped quickly and methodically, eating up the ground in front of her. She was running blindly, anxious only to put distance between her and the man with the knife.

Images of William's blank, dying eyes—Danny's teasing smile—Liza's yearbook photo so full of life—her own bloody hands—bombarded her vision even as the sound of death trampled the earth behind her. The pounding footsteps became more of a sensation than a sound as a grinding roar stopped up her ears. She was gasping for breath now, the thin, high air turning her healthy lungs and fit body into a weaker, aching version of herself.

"Faith!" A dark growl pierced the oxygen-starved haze of the chase. A foghorn shattered her eardrums, snapping her into a moment of heart-stopping clarity. Darkness loomed behind her. The knife she'd seen—a big, wicked hunting knife—sailed through the air past her shoulder and speared the bark of an aging pine.

She screamed in the instant she felt the heat and heard the roar at her back. The horn blared again. Awareness of the real danger at her heels came too late.

She veered to the right, but a timber-size vise clamped around her waist and lifted her off her feet. Dragged up hard against a wall of muscle, Faith went airborne, flying toward the ditch. The truck with the red car in tow blared past, close enough to feel the rush of wind left in its wake.

Faith and her rescuer hit the ground with a jarring thud. And then they were skidding, tumbling, rolling. Locked

tight in the clasp of strong, sturdy arms, she realized that
he was taking the brunt of each hit, each scrape of exposed
rock, each splash of standing rainwater. When they finally
came to a stop in the muddy debris at the base of the ditch,
they were a tangled clinch of arms and legs.

For a moment, all she could do was lie there and catch
her breath, letting her swirling vision come to a standstill,
taking note of each bruise and ache along her legs and hips
and back. Taking note of the fact she was still alive, still
in one piece.

Still in danger.

Faith squirmed beneath the crushing weight of the man
lying on top of her. "My car," she wheezed. She shoved
against his shoulders. "He's stealing my car."

The man's weight shifted onto the cradle of her hips as
he pulled his arms from beneath her and propped himself
up on his elbows at either side of her. Faith's lungs filled
with precious air and Jonas Beck's craggy, scarred face
came into focus above her. He, too, was breathing hard. His
broad, hard chest expanded in a deep, quick rhythm that
matched her own, brushing against the sensitized peaks of
her breasts with each and every breath.

Oh, God. That…tingled. She tried to suck in her stomach, to lessen the contact she couldn't escape. But when
she needed to breathe deeply again, her breasts thrust up
against him, and the tingling became a distracting, drizzly
warmth that poured throughout her body, gathering in force
beneath the pressure of his hips on hers. What was wrong
with her?

"Son of a bitch."

That doused her body's untimely response. "Mr.
Beck—"

Faith turned her face from the damning tirade that flowed
from his lips. His first words were the kindest he uttered
about the barreling truck that had almost flattened them like
pancakes. "It's practically impossible to stop on this grade,

but he didn't even slow down." Five callused fingers grabbed her jaw and angled her face back to his. He wasn't hurting her, but she couldn't free herself from his steely grip. "Didn't you see him?"

Above her, those ice-blue eyes glittered with an emotion that mystified her. He was communicating something more than a taunting reprimand, but she couldn't answer what she didn't understand. Faith's anxiety shifted from thoughts of lost freedom to something much more immediate. "I came down to check the car. He was headed up the mountain. He must have turned around. I think he tried to…on purpose."

Her voice trailed away. She already felt helpless and small, pinned beneath Jonas's body and trapped within his grasp. He didn't show any signs of getting up, of trusting her on her own two feet. How could she explain her fears about what pursued her without sounding crazy or paranoid, to boot?

"He did that deliberately?"

"I don't know. I'm not sure."

The grip on her jaw tightened enough to demand her attention. "That's a hell of an accusation. Did he or didn't he?"

Not the most persuasive way to earn her cooperation. A flash of self-righteousness, fueled by embarrassment, sparked her temper. Even though it was a futile effort, she wrapped both hands around his wrist and tugged against his grip. "Get off me."

Foolhardy never even crossed her mind as she gave vent to her frustrations and struggled against him. Her body lurched beneath his and his eyes squeezed shut. The scar that bisected the upper half of his face furrowed as he winced. "Shit."

His hand clenched around her chin, then quickly released her, as if suddenly remembering his considerable ability to inflict pain. He dug his fingertips into the mud beside her head, clutching the very ground itself to control… To control what? What did he have to be so upset about? She was the one with a murderer on her heels.

"Why don't you watch your mouth?" she challenged. "Expand your vocabulary to something nice. You sound like an R-rated movie."

"Watch *my*—?" His eyes popped open, bathing her in a sea of crystalline fire. "You're the one with some explaining to do. Why the hell did you run from me?"

"What were you doing with that knife?" she countered.

"You asked for my help."

"I asked to stay the night."

"You screamed."

"You scared me."

"You almost got yourself killed!"

Jonas got the last word with that one. Their rapid-fire expression of pains and tempers fell silent at the import of just how close she'd come to death. Again.

Shocked by the bottom-line truth, she opened her fists and mindlessly tangled her fingers into the soft, faded folds of his chambray shirt. She felt nothing soft beneath the material, and trembled at the dangerous illusion of power she felt at touching all that brute strength without being harmed by it.

He'd shielded her with that very strength. It was a heady, humbling feeling.

"You saved me." She swallowed hard, fixing on the beating pulse along the column of his neck, as she worked through the terrible risk this stranger had taken to protect her. "You could have been killed, too." Through the barrier of cotton, her fingers brushed across that sculpted wall of strength. "Thank you."

The words felt inadequate. But as her fear and anger receded, other thoughts, more startling, more pleasurable, crept back into her conscious mind. His face might be initially shocking to look at; with its strikingly harsh expression she suspected one grew accustomed to it rather than learned to love it. But there was something utterly fascinating about Jonas Beck's body.

With his hips pinning hers in the soaking mold of mud and water, she realized her legs had veed apart and his trunklike thigh was wedged at her most intimate place. His scent, intensified by the exertion of his efforts to save her, was simple and fresh. Plain soap and musky man. And despite the rough angles of his face, the texture of the skin itself was remarkably smooth. Up close like this, she was learning firsthand about the taut, broad muscles of his arms and chest—and how precisely he controlled them.

Mammoth as it was, there was an artistic proportion to his body that made her feel as if she'd been wrestling with Michelangelo's statue of *David*. She was vibrantly aware of the raw potency of his overwhelming masculinity and how completely feminine that made her feel.

Her body's softening, feverish response distracted her from both her violent past and shaky future. For a few moments she savored the surprising sensations that warmed her body from the inside out. And she pondered the notion that this beast of a man with the scarred face and foul mouth and brutish temperament should be the one to awaken such a curious warmth inside her.

But this was neither the time nor the place—nor the man—to discover the extent of her body's sexual awakening. She needed to focus on staying safe, and on finding the truth and clearing her name with the authorities. What her body thought she wanted wasn't important. She resolutely lifted her gaze to his face. "I think you'd better get off me now. Please?"

His eyes had closed, his mouth had squeezed into a grim line, but he nodded. "I'm working on it."

Faith tried to wiggle free, immediately feeling less concerned about escaping her own wayward thoughts than by the reason he'd been lying so still for so long on top of her. "Are you hurt?"

"It'll pass." He placed an encompassing hand at her waist to hold her still. Long, callused fingers sizzled against the bare skin of her back as they slipped beneath the tied hem of her voluminous shirt.

Faith ignored her impulse to scoot away from the overly familiar touch. The big man was in pain. "Did the truck hit you? A rock? Are you cut?"

His eyes blinked open. "You nipped me with your knee on the last bump."

"Nipped you?"

"In the crotch, lady."

"Oh." Embarrassment flooded her own cheeks. He could be hurt by something so basic? She'd somehow imagined him to be impervious to injury. Except for that scar. "I'm sorry."

"I'll be fine in a minute. Let's just move slowly until then, okay?"

"All right. Can you roll to the side and I'll sit up?"

"Yep."

With his steely control evident in the tight clench of his jaw, Jonas shifted his weight onto one elbow and tilted his hips off Faith. A breeze of cool air swept over her body, chilling her with goose bumps. When she was sure it was safe, she slipped across her bed of mud and beaten-down leaves and sat up across from him. The September morning felt colder than it had earlier, now that his body wasn't shielding her with its strength and heat.

She watched Jonas take in steadying breaths of air and slowly exhale while she huddled inside her wet clothes and mud-spattered skin. With the equally powerful rushes of adrenaline and unexpected desire waning, Faith was able to think rationally again. She wiped a splotch from her cheek and tucked her hair behind her ear, leaving her hand to rest against her neck. "I'm sorry I got you involved in all this."

"Just what am I involved in?" His blue eyes were piercing as they searched her face.

She slipped her hand down to her right front pocket, double-checking the condition of the hidden disk. Those ice-blue eyes followed the movement, but asked no more questions. Faith pushed herself to her feet and busied herself straightening her sticky clothes, uncomfortable with his perception that seemed to know a lot more than his silence let on.

He probably thought she was an idiot or a crazy lady already, and any explanation resembling the truth of her predicament would only cement that opinion of her. She summoned her best young executive tone instead, coming up with a halfway decent excuse. "I borrowed that car from a friend for my vacation. First, I let it run out of gas, and now I lose it. I'm not sure how I'll explain my lack of responsibility." The sheriff had already said the car belonged to a dead woman. "Explain it to my friend's family," she hastily amended.

"I thought you were raised to be responsible." He mocked her with the assertion she'd made at breakfast. "What about the truck trying to run you down?"

"My tired imagination."

Jonas rolled to his feet, not buying her bull. "So the big man with the big knife you thought was chasing you through the woods had nothing to do with you running out into traffic?"

She felt the color draining from her cheeks and turned away. "Maybe you did spook me a little."

He stalked past her to the tree where his knife was imbedded and wedged the blade free. "You're a lousy liar. You're scared of something. Scared shi—spitless." He wiped the knife clean on his pant leg and snapped it into the leather sheath at his waist. "And until you learn to take care of yourself better, I'd stay out of the middle of the road and I'd stick to the truth. Chances are the sheriff hired someone at a local garage to tow your car. The driver went up to the next turnaround because the road's narrow here. Either he didn't see you, or you do have something serious to worry about.''

He turned his back on her and strode toward the path through the trees where he'd descended earlier. Faith ran to catch up to him, then marched in doubletime to match his pace. ''But why would the sheriff do that? You told him you'd fix the car. Why would he take it without my permission?''

''I don't know why, I'm only suggesting a possibility.'' If he was feeling any of the suspicions she did, he didn't show it. He started up the incline and Faith scrambled up after him. ''Maybe Prince was trying to be neighborly. He doesn't like that you stayed the night with me.''

Using her hands as much as her feet, she fell into step behind him, too confused to argue the point. Jonas handled his knife with the cool efficiency of a hired killer. His antisocial act could be the ultimate cover for a man as lethally deceptive as Copperhead seemed to be. Maybe Jonas Beck was the very thing she needed to fear most—Sheriff Prince and his deputy did. But the logic of it didn't make sense. ''If they took my car, they've virtually abandoned me with you. How is that safe?''

He halted above her and turned. Faith pushed herself to a standing position, eliminating only a fraction of the height difference between them. He shook his head. ''I don't have answers for you.''

Then he did the most surprising thing. He held out his hand. To help her make the climb. Faith stared at the big hand, feeling an unexpected comfort in the polite gesture, yet she was very sure that *comfort* was not what he'd intended to offer.

A bone-deep need to connect with another human being and ease some of the terror and isolation that consumed her had her reaching out and laying her palm against his. His big, impersonal fingers folded her up in his grasp and he turned toward the path. But Faith tugged against the pull of his strength, refusing to blindly take even the little support he offered.

He paused and looked down at her expectantly, neither forcing her to follow nor releasing her.

"How do I know I can trust you?" she asked, looking for the answer in the icy shallows of his eyes.

"You don't."

She pressed her lips together, hesitating. Then she took a deep breath and spoke her heart. "I need to trust someone."

His eyes shadowed before he blinked, and then they were clear. Deep lines grooved beside his mouth as it curved into a humorless smile. "It's a kicker, isn't it?" He answered without giving her reason or permission to trust him.

Faith frowned. "What does that mean?"

"It means we're going back to the cabin to wash up. I'll call the sheriff on my cell. Then I'll drive you into town and we'll track down your *stolen* car."

"Mr. Beck, I—"

"Save it. I don't want to know your story. I don't want to be a part of your lies. I don't care what you need. I just want you on your way so I can get back to my life." He pulled on her hand. "Let's move it."

His life?

Just what kind of life did a recluse with such a hard face and even harder heart have?

But though his words held no comfort, his grip was gentle and his strength unwavering as he led her back up the mountain.

"Where is she now?"

The two executives strolled down the concourse of the Washington, D.C., Reagan International Airport, dodging tourists with too much luggage and commuters hurrying to make their morning flights. They looked like any other pair of politicians or CEOs discussing the business of the day. It was an easy role to assume. Easy and inconspicuous. Definite necessities given the circumstances.

"We had a sighting on the car in Wyoming. We had a man in place who confiscated the vehicle, but failed to neutralize her."

"I want you to handle it personally." The traveler with the senior authority plucked a shred of lint from the taller one's sleeve. "She may have switched vehicles again. Once she's located, use whatever assistance you need to keep her under observation until your arrival. I don't want to lose her this time."

"Understood." The taller one nodded. He was all business, never joking, never wasting words. He was well worth the considerable expense he was being paid. "The plan will be delayed with the added travel," he cautioned.

The one who was paying all that money shrugged. "I've been waiting a long time for this to come together. I can wait a while longer. I'll make the necessary calls."

They stopped at the baggage claim carousel to pick up their luggage. Not another word was spoken until they were on the move again. The shorter of the two flagged down a cab outside the terminal and asked, "Are we sure she has the disk?"

"Most likely. It hasn't turned up at the lab or her home or at any of her usual contacts. Perhaps her uncle?"

The short one's head moved from side to side, negating the possibility. "We have him under surveillance. Nothing yet. And Miss Monroe seems to be the type of woman who would endanger herself before allowing her family to be harmed. She won't go back to the farm any time soon."

"Perhaps she doesn't know what she's holding on to."

"Rutherford told her something, I'm sure." That was the real concern. How much did Faith Monroe know? Would she use it as a bargaining chip to ensure her and her family's safety? The idea of blackmail and exposure didn't sit well. Not as the potential victim, at any rate. "It could have been everything. It might have been nothing more than an old man pouring out his affection."

"Then why run?"

"You can be a very intimidating man."

A yellow cab jerked to a stop in front of them and the cabbie jumped out to take their bags and load them in the trunk. Public transport was such a step down from the usual limo ride. But this was part of the cover. It was a necessity in order to complete the plan. And nothing—no one—would stand in the way of the plan.

While the cabbie was arranging the trunk, they climbed into the back seat. The short one handed over an attaché case to the tall one. "Severing our connection to Eclipse Labs was too messy. This time, I want it neat."

"Dead bang," the tall one promised. He knew what was inside. He didn't have to count it. He wasn't the sort of man that one shortchanged.

His employer smiled. "Good. I don't care how you do it, I just want to know when it's done."

The tall one nodded. "Your problem will be resolved within seventy-two hours, and the disk will be returned to you."

"That's the best news I've had this week." It actually felt appropriate to smile. "This mission has been planned from start to finish. Now that we're so close, I won't let some dewy-eyed hick of a girl stand in my way."

"She won't be a problem much longer."

The tall man slid out of the cab with his money, gave the cabbie a generous tip and asked for his suitcase to be returned. By the time the befuddled driver had slid behind the wheel and pulled into traffic, heading for an office building near the Smithsonian, the tall man had disappeared inside the crowded terminal.

"Faith Monroe isn't any real threat." The cab's remaining passenger leaned back against the stiff vinyl seat, risking a smug smile at the prophetic turn of events. "Her father wasn't, either."

"WHY DIDN'T YOU call before towing my car? We could have avoided this whole misunderstanding."

"I'm telling you, lady, I didn't tow your car." Faith had yet to get a satisfactory answer from the gum-chomping teenager in the grease-stained coveralls at Bill's Tire and Garage. "The guy who dropped it off said he was from Beaverton. He was passin' by, thought it looked like a hazard. There's hardly any shoulder up there as it is. I only put it up on the rack for repairs like he told me."

Faith schooled her patience on a deep breath and tried again. "All it needs is a tank of gas. There's nothing that has to be fixed." She gestured up toward the suspended car. "Bring down my car. I need it."

But Bill Jr. was more concerned about the giant blocking the front entrance of the shop than Faith's complaints. "It's thirty-five bucks for the tow," he mumbled. "I can't release it until somebody pays the fee."

"You just said you didn't tow it."

"I didn't say I didn't have to pay for it." Maybe the fact he never looked her straight in the eye made her doubt his sincerity. "The guy charged me thirty-five bucks."

"Some favor." The fear of being stranded and at the mercy of any more close calls like a mystery driver in a runaway truck fed her frustration. "What's the name of the garage in Beaverton?" she demanded. "This whole thing sounds like a scam to me. Are you sure you weren't driving? Maybe you're making up this whole blackmailing, good-neighbor story because you nearly ran me down and you're afraid of losing your license."

Jonas, standing off to the side with his hands hooked into the front pockets of his jeans, filled the doorway from frame to frame. His silver-dusted hair brushed the crown of the open archway and his tan leather work boots were rooted to the concrete floor. But no matter how casual his stance might be, his imposing size and grim countenance gave the impression he was unhappy about not only putting her up for the night, but chauffeuring her back to town.

Bill Jr. wasn't the only one unnerved by Jonas's brooding silence. He shoved his hands deep into the pockets of his tan coveralls and shifted on his feet.

While Faith took perverse comfort in the fact Jonas hadn't tried to charm or befriend her and ask curious questions, she was beginning to wonder why he hadn't. How could a man chew her out for talking too much in the morning, then turn around and dive in front of a speeding truck to save her life? What peculiarities made a man defy the local authorities, open up his home to a stranger and then raise a stink about thank-yous and paybacks? It was a strange code of honor Jonas Beck lived by, the tenets of which Faith was certain were inviolate.

The man drove her nuts, frightened her and fascinated her by turns. He wielded that big hunting knife with the finesse of a killer and had the strength to break her in two. Yet she'd caught herself sneaking peeks at the controlled power of those very same hands on the steering wheel as they drove into town, and remembered with vivid detail their shielding, possessive grasp on her as they tumbled down into the ditch. What would those hands be like as they held a woman in the throes of passion? What would they be like clasped around the neck of her enemies?

And did any of it really matter? As soon as she had her car, she'd be moving on. Before Sheriff Prince and his friend-in-need act could alert the Saint Louis police or the FBI or anyone else of her whereabouts. Jonas Beck, reclusive man of the mountain, would simply be another less-than-friendly chapter in the bizarre nightmare of the past two days.

She'd seen a man die. She'd cost a friend her life. A

security guard was dead. Her uncle and grandmother were missing and she'd nearly been flattened like a pancake. She had a disk to protect, a name to find and an unspoken promise to keep. She should worry less about Jonas's snarly moods and sexy hands, and worry more about her own survival.

"Were you driving that truck?" Faith prompted, drawing on what reserves of energy she had left.

But Bill Jr. chomped his gum and refused to look her in the eye.

"Answer her." Jonas took one step into the garage and the teen shot to attention. Then he doubled up in a fit of coughing. Had he swallowed his gum?

As annoyed as she was that two words from Jonas could accomplish what a tirade from her could not, the intimidation factor worked. As soon as the boy recovered, he started talking.

"No, sir. The man drove in early this morning, just like I said, and left the car. Said he was saving me a trip up the mountain and charged me thirty-five bucks. He said to be sure the little lady paid me back." *Little lady?* How far back into the hills had she traveled? "Look, I got a pump out back. I can fill it up for you if that's all it needs." He backed off a step when he raised his gaze to Jonas again. "But it'll still cost you thirty-five dollars for the tow. Otherwise, Dad'll have my hide for paying it."

Faith squeezed the purse at her hip in fists of frustration. Thirty-five dollars might as well be thirty-five thousand. Probably because she'd run from the police in Saint Louis, her credit cards had been canceled. And when she'd tried to get cash in Scottsbluff, Nebraska, the ATM ate her bank debit card. She forced a smile onto her face. This boy was in a bit of trouble himself. Maybe he'd give her a break. "Would you take a check?"

Surely, by the time the draft cleared, she'd have this mess straightened out. It didn't feel like a sure thing, though.

Bill Jr. confirmed it. "I can't take an out-of-state check."

"But—"

"Your plates say Missouri."

"Here." Jonas intervened, thrusting a handful of cash at the young mechanic. "Here's thirty-five to get the car out of hock." The teen's eyes swelled as Jonas unfolded more bills from the wad of cash in his money clip. Faith's eyes rounded, too. Where did Jonas get that kind of cash? "And another forty to put gas in the tank and drive it back to my cabin. And I wouldn't recommend handing out any more money to strangers."

"Sounds like good advice, Beck." Sheriff Prince sauntered through the doorway, his face wreathed in a good-ol'-boy smile as he tipped his hat to Faith. "Ma'am. I'm glad I caught you." She hoped that was just an unfortunate choice of words. As she shifted to face him, he nodded at a point over her shoulder. "You take your thirty-five dollars and run along now, Billy. I'll handle this."

Bill snatched the cash from Jonas and dashed into the office adjoining the garage. Faith hadn't realized what a big man Hamilton Prince was. Portly rather than muscular, he carried an air of authority that said he ran this town. Elk Point was his kingdom. She was not only a peon, she was an outsider. And despite his benevolent expression, his hand rested on his holster.

Whether the warning was intentional or not, Faith hugged her arms in front of her and retreated.

And nearly laughed with crazy relief when she bumped into Jonas. Sheriff Prince might be big, but he wasn't even in the same class.

There was something at once confining and reassuring, knowing there was a solid wall of man standing right behind her. There was no escaping her position now. But then, maybe she didn't want to. She could feel Jonas's breath lightly stir her hair. And she was warmed by his abundant heat. It was a good thing, too. Her knees couldn't seem to stop shaking and her skin was a sea of goose bumps.

"Did you need something from me, Sheriff?" she asked, gathering her composure.

He shrugged. "'Fraid you're gonna have to enjoy our hospitality for a bit longer. I got a wire this morning. I have to hold that car as evidence. Seems the woman it's registered to isn't just dead. The Feds say—"

"She was stabbed to death." If Prince wanted to make casual conversation out of Liza's senseless murder, she wasn't about to oblige him. Anger and grief battled inside her. "Liza Shelton was a good friend of mine. I haven't even come to grips yet with the fact that she's gone. She was funny and outrageous and the most generous woman I've ever met. Is that what you want to know? She loaned me her car, and a few hours later I see a federal agent on the news talking about her death."

Faith swiped her fingers through her hair and caught them at the side of her neck, hugging herself even tighter. "She was fine when I talked to her yesterday morning. She was alive and happy and eager to make the acquaintance of a cute guy who lives in her building. I borrowed her car. I gave her mine. I didn't kill her."

"I didn't say you did." The sheriff tilted his head and nodded, doing a poor job of acting as if the accusation hadn't already crossed his mind. "It's funny, though, the FBI getting involved in a local homicide. Must be something more going on. Can you prove you didn't steal this car? And how come you're running so hard and so fast to get away from your *good friend's* murder?"

Faith didn't know whether to slap that patronizing smirk off his mouth or burst into tears. "I didn't kill her."

"Well maybe, since she had *your* car, somebody thought they were killing you." She felt light-headed at the possibility that Liza's death had been a case of mistaken identity.

It went down about as well as the idea she'd been murdered in retaliation for helping Faith escape.

She fought through the haze in her brain to say something to defuse the sheriff's speculations. "Why would someone want to kill me?"

"Why don't we go over to my office and relax while we wait for the Feds to arrive," Prince offered. "Maybe they want an answer to that question, too."

"The Feds?"

The sheriff nodded. "They said they're sending someone to follow up on my lead."

No. She had to leave. Going with the sheriff meant surrendering her freedom. It meant losing what little chance she had left to find out the truth. She had to find Darien Frye and give him the disk and get her life back. "I can't—"

"Do you have a warrant, Sheriff?" Faith's breath rushed out on a startled gasp as Jonas's heavy hand settled over her shoulder. "A subpoena for her testimony?"

"I…" Put off only for a moment, the sheriff rebounded with an all-knowing smile. "You're looking mighty chummy there, Beck. She an old friend of yours? Now that *would* make me curious."

Her panic dulled beneath the support of Jonas's hand and the blatant challenge in his voice. "Are *you* conducting an ongoing investigation that involves Miss Monroe?"

Faith let her hand slide down her neck. She latched on to Jonas's hand, not yet realizing the significance of turning to him for security and comfort. But the sheriff's gaze zeroed in on the tangible connection. "It sounds like the Feds might."

"Then the Feds can come ask her questions." Keeping his hand linked to hers, Jonas pulled her into step beside him and steered her out of the garage. "We're out of here."

Chapter Four

"Where are we going? Your car's back there."

Jonas didn't answer. Faith trotted along beside him in double-time to keep up with his long strides as they passed by the brick facades of antique shops and souvenir stores. Right now, he needed distance and time between them and the enemy. He couldn't think of the sheriff in any other way. Prince knew something about Faith. Some damn secret that could get her into a lot of trouble.

And she was definitely in trouble.

For a few conscientious seconds back in that garage, he'd tried not to care about her trouble. She was stranded. She was broke. She was dirty and exhausted. He'd tried not to react to the sweet curve of her rump brushing against his thighs. But leaning into his stomach and chest had been a purely innocent, maybe subconscious, plea for help. And while he could control his emotions and ignore his libido, his training had leaped to the fore.

Jonas refused to question how easy it had been for him to slip into protective mode with her. The idea of having feelings—protective or sexual or otherwise—for this young, ingenuous woman was too dangerous for him to dwell on.

Yet here he was, paying her debts, going toe-to-toe with Hamilton Prince—and touching her—because she needed a champion.

"You can let go of me now." She released his hand and pulled away, dropping a step behind.

Jonas clamped his fingers around her upper arm and hauled her back to his side. "What the hell is going on with you?" he demanded. "Do you have any idea how much trouble you are?"

"Don't cuss." She shoved a fist at him. It was a half-hearted wallop that bounced off his shoulder. "I don't think I'm the problem here. You're the one dragging me down the street."

"Do you know something about that murder? Because someone sure as hell knows a lot about you, *little lady*. Any clue how a stranger from another town knew that car belonged to you?"

She froze for an instant. Her eyes widened like saucers. And then she smacked him for real. "Let go of me."

For a mouthy bundle of femininity who didn't even reach his shoulders, she was one hell of a handful. Suddenly she was all arms and legs and twisting hips. A sure sign of desperation. Jonas didn't want to hurt her. But he had to protect himself. Protect her. He had to get her quiet and out of sight before anyone questioned what was going on.

He picked her right up off the ground, pinning her arms between them, and carried her into an alleyway between two buildings. He backed her up against the brick wall and hugged her tight to his chest, absorbing her struggles into the ample strength of his body.

"Faith. Faith!" He tried to reason with her, but she wasn't listening. "I know I'm not wearing a badge anymore, but I'm not the bad guy here. If you run from me, Prince'll pick you up and slap you in a cell so fast you won't have time to catch your breath, much less explain whether you're innocent or not."

Her struggles ceased instantly. She was afraid. As afraid of whatever pursued her as she'd been of him last night in the storm. They stood there for several moments, the only sounds were stuttered gasps for air as they caught their breaths. Jonas didn't dare move, in case this surrender was a decoy to gain her freedom. He held her still, in what might have passed for an embrace to any curious onlooker. Her fingers splayed against his chest, his hands cradled her neck and back, his hips pinned hers against the wall.

For one dangerous moment, his body reacted as if this *was* a real embrace. She was firm and round in his hands, not skin and bones. She was soft and yielding in every place that was hard and yearning on him. His mind might be warning him to keep his distance, but his body was begging him to seize the temptation of the proud, pert breasts that branded his chest, or the cradle of full, succulent hips that framed so perfectly within his own.

But it wasn't real. Innocence—even Faith's frustrating, seductive version of it—no matter how tightly he held it in his arms, would never be his.

"Someone tried to kill you this morning up on White Horse Road, and it wasn't me. Maybe you'll want to pick your fights a little more wisely next time."

Faith tipped her head back against his hand, letting the silky tendrils of her hair slide across his fingers like a rare caress. But there was nothing tender and shining in her eyes, and he was doubly sure there was nothing soft and understanding shining from his.

"I'm sorry. I shouldn't...I shouldn't have hit you." She hadn't inflicted any damage. He held her, suspended six inches off the ground, and *she* was apologizing to *him.* "I already hurt you this morning when...you saved my life. I don't seem to be doing a very good job of repaying you for your help."

Jonas's lust faded beneath his cynical thoughts. Did she see everything in black and white? Think that for every gift there should be a reward? For every slight there should be punishment? In the real world there were givers and there were takers. And he'd seen a lot more of the latter. He'd tackled a lot tougher adversaries than she was without an apology or a thank-you. Still, the effort she made to treat him like any other human being helped him find a bit of patience.

"You want to tell me what's going on now?" he asked, lowering her to the ground and backing off far enough to let her breathe normally while keeping her in place.

Her fingers curled into the loose cotton of his shirt, pulling it taut at the center of his chest. Her gaze focused there. "You said you didn't want to get involved."

"You didn't leave me a choice, lady. Prince thinks we're an item now."

She frowned. "An item?"

"Yeah, I know. You and me—it's hard to stomach." He and anyone as fresh and pretty as Faith Monroe was never going to happen. But reality was beside the point. Jonas had publicly staked his claim. And Prince, for now at least, was buying it.

Now that she was calm—physically, at any rate—and he was in control of his hormones, he nudged his hand beneath her chin and tipped her face up. "So what's going on?"

For the longest moment, long enough for him to discover the warm, velvety texture of her skin along her jaw and throat, her wide green eyes searched his face. She skittered away from the scar, then bravely returned to study it. Her gaze dropped to his mouth, skimmed over the bump at the bridge of his nose, then looked deep into his eyes. Jonas held himself in unblinking stillness beneath her scrutiny. She was searching for something. Trust. He could see the debate warring in her own eyes. She was deciding whether or not she could trust him.

He made no effort to sway her one way or the other. People either accepted the beast for who he was and dealt with the looks and the moods, or they ran in fear of him. If she accepted him, he would be her ally. The kind of ally who would place her life before his own. The kind who would exhaust every avenue to keep her safe and uncover the truth.

There didn't have to be any friendship or camaraderie or even payback to make the alliance work. It was just what he did. What he knew. It was the kind of man he was.

If she didn't accept him, then he'd walk away without a backward glance and let her face her demons alone. The same way he'd walked away from the family who'd rejected him. The same way he'd walked away from the career that no longer wanted him. The same way he'd walked away from every snide remark or teasing laugh or fearful look since the time he'd learned that fighting back only made him more of an outcast.

Truth be told, though, there was a tiny part of him—a remnant of a heart that very long ago used to believe he could be just like any other man—who didn't want to walk away.

But it would be her choice.

She unlocked her grip on his shirt and, for a few moments, focused on smoothing out the wrinkled denim. Lightly stroking his chest, petting him, soothing the big, scary man who picked her up like a sack of potatoes and dared to hold the fair maiden in his arms.

Though his muscles jumped beneath her tender touch, Jonas braced for her negative decision.

He was wrong.

"*Anymore*. You said you didn't wear a badge anymore." Her voice was hushed and throaty. "Did you used to be a cop?"

She raised her gaze to his again. Something inside Jonas paused and tried to make sense of her guileless question. Certain rejection had become cautious consideration. An emotion he wasn't very familiar with tried to kick in. But he couldn't tell if it was amusement or admiration or relief. He'd let something slip and she'd picked up on it, despite being upset. He'd have to watch himself more closely. Not lull himself into thinking she was a harmless interruption to his solitary life who would go away if he just ignored her.

But he supposed she deserved an answer. "No. I worked for the government."

"FBI?"

"No." He could tell his answers confused her.

But he wasn't going to talk about it. Not in any detail. And not in an alleyway in the middle of Ham Prince's town. Not while every cell of his body was screaming with the urge to touch her, kiss her, take her.

Not when a quick glance took note of the two women standing across the street at the grocery store. Judging by their bent heads and sly looks, they were trying to decide whether he was committing a crime they felt honor bound to report to the sheriff's office, or if they should warn the new girl in town about Jonas Beck's dangerous reputation. The fact that Faith still wore her muddy jeans from their dive into the ditch probably compounded their low opinion of him.

"C'mon. You and I both have some explaining to do." He took her by the arm and pulled her back onto the sidewalk. Out of the shadows and into the noonday sun where those two busybodies could see them clearly and he could think without the distraction of Faith's body pressed into his. "For what it's worth, most of the time, I am the good guy."

"Most of the time?"

"Take what you can get, honey."

A quick scan of Main Street told him the sheriff's car was still down at Bill's Garage. The two ladies had ducked into the grocery store to spy through the window. And Hamilton Prince had called in a couple of his deputies.

Faith had seen them, too. "Are they watching me?"

"Both of us, I'm sure. Prince doesn't like to be told no." Jonas intended to give them all an eyeful. Of two law-abiding, worry-free citizens. He summoned some long un-used muscles and managed what passed for a smile. "You hungry for lunch?"

He felt her tension immediately. "You've already spent too much on me, and I can't afford it."

The two deputies parked outside the town's only restaurant and made a show of adjusting their badges and belts when they climbed out. "We *need* to have lunch."

"Oh. I don't know which sounds harder—hiding from the cops, or pretending I don't have to hide." Now she got it. "Okay. But I'll pay you back."

"Whatever." Jonas headed for the crosswalk. They could debate money matters later. They needed to get this show on the road.

"Wait." He let her pull away from his grip when he realized she didn't intend to bolt. Instead, she reached for his hand and laced her fingers with his. What was she doing now? She offered him a lopsided grin that was half apology, half coy request. And beautiful as hell. Damn. He shouldn't notice or care about stuff like that. "Couples who are an *item* don't walk through town dragging one behind the other."

If this was some charm or feminine wile thing to distract him so she could escape, he wasn't buying it. "You don't have to look too friendly. That's not believable, either."

"You can't keep picking me up like a chess piece and moving me to wherever you think I need to be."

"It gets the job done."

"Not every time, it won't." She squeezed tighter, her reprimand taking him by surprise. Though her hand was half the size of his, her grip was strong, confident. He liked the feel of her hand in his. But he let the feeling pass without reading anything into it. He was working. Sticking it to Prince and taking the heat off Faith. Nothing more. Nothing personal. It was something he knew how to do.

All too well.

NOT EVERY TIME, it won't.

By the time they were seated at a table across from each other at the Sweet Treat Café, Jonas had tried to come up with a situation in which his brute strength and superior training hadn't served him well. The results were few and far between, but each of them had been disasters.

His family.

The one criminal who'd always stayed half a step ahead of him.

Anything having to do with a woman.

Tenderness and compassion had been denied him as a child. And they didn't come naturally to him now. Maybe that's why nothing had lasted beyond a one- or two-night stand with a willing female. Why his stepsisters never did more than send him a Christmas card. Why a criminal legend had made Jonas's forced retirement such a bitter pill to swallow.

But his strength and cunning were more than enough to handle Mel Prescott and the other deputy Sheriff Prince had hired. They sat at the far end of the café, sipping coffee and laughing loudly to mask their scouting assignment. Faith sat with her back to them, but more than once, their gazes collided with Jonas's. Their jovial conversation would cease for a moment, then start up with all the more fervor, as if he couldn't spot them for the spies they were.

''So, who's picking up the tab?'' The waitress who'd served their meal beamed a smile. But her attempt to sound bubbly instead of nervous fell flat. She turned all her attention to Faith and tried to pretend her oversize customer with the permanent scowl wasn't there.

She was better than some. The service had been fine, though Jonas had seen her reluctant whisper to the hostess when she saw he'd been seated at her table. She hadn't said anything wrong, but she'd found a way to take his order, fill his coffee mug and clear the table without once making eye contact with him. It was no big deal.

To him.

Faith cleared her throat, looked the waitress in the eye, and pointed across the table, forcing the woman to look his way. "*He* will take the check."

This wasn't a matter of running out of money. He'd heard mothers teach their children the polite rules of society in that same tone of voice. Jonas resisted laughing at Faith's stalwart defense of him and held out his hand for the bill.

The waitress muttered, "Thank you, sir," and slipped the paper on the table beneath his outstretched hand, managing not to touch him before darting away.

He picked up the check and reached for his money clip. Faith rested her forearms against the table and leaned forward, her expression reminding him of a golden tabby with her dander up. "Is it my imagination, or was she rude?"

"That was typical."

"I think she's afraid of you. It must be awful to have people stare at you and whisper behind your back. You can't help the way you look." Faith squinched up her face and sank back in her chair. "Sorry. That didn't come out right. I meant…people shouldn't judge anyone else…." She sat up straight again, her mouth crooked into a beseeching smile. "Please help me out of this one."

He tossed a couple of bills onto the table, unfazed by the insult. "Don't apologize for being honest. *You* can't help the way I look, either. I wasn't born handsome. And after a face gets cut and broken a few times, you figure out it's never going to transform into handsome, either."

She didn't laugh. But then, maybe that hadn't been his intention. He couldn't intimidate the hell out of people *and* be accepted by them. She needed to understand that.

"How did you get that scar? It looks as if the injury was horribly painful." He'd endured worse physical pain than the night he'd received his devil's mark. But the inner scars it represented were ones that would never heal. "Sorry. I shouldn't ask that."

"No, you shouldn't." He rarely allowed himself to think about that fateful night. He wasn't about to comment on it now. "This conversation is about you. Not me."

"Right." She combed her fingers through her hair, leaving a wisp of it clinging to her brow. His fingertips itched to brush it back into place, to touch those fine, silky waves again.

But he folded his hand around his water glass instead. She was buying herself some time and emotional distance, not trying to entice him. There was no real personal relationship here, only the professional relationship that had cropped up since their accidental meeting on his porch last night.

She seemed to think he was a last-chance lifeline of sorts. And with a naive hope that he had never known for himself, she'd cautiously accepted his brief explanation about once working for a government security agency. She'd decided to trust him—to keep her safe, at least.

With that demonstration of optimistic faith, he wondered who else she'd blindly given her trust to before yesterday. Someone who'd taken advantage of her youthful beliefs and set her up to take the fall for the heinous crimes she'd described while she'd picked at her soup and salad.

With an unexpected detachment, Faith had recounted the past thirty-six hours of her life, from finding her boss's office ransacked to pounding on Jonas's door at three in the morning because she was afraid Hamilton Prince was going to arrest her for three murders she hadn't committed. She claimed she didn't have a motive, but circumstantial evidence put her at the scene of all three deaths.

All of the old suspicions twisted in his gut, warning him this was something big. Something deadly. Faith Monroe was caught up in the middle of a big picture she didn't understand. She was outlining possible scenarios that sounded way too familiar to him. Conspiracy. Organized crime. Government cover-up.

Those were the kinds of corruption The Watchers had tackled. Those were the types of witnesses he'd protected, the killers he'd brought to justice.

He didn't want to do this. He didn't want to be a part of her life.

But he already was. He'd become a part of it the minute he'd decided to answer her frantic knock.

"And you didn't recognize the truck driver?" he asked again. The simplest scenario was that whoever had killed the others had followed her to Wyoming to finish the job by killing her. "He didn't seem familiar to you?"

She shook her head. "It happened too fast. All I saw were those tan coveralls, like Billy was wearing." She was thinking, replaying the images in her mind. "But he had a sweatshirt on underneath. With a hood. It covered his face from the angle I saw him."

"And there were no markings on the truck?" She shook her head again. "I didn't see anything except the Wyoming plates myself. It'll be simple enough to get a Beaverton phone book and check out the kid's story."

"And then what?" she asked.

Jonas lowered his voice in case Prescott and his buddy stopped their put-on laughter long enough to listen in. "We go to the library, of course."

MAYBE SHE SHOULD HAVE been the one to call the Beaverton Garage, thought Faith. According to Jonas, they had no one on a call near Elk Point. They claimed to have only two trucks, and both of them clearly bore their business logo. According to Jonas.

An unidentified man in an unidentified truck? Maybe she shouldn't be so ready to trust him. Of course, he had thrown himself in front of the truck to save her. But if he knew something and wasn't telling her, if he even suspected what was going on—shouldn't she be wary?

None of the other patrons seemed to be concerned by

their presence in the Elk Point Community Library. Of course, since only the quietest of hushed conversations were allowed, there wasn't much opportunity to gossip about the grizzly-size mountain man and his mud-stained companion, sitting at the bank of public-access computers.

Faith, however, grew increasingly nervous as each minute passed. Had she made a huge mistake in sharing her story with Jonas? She couldn't even think of him as Mr. Beck anymore. He now knew what frightened her, what haunted her footsteps. They'd created an odd sort of intimacy by trading secrets.

Not that he'd shared much. She still wasn't sure who The Watchers were. Or rather, who they used to be. She'd never heard of the top secret security organization. And Jonas had warned her that the government would deny its existence and his own if she got curious enough to check out his story. And now that The Watchers were supposedly disbanded, there would be no one around to verify his background, anyway.

He looked the part of a security operative, the kind of man who could save lives and mete out justice with equal skill.

But he could just as well fit the image of the man who pursued her.

In one horrible version of her imagined future, his former job as a security agent was just a story he'd made up to get her to talk. Even if he wasn't Copperhead, intent on retrieving the disk and killing her, he could still use the information to take advantage of her. He could trade her in to the sheriff in exchange for leaving him alone to grouch about his mountain in peace.

He could blackmail her, force her to become some sort of servant to his desires. Though he hadn't touched her sexually in any way, she'd seen the fire blazing in his eyes. In the alley, when she'd been so frightened, he'd touched her gently and stroked her beneath the chin. He hadn't been angry then. He'd been...hungry. For her? For any woman?

Now that was an unsettling prospect.

Faith glanced over at the man in the cubicle beside her. With Jonas intent on the information scrolling by on his monitor, she had a few moments to study his harsh profile. The strands of life experience that peppered his short, dark hair. The immense strength of his shoulders. The straight line of his back. The power and dexterity of his large, well-shaped hands.

Faith's pulse hummed a little faster through her veins. Though she would be slave to no man, the idea of being the object of Jonas Beck's desire wasn't an altogether objectionable idea. At once daunting and thrilling, she imagined making love to him would be like riding a wild tornado. There'd be little finesse. But there'd be no mistaking his desire, no denying his need.

In her sheltered life and limited experience with men, she'd never really fantasized about a lover. But the idea never seemed far from her mind now that she'd met Jonas.

Maybe that was all the more reason she shouldn't trust him.

"Any luck?"

Faith suddenly felt herself bathed in a gaze of clear icy blue. She blinked rapidly and turned back to her own computer as she realized Jonas had caught her staring. Fortunately, he didn't call her on it. "No, not yet. It takes several minutes to run each search. He wasn't listed under *scientist* or *engineer* so I'm running a more general search. If nothing shows up this time, I'll include other countries besides the United States. Or a deceased list. Maybe Dr. Rutherford's friend passed away and he didn't know it."

"Who would you give the disk to, then?"

"I don't know." Doubts crept in, fraying the edges of her determination again. "Maybe I'm not supposed to give it to anybody. But locating his friend could at least give me a place to start finding answers. There must be some useful connection.''

"Well, I hope you have better luck than I did.'' He wrapped the minidisk she'd shown him in Dr. Rutherford's handkerchief once more and handed it back to her. "None of these computers will run a disk this size. We need something high-tech.''

Faith lifted the disk and handkerchief to her nose, inhaling the fading scent of her friend and mentor, reminding herself why she was here in the first place. Before she lost the fight to the tears stinging the backs of her eyes, she stuffed the disk into her pocket and shook her head. "I'm not going back to Eclipse Labs.''

Jonas agreed. "I used to have access to the type of technology we need, but not anymore. Not legally, anyway. And there's nothing else we can use here in Elk Point.''

"How close is the nearest university?'' An academic lab or technology school would be likely to have the equipment they needed.

"Laramie.''

"Isn't that on the other side of the state?''

"Pretty much.'' He turned in his chair to face her. One of the craggy lines beside his mouth became a dimple as he tried to smile. "But I don't have any pressing business keeping me in Elk Point. Do you?''

"I can't let you drive me that far.''

His effort at gentling his expression vanished and he pushed to his feet. "Just write the mileage in that little book of yours and pay me back later.''

Faith snagged his wrist to keep him from stalking away. "I don't want to be your charity case. I already feel like I have no control over my own fate. I have to be responsible for something. It helps me believe I'm going to get my life back.''

"Shh.'' The white-haired librarian at the front desk took heed of their raised voices.

Jonas held up his hand by way of apology to the older woman, and Faith released him and spun away. The red-and-white message flashing on her computer screen reminded her just how lost she was: No Match Found.

She propped her elbows on the desktop and her chin in her palms, and considered how the same man could raise her hopes and fuel her desperation in the span of one short conversation. One minute he had her thinking they were a team, that there might even be some kind of friendship or unlikely attraction budding between them. The next, he made her mad enough to spit.

"That's the name you're looking up?"

Jonas's deep, hushed voice cut through her thoughts and alerted her to some unspoken danger.

Faith risked a glance at the front doors, but Mel Prescott and his watchdog buddy were still parked outside, leaning against the hood of their county car, sipping from their cups of coffee. They hadn't moved since she and Jonas had come in half an hour ago. Where was the threat?

A prickle of goose bumps teased the skin along the back of her neck. Maybe Jonas was the only thing making her nervous. "I've tried different spellings. I thought of using the name Darren, but I'm sure he said Dar-i-en with three syllables."

Jonas reached over her shoulder and punched the delete key. "No wonder someone tried to run you down."

"Hey." He clicked another button and her screen went blank. "Jonas—" She swallowed her surprise on a huff of air. "Why did you do that?"

His hands clamped around her shoulders and he was lifting her to her feet before he answered. "You have no idea what you're up against, do you?"

She lowered her voice to counteract his brutish invitation to leave. "We're in a public place. You'd think you could mind your manners here—"

He pulled her along beside him, ignoring the librarian's shocked *O* that pinched her lips. "Mr. Beck?"

"It's all right, Mrs. Curtis. I didn't find any books today, so we're leaving." With that terse explanation, the librarian reluctantly returned to her work as Jonas dropped a harsh whisper in Faith's ear. "Why don't you just send up a beacon and tell him where you are?" he accused.

Accused her of what? "What are you talking about?" Faith asked, trying to decide whether fear or anger was the better response.

Latching on to that now familiar spot on her upper arm, Jonas shoved open the double doors. Faith tried to take hold of his hand, but he was beyond any of the decorum she'd taught him earlier. Driven by some inexplicable demon, he scanned the parking lot and road beyond, then hurried her down the sidewalk toward the parking lot.

There was an urgency to his hold on her. His hand was firm, but not rough. "Dammit. He could have tracked you down through the Internet from the moment you first typed in his name thirty minutes ago."

"Why are you so angry? Do you know Darien Frye?"

"Gentlemen." He halted right in front of Mel Prescott, startling the deputy into dropping his cup and spilling coffee down his pant leg. He purposefully blocked Prescott's escape route to the driver's-side door.

"Beck." Prescott cleared his throat, making a poor effort at hiding his nerves. "Is everything all right?"

Jonas leaned in and Prescott immediately reached for his gun.

"Jonas!"

But his big hand locked down over Prescott's, preventing him from drawing his weapon. "You tell me. Who's your boss been talking to this morning?"

Mel was already shaking his head. "I don't... He just told us to keep an eye on you. I don't know what's going on."

Jonas freed him. His pointed gaze encompassed both men. "You do that. You keep a real close eye on me. Don't let me out of your sight." Even Faith shivered at the warning in his voice. "Or I may come back to haunt you."

"Why, you—" Prescott's useless threats stalled in his throat.

Jonas pushed Faith in front of him, angling himself like a shield behind her. She felt, more than heard, his lips dipping beside her ear. "I know Frye."

He stopped to unlock the passenger door on his Humvee, and Faith shook herself loose to protest being manhandled. "You see? This is why I don't want to owe you anything. I thought you wanted to help me. You can't keep hauling me out on the street and dropping bombshells without—"

"Get in the car." It was an order, not an invitation.

He wasn't even looking at her. Instead, his eyes were focused at some far point on the horizon.

Faith planted her hands on her hips and refused to budge. "I'm not going anywhere with you until you tell me what's wrong."

His answer was to scoop her up in his arms and set her inside.

"Dammit, Jonas!"

"Don't cuss in public," he mimicked her, pinning her to the seat with one arm and buckling her in with the other.

"Sometimes the situation calls for it." She pummeled the big shoulder that passed by her face. But she was trapped, prisoner to his unexplained whims yet again. She really had no way to hurt him, to overpower him, to put a dent in his cold, callous armor. "Jonas, please."

The battle between them ceased for an instant. He turned his head and looked at her. He had the oddest expression on his face. As if there was something softer, kinder, more patient inside him trying to get past the vivid slash of his scar and the glacial tint of his eyes.

Caught up in the mysterious message behind his features,

she didn't immediately see his hand come up beside her face. When her gaze darted to the broad, tanned fingers, he hesitated. His nostrils flared on a silent breath and then he brushed his fingers across the feather of her bangs that had caught in her lashes, and smoothed them off her forehead.

It was an awkward touch, but it was a gentle one. It was a tender gesture that surprised her with its calming effect on her temper, its soothing reassurance to her fears. And it surprised her by triggering something deeper inside. A slow-burning desire to touch him in the same gentle way.

The opportunity passed before she could act on it. Without further word, Jonas pulled away, closed her door and circled the hood of the car. Since he could pretend that charged moment hadn't happened, so could she. "The deputy's on the radio, calling something in," she reported, looking out her window while Jonas started the engine.

"I imagine he's telling Sheriff Prince that I assaulted him." He quickly backed out of the parking space and put the Humvee into gear. "Maybe he's telling him I assaulted you."

"Jonas!" The random bruises on her arms and legs were from their tumble into the ditch on White Horse Road, not anything he had inflicted on her. "I'm alive because of you. You haven't hurt me. And they can't arrest you for rudeness."

He made a grunting noise that she interpreted as a laugh. "That may not make any difference to Prince. It'd be a perfect excuse to lock me up." He pulled onto the highway heading up toward his cabin. "He'd like us to stay in town."

"And we're not going to?"

"Not for long." He checked the rearview mirror and pressed down on the accelerator, pushing their speed up to the legal limit.

She watched him check the mirror again, then grabbed

the armrest for balance as he zoomed around the first double-back curve. "What happened at the library?" she asked.

His voice grew darker, scarier, almost predatory in its warning. "You don't want to find Darien Frye."

"But that's the name Dr. Rutherford told me to remember. He made me say it twice. It's the only lead I have."

"He was probably warning you that Frye was responsible for his death." The Humvee picked up speed as it came out of the turn. "Frye is an old, uh...nemesis...of The Watchers. He has capabilities and influence you can't even imagine."

"Darien Frye killed Dr. Rutherford?" Jonas's next glance in the mirror raised her paranoia another notch. She turned around and looked out the back, then quickly righted herself. "We're being followed."

Jonas eyed the brown county cruiser in his side mirror. "I told Prescott to keep an eye on me."

"You *want* the deputy to follow us?" There was a devilish satisfaction in Jonas's expression when Deputy Prescott turned onto White Horse Road after them. He was playing a game of cat and mouse, only Faith wasn't sure which of them was the prey.

He never answered her question. "Frye wouldn't dirty his hands with the actual killing. But he'd pay good money to have it done. What else did Rutherford tell you?"

Faith closed her eyes and replayed the gruesome episode in her mind. There'd been so much blood. And he'd fought so hard to share a handful of words when he should have been fighting to live. She opened her eyes and watched the forested slope zip past her window. They were picking up speed. "I asked him who'd attacked him. He said a snake had done it, and that I needed to run away before he found me, too."

"A snake?" It sounded as if Dr. Rutherford's delirious answer made as much sense to Jonas as it had to her. She nodded. "A copperhead."

"Dammit." Jonas the beast was back again. He pounded the steering wheel with his fist, swiped his hand across his jaw and swore again. "This just gets better and better. Your boss was stabbed, wasn't he?"

Faith sidled closer to the door, feeling his edgy tension radiating throughout the car. What was going on? What did Jonas know? "The guard was stabbed, too. And Liza."

He shook his head and swore again.

"You're like a roaring animal when you curse like that. You scare me and you don't make any sense. You're a better man than that, Jonas. *I* deserve better." But his string of curses wasn't what made her clutch the door and turn to him. "You know what Copperhead means, don't you?"

His breath rushed out on an angry sigh, but he made a visible effort to curb the word on the end of his tongue. He pulled into his driveway and followed the curving road up to his cabin. Faith held on with both hands to keep her balance on the bumpy gravel driveway. Jonas didn't speak until the Humvee jerked to a stop and he'd turned in his seat to face her. She shrank back against her door, reading cold, unforgiving conviction in his eyes. "Copperhead is the code name for a hired assassin. We never could find out his real identity. Last I knew, he worked for Frye.

"If he's after you, you're as good as dead."

Chapter Five

"You've got ten minutes to get ready." Jonas climbed the steps to his porch in two long strides and opened the door. "Help yourself to anything you need and make a pit stop. We'll be on the road for a while."

Faith ran up the stairs behind him, barely keeping up with his determined pace. "You have some explaining to do." She followed him right into his bedroom. "What do you know about assassins? Who's Darien Frye? Why is he hurting the people I love?"

With methodical precision he cinched a leather sheath onto his belt and slipped in that long hunting knife. He opened his closet and pulled a metal box from the top shelf, unlocked it and pulled out a black leather holster and some type of gun. It, too, was black. Steel. With a thick handle and long barrel. Jonas slid back the top half of the barrel and set it on the bed. He pulled the holster on over his shoulders, stretching it to fit across his back as he returned to the closet.

"I won't let him get to you, I promise," he said, brushing past her without an emotional response or answering her questions. He dumped out a shoe box full of three black cartridges and boxes of bullets and proceeded to load each magazine. Then he shoved one into the gun's handle and tucked the others into his pockets. It was like watching a medieval movie as the knight suited up for battle. Only, these modern weapons were real. The knife and bullets and deadly serious attitude were very real. "It's what I do."

"It's what you *used* to do." He slid the top of the gun back into place with an ominous ratchet and click that meant business. "You can't just uproot your life for me."

"What life?" he challenged. The gun went into the holster beneath his left arm. He pulled a dark brown suede field coat from his closet and put it on, despite the seasonal warmth of the afternoon. But she could see why. It covered him from neck to hip, hiding the arsenal he carried. "The only thing that was ever good about my life was my job. I may have a few years on me now, but no one ever died on my watch."

"No one?" She followed him from bed to closet and back again as he loaded bullets, a change of clothes and other gear into a duffel bag.

He finally stopped when she planted herself in his path. He looked down from his towering height, giving her a new understanding of the phrase *armed and dangerous*. But something hot glittered in his eyes as that indulgent expression he'd shown her at the library tried to creep across his face again. He cupped her shoulders with his hands. "No one I was assigned to protect." Then he set her aside and resumed his packing. "We're down to five minutes. You'd better get moving."

He zipped the duffel shut and slung it over his right shoulder. "I'll meet you at the car in five."

He exited the room, leaving Faith standing alone beside his bed. She hugged her arms close around herself, feeling lost and abandoned in the wake of Jonas the protector. Or maybe it was the fledgling compassion she'd seen glimpses of in his behavior that rattled her to the core.

There was another man hidden inside this beast of the mountain. A kinder, passionate, deeply honorable man behind the looks and the language and the grab'n'go social skills. The man inside was the one who intrigued her, the one she was so inexorably drawn to time and again. *He* was the man who could truly hurt her. Who could make her care. Who could use up whatever reserves of emotional energy she had left.

But he was the same man who could save her life. The closest thing she had to a friend right now. And he'd been her only ally through this whole mess.

She'd thought leaving graduate school and entering the working world in the big city was the biggest risk she'd ever take. But that was before she knew that men like Jonas Beck and Darien Frye and the mysterious Copperhead existed in the world. Before they became a part of *her* world.

No one ever died on my watch.

Faith could endure a lot of things. Her parents had died when she was twelve and she'd grown to love her uncle like a second father. She'd come between a murderer and a tiny, round piece of plastic. She'd made a stranger choose to put his life on the line for her. She owed so many people so much.

But she couldn't make good on a bit of it if she was dead.

Shaking herself from her intellectual debate, she roused herself to action. The clock was ticking.

Four and a half minutes later, wearing one of Jonas's thick, soft flannel shirts as a jacket over her own stiff clothes, and carrying her purse plus a bundle of snacks, water bottles and a first aid kit wrapped up in a blanket, Faith walked out the front door into the crisp September sunshine.

Jonas had the Humvee running with the back open. When he hopped out, she nodded over her shoulder toward the door. "Should I lock it?"

"Don't bother." He met her halfway and took the bundle from her arms. "If they want in, they'll get in." He tossed her parcel in the back and closed the door. "You didn't leave anything of yours behind, did you?"

She snickered at that. "I didn't come with much."

"Let's move it, then." He closed her door, then jogged around and climbed in beside her. "Buckle up."

The lurching ride down to the road was reason enough to take the precaution. When they got down to White Horse Road, a familiar, brown county sedan caught her eye. It was parked on the shoulder near the end of Jonas's driveway. Faith braced her hands against the window and leaned as close as she dared to see if her flare of panic was justified.

She saw two men inside the car: Mel Prescott, slumped over the steering wheel and his deputy buddy, eyes closed, mouth wide-open, as his hatless head fell back against the vinyl headrest.

Faith reached behind her, blindly groping for the man undoubtedly responsible. "Jonas?"

A rough, warm hand closed around her icy fingers and gave them a squeeze. "Don't worry. They're not dead. Just out of commission. I bought us a few minutes of time without anyone tailing us." He released her before she could turn around and verify his reassuring touch with her own eyes. "I like knowing where they are. And knowing they can't call in and say we're on the move."

He turned onto the smoother pavement of White Horse Road, heading away from the town below. Faith settled back into her seat, feeling a margin of safe breathing space she hadn't a few moments ago. "Where are we going?"

"Up into the Tetons. We're gonna get lost."

"DAMN BECK." Hamilton Prince opened the door to the rustic mountain cabin without even drawing his gun as a safety precaution. Interesting. This good ol' boy with aspirations of greatness was either an arrogant son of a gun or just plain foolish. "Yep. He's gone. Cleared out. Looks like he took the girl with him."

The tall man in the suit followed more cautiously. A missing car and quiet yard didn't necessarily mean no one was home. Once he'd ascertained that the main room was clear, he entered. "What can you tell me about this Beck?"

Prince peeked into the bedroom and bathroom before coming back to the kitchen area, where he began poking around in drawers and cupboards. He laughed and shook his head. "Not much. He must be living on a pension of some kind. I never knew him to work anywhere around here. Never made friends with anyone. It isn't right, keeping to yourself so much. I ran a check on him when he first moved here, to see if he was wanted for something. Came up blank. The only info I had on him came from the DMV. I think he changed his name. He's got the look of pure trouble."

"How so?"

"Ugly son of a gun." The sheriff traced a line across his forehead with his thumb. "He's got a big scar down the middle of his face. He could scare kids on Halloween if he was of a mind to."

Interesting description. A detail like that should make Beck easier to locate. If he had indeed *cleared out,* as Prince believed.

"Maybe that's why he keeps to himself." The man in the suit placed his gun back inside his holster and straightened his charcoal jacket, maintaining a friendly yet professional tone. Though Prince seemed ready to return to town to chew out the two deputies who had fallen asleep on the job and lost track of Faith Monroe, *he* was still assessing the situation. He began his own search through the cabin. "Are you sure she was here with him?"

Prince nodded. "Spent the night. I saw them together in town this morning. Maybe they have a thing going."

He doubted it. Miss Monroe hadn't dated anyone seriously since college, according to his quickly scanned information. She'd been all about establishing her career in Saint Louis, not finding a boyfriend. If she had gone somewhere with this Beck, it would put the plan even further behind schedule. His employer wouldn't be pleased. But he agreed, just to keep the sheriff talking. "Maybe."

"I impounded her car, just like you said."

"Good. I'll have one of my men check it out." He'd go over the car himself from bumper to bumper, but he suspected it would be a long shot. If she'd skipped town, she would have the disk with her. "Do you have a make and plate number on Beck's car?"

"Sure thing. Never let it be said that my department won't cooperate with another." He pulled a cell phone from his trouser pocket and placed a call. "If you get anything on Beck, you let me know. A man like that must have something to hide."

Cooperate? The sheriff was still bent on condemning this Jonas Beck. Maybe if he'd paid more attention to his work than his gossip, he'd have kept tabs on Faith Monroe the way he'd been ordered to.

"Must have." While the sheriff talked to his office, the man in the suit checked the other rooms for himself. The bedroom, in particular, was of interest. Beck owned a gun. And he had it with him. He examined the metal lock box lying open on the bed and sniffed the distinct smell of gunpowder in the empty shoe box beside it.

The bathroom was a stark example of simple living. No clues of any kind beyond a mud-stained denim shirt stuffed into an otherwise empty laundry bag. He caught a whiff of something peculiar and raised the shirt to his nose again. Hmm. Beyond the earthy scents of pine and dirt he detected the faint odor of something citrusy. Something fresh. Perfume. The tall man smiled. "Not exactly Mr. Beck's scent, I'll wager."

But the bathroom in Faith Monroe's house had been

filled with the same smell. Her shower gel. Oh, yeah. He was on her trail again.

And he wouldn't have to rely on the bumbling *cooperation* of Sheriff Prince and his incompetent band of merry men. He needed to track this Jonas Beck for himself. And a man with a scar down the middle of his face shouldn't be that hard to find.

He checked his weapon of choice and masked his smile. He clutched the shirt in his fist and joined the sheriff out in the kitchen. "I think I've seen enough. I'd better get on the horn to my superior and report in."

The sheriff nodded. "Did you find something?"

The tall man shrugged. "We might run some DNA samples on this Jonas Beck, see if we can uncover an alias and put together a history for him."

"Man, I wish I had your resources. Keep me posted on your case, will you? Here's the plate number you asked for. Beck drives a black Humvee." Prince handed him a slip of paper and patted his belly above his belt buckle. "What do you suppose a girl like that sees in a man like him?"

He pocketed the paper inside his tweed jacket. "Women are unpredictable, aren't they?"

"That one sure is," agreed Prince. He turned toward the front door, shaking his head. "You know, I offered her a night in a motel down in Elk Point. But she wanted to stay with Beck."

"Is that so?" The man in the suit picked up the wooden chair at the table and swung it at the back of Prince's head. The stout sheriff crumpled to the floor with a noisy thump. He rolled him over and knelt on top of him before he'd blinked open his eyes. "Are you telling me a twenty-four-year-old blonde with no money and no transportation got away from you? How'd she manage that, big guy?"

The sheriff's dazed eyes tried to focus.

"You didn't get the job done. And you made mine a lot more difficult." He covered Prince's slack mouth with the wadded-up shirt while he was still too out of it to fight back. Then he pulled his knife from the pocket of his suit and flipped it open.

He plunged the blade into the sheriff's pudgy belly. His victim's groggy eyes widened with the awareness of pain.

The tall man twisted his wrist. He muffled Hamilton Prince's last cries beneath the palm of his hand.

When the sheriff's eyes closed, he pulled out the knife and cleaned it. Then he dropped Jonas Beck's sweet-smelling shirt over the man's face and drove away in his unmarked black car.

SOME TIME LATER, FBI Agent Rory Carmichael stormed into the door of the Elk County sheriff's office and flashed his badge at the two startled deputies. "Where's Sheriff Prince? I've got some follow-up questions about that red compact car over at Bill's Garage."

The deputy with the stained pant leg stood up. "He drove out to Jonas Beck's place two hours ago."

"And he hasn't returned?" The deputy shook his head. "Don't you think we'd better go find him?"

"MY GOD, this is gorgeous country." Faith lingered on the observation patio of Jackson Lake Lodge in Teton National Park, watching the sunset cast dusky blue shadows over the craggy peaks of the Tetons. Below the snow-studded mountains, Jackson Lake reflected the dramatic thrust and cut of granite and dark green pine. Closer to the lodge itself, the still lake glimmered a clear, icy blue. She inhaled deeply, absorbing the pristine air and enhancing her perception of the park's beauty. "I can see why you'd want to live out in this part of the country."

"You ready to go?"

She shook her head at the unmoved voice beside her. Jonas cast a pretty large shadow himself. In more ways than one. He'd granted her a five-minute reprieve from her assigned list of tasks so she could act like a tourist and actually enjoy the historic lodge and its spectacular views, renewing her spirit in the process.

"Aren't you affected by the beauty here?" she asked. "Mother Nature's outdone herself."

Jonas leaned on the rock and timber wall beside her, but his back was turned to the mountains as his gaze continually scanned the crowd outside with them, as well as those behind the sixty-foot observation windows of the lodge's guest lounge above them. "I like the open space of the mountains."

Faith glanced up at her companion. She hadn't expected a meaningful response. But she had a feeling his answer was based more on his life experience than on the scenery. "You prefer being by yourself, don't you?"

"It's easier."

"In what way?"

When he tilted his head down to face her, not even the bill of his black ball cap could shade the icy blue light shining in his eyes. "I'm not the kind of man most folks want to be around. I make them uncomfortable, even the ones who mean well."

Faith's admiration for the landscape around her shifted in a new direction. Craggy features. Flecks of silvery white on top. A lake—make that eyes—of shimmering blue. The unmoving strength of the Tetons was a perfect metaphor for the man beside her. "That sounds terribly lonely."

"You'd be surprised what a man can live with. Or without." He straightened, turning a subtle 360 without explaining his cryptic response.

Or denying that he was lonely.

The defunct Watchers had been aptly named, thought Faith. There didn't seem to be a moment when Jonas hadn't been scoping or scanning or checking their surroundings. Each turnoff on the highway, each face in the crowd, each closed door or obscuring landmark had been assessed by his all-seeing eyes. If the enemy was here, he would know. She wasn't quite sure how he would recognize a faceless killer known only by a code name, but she was beginning to understand that Jonas and danger were old friends. And that, even if he didn't know the face, he'd know a threat as soon as it appeared.

Had anyone ever watched over Jonas so diligently? A parent? A woman? A professional partner? Or was he the type of man who had always worked alone? Had always been alone?

An incredible sadness touched Faith's heart. What Jonas lacked in social graces he made up for in honor. In putting his life on the line for another human being. In serving his country. In understanding the misconceptions of others so that nervous teenagers and skittish waitresses and curious librarians didn't really have anything to fear from him.

He didn't deserve the startled glances and evading looks and outright stares from others when he walked into a room. His strength should be respected, yes, but he didn't deserve to be unwelcomed by a society he'd been trained to protect.

"Let's go." His broad hand closed around her upper arm. "We've been in one place long enough. Now that we've set up a campsite and dropped my name at a few of the shops here, I want to put some distance between us and western Wyoming."

"Jonas." Without any more of a rebuke than that, she twisted her arm free and reached for his hand. "Do you really think that will work? That they'll think we're staying here in the park?"

They mounted the wide, deep steps that led up to the observation lounge. "That's the idea. The FBI will send their people to Elk Point to inspect the car first. And then, even if Sheriff Prince doesn't give them a runaround, it'll take a few hours trace us to the lodge. It'll be late by the time they locate our tent. And I'm not leaving a forwarding address."

"What about Copperhead?"

"Striking in the dark of night in unfamiliar territory isn't his style. That at least buys us until daybreak."

"And tomorrow?"

A tug of resistance on her hand stopped her.

Even standing one riser above him on the steps didn't put her at eye level with Jonas. But it did put her very close to his mouth when she turned to question him. Or maybe he was leaning in. It seemed as if that mouth was suddenly very much in her personal space. And she didn't seem to mind. Of all the curved and jagged lines that made up his face, his mouth was beautifully shaped. A thin curve across the bottom, an arrogant arch at the top. Powerful and masculine like the rest of him. She felt a little breathless, a little eager and…and maybe she was the one leaning toward him.

But a whisper of the chilly evening air fanned between them, and the rugged landscape of his face drifted out of reach. "Let's get through tonight first, shall we?"

She nodded dutifully. Though she was long past the awe-inspiring moment of watching the mountains, she made a concerted effort not to let her fears wander into the future. Her hand clutched convulsively around his.

"Why do you do that?" he asked, extricating his fingers from hers and shoving his hands into the pockets of his jacket. "Does it really make that much difference to you whether or not I hold your hand?"

What kind of question was that? Faith shifted her hips to one side and crossed her arms in front of her. "Yes, it does." His eyes were narrowed in a quizzical frown, as if he was expecting to learn something insightful from her answer. "It allows me a little control. Even if it's an illusory thing. It's one little something I can choose to do while the rest of my life spins out of my hands. Plus, it gives me something to hold on to. I know you didn't want the responsibility of helping me, but…it's reassuring to have something to cling to."

Maybe he hadn't been expecting a philosophical discussion, after all. Judging by his stony expression, she didn't seem to be making any sense. Time to lighten up. Faith shrugged and offered him a conciliatory smile. "I'm sure it draws a lot less attention to us than when you pick me up and set me down somewhere else."

"That's a little Neanderthal of me, huh?"

"Yeah." She laughed a beat, then stopped abruptly. Neanderthal. Jonas. Maybe she shouldn't be laughing. "I didn't mean—"

"Like this?" He slowly, deliberately, took her hand and held it up between them, moving her past the awkward moment.

She rewarded his kindness with a grateful smile and tightened her fingers around his. "Just like that."

Three hours later, Jonas woke her to check them into a roadside motel in a small town at the end of the Wind River Valley called Lander. He'd paid a park visitor from Arizona a thousand dollars for his beat-up Chevy truck, with no questions asked, no papers exchanged. They'd left Jonas's Humvee parked in the lot at their remote campground.

Hopefully, the diversion would work and Copperhead would lose their trail, granting them enough time to find out the contents of the disk, establish Darien Frye's motive for the string of murders and find an unbiased official to report her story to who would make Frye the number one suspect instead of her.

And hopefully, she'd find a way to repay Jonas. Not just the money he was spending on her, but for his time and expertise. And the kindness he'd shown her—taking her in, supporting her, keeping her safe—kindness Jonas Beck probably didn't think, or wouldn't admit, he possessed.

Faith carried her purse and her bag from Jackson Lake Lodge into the room and tossed them onto the bed. Running on catnaps in the truck and two hours' sleep from the night before, she was too far beyond tired to immediately notice a problem with the room. But a jolt of adrenaline sharpened her powers of observation. "One bed."

Jonas locked and bolted the door behind him, then swung his duffel down onto the floor and deposited the foodstuffs she'd brought on the desk beside the TV. "Don't worry." He slipped off his jacket and draped it over the back of the thinly stuffed chair in the corner. "We'll be sleeping in shifts, so you won't actually have to go to bed with me."

"Well, I wasn't worried..." How shallow did he think she was? She'd only been with one man before in her life, but that didn't make her a prude. He'd registered them as Mr. and Mrs. Jones, so she supposed that's why they'd been given the single bed. But did he intend to camp out on the floor to protect her virtue as well as her life? Was he worried about her waking up in the middle of the night, startled and screaming because of the scary monster in her bed? Was he so conscious of his looks that he was trying to spare her the fright? He had to be as tired as she was. She'd been raised to be practical, to put up and make do if and when she had to. Her decision was firm. "We'll share the bed."

"We won't—" Jonas tossed his cap onto the desk and scuffed his hand over the short crop of his hair, emphasizing the slash of scar that grazed his forehead "—be sleeping together."

Faith stiffened up at his pinpoint glare. He'd zeroed in right on her mouth, as if her lips were somehow to blame for his surly mood. She pressed them tightly together, then moistened them with the tip of her tongue, feeling suddenly parched beneath his heated scrutiny. His eyes flinched at the tiny movement, and his nostrils flared.

She turned away, busying herself with unbuttoning the flannel shirt she wore, trying to ignore the edgy shards of heat that pulsed through her. Maybe it wasn't a self-conscious fear of startling her in the middle of the night that made him so adamant about keeping distance between them. Maybe it was just the opposite. Was he concerned about the kiss that had almost happened at Jackson Lake? She was. She seemed to lose her focus whenever she got too close to him.

Maybe he was worried that something *would* happen.

"This is fine. I was thinking more about comfort than propriety." She opted for a half truth. "You look like you take up a lot of space."

"I do." If there was any self-inflicted insult implied in that comment, it didn't reflect in his tone or actions. "We'll sleep in shifts."

With yet another decision taken out of her hands, Faith sank onto the side of the bed and kicked off her tennis shoes. Her stiff sweater and muddy jeans had grown increasingly uncomfortable, yet she was more distracted by the purposeful stride of her roommate than by her chafing clothes.

The whitewashed concrete block walls seemed to close in as Jonas moved about the room, checking the bathroom and closet, peeking through the closed curtains to the parking lot out front, opening and closing every drawer in the room.

"What are you looking for?" she asked, clinging to her spot on the bed.

"I don't like surprises." He flexed his shoulders to relieve an ache or fatigue, stretching the leather and elastic bands of his holster and reminding her all too clearly of the danger that stalked her. "It's nothing fancy, but it's clean. You want to wash up first?" He angled his head toward the door. "I have an errand to run. You could be settled in by the time I get back."

"You're leaving me?" Faith shot to her feet. He was that desperate to avoid close contact with her?

"Just for a few minutes." He shrugged into his jacket and adjusted his gun beneath it. "I saw a convenience store on the way in. I need to pick up a few things for us."

"Is it safe?" She hurried to his side, ignoring his unspoken request to keep distance between them.

He pulled on his cap. "You'll be fine. Just don't open the door for anyone but me, and don't use the phone. Even if it rings, don't answer it."

"I meant you." She reached for the bill of his cap and pulled it low over his forehead, hiding his most noticeable feature. "What if someone sees you?"

He snatched her wrists and pulled them down from his cap. "Darien Frye isn't looking for me."

"But—"

"But nothing." He released her and turned and unlocked the door. "I've got a few more tricks to put Frye and his man off your tail. In the meantime, why don't you wash off this morning's mud so you can get a good night's sleep?"

Faith held on to her side of the door when he tried to leave. For one long, shaky breath, she stared into those ice-blue eyes and begged for some sort of promise that he would return, that he would be safe, that they would beat this thing together. A wink, a smile, that brush of his finger across her forehead again—that was all she needed. Some tiny reassurance.

But there was none. For a man who was just now learning the finer points of holding hands, there was no reassurance he knew how to give. "Lock the door and bolt it," he ordered. "I'll be back in fifteen minutes."

After pushing the door shut, she did as she'd been told. He waited until she'd twisted the dead bolt into place. Then she heard him drive out of the parking lot in a spin of speed and gravel. Faith leaned her back against the steel door and hugged her arms across her stomach, feeling as alone and unsure of herself as she ever had in the past forty-eight hours.

She'd come to rely on Jonas so quickly, looking beyond his grizzled appearance and gruff manner to see the fiercely protective hero he was inside. When he was with her, she felt safe. And though her quiet upbringing hadn't prepared her for a man who was so much, well…man, she felt a kinship to him she hadn't found anywhere else.

One chair at his table. Jonas Beck understood what it was to be alone. Maybe that's what made her reach out to him again and again. He understood the loneliness of her quest, of having nowhere to go and no one to turn to. And though her heart ached with pity for his solitary life— shunned, feared, forgotten—it was the thing that made her believe he understood her as well.

He'd come back. He'd keep her safe.

And she'd do everything within her power to help him, and thus, help herself.

Resolved to carry out even his simplest requests, she pushed away from the door, stripped off the rest of her clothes and headed for the shower.

"Yum." The reviving spray beat down upon her weary muscles, washing away the tensions of the past two days— stolen cars, runaway trucks, nosy deputies—and Jonas's certainty that Copperhead was every bit the threat to her life she'd imagined him to be.

Faith pulled her comb through her towel-dried hair and relished the gentle massage across her scalp. Though she had new, clean clothes to wear tomorrow, she'd opted to slip back into Jonas's flannel shirt and a pair of clean panties to sleep in.

She was comfortable, she was warm, she was clean. But she didn't want to think about falling into bed until she knew for sure that Jonas had safely returned. She eyed the clock. There were still a few minutes left before the time he said he'd be back.

In normal circumstances, she'd curl up with a book until sleep claimed her. But she had no book, and there was nothing normal about hiding out in a motel room, waiting for her unofficial bodyguard to return. She turned on the television for some background noise, and set about packing her things inside her sack for tomorrow's departure. She turned the NT-6 disk over in her hand. It was just a small, shiny piece of plastic. But three people had died for it already.

Four.

Faith slowly turned toward the television and focused her attention on the words that had registered in her subconscious mind. "Elk Point's county sheriff, Hamilton Prince, was found stabbed to death inside the cabin of a local man, Jonas Beck. The cabin is located approximately fifteen minutes outside of town. According to FBI spokesman, Sheriff Prince was assisting federal authorities with an investigation involving three deaths in the Saint Louis area. Anyone with information regarding—"

"Oh, my God. Not again." There was her picture, staring back at her from the TV screen just as clearly as her reflection had stared back from the mirror only moments ago. "No." She was shaking her head and moving away from the set, gripped in a new horror that made her feel as if the concrete wall she'd pressed her back against was caving in on her. "Not again."

She watched the story play out as if she was witnessing it in person. "...wanted for questioning, along with Mr. Beck." The photograph of her finally left the screen and was replaced by a shot of Jonas's cabin, its rustic seclusion hidden behind a crowd of official vehicles and yellow crime scene tape. The reporter turned while the camera shot panned up the steps behind him to the porch where county paramedics were carrying out a large body in a black bag strapped onto a gurney.

If her family was seeing this... If they were part of this... Faith swallowed hard and tried to keep it together.

The reporter had a grim face as he turned back to the camera. "Special Agent Rory Carmichael is joining me to make an official statement to the press." Tears stung Faith's eyes as she riveted her focus on the television across the room. The reporter stepped to one side and Agent Carmichael moved into the picture.

Faith squinted, trying to align the man's image with a hazy memory. "I know you," she whispered.

It was the same man she'd seen on the television in Kansas City. The man talking about Liza's murder. Tall, thin. Reddish-brown hair slicked back from his forehead. He wore a gray suit with his badge hanging from the front pocket of his jacket. "…circumstantial evidence places her at the scene of each crime…"

"But I wasn't." Faith's knees wobbled and she sank to the floor, the disk clenched in her shaking fist. "I didn't do anything wrong. I tried to help."

A knock at door the door startled her. She stifled a scream on a gulp of air. Goose bumps tingled across her skin.

Jonas wouldn't knock. Had they found her? Copperhead? The FBI? The police?

She huddled against the wall beside the bed, staring at the metal door. What to do? What to do?

"Mrs. Jones?" The person outside knocked again, urgent this time, demanding. "Mrs. Jones? It's Alice from the front desk. I brought some extra towels. Figured there weren't enough for that big hubby of yours."

Faith breathed hard, in through her nose, out through her mouth, forcing herself to stay calm and in the moment. *She* was Mrs. Jones. And Alice, she'd seen Alice through the window when they'd checked in.

Towels seemed safe enough.

Don't open the door for anyone but me.

She slipped the disk into her purse and slid it under the bed. She had to wait for Jonas. But the light was on. The TV. Alice knew she was in here.

Alice was a woman. The night clerk. Not Copperhead.

Not the FBI. She wouldn't hurt her. She could just answer the door and send her on her way.

Agent Carmichael was staring at her from the TV. Telling anyone who would listen about the young blond woman he was searching for.

She jumped at the next knock. "Mrs. Jones? Are you in there? I have a key. I can just set the towels inside the door."

"No." She breathed the word, too softly for anyone to hear.

Run.

She scanned the thick block walls. Not an option.

She could fight. She could take another woman. But if the other woman had a knife… Faith scanned the room for anything resembling a weapon. The lamp. Blunt object. She scurried across the room on her hands and knees and pulled out the plug, plunging the room into instant darkness. She froze.

"Mrs. Jones?" The voice hesitated. Sounded concerned.

Faith pulled the shade off the lamp and turned it around in her fists, arming herself with a club. A crunch of gravel and squeal of brakes drew her attention back to the door.

"Mrs. Jones?" One more knock.

A car door slammed. Faith heard a garble of voices. Then one became more distinct. "I'll take them."

Jonas.

Her relief was so intense, Faith felt light-headed. She pushed to her feet and stumbled toward the door, flipping aside the dead bolt as she heard the key slide into the outer lock. "Faith?" She dropped the lamp at her feet and the bulb shattered. "Faith!"

She twisted the knob and the door swung open. "Jonas!"

She flew into his arms. She wrapped her arms around his neck and climbed right up the front of him, burrowing against him. He looped one arm around her hips as he shut and bolted the door behind him with the other.

"Faith, honey. What is it? Tell me what's wrong." He tossed the towels and a sack onto the chair and gathered her up in both arms. "Are you hurt?"

She shook her head, fearing tears would burst out if she tried to speak. He was strong and he was solid. He was warm and she was safe. And it was all she could do to press her cheek against his neck and hold on.

He carried her with him as he checked the bathroom and closet to ascertain that no one else was there. "Honey, what happened?"

She moved her lips against the warm, musky smell of his collar. "He's dead, Jonas. He's dead. And they think we—that I—killed him."

He tossed aside his cap and sank onto the edge of the bed with her in his lap. "Who's dead?"

Chapter Six

The woman was shaking. And cold. Plastered to him like a second skin. She was spooked.

"Dammit, Faith, what's wrong?"

"Jonas!"

She wanted to worry about his vocabulary now? "You need to talk to me."

When he'd first driven up, his senses had buzzed with caution. Something wasn't right. The room was dark through the curtain cracks and he could read the concern in the desk clerk's posture. Her *No one's answering. Is your wife a sound sleeper?* had shifted him into full alert. He was damn sure they hadn't been followed to Lander. But Frye had connections even he might not know about. Maybe she'd picked up a phone call when he'd warned her not to. Or a tracking device was somehow planted on her, or hidden in the disk itself. And then he'd heard the crashing sound inside the room.

If Faith hadn't opened that door, he'd have kicked it in himself.

But the room was clear. The lamp had fallen to the floor beside the door, but he'd seen no signs of forced entry. She wasn't crying, but she sure was holding on as if he was the prize of the century. Which he knew he wasn't. He sensed the danger, whatever it had been, had passed. But, hell, he could have handled an intruder. What was he supposed to do with her?

He shrugged out of his jacket. In the instant he had to let go of her, her fingers clamped around his neck and she tried to find a footing to keep herself pressed against him. "No, don't."

"I'm not going anywhere." The effect of all her struggling was that her long, creamy thighs, exposed all the way up to the elastic strap of some pale-blue panties, kept rubbing against his lap. She was scared and craving comfort, but his body had gotten the fool notion that this was the time to perk up and respond to the press of breasts and bottom against him.

"Be still," he ordered. He draped his suede jacket around her back and shoulders and wrapped his arms around her again. She settled against him, her rump nestled squarely against his groin. He squeezed his eyes shut and breathed through the flooding rush of heat, praying she wouldn't notice his rigid response. Probably not the kind of comfort she wanted from him.

Jonas concentrated on an image that had always cleared his mind of distracting thoughts—his stepmother's damning eyes and his father's back turned on him, letting him take the blame for something he hadn't done. Letting him become the monster.

Better. He could feel himself filling with anger and hurt—emotions that sharpened his senses instead of handicapping them. But it was hard to keep the image and maintain the resentment. Not when he held this soft bundle of woman in his arms. Not when she smelled so clean and sweet. And scared. He needed to do his job, and move past the warm, peaceful feeling that tried to take root inside him. "What happened?" he prodded. "Tell me who's dead."

"I was watching the news on TV," she began in a halting voice. "Sheriff Prince was stabbed. They found him in your cabin."

He could feel her fingers toying with the front of his shirt, tracing buttons, smoothing the material. Each tiny caress was an unexpected torture. But he could stand it. He could sit still and hold her if that was what she needed from him.

No one had ever needed him for this kind of thing before. They called on him for strength, protection, expertise, knowledge, experience. No one had ever demanded comfort before. He wasn't sure what to do. He'd provided the basics—warmth, security. But what next? Pat her back? Say something nice?

"The FBI was there." The tiny touches continued, but she'd stopped shaking. "The same agent who was investigating Liza's murder was on the news. Every place I go, Copperhead finds me. But the police, the FBI, they think I'm doing this."

"And you thought the lady with the towels at your door meant Copperhead had found you here?"

"Yes. No." Her teasing fingers curled into a fist and she pushed away, tilting her face up to his. "I'm such an idiot. He couldn't have found us here. Not so soon. Alice must think your Mrs. Jones is crazy. Being afraid of a few towels." Though she tried to find some humor amidst the irrational confines of fear, she didn't smile. "Why is this happening to me? I mean, why *me?*"

"First, you're not an idiot. Most people never have to learn how to handle this kind of thing." He found it hard to look into her earnest green eyes without thinking things he shouldn't, without wanting things that weren't his to take. He palmed the back of her head and pulled her face back to his chest. But that wasn't much better. Now the dark gold strands of her freshly washed hair clung to his fingers like strands of damp silk. He'd never touched anything so soft.

But he ignored the desires that were stirring despite his best intentions and focused on reasoning with her. "Second, if you didn't care about your boss, you wouldn't have helped him. If you didn't care about your friend, you wouldn't feel guilty. And as for Prince? Hell, even I didn't want him dead. He's nosy enough that he either saw something he shouldn't, or he made someone very unhappy. You're just young, and you care about things. You see the good in people, and then it surprises you when you learn how mean some of them can be.''

Damn, what was he talking about? Why was he rambling so much? She pushed against his hand and leaned back into his arms. He caught his breath halfway down his throat. He was doing something right. She was smiling. Actually, it was more of a crooked smirk, but her eyes were bright again. "So you're saying I'm young and foolish?"

He hoped it came out better than that. "You just have a big heart. You trust people. That'll get you into trouble. Others will take advantage of that.''

"But I'm not an idiot," she challenged.

"Hell, no." She raised an eyebrow at the curse word. He repeated himself—the way she wanted to hear it. "No."

That tantalizing smirk blossomed into a full-blown smile. His whole body lurched as if she'd just issued an invitation. Damn. Had he ever wanted anything so badly?

He slid his hands up and down her spine, working off some of the tension that was battering inside him. If he could just taste her once. Know what it felt like to kiss a woman who wasn't afraid to be kissed by him.

But then, that might be the very thing that would make her afraid of him. That should make her afraid.

"Jonas?" Her eyelids veiled, leaving only a glimpse of green shining through her thick, long lashes, but she was studying his mouth. "Thank you."

Even through the thickness of his jacket, he could feel the womanly shape of her. The indention of her waist. The flare of her hips. That sweet, round, beautiful butt.

His lungs swelled painfully in his chest as he bravely

fought the need to pull her closer, to feel her—skin to skin, to bury himself deep inside the most feminine part of her.

He tried to come up with something to say. *Thank you for what?* or *You're welcome* or *It's no big deal.* But his mouth wouldn't form the words. All he could seem to do was bend his head and drift closer to those untinted pink lips.

Her hands started to move on him, sliding around his neck and against his hair. It seemed that this new position was less about comforting and more about... Hell. How long had it been since he'd kissed a woman? How long since he'd even considered it a possibility? Or was this warming trend just a cruel illusion concocted by his feverish hormones and wishful thinking?

He tried to distract himself. To think clearly for a minute. To misread Faith's emotions and force himself on her would be a disastrous mistake. The kind of thing that could shatter the blind trust she had in him. The kind of thing that could send her running, straight into the waiting clutches of her enemies.

He shook his head, not liking that idea at all. "He'll never get to you, I promise." But he was still moving closer, catching her soft, warm breath on his own. "You have such pretty hair. Like cornsilk." He sifted the ethereal weight of it through his fingers. He tried to think of practical things, but he still wasn't moving away. "You'll have to dye it. Your description's out on the wire. On TV now, too, I guess. I bought something red. I thought it would look more natural. With your green eyes..."

He'd noticed the color of her eyes?

It was silly how such a little thing could make her feel so pretty. So curious about the man who'd noticed.

Faith wondered if her pupils were dilated with the same drugged arousal that darkened the centers of his cool blue eyes.

Cornsilk. What a sweet, sweet compliment. Simple. Evocative. Sincere.

What else had Jonas noticed about her?

She'd melted into a delicious putty, surrounded by the strength and piney scent of his coat and arms and chest. Her fears had been forgotten, soothed away by his blunt words and sheltering touch. And now she wanted more. She wanted to kiss him. And, if she could count on any of her neophyte skills with men right now, he wanted to kiss her, too. She stretched the length of her torso, tipping her head back against his hand. Reaching, encouraging.

"I hate to change the color, but…" His voice trailed away. Faith closed her eyes as his mouth drifted toward hers.

A horrendous groan rumbled in his throat. She felt two hands beneath her, one on her bottom, one on her thighs. Jonas lifted her off his lap, nearly spilling her into the desk in his haste to move away from her.

Faith's anticipation crashed so hard, she grabbed on to the back of the desk chair to steady herself. Jonas's jacket pooled at her feet. Goose flesh popped out all over her skin as her overheated body shivered with the unexpected jolt of rejection.

But her embarrassment was short-lived. Jonas's big hands shook as he tore through the bag from the convenience store. This man who could stand down the barrel of a gun and the gawking looks of a townful of small-minded people couldn't even look at her as he stalked back across the room. Her feminine intuition was slow, but not stupid. Of all the noble…

"Here's the hair—"

Faith reached up and caught his face between her hands. Doing for him—for them—what he would not do for himself, she tugged his mouth down to hers and kissed him.

At first he simply stood there, his head bent low, his lips stiff beneath the pliant quest of her own.

But then, it was as if the leviathan had been unleashed. Jonas's chest swelled with a mighty breath. Something low and earthy growled in his throat. And after that first stunned moment, his mouth opened over hers. He grabbed her hips and dragged her body against his, forcing her softer curves to conform to his hard angles.

Without any finesse or fanfare, he plunged his tongue into her mouth, deepening the kiss from sweet and tender to coarse and erotic.

Oh, yeah. He'd wanted to kiss her.

Faith caught her breath. There was nothing she could do but hang on. The instantaneous passion was overwhelming yet empowering. Jonas's raw, sensual assault on her senses left her no room to question her initiative, no need to doubt his desire for her. What had begun as an invitation to acknowledge their mutual attraction and assure him of his welcome had become a physical expression of every hurt and fear and unspoken need between them.

Sensation after sensation pounded through her with the speed of a carnival ride. The prickle of his late-night beard stubble abraded her sensitive palms. The velvety texture of his hair soothed them. The utter hardness and sinuous strength of his chest and shoulders was a savage landscape to touch and explore. The rough need of his hands, sliding up beneath her shirt, scorched the bare skin of her back, then squeezed her bottom and lifted her up against his unabashed arousal.

Faith moaned at her body's wanton reaction to his unfiltered sexual appetite. The tips of her breasts tightened to painful nubs that could only be eased by the friction of rubbing against him. Her toes curled, her hands grasped. And her mouth opened to grant him every driving wish of his tongue.

A tamer kiss might have given her time to second-guess her ability to take on a man like this. A man of animalistic power who could consume her diminutive size, by comparison. A man of the world who had seen more and survived more in a matter of days than she'd known her entire life. A man who belonged to no one and followed no rules except his own.

But Jonas wasn't tame. He was the beast who lived alone on the mountain above a tiny little town that feared him. He was a man who would throw himself in front of a speeding truck or uproot his home to save a woman's life. His manners were unpolished, his language crude and his kisses out of this world.

As his mouth drove her head back against the supporting cup of his hand, Faith didn't see his scar or the unflattering angles of his face. She felt the power of his unleashed need throbbing at the aching juncture between her thighs. She tasted the heat of his consuming mouth. She smelled the musk and pine that radiated from his skin. She heard the urgent hunger noises in his throat.

She sensed the huge heart that lay well guarded and untapped inside him. And she forgot she was supposed to be afraid.

In her humble effort to give him everything he asked for in this wild kiss, Faith pulled her hands to the front of his shirt and worked open the top two buttons. She slipped her fingers inside, gasping at the tempting contrast of crisp hair and hot skin beneath her palms. She pushed the denim aside, wanting to learn more about his masculine textures, but her fingers jammed beneath a wad of cotton material. Frustrated, she tugged the material free and tried again, sliding her fingertips into the tight squeeze between cloth and skin before she met another dead end. Trapped again, she moved her hands to the outside to find the impediment, and brushed against the cold, smooth strap of his holster.

The ride crashed to a halt.

All at once, the hands that had held her so eagerly, so passionately, closed around her upper arms and pushed her away.

"Damn, damn, damn."

Jonas heaved a massive breath and set her feet firmly on the floor and backed away, his voice hoarse. As Faith withered into herself, his hands splayed open, palms high, at either side of her—supplicating, surrendering—as if he'd been caught defiling a temple and was to be damned to hell.

"I'm sorry. I don't mean to say— I— That shouldn't have happened."

"I—I'm the one who's sorry," she stuttered, hugging her arms around herself in a futile effort to be warm again. "I didn't mean to embarrass you."

"Embarrass? Crap." He swiped the back of his knuckles across his mouth and jaw. His shirt gaped open, wadded beneath the strap of his holster and the gun at his side, exposing a mile of muscled chest and a vein that throbbed at the base of his throat. Faith looked at it instead of the eyes she could feel boring down on her. "Honey, right now I want you like hellfire. You shouldn't give a man everything like that. It'll make him think…"

Instead of finishing his sentence, he pinched a thumb and forefinger around her chin and tipped it up. He'd already released her by the time she jerked away from his touch, but the demand to look him in the eye had been made. She saw shadows amongst the ice. Shades of darkness that contrasted with the sharp white line of his scar and hinted at his emotions without revealing them.

"You are everything pretty and perfect and pure that I can taint. And I couldn't forgive myself if I did." He made a chore of buttoning his shirt and arranging the weaponry he carried. "You can call me a son of a bitch for going after you like that. I don't deal with women much—with anyone… Hell. Temptation doesn't normally drop into my lap, and it's hard to resist when it does. But it shouldn't have happened. It *won't* happen again." He braced his hands on his hips, his chest heaving in and out with an energy that seemed to have been drained from her. "I'm sorry," he stated finally. "This has nothing to do with you."

But it felt like it did. She was cold. Shocked. Shaking. Her body was aching with unsatisfied need. Her senses were still spinning, her equilibrium shattered. Her heart and soul left hanging wide-open.

"You can hit me if you want. Tell me to go to hell."

The offer startled her from her lost stupor. Faith blinked and studied the expression on his face more closely. He was serious.

She clutched the shirt she wore in a fist at her collar and hugged herself more tightly. She shook her head. "No. I wouldn't do that."

Why would he think such violence would be the answer?

"You're too nice for your own good." It sounded less like a criticism than a sigh of regret. But he gave no explanation. He spun around in his tracks, spotted the box of hair dye where it had fallen beneath the desk, snatched it up and thrust it at her.

"Here. I'm going outside for a walk. I expect you to be a redhead when I return."

She took the box and nodded.

He slammed the door behind him and entered the chilly autumn night without his coat.

Faith stood in the darkness for several moments, contemplating the extremes of compassion and passion, confusion and curiosity that filtered through her mind and body.

Had she ever thrown herself at a man like that before? Ever ached so much to have a man hold her? Ever hurt so much for another human being?

Were the strenuous events of the past two days making her behave in a way she never would have in her quiet, predictable former life? Or were they bringing out a part of her that had always existed—a woman who took risks and cared deeply, and either paid the consequences or reaped the rewards?

Her old life made sense.

Her relationship with Jonas didn't.

A glimpse of her old life might set things straight again. And it might alleviate some portion of her guilt.

She turned on the light over the bathroom sink and set the hair dye on the counter. It added just enough illumination to the main room to allow her to clean up the broken lamp and retrieve her purse. She pulled out her cell phone. Jonas had warned her not to answer any call, but he'd never said anything about making one.

Still, she kept her eye on the door as she punched in the number to her uncle's home in Missouri. The phone rang and rang. Each ring made her a little more nervous. What if her family didn't answer? What if someone else did?

When the answering machine clicked on, she sighed with a mixture of regret and relief. It was heartening to hear Wes Monroe's no-nonsense baritone voice again, even if it was only on tape. When the machine beeped, Faith spoke. "Hi, Wes. Gran. It's me. I miss you. I wish I knew that you were safe. I'm…" She couldn't truly say *okay*, not after what had just happened. Not with all that had been happening. "I'm safe. I love you. Bye."

Faith disconnected the phone and headed for the sink. Her relationship with Jonas Beck might not make any sense. But right now, it was the only one she could count on.

JONAS SAT in the veil of darkness and listened to Faith sleep. Toss and turn was more like it. After her soundless *good night* near 11:00 p.m., she'd climbed underneath the covers. Exhaustion had claimed her quickly, judging by the hushed, even breathing from her side of the room. But less than an hour later, a nightmare was tormenting her slumber.

The chair in the corner was too cramped to sleep in, and the motel's idea of reading material was a listing of local restaurants. He'd untucked and unbuttoned his shirt, and set his gun on his lap and his knife within easy reach, should anyone manage to get through the bolted steel door or double-paned window. But guilt would have kept him awake, anyway.

He was helpless to sit there and listen and damn himself for causing any bit of the grief that troubled her. But he couldn't go to her, he could only watch over her.

He'd made a huge tactical error in kissing her, consuming her. Putting his rough hands and hungry mouth all over her. God, he'd been a brute. Not one sweet word. Not one tender touch. It had been all about need. Even the knowledge that she'd initiated that embrace didn't ease his conscience. He'd left beard marks around her mouth in a paler shade of her new auburn hair. He'd wanted her so badly. His body craved her. His soul needed her.

His brain had kicked in too late to warn him of disaster. If he didn't hurt her, he sure as hell would get hurt himself. And he'd endangered them both by allowing that seed of sexual attraction to be acknowledged. His enemies, her enemies—their enemies—would jump all over that kind of vulnerability. And the unaffordable distraction it presented would bias his strategy, compromise his objectivity.

He needed help if he was going to pull this off now.

And that meant swallowing his pride and going back to the man who had put his old warhorse butt out to pasture in the first place.

Faith thrashed her pillow off the bed and moaned in her sleep. Jonas squeezed his fist around his cell phone and breathed through the urge to go to her. He'd held her once already, and what had started out as a healing reprieve for them both had transformed into combustible passion.

She was bold, yet innocent. Soft to the touch, yet strong. She'd tasted like the fresh mint of her toothpaste, yet there'd been something much more potent in that luscious mouth that he hadn't had the strength to resist.

So let her moan in her sleep. The best thing he could do for her right now was keep his distance. He'd sworn, long ago, that he would never get involved with an innocent woman. And he'd never broken that vow. Not once. The world wouldn't let him. Not since…

Jonas grunted a sigh. He wouldn't go back there again. He was preoccupied enough already on this unofficial mission he'd assigned himself, without thinking back to that fateful night when he'd first been made to understand his curse. To keep Faith safe, he definitely needed help.

He punched in a number he knew by heart.

It rang only once before a voice from his past answered. "Murphy."

The voice was as sharp and clear and authoritative as Jonas remembered. And even though it was 2:00 a.m. on the East Coast and George Murphy had probably been sleeping, there was no doubt that his former boss had awakened with every keen sense and his considerable intellect on full alert.

"Beck here. I need to know if there was ever any resolution to the Frye investigation."

The other man laughed. He'd always been able to make nice, even when the chips were heavily stacked against them. Probably why he'd been put in charge of The Watchers project. "What? No 'Hello'?" asked George. "No 'How's the wife and kids?'"

Jonas shook his head. "You're divorced and no sane woman would have me." He paused only long enough for a breath and went on. "I know the program was put out of commission, but you managed to come out in the thick of things. I also know you still have your connections at the Bureau. Did anyone ever get a conviction or DOA on Frye?"

There was a thoughtful pause at the end of the line before George answered. "I'll call you back on a secure line."

Damn. That meant the Frye case was still active.

Jonas relayed the information and hung up. He swiped his palm across his beard-roughened jaw and rested his chin there. The tension within him was humming at the same frequency of dread and anticipation that he'd feel knowing the enemy was right on the other side of that door.

Darien Frye had stirred up someone else's attention besides his own.

When his cell phone rang a few minutes later, it woke Faith. Startled from her fitful sleep, she sat up in bed, shoving her russet hair off her face and hugging herself around the neck and waist in that self-protective stance of hers.

"What is it? What?" she whispered.

Silhouetted against the light from the bathroom sink, he could see she was shaking. Though whether it was from alarm at the late-night call or remnants of her nightmare still working through her system, he couldn't tell.

Steeling himself against the urge to tuck her back into bed and promise her sweet dreams, he punched the button on his phone and put it to his ear.

"Beck."

When she swung her long, bare legs to the floor from beneath the twist of sheets, Jonas raised his hand, indicating everything was okay and that she should lie back down. She didn't, of course. He could count sweet, soft and innocent among her many attributes, but stubborn was right in there with them. She picked up the fallen pillow, hugged it in her lap and listened in.

"I'll skip the amenities myself." George Murphy sounded like a man on a mission. "Darien Frye's been underground for two years now. Once we exposed his operation, the FBI signed back on, but had about as much luck as we did bringing him in. Of course, the market for the kind of armaments he could put his hands on declined there for a few years. Maybe he made enough and retired to some sunny country without an extradition agreement with the U.S."

Jonas might have been discharged from the game, but he read enough to keep up with the times. "The illegal arms market is booming right now. The Bureau hasn't picked up anything on him?''

Faith watched intently, as if she could understand the details of George's answer by watching Jonas's steely expression.

''He's officially listed as MIA with the Bureau,'' Murphy reported. ''Of course, they'll deny that. It's embarrassing for one of your own to sell out and get away with it. But I haven't heard talk of any recent activity attributed to him. I think the Feds are hoping he had a heart attack, or died of natural causes. They'd love some information so they can close the case.''

Jonas stared right back at Faith, revealing nothing of the edgy turbulence inside him. ''You know I'd love to stick it to Frye. Look him in the eye and see his reaction when he knows he's finally been caught.''

''You and me both, buddy. But you're out of commission now. You can't go after him. Not legally.''

''What if he comes after me?''

George's succinct curse would have earned a reprimand from Faith. ''You've heard from him recently?''

Jonas looked across the room, drawn to the luminescent sheen of Faith's skin in the dim light. Her trembling had stopped, and if he could judge anything simply from the stillness of her silhouetted posture, she understood this phone call was, ultimately, about her. ''A friend of mine has.''

He could hear George up and moving now. ''I don't know if I can give you backup.''

He might as well give him the rest of it. ''A local sheriff was murdered in my cabin. It looks like Copperhead is back in business, too, and that he's working for Frye.''

George said every foul word Jonas was thinking. He took a deep, calming breath. ''What do you need from me?''

''Can you call off the Feds?'' Jonas asked. Reducing the number of parties pursuing them would make this a whole lot easier. And eliminate the potential crossfire that could prove deadly for Faith—and himself. "Give me a chance to work this on my own?"

"Let me make some calls and get up to speed on this. I'll see what I can do."

"Keep me posted."

Things would be stirred up in Washington by sunrise if George Murphy was planning to *do* something. "Is your friend safe?"

"She's with me."

She. That word should give Murphy pause. A beat of silence passed before he responded. "Then she's safe. Beck?"

"Yeah?"

"If you bring in Darien Frye, maybe we could get The Watchers back." The top secret organization had been Murphy's baby from the start. He'd created the concept. He'd recruited the manpower. And he'd treated the odd assortment of misfits under his command like family until the project had been taken out of his hands. "Maybe *you* can come back."

It was the best form of *good luck* Jonas could hear.

"Find out what you can and call me."

There were no goodbyes. That wasn't how their relationship worked. He turned off the phone, stretched his long legs in front of him and processed the conversation in silence.

In his long career, there was only one man who'd ever gotten away from him. One mastermind who'd changed his identity so many times that The Watchers couldn't track him down. He'd murdered and swindled and taken what he wanted without anyone to question his actions until Jonas had been assigned to investigate him.

He'd nailed every other case in his career. Kept the witnesses alive. Eliminated the traitors. Found the evidence to prove when men belonged behind bars. Every case but one.

The one who got away.

Darien Frye.

Now was his chance to make it right. But the idea of going back to complete his career with a perfect record wasn't giving him the satisfaction he would have expected, even a few days ago.

"Was that...The Watchers?" Faith's soft voice hung still in the air, reminding him very plainly why the opportunity to catch Frye wasn't as appealing as it once might have been.

"The Watchers don't exist anymore." He squeezed his shoulders into the back of the chair, trying to find a comfortable position.

"But the friends you worked with do. They think Darien Frye's a dangerous man, too, don't they?"

"Yeah."

She couldn't let a thing rest, could she. "He sells illegal weapons?"

He shifted again, crossing his legs at the ankles. "It's a little more complicated than that, but, yes."

"Will your friends help us?"

"They'll do what they can from their end." George Murphy would be more than thorough. "We still have our work cut out for us."

"Then you'd better get some rest. That chair's not big enough for you to relax in." She tossed the pillow onto the bed and stood up. "You said we'd sleep in shifts. When do I take over?"

"Take over what?"

"Watching over you so you can sleep."

"You don't."

She balled her fists at her hips and tried to look all tough. "You can't stay awake twenty-four hours a day."

"If I have to, I can."

She turned her face into the curtain of light from the bathroom, giving him a good look at the taut line of her mouth. He didn't have the heart to tell her that her sleep-tousled hair and shapely legs beneath the hem of *his* over-size shirt that she wore spoiled her tough act.

"Well, aren't you just the big manly man? I've seen you in the morning when you've had sleep. I don't know if I can stand to be around you when you haven't." He raised an eyebrow at the obvious taunt, but ignored her. "At least lie down in a comfortable position so you don't wind up with a crick in your neck. The bed's big enough for both of us."

That he couldn't ignore. "Faith, that's hardly appropriate, considering—"

"It's practical. I want you sharp if you're watching my back, not dozing because you were too bullheaded to sleep." Then she seemed to remember that same explosive kiss that was keeping him rooted to the chair. She hugged her arms around her waist, and he expected her to retreat. Instead, she crossed the room and stood beside him. Close up, he could see there was no anger in her expression, no teasing. But she was clearly distressed. "I promise I'll stay on my side of the bed. And I don't snore. Much."

Logic and humor? He weakened in the face of her tentative smile. But he clenched his fists around the arms of the chair and stayed put. "No."

She brushed her fingertips across the back of his tight, white knuckles, and Jonas jumped in his skin at the gentle touch. "Get some sleep, Jonas. Or neither of us will. I'll worry about you."

He grabbed the gun and lurched to his feet, towering over her by a good foot or more. Maybe a little intimidation would remind her that kindness was wasted on him. "I'm not getting in that bed with you."

"Please?"

Sucker.

Every self-preserving instinct inside him melted at that one word.

"Fine." He grabbed his knife and stalked to the bed, pointing with the sheathed blade to the far side of the sheet and blanket. "Get in and cover up."

For once, she quickly did his bidding, sliding across the bed and pulling the blanket up to her chin. He tossed her the pillow, then laid the knife on the bedside table. He propped up the two remaining pillows against the head-board and deposited his gun underneath them.

Still wearing his jeans and unbuttoned shirt, he sat on the edge of the bed. He paused at the protesting creak of springs and waited to verify its strength before turning and leaning back against his pillows. The soft mattress bowed beneath his weight and Faith tumbled down into the valley beside him.

The instant impact of hips and legs pressed against his side made him question the wisdom of giving in to her request.

But in the next breath she was scrambling away with a hasty "Sorry."

This was only slightly more comfortable than the chair. Here he could stretch out, but once he did, he held himself perfectly still, avoiding another meet-in-the-middle with Faith.

By the time he realized she was clinging to the opposite side to keep from rolling, she spoke again. "Were The Watchers a branch of the FBI or CIA?"

He'd add *curious* to *stubborn* when it came to her more trying personality traits. "Neither."

"Defense department?"

He'd never really done pillow talk, but he had a feeling this wasn't how the usual conversations went. Still, talking about work beat thinking about the half-naked woman be-side him. "I always thought of ourselves as internal affairs for the legal agencies that protect us."

"How do you mean?"

He sagged into the pillows, surrendering to a will that

seemed stronger than his own tonight. "What do you do when a chief of police is corrupt? He has the means at his disposal to silence anyone who threatens to expose him. When a high-ranking CIA agent's cover is blown, how do you get him out alive? Whose information do you trust when an FBI agent has turned?"

"You did all those things?" Awestruck by the scope and danger of his former job, she released her grip and tumbled back into him. This time it was a breast that teased the skin at his rib cage. Jonas hissed a breath at the forbidden stir-rings inside him. She climbed to the other side, dragging the blanket with her, and held on again. "Sorry."

"I worked mostly in tracking down rogue agents, and either exposing or neutralizing them."

"Neutralizing?" He could hear the shock in her voice. Good. Remind her what kind of monster he could be. That should wipe out any feelings of lingering passion or pity she had for him.

"Darien Frye is an agent I was unable to neutralize."

She lay there in silence for so long that Jonas was sure she'd drifted back off to sleep. But a tiny voice, muffled by her hand or pillow, finally spoke. "Jonas? I'm just a means to an end, aren't I?"

If he was truly back in Watcher mode, he'd have let her question pass without a response. But something about the vulnerable beauty who had more guts than sense was work-ing its way beneath his tough exterior and objectivity. He shouldn't give a damn that she was worried or hurting or afraid. But he did.

He'd find a way to distance himself from her in the morn-ing. But right now he *was* tired, and she didn't deserve to think that he was using her just to get to Frye.

He reached across the bed and palmed her hip. She jerked at the unexpected touch and released her grip. This time, as she rolled into him, he caught her in his arms, blanket and all. Her token struggle lasted only a matter of seconds.

"I thought the idea was to get some sleep," he stated, using the logic of her earlier argument against her. "If you want me to rest, you're gonna have to stop talking and be still."

She had somehow propped herself up on one elbow atop his chest. It was too dark to see the color of her eyes, but he could hear the weary distress in her voice as she looked up at him. "But I promised to stay on my side of the bed."

He brushed away the hair that had fallen across her brow. "I didn't."

"You should have asked first."

"I know." He waited a moment, surprised at how important the answer to his question would be. "Do you want me to let go?"

"No." She burrowed into him, using his chest as a pillow and his bare stomach as an armrest. She settled quickly into a deep, quiet sleep.

Jonas followed soon after.

Chapter Seven

When the first ray of sunshine hit Jonas's face, he blinked one eye open. For a few dreamy moments, he breathed in gently, warming to the fresh, unfamiliar scents on his wrinkled clothes and the bed that were not his own.

But then the coolness of the sheet draped across his stomach registered. His arms were empty. The bed was empty. Though it was no more than he deserved, the awareness of where he was and that he was alone careened through him like an out-of-control train, jolting him into another day.

Another reason not to like mornings. Faith was gone.

And it wasn't just his arms that felt empty.

He rolled over quickly, squashing the feeling. He clutched the cold leather and steel beneath the pillow and visually verified the location of his knife and his roommate. He stood up fast enough to give himself a headache, plopped back down on the side of the bed and cursed.

"Good morning to you, too."

The gentle ribbing in Faith's voice from across the room managed to reassure and annoy him at the same time. At least she was safe. Good Lord, she was dressed, too. She wore a new pair of jeans and an aqua sweatshirt with the Teton National Park logo that would have been gorgeous with her golden hair. He blinked and looked again. He supposed it went all right with that bright coppery color. But it just wasn't...

Jonas shook his head. With a hired gun after her, she might have to change more than her hair before this was over. And personal opinions on what he liked or didn't like couldn't get in the way. "Whatever."

He must have done an adequate job of keeping her nightmares and waking doubts at bay since she'd cuddled close through most of the night. Who could see his face then? And the darkness blurred the true dimensions of his body.

But he was a scarier prospect in the bright light of day, and regrets or embarrassment must have had a pretty easy time taking over even Little Mary Sunshine's best intentions. It was just past 7:00 a.m., but she clearly had no desire to linger in bed. Not with him there with her. He idly wondered if it was the face or the scar or the personality that had turned her off.

He pinched the bridge of his nose between his thumb and forefinger and waited for the throbbing tension to fade. Once the worst of it had passed, he dragged his hand down across his rough, stubbly face.

Jonas stood more slowly this time, grabbing the knife and looping the holster over his shoulder. She sat in the chair at the far window, holding back the edge of the drape so that a long, narrow chunk of sunlight flooded the room. "What are you doing?"

"Watching the sunrise. You have pretty ones here in Wyoming." She glanced over her shoulder, looking his way without looking at him. "I made some bologna sandwiches. It's not breakfast at Tiffany's, but it's all we have. And it's filling. I saved the last bottle of water for you."

He scanned the desktop to the neatly made meal, resting on a washcloth-turned-placemat. He went over and grabbed the first sandwich, taking away a third of it in his first bite. "What's your fascination with mornings?" he grumbled as he chewed. "Don't you take it for granted the sun's going to come up?"

"Not recently." She was still peeking through the edge of the curtain. "I did the same thing for months after my parents died, too. I find it reassuring to see proof there's going to be a new day."

That was a little fatalistic, even for his morning mood. "What happened to your parents?"

She let the curtain fall back to the window. "Died in a car accident twelve years ago. I was only twelve," she stated matter-of-factly. "It was a rainy night. They lost control on a bridge and plunged into the river below."

"That's tough." Jonas cringed as soon as he said the words. He couldn't come up with *I'm sorry* or *That must have hurt?* He'd better stick to keeping people safe and steer clear of the touchy-feely stuff.

But Faith turned and gave him a beautifully serene smile. "It was. Thanks."

Jonas chomped another bite of the sandwich, unsure what to make of the inexplicable warmth coursing through him. But the good feeling didn't last long.

He could see now that Faith held a small notebook and pen in her lap. She opened the book to a well-marked page, clicked her pen and prepared to write. "When you worked for The Watchers, how much were you paid per day? Or did you get paid by the job?"

"What?" Jonas stopped chewing and swallowed the food that had suddenly lost its flavor. "I'm not expecting you to pay me."

"I'd like to know so I can keep track." She jotted something in her notebook and then stared down at it. "I don't want to confuse our working relationship with anything else."

He tread cautiously around that one. "What other kind of relationship do you think we have?"

She stood up, crossed one arm around her waist and

tapped the pen to her mouth. "Well, we did share a rather—" she cleared her throat "—exceptional kiss last night. I don't know about you, but I think there's some sort of...chemistry between us."

Right. The explosive kind. The kind that made him forget who he was and think he could be something human again. He needed to crush that idea before she realized how on the money she was. "That kiss was a pretty woman and a horny guy and way too much tension in the room. It's not a relationship."

She pressed her lips together into a tight line, but wouldn't let it drop. "I agree. We were running on frayed nerves and shared fears and not enough sleep. Our guards were down. And you said that wouldn't happen again."

"I meant it." He didn't like it, but that's how it had to be. Hands-off. No contact beyond what was necessary for the job.

Faith might be young, but she was no dummy. She called him on the corner he'd just painted himself into. "So then you hold me through the night. How is that different?"

He glared at her for several long heartbeats. But it wasn't exactly temper that was brewing inside him. "That was practical. We both needed our rest."

"It didn't feel practical to me. You can be very gentle when you want to be. And when it's wrapped up in all that strength, it's kind of, well... It felt like you were taking care of me. And I'm grateful. I've never slept with a man that way before. I mean, I've *slept* with a man. Once. But he didn't. I mean, we...it wasn't—"

"I get the picture." More than he wanted to, actually.

Her cheeks spotted a bright rosy color. She combed her fingers through her hair and cupped the side of her neck, working through her embarrassment while Jonas simmered with a blend of jealousy that she'd been with another man, and something much more territorial. A perverse male pride that she appreciated their night together, while that other jackass—who didn't know what a special woman he'd had in his arms—had left her wanting.

He should tell her what it meant to him. The trust she'd shown him. How *normal* it felt to hold someone soft and warm throughout the night. How—

"But if it's all part of the job, I want to make sure I'm paying you what you're worth, so there won't be any misunderstanding when this is all done."

Sometimes, the worst part of his curse was in mistakenly thinking that it could somehow be lifted from him.

As reality crashed in around his softening feelings, he downed the last of the sandwich and stalked over to the sink. "You don't have that kind of money," he spat out bitterly.

He watched her reflection in the mirror follow right on his heels. "Then I will find some other way to pay you back."

"You don't owe me anything."

"I owe you my freedom." She stopped beside him in the mirror. But she was looking up at him, not his reflection. "I owe you my life."

Jonas turned and braced his hip on the counter, bringing his face a few inches closer to hers.

"So what are you offering as payment?" If she expected him to be crude and cutthroat about helping out a woman in need, then he'd be as crude as he could be. He brushed his knuckles beneath her chin and slid them along the smooth heat of her throat. "Another kiss, maybe?"

The color washed from her cheeks, but she didn't move away. "I...I could do that."

Damn, the woman had soft skin. Touching her like this made him think...made him wish... Hell. He steeled himself against betraying any tender feelings. "You'd do that to pay a debt?"

She nodded.

"How about a night in bed where we do more than

sleep?'' He ran his hand down between her breasts. Paused at her sharp intake of breath. Then took his sweet, deliberate time tracing the flat of her stomach. He circled the waist of her jeans, cupped her rump and pulled her into the vee of his legs. Every nerve ending in his body leaped to life at the suggestive contact, challenging him to seize what he could so easily take. He tortured himself by refusing to act on the impulse. ''Is your life and your freedom worth that?''

She braced her hands, still clutching the pen and notepad, on his chest and tilted her guileless green eyes up at him. Her breath was but a husky whisper. ''Is that what you want?''

Yes. He wanted her. He wanted that reckless determination and brave heart and beautiful body to be his completely.

But not like that. Never like that.

Or else he'd never be free of his curse.

Unable to sustain his temper or his resentment a moment longer, he turned her around, swatted her rump and sent her back into the main room. ''Go. Pack your stuff while I grab a shower.'' The coldest one he could stand.

''But Jonas—''

He couldn't let her reason her way out of this one. ''You're right. We do need to set some ground rules regarding our relationship.''

He held up his hand when she would have interrupted. ''I'm in charge. What I say goes. You are not a means to any end, you are part of the job. You don't write another penny in that book of yours because you don't owe me anything. And we don't have any more deep, meaningful discussions like this one. Especially in the morning. Am I clear?''

''Crystal.''

HE'D SAID IT ALL without a single curse. Chastised and reassured her in one long breath. Her tough guy was mellowing. Or maybe he'd never been as tough as he claimed to be in the first place.

Faith didn't understand the mix of emotions tumbling through her as she crouched in the dark behind Jonas outside the University of Wyoming's engineering classroom and computer lab. But she did understand one thing. Jonas Beck was a good man, even if he refused to believe it. In a span of less than forty-eight hours, she'd been saved, comforted, protected and almost seduced by the big, bad beast of the mountain.

His bad-boy style and rock-hard body should have sent her running as far from him as possible. But the glimpses of wounded insecurity, fierce protectiveness and blatant desire that peeked through the cracks of his harsh exterior were stirring up some unexpected feelings of her own.

Jonas wasn't as invulnerable as she'd first thought him to be. He could be hurt—by insults and ignorance. By failing to meet the lofty expectations for behavior he set for himself.

He could be hurt by her.

He liked her, she was sure of it. In a sexual way, at least. That torrid kiss, his wicked suggestion that she use her body to pay him for his protection, were definite clues.

Though she now understood he'd said those things to shock her, to prove his point about how little he needed from her—or anyone—she'd been tempted to consider his invitation. Not to repay any debt, but because she liked him, too. He was more raw, honed man than any she had ever seen before. And touching him, being touched by him— knowing he could channel every bit of his strength and passion and even tenderness onto the woman he was with— was a heady consideration.

She'd be a fool to give him her heart, though. He'd be a hard man to love. She likened him to a wounded warrior who had seen and survived unknown horrors. Back in civilized society, he could be trained to watch his mouth and mind his manners, but there was so much hurt inside him that she didn't know if he could ever be completely healed.

Faith tried not to think of the bigger picture. She tried not to consider her future or Jonas's. She tried to stay right here in the moment. To keep her wits about her and her senses sharp.

It wasn't hard to focus on the predicament she was in right now. Once the sun had set and the wind picked up, the temperature in Laramie had dropped steadily. She shivered beneath the tent of Jonas's brown jacket, but admitted her shaky composure might be from nerves as much as the cold.

They huddled between a hedge and a brick wall while they waited for the campus security guard to finish his hourly check on the outside doors and windows of the building. They'd walked through the building that afternoon to learn the layout of the lab and find the best way in. But since the lab required a valid student ID to even enter, Jonas had decided they would come back late at night and break in instead of causing a scene and drawing unwanted attention to themselves.

Faith lightly tapped on the broad back that faced her. "Are you sure this is a good idea?"

He glanced down at her over his shoulder. "We won't get caught."

"That's not what I asked. Technically, I haven't broken the law yet. And breaking and entering is definitely against the law."

The shadows masked the expression on his face, making it difficult to tell whether he was amused or annoyed by her attack of conscience. "If it'll make you feel better, we'll send a little extra money to the university for its electric bill. All we'll be doing is running one of their computers. I don't plan to do any damage. We'll slip in, slip out, and they won't be any wiser."

"In and out," she repeated, drawing the corduroy collar of his coat up around her neck and gathering her courage.

"Cold?" She heard Jonas move in the shadows an instant before two strong arms pulled her up against his chest.

She was startled for a moment, but quickly took advantage of his abundant heat and burrowed against the chest he offered. He wore a black, body-hugging sweater that tickled her cheek and snagged some strands of her hair. But it smelled heavenly—like musky man and a clean, warm blanket. "Better," she approved, finding strength as his warmth seeped into her. "Is covert work always like this?"

"No. Usually, you have to deal with the cold on your own." But the long hours and constant alertness and threat of danger always remained? She got the joke, but the unspoken balance of his answer weighed on her compassion.

Faith curled her glove-sheathed fingers into the front of his sweater, feeling for all the long, lonely hours he'd spent doing this same kind of work to protect others. To protect her country. "Thank you," she murmured against his chest.

"For what?"

How did she answer that one with sounding like the naive sap she was? She finally opted to be as vague as he had been. "For keeping me warm."

"There." It was a whispered alert, not a comfort word.

Faith pulled away, brushed the loose hair off her face and tucked it behind her ear. "What is it?" she asked, keeping her voice equally low.

He pulled a slim flashlight from his coat and turned it on to check his watch. "That's it." Jonas turned off the light. "The guard will be back in twenty-five minutes if he sticks to his schedule. That's our time slot." He folded his hand around hers and pulled her along beside him. "Let's go."

She patted the disk that was wrapped inside her pocket and quickened her pace to keep up with Jonas's long, crouching strides. He hurried behind the wall and hedge that encircled most of the engineering building and headed for the structure's side entrance. The decorative wall was both a blessing and a curse, according to Jonas. It would hide them from passersby on the street and sidewalk, but it would also hide their view of the guard when he made his next security check. Hence the need for timing their little visit down to the last minute.

"Can I help?" she asked after they ducked inside the door's protruding archway.

But Jonas already had the situation well in hand. He twisted the flashlight on and stuck the handle in his mouth. Then he drew out a wallet filled with thin metal tools. The items he pulled out looked like toothpicks in his big, gloved hands. But he used them with the dexterity of a surgeon. She marveled at the speed and stealth he used as he inserted them into the lock—twisted, jimmied, snapped—and then he was ushering her inside and closing the door behind them.

"Upstairs." He nodded toward the half staircase ahead of them. With his hand at the small of her back, he quickly guided her up the stairs and down the long dark hallway toward the computer lab entrance at the far end.

They hurried along in a whisper of movement through the tomblike interior of marbled floors and high ceilings. At every juncture with another hall or lecture room, she'd feel Jonas's fist at her neck, latching on to the jacket's collar and pulling her back a step as he scanned for any signs of company.

Faith took up the sentinel role when they reached the lab and Jonas opened the door with the same swift, silent process. "We're in."

He pushed open the door and guided her inside. "Twenty minutes," he announced, checking his watch and reminding her of the time crunch before handing over the flashlight and letting her scan the computers to find the one most likely to suit their needs.

She knew in a minute that the only one with the proper

disk drive and software program would be the one at the front desk—in clear view through the glass door should the guard decide to run a check inside the building. She offered Jonas an apologetic smile, even though he probably couldn't see it. "I'm afraid that's the one we need."

The risk of it didn't phase him. "Get to it, then."

He headed back to the door while she sat down and booted up the computer. Faith's heart pumped a little faster as the monitor came on and filled her workspace with a small puddle of light. "I won't need the flashlight now. Do you need it?"

Jonas zipped back to her side, took the flashlight, but remained, putting a physical blockade between her and the door. Her protective shadow raised the tension another notch. Faith clutched her fingers into fists, them wiggled them straight, wishing her pounding pulse wouldn't manifest itself in the form of shaking hands. "Are you sure I can't take my gloves off?" she asked.

"We're not leaving any fingerprints." A familiar logo from Eclipse Labs blossomed onto the screen. "There it is." He squeezed his hand over her shoulder and Faith jumped at the contact. "Easy," he crooned in a bone-deep pitch, leaving his hand in place and drawing out some of her tension. "Can you make it work?"

Faith glanced up, marveling at his patience in the face of a ticking clock. His glacial eyes caught the light from the monitor and seemed to glow in the dark. But she found it comforting rather than eerie, knowing that those eyes would spot any danger long before it got to her.

She inhaled a steadying breath and placed her hands on the keyboard. "Everything's on a network. Someone will know that we were here."

His grip tightened in a comforting squeeze, then disappeared. "They'll know when, but not who. And we'll be out of town before anyone questions it."

She nodded and began to type. "The disk is encrypted.

But I know most of Dr. Rutherford's entry codes.'' She quickly typed in several, but as she suspected, nothing opened the secret files. ''What would you use?''

She typed in *Darien Frye*. Error. She tried *Frye*. Error. *NT-6*. Error.

''We're down to fifteen minutes.'' Jonas was circling the room now, a noiseless wraith checking windows and doors and keeping the outside world at bay. ''Got anything yet?''

She was taking quick, deep breaths now, suppressing the urge to panic. She typed in his granddaughter's name. His late wife's. *Eclipse. Doomsday.* Faith clapped her fists together. ''Dammit, it won't open.''

''Easy, honey. You'll get it.'' She looked up, searching the darkness for the source of the husky endearment.

A skittering sensation of soothing heat short-circuited her frustration. She turned her attention back to the keyboard. ''Does it mean anything when you say that?'' she asked, expecting him to call it a slip of the tongue or to say nothing at all.

He didn't. He was back at the door now. ''Just keep working. We have twelve minutes.''

On a whim she typed in *honey*. Error. She could hear the word playing through her mind in Jonas's deep, dark pitch.

And she could hear another voice. An older voice. *Faith, honey, have you seen my notes on the Ryan project?*

''He wouldn't,'' she breathed out loud. It would be too much of a cosmic twist to this whole nightmare. An expectation that Dr. Rutherford knew she'd be involved up to her eyeballs in NT-6. Whatever it might be.

She slowly typed in a word. *Faith.*

Goose bumps prickled along the surface of her skin as a series of numbers and letters scrolled across the screen. ''I'm in.''

Jonas hurried to the desk and squatted down beside her. ''We've got ten minutes. Let's take a look.''

Faith skimmed her finger down the screen, evaluating their choices. "Design specs?"

"Sounds good to me."

She selected the file and waited for it to load. "He used my name, Jonas. The password. Why would he use my name?"

"Probably because you were important to him. Wait." Jonas had spotted something. Her nerves tightened into knots. But his narrowed eyes weren't looking at the door, they were looking at the screen.

Faith looked too. "What is it?"

His fingers brushed along the hair at her temple, tucking it gently behind her ear. Now she was really worried. "It's nothing."

"You're a terrible liar."

His fingers slipped around to cup the back of her neck. "It's nothing we'll talk about now," he amended. "Our time's running out."

She intended to hold him to that promise. Scaring the bejesus out of her without saying why? He'd need a little lecture about that. Later. But drawings and formulae were coming up on the screen now, and she diverted her attention to study them.

"It looks like some kind of storage container." She scrolled down to the next image. "Something that can be converted into a—"

"A weapon." Jonas said it with such drop-dead certainty that it chilled her to the bone. "It's a freakin' bomb."

"A bomb?" Faith shook her head. That didn't make sense. "Dr. Rutherford was such a gentle man. He designed toasters for NASA, not bombs."

"Looks like he designed this one." Jonas checked his watch again. "Can you print that out?"

"Yeah." She hit the print command and closed the file. The printer beeped and clicked and whirred to life. "Oh, my God. That's loud."

Faith instinctively reached for the off switch to silence the cranking noise that would surely give them away. Jonas grabbed her hand and turned her back to the keyboard. "We've got a few minutes. See what else is on the disk."

"But—"

"Just do it." His voice was calm and assured. She wished she was, too.

"How much time do we have before the guard comes back?"

Jonas didn't answer. He pointed to a file labeled NT-1-5. "Open that one."

Feeling the knots twist ever tighter in her stomach, she clicked on the icon and opened up a list of scientific formulae.

"Do you know what they are?" Jonas asked.

Faith scrolled through the pages. "They look like chemical compounds for metal alloys." One line of figures jumped out at her and she frowned. "But this one wouldn't work. Extreme temperatures would break it down. It'd crack. Crumble into dust. He must have labeled the project NT-6 because that's the compound that worked."

Jonas leaned back, resting his elbow on the desktop, and looked right at her. "What kind of engineer are you?"

She grinned at the awed skepticism in his voice. "A smart one. Who aced chemistry." For a few moments, his obvious admiration chased away thoughts of ticking clocks and security guards. "Do you want me to print this off?"

"No." He checked his watch again and vanished into the darkness. Her stress-free reprieve vanished with it. "Is that thing done printing?"

His voice was near the door again. Faith checked the page count. "It's got a couple more to go."

"We can't wait that long. Our twenty-five minutes are almost up. Turn it off and kill the noise."

"But it'll still be queued up in the printer. Someone could see—"

"Then clear it out."

"That'll take some time—"

"Now's not the time to argue with me."

She was already clearing the print command. "I wasn't arguing. I was pointing out—"

A toilet flushed somewhere down the hall.

Faith froze.

But she could hear Jonas moving. "Shut it down now. Our guard just took a potty break. He's two minutes early."

Her fingers flew frantically over the keys as she commanded everything to shut down. "C'mon." She tapped her feet nervously on the floor. Why was it taking so long? She saw a beam of light through the glass door. "There's a light in the hallway."

"Grab the disk."

The next half minute rushed by too quickly for Faith to take note of everything that happened. She snatched the disk as it slid out of the computer, stuffed papers into her coat pocket. And then she was across the room, jammed into a dark doorless closet with Jonas at her back and his hand clamped over her mouth.

Her pulse hammered in her ears and her heart felt as if it would pound right out of her chest. The lab door was opening and light from the monitor was pouring into the room. It clicked off the instant before the beam of light swung across the computer terminal she'd been using. The sudden shock of light and dark and light again startled her. But her gasp was muffled by Jonas's broad hand. His left arm closed more tightly around her waist, pulling her up against the heat of his body as if he could sense the responding chill bumps that made her shiver.

She tried to breathe deeply, silently as the guard stood in the doorway and inspected the dark room with his flashlight. The pungent scent of Jonas's leather glove warred with the smell of her own fear. But Jonas breathed slowly, steadily behind her.

But when the guard took a step into the room, she felt him shift. He was pushing her behind him, reaching for his knife.

"Is somebody in here?" asked the guard.

"No—" Faith jerked free of Jonas's restraining hand.

But she wasn't warning the guard.

She wrapped both her arms around Jonas's biceps and pulled against him for all she was worth. She couldn't let him out of this closet. She wouldn't let him kill an innocent man.

Chapter Eight

"Dammit, Faith." Why was she fighting him?

Jonas latched on to a wrist and a shoulder and tried to push her out of sight into the recesses of the closet.

But she had braced her feet and was shoving against him. "Sit down."

"What?" Of all the damn dumb times to teach him a lesson on manners— "Get back—"

The guard stepped into the room and Jonas's senses screamed into defensive mode. He hadn't discovered them yet, but unless he was deaf, he could hear the shuffles and whispers of noise. He unsnapped the sheath of his knife.

"Sit." Faith shoved at the middle of his chest. The backs of his knees hit something solid and he plunked down into one of the rolling computer chairs. The immediate disadvantage had him pushing to his feet. But he never got there. Faith climbed into his lap, facing him, straddling him. The shock alone stopped him for an instant. Her brazen bad timing would get them both arrested. Or worse.

"Try it my way. Please?" she begged before framing his face between her hands and kissing him.

"Fai—" His body exploded with a fiery response at the insistent urging of her lips on his. His hands that had flown to her waist to lift her off him splayed across her bottom, dragging the swell of her breasts against his harder chest.

But his brain responded with an equally urgent protest. Escape.

A beam of light reflected off the radiant skin of her forehead. "Hey!" They'd been found. "What are you kids doing?"

Kids?

Overhead lights flooded the room, temporarily blinding him. But the kiss didn't stop. If anything, her soft, full mouth took on a taste of extra naughty. She cooed something seductive in her throat and leaned in closer, wrapping her arms around the back of his head. They slid up to scoot his hat down low over their faces.

And then he understood.

Of all the crazy, misguided—

Jonas wrapped his arms around her waist and joined the charade.

He heard a man's voice behind him, clearing his throat. "It's after hours. I'm afraid you kids will have to leave."

Jonas urged her mouth to open and delved inside with his tongue. She was hot to the touch and sweet to the taste. She wiggled her hips and he groaned, forgetting for the moment that this bold seduction of hers was for an audience.

But at the sharp tap on his shoulder he stilled. "I said you kids will have to leave."

Jonas recognized the voice of authority when he heard it. And even though it was the throaty timbre of an older man, it was the tone of a man who was used to being in charge. He moved his hands back to the neutral territory of Faith's waist and reluctantly broke off the kiss. He was a sorry son of a gun to react so strongly to a fake embrace, and Faith was one hell of an actress to make their impromptu cover look—and feel—so convincing.

"But we were just getting to the good part."

Jonas's eyes opened wide at the breathy sigh in her voice. She was playing this thing to the hilt. Sneaking into an off-limits room to fool around. He wondered if the white-haired guard with the still-holstered gun was buying it.

"Come on now, you two." The man's grandfatherly voice had an indulgent ring to it, as if they weren't the first couple he'd caught using the facilities after hours. "Time to go home."

With a disappointed moan, Faith finally moved. As she pulled her hands away, she slouched Jonas's hat down over his face and turned sideways in his lap, facing the guard, trying to camouflage him. Didn't she know? A face like his just didn't blend in.

The guard was backing up, feeling more assured of their cooperation. "I'll have to write this up, you know. Just give me your ID numbers and I'll take care of it."

Enough of this game. The old guy was sly, sounding friendly enough, but working in a subtle request to prove they were who they claimed to be. Jonas stood and set Faith on her feet.

"Whoa." The guard backed off another step, his face reflecting his concern. "You okay, miss?"

Faith flattened her palm across her heart and looked properly affronted. "Of course, I am. It's just—" She giggled like a school girl. "Your timing sucks. If you know what I mean."

The guard meant, *Is the big guy forcing you to do anything you don't want to?* "I know it's a thrill to try to get away with something, but I can't allow this...public display of affection to continue."

Any chance at a distracting cover was blown. She was laying it on too thick for the old codger to buy it. Faith's kiss-swollen lip pouted out in a frown. "I just wanted to try it someplace different."

"I'm going to need the two of you to come down to the security office and file that report. You grad students?" He looked up at Jonas. Probably noticed the gray in his hair. Or the lines beside his eyes and mouth.

"He's my professor," Faith piped in.

Way too thick.

"Professor?" The old man stuck the flashlight right in Jonas's face. Now he probably thought he was breaking all kinds of campus rules. "What do you teach?"

Forget it. The guard had already seen too much as it was. Jonas reached out and twisted the man around before he could reach his gun.

"Jonas, no!"

He pinched his carotid artery until the man passed out.

Faith was beating at his shoulder, tugging at his sleeve, as he lay the unconscious man on the floor. He stepped over the body and reached for her hand. "Let's go."

But Faith dropped to her knees beside the guard's body. "You didn't have to hurt him."

What was she on about now? "Relax. He's not dead. He'll wake up in a few minutes."

"He was just doing his job." She had two fingers pressed against his neck, feeling for a pulse. "Danny Novotny was just doing his job, too."

"Who's Danny—?" Damn. He breathed in deeply. He'd lost control of this situation long ago. He took it back. He picked Faith up by the arms, lifted her over the body and headed for the door. "I'd like to be out of here when he *does* wake up."

She fought against the grip on her arm. "He was afraid of you, that's all. That's why I tried to hide you. So he wouldn't be so intimidated. We could have talked our way—"

Jonas stopped in his tracks. He grabbed her by both shoulders and pulled her up onto her toes, jamming his face right down into hers, demanding her attention. "We don't know if he radioed in whatever suspicious noise or light brought him down here in the first place. This building could be swarming with campus and city cops any minute. Now, do you trust me or not?"

Her voice was small and quiet. "He's not hurt?"

"No."

Her hands came up and rested lightly against his shoulders. "Then let's go."

"If you insist."

"IF THAT SWEET old man turns up dead after talking to me, I'm going to go straight to the police." Faith still held the tepid coffee she hadn't touched between her hands as they sped along the back roads of northeast Colorado toward Denver. This was getting to be too much. She was going to lose it. "Not the Saint Louis police. But somewhere. I swear, Jonas, I'll turn myself in."

The battered green Chevy's engine hummed with power, the only sound besides her own voice in the dark of the night.

"It won't come to that," he finally answered. He drove with one big hand in a comfortable grip on the wheel, and the other resting on the door beside him. He looked straight ahead, his icy eyes focused on the road before them. "If Copperhead killed Sheriff Prince, he might have reached a dead end and is waiting for further instructions. Frye has the connections to place us in Laramie, if he's smart enough to put the pieces together without the names. That should buy us a day or so. I'm more concerned about our descriptions being out on the wire now. Some local hotshot might try to detain us."

"And hand me over to the FBI?"

His big shoulders shrugged, disturbing the atmosphere within the cab of the truck. Disturbing Faith's equilibrium as well. Once she'd turned herself over to Jonas's judgment, he'd sneaked them out of the engineering building, shuttled them off campus and out of town before campus security alerted anyone else.

"Once we expose what's on that disk, you'll be safe. The Bureau will be knocking themselves out to protect you.

The information there is the kind of thing the government wants to contain. A bomb like that would be a big ticket item for a terrorist or third-world revolution market.''

A shiver of dread rippled down Faith's spine. ''But its design specifications are so small.''

''It's not the type of bomb you strap onto the wing of a fighter jet. It's the kind you sneak on board an airplane. Or smuggle into a police station. It's not one you see coming.''

She nodded. ''It looked like Dr. Rutherford was developing an alloy that could pass through an X ray or metal detector.'' She set her cup in the holder on the dash and hugged herself, willing the goose bumps to go away. ''I still can't believe he would invent something like that.''

''Maybe he was forced to. Or he stumbled upon the formula accidentally, and someone else came up with the idea of using it for a bomb housing.''

Faith yawned through her smile. He really was trying to say nice things, to carry on a conversation to distract her from the terrible fears that dogged her every waking thought. He'd talked a lot for a man who didn't like to socialize. She should give him a break. Except she liked it when he talked. His deep, resonant voice, his intelligence— it made him seem so human. So normal.

''My dad used to work with metals and plastics.'' She moved on to a lighter topic. ''He'd take me to his lab in the summers when I was off school and let me do a few experiments of my own. I poured molds and built models. I guess that was my inspiration to go into engineering.''

Jonas reached down and adjusted the heater, which was running with the same top-notch efficiency of the engine. ''Your father sounds like he was a good dad.''

''He was.'' Faith settled back into the seat, feeling a moment of contentment as she remembered some of her favorite experiences with her father. ''What about you?'' she asked, after several miles had passed. ''What was your dad like?''

A long beat of silence passed. "Not like your dad, I'm sure." He scrubbed his free hand across the stubble that lined his jaw. "I think my friend, Murphy, knows the right people in Washington who can help us. We'll catch a flight out of Denver tomorrow. I can pay cash and get us fake IDs."

The awkward shift in their conversation was hard to miss. But if he didn't want to talk about his father, she wouldn't press him. Maybe there was a conflict or loss there that had helped steer him toward the hard man he'd become.

"And then it'll be over?" she asked.

She'd like to meet this George Murphy from The Watchers. Maybe he could shed some light on Jonas's past, his personality, his future plans. She'd like to meet anybody who could help her understand this giant enigma of a man whom she was learning to appreciate and enjoy spending time with. Who made her feel a little less lonely and a whole lot safer. And who stirred things inside her that no man had ever touched before.

"It'll be over when Frye and Copperhead are in prison or dead." He surprised her by reaching across the seat and catching her hand up in his. "But that'll be soon. We're going to get them, honey. One way or another. I promise."

Honey. There was that word again. Sometimes it rolled off his tongue as if he hadn't given its significance a thought in the world. And other times, like just now—in the warmth of the truck and the cloak of the night—it felt very, very significant.

It scared her how off-kilter, how feminine, how treasured this man could make her feel.

But before she got too deeply in touch with emotions she wasn't sure she wanted or was ready to feel, she squeezed his hand and then released him. She snuggled down into his jacket, which she wore draped around her shoulders, and stared out her window into the passing shadows of the autumn night.

Lord, she was tired. It seemed she'd been spending her whole life driving, running, hiding. For the sake of her conscience and a good night's sleep, she needed this nightmare to be over.

"Are you sure that old guy you did the neck thing to will be all right?" she asked, rehashing a topic that still worried her.

Jonas shook his head, his mouth curved into something almost like a smile. "That old guy was a retired cop or military man. He might have snow on the top, but he was in good shape. He'll recover just fine. Probably well enough to be pretty pissed that I got the drop on him."

"Really?" He'd looked more like someone's grandfather to her, someone who should be playing with grandkids and going fishing. "He wasn't anything like the cop who interviewed me in Saint Louis. He didn't look like he could defend himself."

"The cop in Saint Louis?"

"No. The campus security guard." A clear image of Jermaine Collier was emblazoned with fear on every memory cell in her brain. "Detective Collier could definitely defend himself. Even against you, I think. He was almost as tall as you, built like a streamlined tank. And the gun he carried was right out of a *Lethal Weapon* movie. Of course, he groomed himself to look intimidating—shaved head and a mustache and goatee."

Jonas glanced her way. "He was a detective?"

"Uh-huh. Slick suit, badge and everything." She glanced back. Was he just making more conversation? Or had she said something important? "Why?"

He returned his attention to the road. "It's just unusual for a detective to wear facial hair—unless he's working an undercover assignment. Most departments have dress codes."

"Come to think of it, I guess none of the other men there did."

"There were other detectives?"

She shook her head. "The crime lab. The technicians who dusted for prints and went through my house taking pictures."

"Detectives don't usually work solo, either."

It was the second thing that didn't seem to fit Jonas's idea of a cop. "Okay, you're officially scaring me. Detective Collier creeped me out enough, already. He was all smooth talk and intimidation. What are you trying to say?"

He looked at her across the seat, his eyes seeming to glow in the lights from the dashboard. "I'm not saying anything. I'm just thinking out loud."

He reached his long arm clear across the seat. His fingertips hovered close to her face, as if he wanted to touch her, but wasn't sure the touch would be welcome. Faith encouraged him with a gentle smile and he brushed a lock of hair off her forehead. The pads of his fingers were like the stroke of a cat's tongue, a mesmerizing touch that managed to be soothing and stimulating at the same time.

"Hey, you were a trouper tonight," he praised. "Thinking on your feet, keeping your cool."

"Keeping my cool?" She yawned.

He grinned and pulled both hands back to the wheel. "Most of the time. You weren't bad for a rookie." He nodded toward her door. "I'll leave the heat running and you can use my coat for a pillow. It'll be a while before we check in to a motel. Why don't you get some sleep."

The compliment made her suspicious. It was a little too long-winded for Jonas. But she *was* tired. And the warmth of the truck's cab and the security of his company relaxed her weary muscles and made her drowsy.

"Okay." She folded the jacket and tucked it between her ear and the door. "Promise to wake me when we get to Denver. Good night."

"Good night."

She was on the fringes of sleep when she heard the tone

of his cell phone and listened to him begin to talk. But she was in a safe, cozy dreamland before she could make much sense of the conversation itself.

"COLLIER. I don't have a first name. Claims to be a detective with the Saint Louis police department. Check him out."

George Murphy jotted down the information. "Collier. Got it. I'll run it through with the description you gave me and have something for you tomorrow. You think he works for Frye?"

"I don't know anything for sure yet. I'm just covering my bases."

"Sounds more like a hunch. Wanna share?"

Jonas glanced over at Faith. She seemed so young and small curled up in the corner of the truck's bench seat. So innocent. But as the pieces of the puzzles began to emerge, he was getting a very sick feeling that her involvement in all this was not unfortunate coincidence, but something much more sinister. A conspiracy set into play long before his lusty little brainiac with the just soul and sexy mouth ever entered the picture.

"Not yet," Jonas answered, turning his attention back to the phone and his midnight call. "Any luck with the Feds?"

George *had* been a busy boy. "I got a friend of mine to agree to stall the investigation. As long as we give him everything you find when all is said and done. He does have a man in the field who's been tracking your friend in relation to the string of murders in Saint Louis. He—"

"Is his name Rory Carmichael?"

"How'd you know?"

"Faith told me about him. She's seen him on TV a couple of times. He put the description out on us after the murder in Elk Point."

"Carmichael's a rogue warrior, according to my contact.'' George's deep breath warned Jonas to brace himself for unwelcome news. ''He's got a rep as a straight arrow. But he's like a dog with a bone. He won't let go of a thing until he thinks it's done. If he followed her trail to Wyoming, he'll find her again.''

Jonas wanted to swear, but he was worried that Faith's finely tuned radar would hear him, even in her sleep. ''Can't they call him back in from the investigation?''

''The order's been issued. But we'll have to wait and see how long it takes Carmichael to follow it. He wants Faith Monroe.''

So he had one gung-ho FBI agent on their tail he'd have to watch out for. But it would be a little easier to avoid one man than a nationwide manhunt. ''What about Frye?''

Murphy's report was quick and concise. ''Like I said, he hasn't actually been seen for a couple of years. But some of his old networks have been showing activity the past few months. Word is out that the DeLeone terrorist cell in Central America has been amassing a lot of cash and is looking for some high-tech weaponry. The sort of stuff Frye used to pedal to them.''

''Like our nontraceable minibomb?'' William Rutherford's disk supplied an apt acronym for what Frye was selling. NT-6. A bomb that couldn't be detected. Small enough to carry in a purse or briefcase, but packing enough payload to destroy a city block.

''Just like.'' There was an uncharacteristic hesitation on the other end of the line. ''Beck?''

''Yeah?''

''Will you recognize Frye if you see him again? Or Copperhead? It's been a lot of years since you worked the Frye case. You might not see them coming.''

''I'll know Frye.'' He'd know those eyes anywhere. His stepmother had claimed he had devil eyes because of their ultralight color. But Darien Frye's ordinary brown eyes had reflected something that wasn't human. No heart. No conscience. He could cut a business deal or cut a throat with equal indifference. Jonas had no doubts. "I'll recognize him."

"And Copperhead? He could be anybody." George wasn't telling him anything he hadn't already considered. "Your girl has seen him, even if she doesn't know it. Someone she trusted. Someone the people he kills are willing to trust."

A cop. An agent. A woman. An old man. Hell. An old woman. Anyone who might not be perceived as a threat could be the biggest threat of all.

"I know." The lights of the Denver metropolitan area were glowing on the horizon. He hadn't told Murphy where they were. He wouldn't trust anybody right now. Not completely.

Faith stirred in her sleep, as if he'd transmitted the thought telepathically. Not even her. He was falling hard for his protected charge. He was becoming less of a guardian and more of a man the longer he was with her. He'd lost his objectivity somewhere along the line. And though he couldn't pinpoint the exact time when he'd started to care, he could predict exactly when it would end.

The moment this was over. The moment she no longer needed a guardian. The moment she realized she could return to normal life and the real world, but he could not.

"Beck? You still there?" Damn. He was really losing focus. George had asked him a question.

"I'm here."

"Are you sure you don't want me to meet you somewhere? I might be rusty from all my years behind a desk, but at least I'd be another set of eyes."

"No. You're more help to us in D.C. We're coming to you. If I can get Faith and this disk to you, we can get her into some kind of witness protection program. Her testimony can clear her name and put Frye away for good."

"If we can find him," George cautioned, ever the voice of reason.

But Jonas was a man of instinct. "I'm not worried. He'll find us.

"I just need to make sure I'm good and ready when he does."

"WHICH BED do you want?" Faith asked, more disappointed than she cared to admit to see that Jonas had booked them a room with two double beds. She shrugged out of his jacket and hung it over the back of the chair at the desk. "It doesn't matter to me, I'm beat."

But Jonas had no trouble making a decision. "I'll take the one closer to the door. It's the only entrance."

"Fine."

Making quick work of washing her face and brushing her teeth, Faith stepped into the bathroom and changed into the flannel shirt she'd borrowed from Jonas. The shirt was big and warm and it carried a trace of masculine musk from Jonas's skin. And while it was a comfort to wear it, or to snuggle in his coat, it wasn't the real thing. And she felt vulnerable, incomplete without him.

She came out and climbed beneath the covers while Jonas took his turn in the bathroom. Though sturdier than the bed she'd slept in last night, this one felt just as empty. Just as lonely.

Jonas repeated the same ritual he had last night, checking the locks and window and turning off all but the bathroom light before removing his knife and holster and arranging them beside the bed and under his pillow. He climbed on top of the flowered bedspread, still wearing his jeans, and unbuttoned his shirt.

When she could hear him settling in to a more comfortable position to watch and doze, she rolled over to face him in the darkness. "Talk to me, Jonas. Tired as I am, I don't think I could sleep right now."

"What's wrong?" His body might be a vague shadow on the other side of the nightstand, but his voice was deep and smooth and clear.

"Nothing new." She pulled the covers up around her chin and wished he'd invite her to cuddle with him instead. "I can't believe that I'm carrying around the design for such a destructive weapon." She hesitated a beat before asking the next question. "How many people could be hurt if a bomb like that was detonated?"

"A lot."

She rolled onto her back and stared at the nothingness above her. "And neither the police nor airport security nor anybody else would have a chance to detect it or stop and defuse it."

So much devastation for such a small, unassuming disk. She thought she could relate.

"Can't I just destroy the disk?"

"No." His sharp answer took her by surprise. "Right now, that disk is probably the only thing keeping you alive. Frye doesn't have it. He wants you to lead him to it."

She shook her head. "But if we tell him it's gone, that it doesn't exist—"

"Then he'll be pissed off and have you killed for messing up his plans."

Her deep sigh filled the silence of the room. "Is there anything I can do to stop him? Besides keep running with the disk?"

He took so long to answer that she thought he might have fallen asleep. "You could hand over the disk to the FBI counterterrorist division as evidence. Give a deposition about the break-ins at your home and the lab. Testify to whatever Dr. Rutherford told you. Combined with what The Watchers have accumulated on Frye in the past, it'd be enough to put him away."

"Wouldn't my testimony be hearsay?"

"The courts are more lenient with deathbed confessions.

Rutherford told you who killed him and who hired the hit. And he indicated that they would be coming after you, too.''

Run.

Faith shivered and curled into a ball beneath the covers, seeking, but finding little warmth. ''I don't want to run forever. I have family. I had a career. I'm missing a friend's funeral. I don't know how much longer I can do this.''

''You got guts, lady. You're strong.'' She heard him shifting on the bed. Without any sort of segue, he switched from boosting her confidence to acting like the agent he'd once been trained to be. ''Faith, were you recruited to work at Eclipse Labs when you graduated?''

''I was recruited by a lot of places.''

''But Eclipse really wanted you, I bet.''

What was he getting at? ''Yeah. They offered the best salary and benefits. But the opportunity to work with William Rutherford was what cinched it for me.''

''I'll just bet.'' That sounded ominous. ''I think you can testify to a conspiracy that's been going on for over half your life.''

Faith sat up in bed. He was making no sense. ''What are you talking about?''

''When we were looking at the disk tonight, did you notice the dates on some of those documents? Not the file names themselves, but inside, on the specs and formulas you were reading.''

''No. I was a little preoccupied. Why?''

''They were dated twelve years ago.''

Twelve. The significance of the number toyed with her comprehension. ''Maybe they were old designs that Frye just found out about. Dr. Rutherford certainly wouldn't advertise that he'd invented something that could be used for such a purpose.''

Jonas's uncharacteristically patient voice told her he wanted her to reach a different conclusion. ''You said your parents died about twelve years ago. And that your father did the same kind of work that you and Rutherford did.''

She pulled her knees up to her chest and hugged them. She didn't want to even consider the possibility of what he was suggesting. She shoved her fingers through her hair and cupped the side of her neck. ''My brain's too tired and my heart's too afraid to put together what you're asking me to.''

But Jonas was determined to spell it all out. ''I'm guessing that William Rutherford knew your father. Maybe they even worked together on the project.'' Faith resisted the urge to cover her ears. ''And Rutherford didn't put your name in as the encryption code—''

''My father did.'' She threw back the covers and climbed out of bed. Sleep was out of the question now. ''Are you thinking my father was killed, too? That he somehow gave the designs to Dr. Rutherford, and Frye killed him?''

Her skin was a riot of goose bumps, and no amount rubbing her arms or pacing was bringing any heat back into her system. ''I hate what you're saying. I lost the two people I loved most. And you're suggesting they were murdered over that same stupid disk?''

She was getting frantic now. No way was she strong or gutsy as Jonas had implied. She was falling apart. ''And that I was set up before I ever went to work at Eclipse?''

She whirled around, seeing Jonas's silhouette on the bed as a lighter shadow in the darkness. ''Why would anyone do that? Did they think my father had given me the disk? Why would Dr. Rutherford lie? He was always so nice to me. Why would he—?''

''Maybe he thought he was protecting you by keeping you close.'' Jonas the shadow was up and moving now, with a stealth that matched his catlike eyes. ''Maybe he needed you there to divert suspicion from himself. Frye must have suspected he had that disk, or they wouldn't have searched the lab and killed him.'' Big, strong hands closed around her shoulders. "Maybe Frye and Rutherford didn't know the codes to get into that disk, but as your father's daughter, you might. Without realizing it, you could be the key to unlocking all that information."

She shook off his hands, refusing to be comforted, and walked away. "I want to go home. I don't want to be a part of this anymore."

But he wasn't done tormenting her with possibilities yet. "Do you remember anything that was on the disk? The designs? The chemical formulas?"

"Sure." She didn't have a photographic memory, but a lot of it she remembered well enough to recreate on her own computer. But she understood why Jonas had asked. "I understand my dad and Dr. Rutherford's notes well enough that I could sell the design to someone else. The competition." Charming. "So, no matter how this conspiracy plays out, I'm dead if I do, and dead if I don't."

"You won't die." She could hear the rustle of denim as he sighed or shifted or steeled himself behind her. "I won't let you die."

"Don't make promises you can't keep." She wasn't sure if she sounded sarcastic or sad.

Jonas's hand wrapped around her upper arm with the controlled force he'd used before making the effort to civilize himself for her sake. In one swift motion, he turned her, catching her chin between his finger and thumb and tilting it up. A glacial light blazed in the depths of his eyes. "I will die before Frye or Copperhead gets to you."

His voice shook with the power of his vow.

"And that's supposed to make me feel better?" The first glimmer of tears stung her eyes. She blinked and let them spill onto her cheeks as she raised her hand and traced her fingertips across the shocked expression on his sensual lips. "Haven't I lost enough people I care about already?"

As the tears overtook her, he scooped her up in his arms and carried her back to her bed. He tucked her in beneath the covers, then crawled on top and lay down beside her. He gathered her into the heat of his arms and body, and pressed her face against the sizzle of skin at the center of his chest.

He consoled her the way the big brute did best. He held her close and let her cry herself to sleep.

And he never confirmed nor denied that it was okay for her to care.

Chapter Nine

Faith awoke in the wee hours of the morning, filled with an unusual, erotic heat.

Her bottom was on fire. As she squirmed away from the burning warmth, a deep-pitched moan hummed beside her ear. The sound snapped her into full consciousness, and she made a quick assessment of where she was. And who she was with.

That's when she realized that Jonas's hand was cupped very intimately, very possessively around the curve of her buttock. He was holding her close, even in his sleep, tangling his legs with hers and the blanket.

It was a heady experience to feel so treasured, so sheltered. She couldn't read his expression in the shadows, but his deep, even breathing told her a lot. This was a good place for him, too.

But her sinuses were plugged from the emotional release of all those tears, and her bladder was annoyingly full. She didn't want to leave. She was afraid she'd never find this particular contentment again. But when nature called...

She reached behind her and gently picked up his wrist. But his arms snapped back into place, almost lifting her from the bed. "Don't go. I don't want you to leave me. Not yet."

"Jonas?" She shook him lightly at the shoulder.

All at once his arms unfolded and he rolled away from her. "I'm sorry. I didn't mean to scare you."

She frowned, missing his uncensored feelings as much as she missed his warmth. "You didn't scare me."

But he was already up and moving away. To the other bed.

Perplexed and concerned as to why he'd automatically assumed she wouldn't want him there with her, she let him have his distance. She pulled her shirt down to a more modest level and got up to use the facility and splash cold water on her face.

When she returned, they were both wide-awake, both sitting in the darkness. "You didn't scare me." She repeated herself, knowing he wouldn't listen this time, either. She leaned back against the headboard and pulled the pillow into her lap. "I'm sorry I made such a fuss earlier. I guess it all caught up to me. I didn't realize how much I was up against."

"We don't know for a fact that Frye murdered your father."

"But you think he did."

"The pieces are all about to fall into place. I can feel it. And then all hell is gonna break loose."

She kneaded the pillow in her grasp. She didn't want to talk about herself anymore. She wanted to know why a man who could be so tender and passionate and protective in the dark of the night always woke up in such a mood. "Why did you think you'd scared me?"

"I scare everybody."

"That's not true." She sat forward and looked at him across the gap between the beds, waiting patiently until he looked at her before going on. "People who shun you because of your face haven't really looked into your eyes."

The ice-blue windows shut and he turned away, refusing to accept kind words. "My stepmother called them devil eyes. They made her nervous."

Devil eyes? Faith's heart lurched in her chest. "She must have been very unhappy to say such a cruel thing to a child."

"She and my dad kicked me out of the house when I was fourteen. But I looked like a man. They said I could take care of myself." His matter-of-fact recitation of such a heartless act spoke volumes about how much he'd hardened himself to his feelings over the years. "My stepmom said I was a threat to her children."

"You have brothers and sisters?" That surprised her. She'd never imagined him to have any family. He'd always seemed so completely alone.

He stood up, peeled off his shirt and tossed it at the foot of his bed. "Look. This is not something I talk about."

He should. She had a feeling he needed to. Desperately.

He lay back down and rolled away from her, pretending he was going to sleep.

He'd been so understanding of her pain, of how lost she'd felt to learn her entire life she'd been the pawn of some larger conspiracy. "My past is an open book to you. I'm game to listen if you want to share some of yours."

Faith leaned back in the bed, wishing they could go back to sleep together. Jonas holding her was when she felt the safest, the most secure. And, apparently, that was the only time he felt comfortable enough to drop his guard with her.

The clock on the bedside table flipped over to 3:00 a.m. before he spoke again. His voice was a toneless sound, as dark as the night itself. "They were hers from her first marriage. Two girls. Both younger than me. According to my stepmother, I gave them nightmares."

He rolled over, facing her now. Faith rolled onto her side to watch and listen as well. In the dim light from the bathroom, she saw him point to the scar on his forehead. "That's how I got this. Everyone thinks it's a war wound. Something I got on a mission, or from a street fight."

She'd assumed as much herself. But, then, she'd misjudged a lot of things about Jonas. "Tell me about your scar," she urged softly.

"Her younger daughter was crying in her sleep one night, having a bad dream. I got left in charge when she went out with Dad. Cindy, my stepsister, was throwing a fit, so I went in to check on her. She was still screaming and crying when her mother came home." He stopped to breathe in deeply; Faith simply held her breath. This couldn't be good. "She accused me of attacking Cindy. Came after me with the fireplace poker."

Faith's breath rushed out in a painful sigh. "Oh, my God."

"She knocked the cap off one of the bedposts, exposed a screw—"

"Jonas." Faith shot up out of bed and crossed the gap between them. She sat on the edge of his bed, massaging his hand between both of hers, reliving the graphic story with him.

"My dad—" He almost laughed. But Faith was dangerously close to weeping again. "—he was almost as big as I am now. He took her side. They wouldn't listen to Cindy or me. He only had to hit me once. I fell against the bedpost. Damn lucky I didn't lose an eye."

"Oh, Jonas." She leaned over and hugged her arms around his shoulders. It was a battle scar of the worst kind, inflicted by people he thought he could love and trust. "How could they?"

"They never wanted me. Once I left, I never went back."

A tight muscle worked along the line of his jaw as he fought to control something. And failed. He wrapped his arms around her waist and rolled onto his back, carrying her with him to rest on top. He squeezed her almost painfully tight as his wry laugh became a silent sob and then a furious revelation of anger. "You know what the irony was? My dad. *He* was abusing the girls. I ran into Cindy a few years later and she told me. It was the last time we talked.''

Faith had thought she was all cried out, but she was weeping now.

Jonas wiped away the tears with the pad his thumb, catching each one in a tender caress. ''Don't do that, honey. Not for me. I should have stayed and protected them.''

''You didn't know.'' She tried to comfort him physically by touching his face and chest. She traced the scar itself, from the bridge of his nose up into his hairline. ''You were a child yourself. They hurt you.''

''I knew I had to make things right. I knew I had to—''

''What? Hide away from the world because of one woman's hateful words? She didn't know what she was talking about. She didn't know you.'' Her tears quickly played out as a defensive sort of anger took their place. ''Do you think you have to protect everyone else now as some kind of atonement? Is that why you joined The Watchers?''

Jonas's hands had started to move, too. They slipped beneath her shirt and drew long, taut circles across her back. ''I took the jobs nobody else wanted. Some of the men had families. And I… It didn't matter so much for me. I never had anyone.''

He'd never had anyone.

''It matters.'' Faith scooted up along his chest, creating an instant friction that pebbled her nipples into rigid knots and elicited a sticky, drizzly heat deep inside her. ''Even then, you were protecting the men you worked with.''

She rubbed her palms along the stubble at his jawline and slipped her fingers into the soft, clipped contours of his hair. She tilted his face and pressed a kiss to the bridge of his nose, the slash across his eyebrow, the heart of the jagged scar itself. ''That's who you are, Jonas. A protector. I'll bet your stepsister knew that, too.''

She hesitated a moment, propping herself up on her elbows above him. "But you're more than that." She stroked her palms across the ridges of muscle at his shoulders. "You're a smart, caring man, who deep, down inside—" she spread her fingers over the strong, firm beat of his heart "—knows he isn't the monster he tries so hard to be."

He lifted his hand to cover hers where it rested against his chest. "Don't make me something I'm not, Faith. I appreciate your fierce brand of kindness, but—"

"Someday, you'll have to start looking after yourself. You'll have to start taking care of what you need. And stop blaming yourself for two little girls you couldn't protect."

His hand had slid all the way up to her neck, cradling her tenderly. "What are you doing to me, Faith?" He lifted his mouth and kissed the tip of her chin. "I can't be like other men. I'll never fit in. I'll always be that monster with the devil eyes."

"No."

Then his fingers speared into the hair at her nape and tilted her head so he could taste her lips. After he'd nibbled enough to ignite an appetite that left her wanting more, he pulled back. His lips still clung to hers, as if he was as loath to break the connection as she was. His chest heaved in a great sigh beneath her. "You make me think about things— want things—I can't have."

Faith could feel the tension humming through every taut muscle of his body. She could feel it in the shaking grasp of his hands as he fought to hold himself in check. She could feel it in the answering need of her own body. "What *do* you want?" she asked, losing herself in the powerful desire blazing in the depth of his eyes. "What do *you* need?"

"Right now, I need…you."

He palmed her head and brought her mouth down to his, taking it in a savage kiss. Faith opened her mouth and welcomed the claim of his tongue and lips.

His hands were all over her, spreading her legs to either

side of his hips, squeezing her bottom, sliding up and taking the shirt with it. "Can you, honey?" he begged, rasping his tongue across the engorged tip of her breast and taking it into his mouth. "Will you?"

Faith clenched her teeth and moaned at the bowstring of pleasure that arced straight down to her core. "Jonas," she breathed, feeling herself lifted to a plane of passion and desire she'd never experienced before. "Kiss me." She strained to reconnect with his tantalizing mouth. "Kiss me again."

"Dammit, Faith, if you don't want this, say so right now and I will leave." But he was kissing her. Touching her. Loving her. "I don't want to frighten you. Ever. I'm too damn big and too damn old and too damn ug—"

She clamped a hand over his mouth to silence him. She rode the ragged rise and fall of his chest, gathering her own courage. Jonas Beck was a man supremely confident in every aspect of his professional life, but who still didn't believe that he could be wanted—that *she* could want him.

He caught his breath and watched her as she sat up straight, still straddling his hips and the ridge of desire straining against his jeans. Faith felt giddy with a power that was every bit as potent as Jonas's physical strength, every bit as true as the hunger shining from the light in his eyes.

She had a rapt audience as she reached down and unhooked the snap of his jeans. "Faith…" he cautioned her.

"Be patient, Mr. Beck." She reached for his zipper.

"You're too pretty. Too sweet." He brushed a lock of hair off her brow, fingered her lips, swept over the tips of her bare breasts. She caught a hiss of breath at the stab of desire that shot to the aching juncture where her heat met his. "You can say no. At any time."

And she trusted him without a doubt to stop if she did change her mind. She never needed to fear Jonas.

But she wanted him—needed him—as much as he needed her.

She smiled and tugged on the zipper. "Does that mean I can also say yes?"

He reached for her then. Pulled her down to his chest. Kissed her wildly. Frantically. Thoroughly.

His hands were on her, skimming her here, squeezing her there. Gentle. Powerful.

They stripped each other of their remaining clothes and then he was on top of her. Stretching her. Filling her. Bringing her to the brink of ecstasy.

It was a trading of comforts, an easing of two raw souls who had exposed their darkest secrets and survived. It was the wildest, most intense ride of her life.

"I want...I need...you...." he whispered between pants, dropping each word like a humble praise against her ear.

When he covered her mouth with his and plunged in for his final release, Faith hugged him close, with her arms and her legs and her heart. And she followed him over the edge into paradise.

JONAS BECK loved mornings.

He loved this one, at any rate.

The sun had been up a good hour by now. He'd watched a bright sliver of changing colors filter into the motel room through the crack between the curtain and window. A sunrise. Certainly not the best view of one, but he'd watched a sunrise.

Of course, waking up with a soft, pretty—naked—woman in his arms had gone a long way toward improving his morning disposition.

With his back propped up on the pillows, he looked down in awe at the utter trust and contentment on Faith's sweet face. She lay draped across his chest, with the long, smooth line of her back exposed down to her waist. Her skin looked as fair as a storybook princess's against his darker tan. Her luscious breasts were flattened against him, and her moist heat was clenched around the top of his thigh beside his body's stirring interest in the sight and scent and feel of her. It was a completely vulnerable position. And he was humbled in the presence of the gifts she had given him.

Her body. Her trust. Her anger for his hurts. Her love of mornings. Her generous spirit.

She made him feel like a man. Not a cursed beast. She seemed to see something in him that he himself had forgotten long ago.

He hadn't made love to a woman since... Hell, he'd had sex before, but he'd never made love. Not like that. Not with a woman whose eyes were wide-open. She'd touched him and kissed him and teased him and offered herself without fear.

And he loved her for it.

Hell. There was a cruel trick for the fates to play on him. To drop this woman on his doorstep and let her get beneath his tough hide and awaken his heart. Because this fairy tale would soon play itself out. He'd turn Faith and the disk safely over to George Murphy and he'd go back to his home in the mountains. There'd be no future for them, only now.

Faith was sixteen years his junior. She was intelligent, pretty, full of life and sass. She could work in the real world and be accepted. She deserved the chance to find a man who wasn't so used up, a man who could give her more than he ever could.

He had no doubt she'd do something crazy like try to stay with him for a while because she felt she owed him something. Her persnickety sense of justice and fair play would keep her at his side, even if life passed her by. But he wouldn't let that happen. He'd enjoy the now. Treasure it. And after she was gone, he'd always remember her precious gift—that for a few days out of time, Jonas Beck was no longer the devil. He wasn't any behind-the-scenes hero. He was just a man.

"Mmm." Every nerve ending in his body shot to life as Faith stretched along the length of him, rousing herself from sleep. "What time is it?"

This was the real test. To see if what she'd made love to in the middle of the night was still appealing in the bright light of day. He stroked the crown of her coppery hair. "It's after eight-thirty. You're a regular slug-a-bug today."

She raised her head and struggled to blink her eyes open. "I guess great sex makes me sleepy." Her green eyes popped open wide and her hand flew to her mouth as her body suddenly stiffened. "Oh, my God. Did I say that out loud?"

Jonas laughed. A deep, resonant sound unfamiliar to his own ears. But it didn't hurt. "Yes, you did, sunshine. But I'll take it as a compliment."

She swatted a hand at his chest. "That's not very gallant. It takes two, you know."

"I know." His laughter faded. He looked deep into her eyes. "Thank you. For everything last night."

Her crooked mouth eased into a beautiful smile. "You're welcome."

He eased his palms along her back and reached beneath the covers to grab a handful of her beautiful bottom. He pulled and she crawled and he tilted his head to capture her mouth in a rich, languorous, life-affirming kiss.

And it started all over again. Her eager palms skimming his flanks, her fingertips digging into the muscles of his chest. Her tongue mating with his. Those soft, mewing sounds she made deep in her throat.

She nipped her teeth around a flat male nipple and he jolted at the sensation. She squeezed his butt and ruffled his hair and kissed him along a line down the center of his chest to his navel. He was beyond feeling now. He was floating. He was flying.

The little witch was seducing *him*. Making love to *him*. When her lips would have moved lower, Jonas could stand no more. He lifted her up and rolled her onto her back. Her arms curled around his neck as he nudged her apart with his knee. But at the moment he would have entered her, he hesitated. He threw his head back and fought for the control that had seen him through so many lonely years.

"Jonas...what...?" She was breathing hard.

So was he. He braced himself above her. "Last night...I didn't...hurt you?" He brushed his fingers across her mouth. "I should have asked. I couldn't...forgive myself...I won't...if..."

She kissed each finger, sucked the last one in between her lips. His body lurched in mimicking response. "You didn't hurt me. I loved it. I..."

Her voice trailed away and her hand took over, closing around him, speaking to him of matching need and desire. Helpless in the face of everything she meant to him, Jonas could no longer resist. She guided him into her and set the pace toward their joint completion.

It was the truest acceptance he had ever known.

THERE WAS NOTHING soft about the sun at eleven. And though he'd gladly volunteer to spend the rest of his life in bed with Faith—making love and holding her and sleeping—Jonas knew the clock was ticking. Reality would set upon them soon enough.

To that end, he flipped off the covers and swung his feet off the edge of the bed. He rolled his neck and stretched and tried to focus his mind on the road ahead of them.

Faith lay on her stomach in the middle of the bed. He leaned over and kissed the swell of her bottom, then gave it a playful spank as he stood. "Time to rise and shine, honey."

She reached for a pillow and plopped it over her head. "You exhaust me, man."

He grinned at the compliment. But she wasn't the only

one whose body was sated by their blissful morning. Still, he'd never let her be hurt in any way. By him or anyone else. And that meant they needed to hit the road and get to the airport. "We have to check out by noon."

"Just five minutes to rest. Please?"

He'd never be able to resist that word, not when it came from those lips. "All right. I'll jump into the shower first, and then you can get ready. But we can't hang out here too much longer."

"I know." With her face buried in the pillow she waved him away. "Places to go, people to see."

Worlds to save. A killer to find. A woman to let go.

Jonas stepped into the shower and let the brisk spikes of water pound against his chest. He'd found peace for the moment, but salvation would be a long time coming.

"This is getting tiresome."

The shorter of the two figures wearing sleek, sophisticated suits paced off the length of the marbled hallway, then returned to the computer lab with a winsome smile for the security guard who should have retired before last night. "You're sure this is the woman you saw?"

The guard took the photograph and studied it. "That's her. Her hair was red, but it's the same girl. She and the big guy who knocked me out ran out of here about 11:20, 11:25. By eleven-thirty, I'd called the cops to report them. I don't think they took anything. I thought they were just in here foolin' around. What's this about?"

About thirty million dollars, you fool. If Faith had accessed these high-tech computers, then she knew what it was they were after now. Their simple pawn had become their greatest liability. The guard returned Faith Monroe's picture and the short one in the suit pasted on a smile. "Thank you for your cooperation, sir. We'll call you if we need anything more."

"You bet." The old buzzard doffed them a salute. "Have a nice day."

"Thank you."

They were out in the parking lot, climbing into their rented car before the tall one said a word. "Old Grandpa in there can ID us now. You want me to take him out?"

The short one grinned. "I think you enjoy your work too much. No, Grandpa thinks we're with the FBI and that we have everything under control. I don't think he'll give us another thought. Besides, we're running out of time."

"But he let them get away. Just like Prince—"

"Sheriff Prince was different. We paid him good money to keep Faith Monroe in town until we could establish your cover there. He failed. Knowing any part of my plan made him a liability." This all made logical sense. "No one else besides the guard knows that Miss Monroe and her body-guard boyfriend were here in Laramie. There'd be no one to divert suspicion onto if we killed him."

The tall one's fist tightened around the wheel. "You should have let me run her down when I had the chance. Saved us a lot of trouble. We could be making the deal with the Central Americans by now."

"Smush her on the road and risk destroying the disk? She might have had it on her. We hadn't had time to search the car or her belongings." The short one offered a teasing grin. "Besides, I didn't think that was your style. I thought you were more of a hands-on man."

The tall one didn't normally lose his cool, but he was starting to simmer. "That guy she's with—Jonas Beck—I don't know who he is, but he knows his stuff. That bogus campsite in the Tetons delayed us a full day. We wouldn't have picked up the trail here if Grandpa hadn't reported them to the cops instead of keeping it a campus security matter." He skimmed his hand across the top of his head and calmed himself. "I like things neat and tidy. This has gone on too long. We've lost our advantage."

The short one bristled in the passenger seat. "You're not thinking of defying my orders, are you?"

"This project should have been wrapped up twelve years ago. Before Jack Monroe developed a conscience and destroyed the NT-6 prototype and blueprints." His big fist looked as if it might snap the steering wheel in two. "And when you found out Monroe had given Rutherford the disk, we should have struck then, not waited all those months for Monroe's daughter to get involved. When it gets personal, it gets messy."

"This project will be wrapped up when I say it is. The Frye name is at stake here. If we want this business to continue, then we have to establish that our reputation is as well earned as ever. That we can produce the weapons and technology to meet the market's demands." The flat, eastern Wyoming horizon blurred before the short one's eyes. But tears were not an option. Not anymore. "Faith Monroe and her family took something from me. William Rutherford tried to keep it from me. That little hick from the sticks is going to pay for all the trouble they've caused me."

The tall man sensed the loss of control, the emotional overload that would make him question the abilities of the leader he followed. "But how are we going to stop her if we can't find her? I know you have men watching the major transportation centers in the region, but we can't just take a chance they'll show up somewhere."

The short one didn't like leaving things to chance, either. "It's simple, really. She has something I want. Let's get something *she* wants." The short one breathed in deeply, feeling the well-planned—and profitable—retribution falling back into place once more. "Then let her come to us."

FAITH SAT UP in the empty bed and reached for the first piece of clothing she could find. Jonas's denim shirt.

Smiling contentedly at what it meant to have their clothes strewn around the bed and floor, she slipped her arms into the long sleeves and fastened a couple of strategic buttons. She caught the collar up around her nose and inhaled the musky scent that was uniquely Jonas's. Heaven. The scent and softness of the oversize shirt reminded her of her night and morning spent in his arms.

He was a powerful lover—honest, intense—nothing fancy—very direct. He'd never left her in any doubt that he wanted *her*, that he found her sexy and desirable. And that she had fulfilled his every need as well. His fears that he had hurt her were unfounded. He'd been passionate, yes, but amazingly tender. She'd been just as eager with him— seeking out his strength, the arousing touch of his hands, his soul-deep kisses. And though her muscles ached from the exertion of seducing and being seduced, and being seduced again, it was a pleasant ache. That of a body unused to making love, not a body used.

Heeding Jonas's warning about the time, she tiptoed over to the desk and opened her purse to start getting ready. While he was using the shower, she pulled out her comb and looked at herself in the mirror. The copper hair didn't seem to fit. Tangled by sleep and Jonas's greedy hands, the strands stood out in wild disarray. But as she combed the waves into order, she realized she still looked different. Something around the eyes, maybe. Less frightened. More mature. Curiously confident.

And while he'd given her such pleasure over and over again, Faith knew they had connected on a much deeper, emotional level. A man couldn't hold her so gently, nor whisper such beautiful things to her, nor love her so well unless he had a heart. Unless he cared.

She'd unlocked the man within the beast.

But before she could analyze her own feelings too carefully, she remembered the reason they were together. She pulled her notebook from her purse and opened it to see the disk she'd stored inside. A chill swept over her body, leaving her bathed in a sea of goose bumps. She held mass destruction in her hands. Something her own father had helped to create. Something friends had died for.

But why had it been given to her? There were too many coincidences for her to believe she'd been a random choice. The dates on the disk, the encryption code, her hiring at Eclipse Labs, her father's death around the time the original designs had been made. But why?

Hopefully, Jonas's assertion that his former boss, George Murphy, could help her was correct. That she could turn over the disk to him and be put into protective custody until this could all be straightened out. Of course, there was the not-so-tiny problem of Copperhead. Had they really shaken the hit man off their trail? Or was it just a matter of time before he caught up with them? And could they get to George Murphy before Copperhead got to them?

Fearing she wouldn't like the answers to those questions, Faith went back to her cleaning and packing, determined to stay focused on survival. She replaced the disk inside her notebook, but had to dump out the contents of her small purse in order to fit everything back inside.

When she picked up her cell phone, she paused. She checked over her shoulder to see that Jonas was still in the shower, then she looked at the tiny screen again.

She had a message.

She'd left the phone turned off as Jonas had asked her to, but her voice mail was still active. She scrolled down to the number on the message and shivered with anticipation. It was a Missouri area code. Had Wes and Gran gotten her message? Were they okay? She didn't recognize the number, but it called out to her like a voice from home.

She decided to take a chance. If she knew her family was okay, she could handle just about anything Darien Frye and the rest of the world threw her way. Listening for Jonas in the shower, she turned her back to the bathroom door and punched in the number.

It had barely begun to ring before someone snatched it

quickly off the hook. A hushed, urgent voice answered. "Hello? Faith? Is that you?"

The voice was too muffled for her to recognize. Was this a trick?

"Faith?" The voice was a little louder this time. A dear voice from a past she'd thought she'd lost forever. Faith stared at her shocked reflection in the mirror until the image was blurred by tears. "Faith? This is your grandmother. Are you there? You won't believe what's happening to your uncle and me. We need your help."

She stumbled over to the bed and sank onto the edge. "Gran?" The urgency in Florence Monroe's voice cut through her shock and enabled her to think instead of just feel. "Where have you been? I tried to find you. I went to the house. It was all—"

"I know. Your uncle Wes suspected something like that might happen as soon as we saw your name on the news in connection to that horrible murder at Eclipse Labs. Oh, honey, we have so much to explain to you." She paused for a breath that sounded more like a sob. "But there isn't time."

"Time? Why not?" Faith stood up and began to pace. "Gran, what's going on?"

The wise, loving voice from her childhood hushed again. "Faith, dear, there's not time to start from the beginning. I'm not supposed to be on the phone at all. But one of the nurses took pity—"

"Nurses?" Faith stopped midstride. "Are you hurt? Is Wes all right?"

She could hear her grandmother's quick breaths and sensed an incredible level of stress—even fear. Faith clutched at her stomach, subconsciously bracing herself. "Maybe we should have told you, but we wanted to protect you. When we lost your father, we swore not to let those horrible people into our lives again."

"Gran." If time was precious and the phone call risky,

she didn't want to waste any time and jeopardize her grandmother's safety. "You can explain the past later. What's going on now?"

Her grandmother took a deep, steadying breath. She never raised her voice above a whisper. "Your uncle and I have been put into protective custody by the FBI. Wes...knows things...about your father. We thought the danger was past. We had no idea he'd come after you."

"Who?"

"Darien Frye, dear. He and your father..." Her voice trailed away. Had the evil greed of a man she'd never met influenced and destroyed her entire family? "Are you safe? Are you far away?"

Faith glanced over her shoulder. The water was still running. Jonas would be furious if he caught her on the phone. She was the unplanned recipient of *his* protective custody, and the risk her grandmother had taken to contact her was as great as her own in returning the call. She dropped her voice to an equally urgent whisper. "I'm safe for now. But everywhere I go people are dying."

"It's his way." Her grandmother's voice sounded cold and flat. "He doesn't like to be crossed. And he doesn't like witnesses. That's why I'm so worried about your uncle Wes and risked calling you. The agents guarding us—they're all around us, disguised as nurses and orderlies."

If Faith hadn't been scared before, the portent in her grandmother's voice would have finished the job. "What's wrong with Wes? He's in the hospital?"

"University Medical Center in Columbia, Missouri." She'd inherited her grandmother's ladylike grace and propensity to express her emotions through tears.

But there wasn't time to cry. "Gran?"

"He's dying, Faith. The doctors don't know what's causing it. He was fit and healthy and working the farm last week. And then we were moved to a safe house. And then he got sick. All of a sudden. Like poison. Only the doctors can't identify it.'' Her grandmother's effort to muffle a sob tore right through Faith's heart. ''I can't lose both my boys.''

''I'm coming, Gran.''

''No.'' She shouted the word over the phone. The sudden volume startled Faith back to her surroundings. The water in the shower had stopped. ''I don't want you in any danger. I just wanted you to know. I needed to hear—''

''I love you, Gran. You be strong. Tell Wes—''

''I have to go. Someone's coming. We love you.''

''I love—'' But the line was dead.

So was she.

''Hang up the phone.'' A chill cascaded down her spine at the dark, frozen voice behind her. Faith slowly turned.

Jonas had emerged from the shower, his body hot and steamy and wrapped in nothing but a towel that didn't quite cinch his waist. But she knew she was in trouble. The expression on his face told her as much. The monster was back.

''Hang it up. Now.''

Chapter Ten

"I swear to God, Jonas, if you don't let go of me, I'll scream."

He didn't think she'd really do it, but he was steamed. She needed to understand the unnecessary risk she'd taken, how she'd put her life on the line for one stupid phone call. He should have been smarter. He should have taken her damn phone and crushed it under his boot as soon as he signed on for this unsanctioned assignment. He knew better than to allow her any contact with the outside world—to allow anyone on the outside a chance to contact her. It was rule one in the protection book. He'd counted on a stern warning and common sense to keep her from making such a foolish mistake.

And that was the thing that steamed him the most. He'd made a grave mistake of thinking of Faith as part of *his* world. For a few blissful hours, there had been no one else, and he'd dropped his guard.

He'd slacked off the hard and fast rules he knew could keep a witness alive. All because she did crazy little things like talking back when others tiptoed around him. Or demanding that he be polite, while offering up *pleases* and *thank-yous* and *good nights* of her own. And holding him close and offering the balm of her body as he exposed the darkest secrets of his soul.

He was angry at himself because he'd let her make that mistake. But he'd made an even bigger one. And now he was scared he wouldn't be able to keep her safe.

"Go ahead and scream." Jonas never broke his stride, hustling her down one of the long concourses of Denver's Stapleton Airport, keeping pace with the steady flow of travelers. With his hand gripped firmly around her upper arm, he carried her as much as she jogged to keep up with him. Something was closing in on them. He could feel it in every pore of his skin.

He might have sensed the oncoming danger sooner if he hadn't forgotten who he really was and spent the morning in bed with Faith—nurturing parts of his heart and soul that hadn't known kindness and trust and fun for so long that they felt like new discoveries for him. Now they might both pay the price for indulging his humanity.

"You might as well shout to the world where you are," he snapped, moving his eyes back and forth in a constant scan of the people around them. Last night, he'd planned to ditch the truck and lose themselves among the crowds at the airport. Now, all he could see were the overwhelming numbers of potential undercover cops and killers who might be on their tail. "That phone stunt could lead Frye right to us. A call like that can be traced. If someone was tapped in to the other end, they've got us nailed. Even if they weren't, they can trace the transmission back to the nearest relay tower. Then it's a matter of hours rather than minutes before they track you down."

"Fine. So I screwed up. You explained that already." But even though she'd been chastised, Faith still argued her case. "It was a risk I had to take. I needed to know about my uncle. My grandmother was distraught. I'm sorry you can't understand how a normal family works. I wish you had known one like mine. But I have a little bit of family left to cling to. And they need me."

He understood all he needed to. "You won't do them any good dead."

"Jonas."

He deserved a reprimand for his callous statement of the bottom line. But it didn't stop him. They stepped onto a moving walkway and Jonas tucked her right up beside him. He dropped his arm around her back and held her close. It was partly a compromise to her objections to his brutish behavior, and partly a concession to the narrow walkspace. But mostly he just needed to feel her warm, breathing body and know that she was still unharmed and in his safekeeping.

"I'm sorry about your uncle." The fear that their morning had temporarily chased away was back in her eyes. Despite her defiant tongue, she radiated her worry as if she was weeping out loud. But though he hurt for her, he couldn't let that sway him from his purpose. "It's my job to keep you safe."

Faith slid her arms beneath his jacket and hugged him around his waist. It was a placating action, whether intended to persuade or apologize or even seek comfort, he didn't know. But her needy touch burned the angry energy out of him, leaving him raw with the knowledge of how far he'd let himself get involved with this woman.

It seemed odd that no one seemed to be paying any mind to the diminutive redhead being swallowed up in the arms of the stern-faced giant. There were a few glances of idle curiosity from the pedestrians outside the walkway, who were moving at a slower pace. But they were watching everyone who went by on the conveyor. And the man who bumped his shoulder, zipping past on the left in an even quicker hurry to meet someone or transfer to his next flight, muttered a polite "Excuse me." But he didn't startle or react as if he'd noticed anything unusual about the man he was addressing.

Strange. It was as if having Faith at his side diminished

his threatening size and the shock of his scarred-up face. He almost felt…normal. As if he really could be like all these everyday, average people around them.

But Faith's next words reminded him he was anything but normal. "It's not your job to protect me. Nobody's paying you."

"Nobody has to." He gave her a squeeze, lifting her up onto her toes, hoping she understood the double entendre of his words. He was a born protector, as she'd stated that morning. But keeping *her* safe was a choice, not a duty. And certainly not a job. "So if I see you writing down one more penny in that notebook of yours—"

"I only put down the cost of the motel this morning." She tried to push some space between them, but he wasn't ready to let her go yet. "I let you buy me lunch."

Small concession. They'd driven through a fast-food restaurant. If he'd waited until they'd gotten to the airport, where the price of one cheeseburger would have been more than the cost of their entire meal, she'd have logged that in as well, he was sure.

Still, it wasn't the price that had concerned him about dining at Stapleton; it was the lines. The waiting. The standing in one place long enough for anyone who might be searching for an unlikely duo to get a really good look at them.

He bustled her off the end of the first walkway belt and hurried her onto the next one. This time he wrapped his left hand around her waist and pulled her back into his chest, forming a shield between her and whatever pursued them. Once he'd situated them well between the couple behind them and the businessman on the phone ahead of them, he rested his right hand on the conveyor's guard rail and resumed the debate.

"And the airline tickets?" He'd called on his cell and made three different reservations under different names on flights to Washington, D.C. Though she'd done her best to eavesdrop, and had hounded him afterward, he'd been closemouthed about the final tally. He didn't want anyone to know which flight they'd be on until he paid his cash at the counter and picked up the tickets. "Are you going to put those in your book, too?"

A beat too long passed before she answered. And though her fingers pressed lightly against his hand at her waist, her body was stiff as a board. He wasn't going to like this.

"I didn't write them down because I'm not going to D.C.," she announced.

Jonas dipped his head and whispered beside her ear. "George Murphy's in D.C." He refused to acknowledge his body's eager interest in the tangy fresh scent of her hair. "The people who can translate your knowledge and that disk into a case against Darien Frye are in D.C." He articulated his authority succinctly enough to remind Faith and his own randy hormones of the gravity of her situation. "The team of professionals who are going to keep you alive long enough to testify against Frye and his hit man are in D.C. That's where we're going."

The innocent little witch turned within the crook of his arm and splayed her fingers across his chest in a tender caress. She tilted those wide green eyes up to his. "Please, Jonas, try to understand. I need to go home."

That *please* word weakened his resolve. He could feel the strain between knowing what he should do, and feeling what he should do, jump in the muscles along the taut line of his jaw. He squeezed and flexed his hand that now rested at the small of her back and offered a compromise to appease her and his conscience. "We go to Washington, first. Then I'll take you to Missouri myself."

"I may not have time for that." Her fingers fisted in the front of his shirt. "He's dying. The doctors don't know what's wrong or how to save him."

"It could be a trap," he warned.

"What if it's not?" she countered. "What if someone's

hurting him because of me? Whatever's going on, I have to be there for him and Gran. Please.''

There was that damn word again. For a man who'd withstood beatings and bullet holes and still come out fighting, that one soft, civilized word always seemed to breach his considerable defenses. He tipped his head up to the skylighted ceiling and inhaled a cleansing breath before looking down into her beseeching eyes. ''You're going to Missouri, no matter what I say, aren't you?''

''If you won't take me, I'll find a way to get away from you.'' He could remind her of the near impossibility of that task. But he was quickly learning that *surrender* and *impossible* just weren't in her vocabulary. ''My family needs me.''

So do I, dammit. But, short of tying her up or holding her at gunpoint, if she was determined, he knew he had to let her go. And the lady was determined.

But once she rejoined her family—or was sequestered away by the U.S. Marshals Murphy would contact to protect her—her need for him would diminish. And without a need...

Jonas swallowed hard. It wasn't her job to save him. He'd survived a long time before she'd ever shown up on his front porch. He hadn't lived. Or loved. But he'd survived.

''Even if your uncle's illness isn't a setup, Frye and his men could find out about it.'' He was making a valiant effort to win this battle with her. ''They might be waiting for you there.''

''But you'll protect me, right?'' She seemed to think he could work miracles. Frye might very well have an army of enforcers waiting to take that disk and destroy her. ''Please, Jonas? I won't ask for another thing. And I'll do whatever you say—when you say it—if you take me to my family.''

He'd already debated too long. Once he'd given an inch,

he'd given her the whole mile. He shook his head, hating and loving the beginnings of that coy smile on her face. She knew she could get to him. He brushed the loose bangs away from her brows, stroking the soft skin of her forehead. He surrendered to her will without actually admitting it with words. "I'm getting too old for this kind of work."

"Thank you." She hugged him tight. Jonas used the leverage to lift her off the end of the walkway and tried not to pay too much attention to the rush of warm, invigorating strength her effusive gratitude triggered inside him.

They'd reached the main concourse and rows of ticket counters. He'd stalled as long as he could, familiarizing himself with the airport, waiting for George Murphy to come through with the proper papers that would allow him to bring his knife and gun on board the plane after signing them over to the pilot. He took Faith's hand and laced his fingers with hers. He needed a free hand as much as he needed to hold on to her. "Columbia, Missouri, right?"

"Right."

He reached inside his jacket, pulled out his cell phone and dialed George Murphy's number. Weaving in and out of the long lines forming to buy tickets and pick up boarding passes, he led Faith past each of the airlines that held their D.C. reservations.

The line picked up. "Murphy."

"Beck. We've had a slight change in plans here."

"Trouble?"

Jonas noted each face as they passed. He briefly filled Murphy in on the phone call and the protective custody that Florence Monroe had violated to warn Faith about her uncle's illness. "We'll be flying into Columbia this afternoon. If you can find any kind of reinforcements, send them there."

"Sounds like a setup to me," Murphy cautioned.

"It reeks of it," Jonas agreed, ignoring the attentive way

Faith followed the terse conversation. "But I swear to God we've already got a tail. I can feel the eyes watching me."

"We're being followed?" Faith whispered. Her fingers bit into to the sleeve of his jacket. He hadn't wanted to alarm her in case she panicked and drew attention to herself. But though her eyes darted form side to side, trying to see whomever was following, the tight clutch of her hands was the only outward sign she revealed. She was a trouper.

Jonas twisted his arm so he could link his fingers with hers and given them a reassuring squeeze. He looked hard into her wide, questioning eyes and tried to silently convey his thanks while he spoke to Murphy. "He's good, though. I haven't spotted him yet."

Jonas heard a flurry of movement on the other end and knew Murphy had risen from his desk and begun to pace. Though only a decade older than Jonas, George was a father figure. He worried like a father, supported and led like a father. Maybe that's why it had hurt so much the day George called him into his office and told him The Watchers had been disbanded and he no longer had a home there.

It wasn't the first time a father had kicked him out of the only haven he knew.

"You're on your own, aren't you?" Murphy chided. "Damn, I wish I was there. You've got to get her here. We can protect her here."

Clearly, Murphy didn't understand the concept of Show-Me State stubbornness. "We don't have any legal leverage to force her to go to D.C. And if you want cooperative testimony, I don't think kidnapping's the answer."

Kidnapping? Faith mouthed.

Jonas reassured her with a shake of his head and reluctantly joined the line at one of the ticket counters. He pulled her around in front of him and latched an arm around her waist. If they had to wait like sitting ducks, he'd shield her from as much scrutiny as possible.

In the background, he could hear George placing a call

on another phone line. While he waited for that party to answer, he resumed the role as unofficial base commander. "I'm calling up a few old friends," he informed him. "Maybe this isn't something we can handle through standard channels."

"Old friends?"

"Some former Watchers. Not all of them retired so far out of society that I can't find them." There was a hint of amusement in his voice. "Unlike you, a few of them actually enjoy the company of other people."

Jonas didn't rise to the obvious bait. "If you can talk them into it, that sounds fine. What about my weapons clearance?"

Murphy laughed. "They'll be glad to see you, too." A reunion of sorts to bring down Darien Frye. Jonas could think of little else that would bring the highly trained and uniquely talented men and women he'd once worked with together again. "I've made an arrangement with the airport authority. Show them your ID. I've listed you as a federal agent transporting a high-profile witness."

Jonas recorded the mental note. It was a cover he'd used before. "Thanks."

"Oh, and Jonas?"

Not *Beck*. *Jonas*. He was immediately suspicious. "Yeah?"

"I found a match for that Detective Collier you asked about. You won't like the results."

Jonas pulled Faith in tighter to his body. "What is it?" she whispered, tuning in to his uneasy tension.

"Jermaine Collier," Murphy explained, "served sixteen distinguished years with the Saint Louis Police Department."

Jonas picked up on the past tense verb. "Served?"

"He was killed in the line of duty three years ago." Murphy stated the obvious. "Whoever interviewed your friend was an imposter."

COPPERHEAD.

It was the only answer.

Faith held on even tighter to Jonas's hand as they jogged around the long, circular concourse of Kansas City International Airport to make their connecting flight to Columbia, Missouri.

She couldn't seem to stop her shivering, even though it was a balmy autumn day outside. She couldn't seem to clear her head, either.

She'd stood face-to-face with a hired assassin in her own home. And while she'd felt vaguely threatened by Jermaine Collier, she'd believed he was a cop. She'd never suspected that he was most likely the man who'd murdered her boss and Danny Novotny. And Sheriff Prince.

If the crime lab team hadn't been at her house to serve as potential witnesses, would she be dead now? Had he tried to kill her with that runaway tow truck? If she didn't have the disk—if she didn't have Jonas—she'd be dead. She stumbled at the thought, but Jonas's steadying hand was on her arm to catch her.

"Easy. I've got you." He slowed his pace to a quick walk and pulled her close to his side.

She willingly leaned into his balance and strength and silently wondered if the man was as invincible as he seemed. And then she remembered how vulnerable he'd been, opening up about his past abuse and the false accusations that had scarred him right down to his soul.

Faith pushed herself away from his tempting warmth and latched firmly on to his hand. "It's bad enough that you're risking your life for me. You shouldn't have to hold me up and carry me along as well."

"I don't mind."

"I know you don't." She reached up and brushed her fingertips across the angles of Jonas's craggy face that, while it would never be handsome, would always be compelling and dear to her. "But I need to be strong, too. I put us in danger. I want to do all I can to make sure that no one else gets hurt because of me or this disk.''

He stopped unexpectedly and turned in front of her. He tipped up her chin with the back of his knuckles. And though his touch was a gentle stroke beneath her jaw, his icy eyes looked tough. ''Remember your promise about doing whatever I say, when I say it?''

She nodded. She'd meant it.

''I'm going to hold you to that promise. If anything happens, I need you to respond without hesitation to my commands.'' His expression softened for an instant before he bent down and kissed her. It was a swift, possessive stamp that chased away the ominous chill of his words. ''*If* anything happens.''

In the next close breath he looked up, beyond her shoulder. And though his expression never changed, she sensed the hyperawareness that seemed to generate its own energy throughout his body. And spark suspicion in hers. ''Jonas?''

His voice dropped to a nearly inaudible whisper. ''I want you to walk with me now, and act as if the only care you have is catching the next plane.''

A sea of goose bumps erupted along the skin of her arms. She clutched at the front of his jacket. ''What's wrong? You know, that really creeps me out when you do that. You say and do things without explaining yourself.''

''You promised.''

She had. His blue eyes held a distinct warning, but the Arctic chill there reflected steely cunning and unflappable confidence. It was a formidable combination that reassured her more than any kind word or tender touch could.

Faith released her grip and stepped out, quickening her stride to match his. He turned around and draped his arm behind her shoulders, subtly offering a protective barrier between her and whatever had caught his attention. ''What did you see?'' she asked, keeping her voice low. ''Detective Collier? Do you think he followed us from Denver?''

He shook his head. "I'm testing a theory."

Terrific time to be testing anything, she thought. Jonas was unarmed, having already transferred his gun and knife to the pilot of their next flight. They'd been delayed while airport security checked his credentials. But then they'd dismissed them with "Good luck" and a mock salute. "Did security change their minds about you?"

Jonas quickened their stride to a pace just shy of a jog. "Only if they've hired a plainclothes detective to follow us."

"It is Collier, isn't it?"

Jonas was scanning from side to side now. "Fewer questions and more listening, please."

Faith clamped her mouth shut, wishing she had the nerve to defy Jonas and spin around to look behind them. But wisdom—and her word—dictated that she stay close and keep moving. "Where are we going?" She thumbed over her shoulder. "We just passed our flight gate."

Jonas grabbed her pointing appendage and pulled her into an open doorway marked Men. The rows of urinals, sinks and stalls were surprisingly empty. Still, Faith dug in her heels and tugged against his powerful grip.

"Jonas! I can't go in here—" The palm of his hand stifled her protest as he dragged her behind a partition of polished white tile and shoved her behind him.

"Not a word," he mouthed. He turned and blocked her into the corner.

Faced with only his broad back for scenery, Faith couldn't see the man who ducked into the rest room behind them. But, seeing the tension radiate through Jonas's stance and the massive fist that curled at his side, she sensed the man was toast.

"Miss Monroe? I need to talk to you and your friend. Just talk. I'm—"

Jonas sprang. Faith could only watch the sudden violence unfolding before her. It all happened so quickly. A series of grunts and breaths and pithy words. A fist to the intruder's gut doubled him over. Then Jonas spun around and closed one massive forearm around the other man's neck.

"Jonas!" Faith yelled. "What are you—?" This wasn't Detective Collier.

But the intruder in the gray suit and tie hadn't been taken completely by surprise. He planted his feet and rammed Jonas back against the wall. Faith cringed when Jonas's head hit the unyielding surface. She reached out half a step, wanting to help but not knowing how.

Jonas's grip loosened and the man pulled free. He swung around and jammed his fist into Jonas's gut.

"Stop it!" Faith yelled. When the man swung out again, his jacket came open, revealing the gun strapped to his side. He'd just evened the odds in this fight. "Jonas!"

But Jonas had seen it, too. And by the time the next fist sailed toward him, he shook his head and met the attack halfway. He caught the oncoming fist in his meaty grip and squeezed.

"Uh! Damn." The man in the suit tried to resist without breaking his hand, but sheer strength won out.

Jonas drove him to his knees. Then in one swift motion, he reached inside the man's coat and pulled his gun from his holster. Jonas stood up straight and released his fist, but trained the gun at the middle of the other man's chest.

"Jonas, don't!" She didn't think she could handle another dead body on her conscience.

"Who are you?" Jonas demanded, his hand and the gun never wavering their aim.

The downed man rubbed his bruised fist. "Damn, you two are hard to track."

"Don't cuss in front of the lady," Jonas snapped. "Who are you?"

"You're right not to take any chances with her safety." The man raised both hands in reluctant surrender. He tilted his head back and exhaled a long, steadying breath, arrogantly ignoring the gun pointed at him. "I have identification in the front inside pocket of my jacket."

But Faith already recognized him. "You're the man on TV."

She snatched at Jonas's arm to pull him away from the fight. "He's the FBI, Jonas. Agent Carmichael." But the fact that she'd moved was motivation enough. The instant she stepped closer, Jonas dashed to her side, angling his body to keep her out of the agent's direct line of sight. She leaned around his shoulder. "You are, aren't you?"

Jonas's voice bristled through the air. "Pull your badge and nothing else."

He grabbed Faith by the arm and shoved her back behind him while the man slowly began to lift open his jacket. A shuffling sound drew everyone's attention to the rest room's open door. An anxious traveler, not more than college age most likely, stood in openmouthed shock in the doorway. A woman in the men's room was nothing compared to one man holding another on his knees at gunpoint. Jonas and the agent turned as one.

"Get out."

"It's occupied."

"Sorry," Faith added as the young man hurried back out the way he came.

The two men seemed to eye each other with a bit of surprise and grudging respect. The cautious male bonding of like minds might be unexpected, but it was hardly Faith's biggest concern at the moment. "Don't you think he might report this?"

Her reminder was enough to speed the conversation along. "I'm Special Agent Rory Carmichael." The man on his knees held up his badge in his left hand.

While Jonas scanned the ID, Faith peeked around to study him. Tall. Lanky. Chestnut-colored hair. Impeccable suit. Well, an impeccable suit that was a little worse for wear right now.

"All right, you can stand," Jonas conceded. But he made no effort to return the gun. "A friend of mine says you've been recalled from your investigation into Miss Monroe. What made you follow us here from Denver?"

Agent Carmichael pocketed his badge and frowned in clear disbelief. "You saw me?"

"I knew you were there." He didn't stop Faith this time from moving around to his side. "What do you want?"

He straightened his sleeves and lapels as he stood. "I need to ask her some questions."

"Ask them. But make it fast," warned Jonas.

Agent Carmichael's warm brown gaze settled on Faith. "The red car you were driving in Wyoming—it had a bug planted in it."

Bug? As in tracking device? In Liza's car? She looked up at Jonas. "What does that mean?"

He answered without taking his gaze, or the gun, off Carmichael. "It means someone could have tracked you all the way from Saint Louis."

Carmichael had a different idea. "Or someone in Elk Point wanted to track you to your next destination. Not knowing you were going to pick up your sidekick here."

"Did Sheriff Prince know about the tracking device?" she asked.

The agent shrugged. "I never got a chance to ask. He was dead before I could talk to him. And the deputies—"

He didn't have to finish describing the deputies' incompetence. Faith nodded. "We know the deputies."

Rory Carmichael smiled. "At any rate, the bug is what changed you from my prime murder suspect to a key witness and probable target."

She couldn't say her change in status with the FBI felt like an improvement.

"Whose murder are you investigating?" she asked, more consumed with a perverse need to know how many deaths she might be responsible for rather than worrying about becoming the next victim herself.

"William Rutherford. We're familiar with his work at the Bureau. We know he worked with your father several years ago. I've filed a request to reopen that case, investigating it as a homicide instead of an accident." Faith hugged herself, trying not to react to the life-altering information he ticked off with such businesslike detachment on his fingers. "Also Daniel Novotny. A security guard at Eclipse Labs who tried to stop the killer from escaping."

Faith nodded, sadly picturing Danny's teasing smile. "I talked to him every morning."

"Liza Shelton—though right now her death is being treated as a local homicide. I looked into it when I found out the two of you had been roommates in college. Their lead investigator said it looked like the neighbor might have done it. A crime of passion or—"

Jonas interrupted. "You have a name for the cop who's running that case?"

Faith answered for him. "Jermaine Collier." She met Agent Carmichael's surprised gaze. "Tall guy with a shaved head and a goatee?"

"Yeah." He shook his head, waiting for more information. "You know Detective Collier?"

She latched on to Jonas's arm before her knees give way. "He killed Liza, too." She had known he was most likely responsible, but to actually hear someone place Copperhead at her friend's apartment...

Jonas's big hand suddenly covered hers, infusing her with his strength. "He hasn't gotten to you yet. And he won't. I promise."

"If Collier's a fake, that would fit in with the lead I'm pursuing." Like Jonas, Agent Carmichael didn't mince words. "There are two people on your tail, masquerading as FBI agents. One of them talked to the deputies in Elk Point. He showed up again at the university in Laramie with his partner. I take it you helped yourself to something in the computer lab?''

Jonas nodded. But Faith could feel the tension thrumming through the corded muscles of his arm. ''You said he had a partner? Let me guess—a man closing in on retirement who looks like he has more money than he can count.''

''No. He was with a woman.''

''A woman?'' Jonas seemed taken aback by the answer, as if he'd been certain he was right.

''What is it, Jonas?''

Another half beat of silence passed before he answered. ''It's nothing. We have a plane to catch.'' He turned the gun around in his hand and offered it, grip first, to Agent Carmichael. ''You. I'm calling a friend of mine for a physical description of Rory Carmichael. If the two of you don't match up, I will hunt you down and you will pay for wasting my time and endangering this woman.''

The agent didn't back down from the threat. ''And if I'm who I say I am?''

Jonas changed his mind and tossed the gun into the nearest toilet. ''Put some ice on that hand and get me a rundown on the agents who are doing guard duty on the Monroe family in Columbia. I want pictures so I can recognize them.'' He took her hand and started to leave. He pulled her close to his side, then stopped for one last directive to the man who'd followed them. ''And find out who screwed up and let her grandmother get a call out.''

''It's not your job to police us. We'll handle disciplining an agent.''

''It wasn't any agent who let that call go through.''

Chapter Eleven

"Are you sure this is going to work?" Faith asked.

I'm not sure of a damn thing, thought Jonas. He hunkered down in the wheelchair that Faith was pushing toward the bank of elevators at Columbia's University Medical Center. Beneath the blanket she'd draped across him, he unsnapped the sheath of his knife and made sure his gun was within easy reach beneath his left arm. "The only thing I'm sure of is that coming here was a lousy idea."

She touched the juncture of his neck and shoulder and gave him a subtle squeeze. "I know this isn't what you wanted. But thank you for listening to what I needed. I'll always be grateful to you for that."

Another damn debt she'd feel obligated to repay.

For one brief, selfish moment, Jonas considered asking her to stay with him. For as long as she could stand him. He could bargain with the money and time and emotional support she thought she owed him. Surely a few days and dollars out of his life were worth some kind of temporary commitment.

But the moment passed. He'd never looked at his future through rose-colored glasses. If he forced Faith to stay, he was smart enough to know it wouldn't be the same. He could never trust the smiles or the touches. He'd become more of a beast than ever, taking—blackmailing—in order to get what he wanted so badly. Love. Acceptance. Salvation.

But a relationship tainted by fear or by force or obligation was no salvation at all.

A man of honor would let her go once she was safe. He'd walk away and demand nothing of her in return. Nothing that would taint the memory of feisty words and fiery kisses, of gentle nights of sleep and sunny mornings of making love.

"If the elevator isn't empty, we'll take the next one," he warned Faith as she parked the wheelchair and pushed the call button for their ride to the third floor. It was easier to concentrate on work than to pay any attention to the impending sense of loss that tightened its grip around his newly awakened heart.

"Okay." He could hear the nervous shifting of her feet in the thick-soled nurse's shoes she'd borrowed from the employee lounge to complete their disguise as nurse and patient. "What if we can't get into room 3116?"

Jonas slipped his hand from beneath the blanket and reached for her hand. "I'll get you in." He squeezed her fingers in a gentle reminder. "But we won't be able to stay long. Five, ten minutes, tops."

He watched the muscles in her throat contract with a hard swallow. "But what if they need—"

"That's the deal, Faith." Her green eyes were clear with reluctant understanding of the plan he'd mapped out on the plane and drive to the hospital. "Whether you like it or not, I intend to keep you safe. And that means getting you out of here ASAP."

Her crooked mouth eased into a beautiful smile and she tightened her grip around his hand. "I like it. Ten minutes, tops."

Every tough instinct inside him melted beneath the warmth of that smile. He had to release her and turn away in order to think straight. ''We'll leave even sooner if I think it's a trap.''

''Let's hope it's not.''

Hope. Now there was something he hadn't believed in for a long, long time. But maybe she could believe in it enough for the both of them.

Without raising his chin from the tuck of blanket at his chest, Jonas swept the waiting area for anyone—anything— that struck him as a little too interested in them or out of place. Carmichael had copied him the names and schedule of the round-the-clock guards who would be watching Wes and Florence Monroe. One was always stationed in each of their rooms—the other two patrolled the floor. Beyond that, there would be doctors and nurses and orderlies and visitors and even other patients who might be something other than what they appeared.

A killer, perhaps. Or Darien Frye himself. Or any of a number of criminal representatives who might want Faith and the contents of that disk for themselves.

The elevator dinged its arrival on the main floor and Jonas urged Faith back behind the wheelchair as it opened. ''Empty,'' he quickly pronounced. ''Let's go.''

The first two floors passed in wary silence. But by the time they slowed for the third floor, Faith had leaned over the back of the chair and was hugging him from behind. ''Thank you for everything, Jonas.'' To his surprise, she pressed a kiss to his craggy cheek. ''The world's a less scary place knowing you're here with me.''

Before he could think of an appropriate response to that kind of trust in him, the door had opened and she pulled away.

The third-floor nurses' station was a beehive of activity. The day and evening shifts were changing, and the men and women in various designs of medical uniforms were reviewing charts and trading gossip. Jonas had timed their arrival for the busy turnover when the majority of the staff would be preoccupied with their work and less attentive to the unfamiliar attendant rolling a patient down the hallway toward room 3116.

The two patrol agents were easy to spot. Green hospital scrubs and white lab coats did little to mask the bulge of a weapon or the communication wires in their ears. If he and Faith slipped in and out quietly enough, they'd never even know their two charges had received visitors.

The guard at the door would be a trickier challenge. Slowly and steadily, Faith wheeled them toward their destination. Jonas checked his watch. Right on cue, the guard's cell phone rang and he reached into his pocket to answer.

Rory Carmichael had checked out. And in exchange for the opportunity to arrest Copperhead and his accomplice, and maybe Darien Frye himself, the federal agent had agreed to help get Faith in to see her uncle.

"Yeah? Yes, sir." The guard at the door acknowledged Carmichael's call and immediately relayed the information to the undercover guards. "We'll check it out."

In the instant the two guards left the floor to investigate the *suspicious activity* in the stairwell, Jonas rose from his chair and walked right up to the guard. The gun that he pressed into the startled agent's ribs was masked by the drape of the blanket.

"I don't want to hurt you," Jonas stated, keeping the agent's hands in clear sight as he reached around him and pushed open the door. "I don't want to hurt anybody." Faith slipped in behind them and closed the door as he backed the man into a corner. "This won't hurt a bit." He smiled, keeping his gun in the agent's gut while he pressed the weight of his forearm against the man's neck.

"Faith?" He heard a woman's breathy voice behind him.

"It's me, Gran."

"Faith!" The unconscious agent crumpled to the floor as a pretty, silver-haired lady wrapped Faith up in a tight hug. "Oh, sweetie. It's so good to see you. What happened to your hair? This is just what Wesley needs. Is the guard… He's not… Who's this?''

Jonas stood after handcuffing the agent and disabling his microphone, realizing he was now the focus of the older woman's attention. Her wide, frightened eyes were just as green and pretty as Faith's. He gave her a curt nod and moved to watch the door. ''Ma'am.''

''It's okay, Gran.'' Faith's tone was bright and full of strength and reassurance. ''That's just something Jonas does. He's a friend of mine. I know it's shocking at first, but the guard will be fine. I have so much to tell you.''

They were both talkers. ''And I have so much—''

He interrupted before either launched into her tale. ''You have however long it takes for those guards out there to realize we sent them on a wild-goose chase.'' He nodded toward the dark-haired man who appeared to be asleep on the hospital bed. ''Make the minutes count, honey.''

Faith nodded, linked arms with her grandmother, and went over to the bed to take her uncle's hand. Then Jonas stood back and watched how a real family worked.

FEELING EACH precious second of time ticking by with alarming speed, Faith bent down and kissed her uncle's wan cheek. She blinked back the tears that wet her eyelashes at the sight of her stalwart father figure lying pale and still upon the bed, his arms and lungs hooked up to tubes and wires and machines. She kept her grandmother's hand clutched tightly within her own and offered them what energy and strength and hope she could.

''I love you, Uncle Wes.'' He stirred in a fitful slumber, but didn't open his eyes. She turned to her grandmother. ''How is he doing?''

It was the first time she'd ever seen her grandmother look old. ''He drifts in and out of consciousness. He's collapsed twice. It's like he can't get enough air to breathe. But the doctors think he's improving. They're treating him with fluids and antibiotics to help him rebuild his strength." She pressed a handkerchief to her lips and stifled a weary sob. "But he's so weak...." Faith hugged her tight. "I can't lose another son."

"He'll pull through. He's tough. You know that. It's a Monroe family trait." She reached for her uncle's hand and connected the three of them together. "He'll come back to us. What happened?"

Gran took a deep breath and composed herself. "Your father got mixed up with some very bad people when you were a little girl."

Faith nodded. "I know about Darien Frye."

Her grandmother didn't seem surprised to learn that Faith knew some part of the truth about her father's death. "Twelve years ago, when Jack died, he'd been working on something at the college. He'd had some sort of breakthrough. He was going to patent the idea and sell it."

But he'd had second thoughts about his undetectable metal alloy. It would wreak havoc on security systems and make law enforcement a nightmare. "I know about that, too. What does it all have to do with Wes?"

"Jack told Wes what he'd invented. Wes is no scientist or engineer. He makes things grow and tends the land."

Jonas's low voice echoed across the tiny room. "We're down to a couple of minutes, ladies."

Faith steered her away from the sentimental journey. "I know he didn't give the plans to Wes. His research partner, William Rutherford, gave them to me a few days ago. I understand what they mean."

Gran's pale cheeks warmed with color. "I should have expected as much from Jack's bright girl." She leaned down and brushed a lock of dark hair off her son's forehead. He stirred in his sleep but didn't awaken. "Wes promised his brother that he'd protect the family if anything happened to him. That's why we took you in and moved away after your parents' deaths. And now, all these years later, he's still protecting us. He heard a report on the news about the murders at Eclipse Labs. We went straight to the FBI. And we asked them to find you, too, to keep you safe.''

Faith slid her gaze across the room to the wary sentry who guarded the door. "I am safe, Gran." For the briefest of moments, Jonas's intense gaze connected with hers, reminding her that *safe* was a relative concept right about now. She turned her attention back to the woman whose hand still clung to hers. "Your house was searched. I'm glad you weren't there. But what happened to Wes?"

The dear matriarch shook her head. "We were holed up in a safe house in central Missouri with three agents. But this morning after breakfast, he collapsed. He couldn't breathe. Air was going in and out, but it was like he was suffocating. One of the agents gave him a shot of something. Epinephrine, I think. We called an ambulance and came here."

"Those symptoms can be induced intentionally," Jonas observed matter-of-factly. "By poison."

"Shush." Faith knew he still considered her uncle's illness a setup to lure her back to Missouri. But her grandmother's stricken expression made his words sound cold and heartless.

But she had underestimated the transformation of her beastly bodyguard. He came to stand on the opposite side of the bed from Faith and her grandmother. "I wouldn't worry, ma'am." He looked at Gran and Wes and finally at Faith. "If he's anything like your granddaughter, he's too hardheaded to give up. I'm sure he'll recover." Suddenly, Jonas's *matter-of-fact* sounded very comforting.

Her grandmother's face lit up with a smile as she squeezed Faith's hand and reached across the bed to Jonas. He stared at the offer of friendship as if it was some kind of trick. It took a reassuring nod from Faith before he gently shook the older woman's hand. Gran held on to his long, strong fingers. "I think I like this one. He called you *honey*, too. Is there something…? He's so big. Nice eyes, though. And that scar. What—?"

"Gran." Faith cut her off before she embarrassed Jonas and forced her to examine and acknowledge her own feelings. Jonas had slipped and used the endearment from time to time the past couple of days. But the checkout lady at the grocery store called her *honey*, too. It might not mean a thing. And her warm, needy reaction to the word from his lips might not be his intention.

The unconscious guard groaned from his corner on the floor. "Time's up," announced Jonas, releasing Gran and turning away.

"Just a few minutes longer. Please?" Faith begged.

But her plea had no effect this time. "What I say, when I say it, remember?" He reached for her hand across the bed. "We have to go now. Nice to meet you, ma'am." He tipped the brim of his low-slung ball cap and pulled Faith around the foot of the bed.

It was too soon. She'd only just arrived. Gran was so worried. And Uncle Wes…

"Faith?" A faint breath of a voice called to her from the bed.

"Uncle Wes." Relief misted her eyes. Jonas let her tug free of his grip and dash to her uncle's side. She scooped up his hand between both of hers and kissed his cheek. "It's so good to see you. I'm so sorry you got hurt. I love you."

His fingers pressed weakly against hers. "Love you, too."

"Faith." Jonas's stern warning chimed like a clock. "Now."

She leaned in closer as Wes tugged the oxygen mask off his nose and mouth, and blinked his eyes open. "…friend says go." He was struggling to breathe now. "Not safe. Guard…poisoned…"

Faith didn't understand. "One of the guards did this to you?"

The agent on the floor was awake. And angry. "Mrs. Monroe? Are you all right?"

Gran puffed up in a ladylike version of losing her temper. "Of course, I'm all right. This is my granddaughter. Stay…"

But he was climbing to his feet. "Reach into my pocket and get my phone. Press the star key to call backup."

"I'll do no such thing," Gran protested.

"Mrs. Monroe—"

Jonas turned on him. "Sorry, pal."

"Go." Wes was trying to warn her of something. "Trusted…friends…not…" His eyes squeezed shut.

"Wes?"

"Mrs. Monroe! Securi—!" Jonas rammed his fist into the agent's jaw, sending him back into the corner and a few minutes of oblivion again. Then his big hands were on Faith's waist and he was pulling her away from the bed.

Her skin blanched in a sea of gooseflesh as the chaos erupted in the middle of her secure, loving world. "No. Don't take me."

Wes opened his eyes and tried to focus. "Frye…dead."

"We've lost control of the situation," Jonas warned. "We go *now*."

"Wes?" She begged her uncle for understanding even as she was ripped from his grasp.

She reached for him. His fingers stretched to meet hers. "…wants you…not formula…blames Jack…you can make…connection…"

"Who blames Dad? What connection? Wes?"

"Go, dear." Gran was pushing her into Jonas's arms now. "I'll be with him. I'll find out what he's saying."

"No," she protested.

Gran smiled gamely through a veil of tears. "We'll see you soon."

"Honey, please." Jonas's arm had circled her waist now. He was taking her away from everything she loved.

"They need me."

"I need you to be safe." He carried her to the door and set her down, trapping her in the vise of his arm and chest as he opened the door a tiny slit and peeked into the hallway.

She twisted around in his unyielding grasp, desperately trying to get back to her uncle. "Uncle Wes!"

Wes's hand fell back to the bed. "Love you."

"No—"

Jonas clamped his hand over her mouth. She beat at his arm, scratched at his hand, hating him for taking her away before she could understand. Before she could make things right. He was taking her away from everything she held precious and dear, everything that mattered.

"Faith." He lifted her off the floor, taking away her leverage to struggle. His lips brushed against her ear in a fierce whisper. "I'm sorry, honey. I have to do this. You have to do this for them, to make this all go away. You have to live."

Faith went limp in his arms. There was no tenderness in his touch, but there was immeasurate strength. It was comfort enough.

She couldn't hate him because he was right.

She couldn't hate him because she loved him.

He had always been strong for her. He had always done the right thing by her. And even if it lacked grace or compromise, it had never lacked heart. *He* had never lacked heart.

Faith nodded her compliance and he released her mouth. "I'm sorry."

She wished there was time and a way to hug him hard enough and kiss him deeply enough and love him long enough to make him understand that he was no monster to her. That he gave her more in a look or a touch than he

ever could with his knife or his gun. He needed to understand that he could be loved. That he *was* loved.

"The other two agents are in the hallway. And they look
a little pissed." Jonas's observation reminded her that survival came first. This wasn't the time to air her feelings.
And he'd never indicated that he'd welcome them, anyway.
Maybe locked up in his secluded mountain cabin was the
only way he felt comfortable with the world. "Better?" he
asked, sparing her an indulgent look, though she could feel
the alert tension humming through his body.

"I'm fine." She stroked her fingers along his arm in mute
apology and breathed deeply, bracing herself for running
the gauntlet or whatever other plan Jonas had in mind.
"What do you need me to do?"

"Jonas, is it?" Gran's voice was hushed, but strong behind them. "The guard's coming to again."

He turned and nodded his thanks, then made a quick
decision. He inclined his head toward the cracked opening
in the doorway and the advancing federal agents. "I'll stall
them. You take the stairs down to the car and drive it
around to the front. I'll meet you there."

"What do you mean, stall them?"

"Now."

Jonas swung open the door and shoved her in one direction. He charged the opposite way.

The agents reached for their guns. "Jonas!"

"Run!"

From the corner of her eye, she witnessed the beast come
to life. With his arms thrown wide, Jonas tackled both men.
All three crashed to the floor, taking a food cart with them.
Faith steeled herself against the gasps of surprise and
smacks of fists and grunts of pain that followed as the three
men fought and onlookers gathered around them.

She turned her back on the danger Jonas faced and ran
down the hall, relieving him of that concern, at least, so he
could concentrate on defending himself. Faith ran past the

nurses' station, she dodged around dumbstruck patients and staff watching the brawl. She hurried past the elevators as one set of doors opened.

"Faith?" A swath of deep brick red startled her with recognition and she stumbled to a halt. "Faith, is that you? What happened to your hair? What's going on? Is that a fight?"

A chattery voice from the grave spun her around in shock. "Liza?" She stared for one long, disoriented moment at the woman framed in the open elevator doors, wearing a nursing uniform much like the scrubs and colorful jacket she herself had on. "Liza?" She took a jerking step forward. "How…? I thought you were dead."

"I'm fine." Her friend's confused smile must have matched her own.

"Liza!" Faith closed the gap between them and hugged her tight. "I'm so sorry I got you mixed up in all of this. Did they put you into protective custody, too?"

Liza wasn't hugging her back. Why weren't the doors closing?

The two facts registered a heartbeat too late. Inside the elevator…with the tip of a knife blade on a button beside the door… Cold, dead fear swept through Faith as she breathed in. Protective fury replaced it as she breathed out.

She pulled Liza from the elevator. "Get out." The tall dark man inside the elevator was no doctor. He wielded death instead of life with his two hands. *Copperhead.*

"He's not a cop. Come with me!"

"No." Something cold and hard jabbed Faith in the ribs and she froze. She released Liza and looked down to see the long, oversize barrel of a gun and silencer pressing beneath the folds of her jacket. When she looked up again, her friend's eyes were devoid of anything resembling friendship. "You come with us."

"Faith!"

She heard her name roared like thunder down the corridor. It was followed by a crash. But she couldn't look.

He'd known. Jonas had known it would come down to this. Maybe not who, but the how. He'd known that death would finally catch up to her. And now she was staring it right in the eye.

"Get in the elevator, Faith. I didn't give your uncle a lethal dose of cyanide this morning. But I can. And I will. Maybe your dotty old grandmother, too." Liza smiled. But there was no humor in her expression. "She likes me since I was kind enough to help her make that call." The smile vanished. The gun bruised a rib. "Now, get in the elevator."

"Faith!"

Jermaine Collier's black, soulless eyes warned her not to respond.

He was coming. Jonas was coming.

Liza linked her arm through Faith's to mask the gun, then guided her onto the elevator. With a nod to Collier, he released the button and the doors began to close.

He raised the knife to Faith's eye level and ran his thumb along the flat of the blade, sending her a deliberate message. "Do you have the disk?"

Faith swallowed hard and forced herself to breathe. To think. To buy Jonas time to save her. "Yes. But I made a copy. Other people have access to that information."

"Who?" Liza demanded.

Collier's eyes glittered with anger. "She's toying with us." He slipped the blade of his knife beneath the thin strap of her purse and lifted it from her shoulder. "She hasn't had time or the means to—"

The elevator alarm buzzed at a jarring decibel. The doors froze open with only a matter of inches separating them. Then they began to shake. Faith knew.

Liza barked an order and shoved Faith against the wall of Collier's chest. The doors parted with a mighty heave.

A cruel arm clamped around her chest, pinning her arms. A knife blade pricked her throat.

"Faith!" The doors sprang open. She caught a glimpse of that beloved, battered face. She saw the blood at his mouth and the deadly intent in his eyes. "Let her go!"

Liza leveled her gun at the opening between the doors and fired.

"Jonas!" Faith screamed as the force of the gunshot threw him back against the opposite wall.

A puddle of blood soaked the shoulder of his denim shirt as the doors drifted shut and the alarm ceased to blare.

"Jonas?"

It wasn't the knife pressing against her vocal cords that choked the volume out of her voice.

JONAS STAGGERED to his feet and peeled off his coat. The motion ached, but there was no sharp, shooting pain. The bullet had gone clean through his shoulder.

He'd left the agents dazed or unconscious, lying on the floor. He'd ignored the shouted threats of hospital security and local police being summoned. Faith needed him. He had to get to her.

He'd gotten a glimpse of a woman with red hair, longer than Faith's. And he'd seen her eyes. The same dead-brown eyes of a father he'd pursued and lost so many years ago.

Darien Frye had a daughter.

And she had Faith.

The bastard with the knife must be Copperhead. He'd seen blood on Faith's throat. A cleansing rush of vengeful adrenaline cleared Jonas's head. He summoned every deadly, covert skill he'd ever used to survive his family and serve his country. He'd promised Faith he'd keep her safe. Hell. He owed her that much. She'd brought three days of sunshine into a life that had been lived in the darkness. He owed her at least that much.

He pushed himself away from the wall. His balance was

fine. He was losing blood, but there was a lot left in him to lose before he'd fall.

There was no opening the elevator doors now. He looked at the numbers lighting up above them. The elevator was moving. Going down. Everything he loved was going down with it.

Jonas pulled his gun and ran for the stairs.

STRUGGLING WAS pointless, but she battled, anyway. Jermaine Collier's grip was every bit as strong as Jonas's had been. But his clasp on her upper arm was rough and bruising as he dragged her out the automatic exit doors and into the dank, fumy parking garage adjoining the hospital.

"How can you still be alive?" Faith's question was all accusation. "Did you kill someone else to take your place and throw off the Feds and the police?"

"Jermaine did, actually." Liza seemed pleased to point out the brilliance of her strategy. "My neighbor, Gabe, was actually Gabriela Montez. I switched places with her and reported my death to the police."

"DNA will prove it's not her. What about her family?"

"She has none in this country. And why run a test? She was positively identified by the police." She smiled up at Jermaine.

Faith tried to face the fake detective, but he held her too tightly. "They'll figure it out," she protested.

Liza hurried her pace. "What's to figure? You're the only loose end left. Once you're gone—"

"You don't have to tell her everything." Jermaine jerked her arm in its socket, punishing her instead of Liza, pricking tears of pain that Faith quickly blinked away.

"Jermaine…" Liza warned.

"I'm telling you to take the disk and off her." Collier's voice was cool and toneless, even when it was angry. "We can frame that mountain man who's already attacked two deputies, a security guard and who-knows-how-many federal agents.''

"Jonas never hurt any of them." Faith felt honor-bound to defend him, even to these murderers. "He's not like you. Killing a sweet old man. Leaving a trail of dead bodies—ow!''

"Shut up." Collier twisted her arm up behind her back, wrenching her shoulder. He sliced through the collar of her shirt and gouged another little nick from her skin. "If you say one more word, I'm cutting your throat."

"Easy, Jermaine," Liza ordered him. With her gun held up beside her face and her eyes scanning the cars and concrete support pillars for hidden authorities or innocent witnesses, she zigzagged across the garage toward the waning sunlight at the ramp that would take them up to the next level or out onto the street. "I've waited too long for this. I'm not going to let your paranoia spoil it."

"If your retribution gets in the way of my million dollars—''

"It won't." Liza's order was considerably more volatile. She shook Faith's purse which she clutched in her fist. They'd already discovered the disk inside. "First, we deliver this. Then we can kill her. And show the DeLeones firsthand how we handle *problems* within the organization. I think my father would have approved."

"You're not doing this for the DeLeones," Collier argued, twisting Faith's arm again, since he couldn't seem to expel his anger any other way. "When I worked for your father, business was business. You blame this bitch's father for Darien's suicide. And you want someone to pay. You wanted to get her so mixed up in this mess that the cops or the Feds or the DeLeones would kill her for you."

"That's not true. I wanted her to take the blame for the theft and deaths so our names would be clear. Then we could kill her."

"She's a liability. She's seen what's on the disk."

Faith took heed of the rift between her kidnappers as Liza pulled out a set of keys and headed for a long black car. It was a long shot, but with Jonas lying wounded or dead in the hallway upstairs, her fast thinking might be her only chance at surviving.

"I have seen the disk," Faith spoke as loudly as the pain radiating up her arm would allow. "I can recreate the formula my father made."

Liza looked over her shoulder laughed. "You're not as smart as you think you are, roomie. You just gave me one more reason to kill you."

"May I?" Collier asked between clenched teeth. Faith closed her eyes and tried to think of anything besides the press of the knife between her breasts and across her belly. She promised herself she wouldn't cry. She wouldn't scream or show the fear that seemed to give him such satisfaction. "You've caused so much trouble that I'm really going to enjoy this."

"Not yet." Liza chastized him and pointed the remote key chain at the car to unlock it. "William Rutherford tried to bargain with that information, too. He said he'd hand over the disk if I promised not to harm you. The old fool thought he could protect you. I guess he forgot the tiny little detail about being able to identify me and linking my father to your father's death." She waved the purse that held the disk in front of Faith's face. "Is that the same deal you're trying to make?"

"Maybe. I—"

Liza stood with the back driver's side door open. "First, I have the disk, so you have nothing to bargain with. Second, you've figured out enough that you're a liability as well. Third—" she smiled over Faith's shoulder "—I'd hate to disappoint Jermaine."

He dragged the tip of the blade across her throat, chilling her with the cold steel, just to emphasize the point.

But Faith wasn't done fighting yet. "I already shared

some of the formula." She was winging it now. "I sent it to an organization called The Watchers. They're a government security agency. They go after men like your father, who sell out their country. They want me alive as much as you want me dead."

Liza's eyes narrowed, considering her story. "You're lying."

Faith tipped her chin and faked her confidence. "About the information or The Watchers?"

"About all of it! You're a naive country girl from Podunkville, Missouri. I deceived you for two and a half years. At college, in Saint Louis." Liza's temper was getting the better of her now. She pointed her gun toward the car's back seat. "Put her in there. Tie her up."

Faith barely had time to duck her head before Collier shoved her inside. She kicked out, connecting with his thigh but missing her target. In the space of a heartbeat, he switched his knife to the other hand and pulled out his gun. "That's it."

She scrambled on her hands and feet toward the other side of the car. But Liza hit a button and locked the door.

"Time to die."

She dived over the front seat, desperate to escape the bead of that gun.

A shot rang out, echoing off the concrete walls and ringing in her ears. The gun flew from Collier's hand. Faith snatched at her chest, but she wasn't hit.

"Faith!" Jonas. Collier's hand hung limp at his side and blood oozed from beneath the crisp white cuff of his shirt. "Get away from her!"

He was alive. Jonas was alive!

Liza ducked behind the open door and fired off countless rounds at their attacker, giving Jermaine enough time to find cover and search for his gun. The deafening sound of gunfire echoed through the garage with the same intensity of thunder in the mountains. Shaking with every tiny explosion of sound, Faith unlocked the passenger-side door and slipped out to the concrete floor.

She crawled along the cold, smooth surface, just getting away from the deadly spray of bullets and spent cartridges and dings of metal and concrete shrapnel. She'd covered the distance of two cars and hidden behind a third when the sudden silence startled her. "Oh, no. No."

Was Jonas dead? She had to help him. Rising to her feet, she tried to spy him through the shadowed garage. The debris of spent cartridges indicated where Jonas had hidden behind a tall SUV. But there was no sign of movement. No sound.

Liza was blocked from view as well. Jermaine Collier was the only one she could see. He had taken cover behind a support pillar, emptying his gun and quickly reloading. "You might as well give it up, mountain man," Collier taunted. "You're hit and you're out of ammo." He swung around the pillar to fire.

"But I ain't dead." A huge knife sailed through the air and pierced the center of Jermaine Collier's chest.

The hit man's eyes and hands popped open. His gun clattered to the floor. Sweat formed a sheen across the top of his bald head. But he didn't fall. Faith watched in tight-lipped horror as he closed his fingers around the handle of the knife, and with a deliberate denial of any pain, pulled the knife from his chest.

Everything around her took on a sudden surreal quality. But it was real. It was all real. The heightened sense of awareness brought on by fear and intense relief. The oily smell of the cars. The vicious barrage of hateful words. The sight of Jonas Beck flying through the air and smashing Jermaine Collier down to the concrete floor before the hit man could react.

Their fight was cruel and intense—two wounded giants battling for their very lives. Faith's heart pounded against the wall of her chest. She had to help. How could she help?

But she was too late. Like every other tragedy of the past few days, she couldn't stop it. She felt the tap of cold metal against her scalp.

"Get up." Liza hadn't disappeared with the disk. She'd come for Faith. "Get up!"

She slowly stood. Liza settled the gun behind Faith's ear. She could see Jonas now, trading punches with Collier, his face bleeding from a cut across his cheek. His shoulder soaked with blood. No. No, he didn't deserve to die. Not like this. Not for her.

Obeying the command of Liza's gun, Faith walked to the black car and climbed behind the wheel. As she slid across the seat, Liza got in behind her and started the engine. She was abandoning her partner.

Faith wouldn't abandon hers.

As Liza shifted the car into Reverse, Faith lunged for the gun. She smashed her foot on top of Liza's on the accelerator. The car burned rubber, then found traction and careened backward, crashing into a pillar. The whiplash momentum threw Faith against the dashboard. She lost her grip and tumbled to the floor. But Liza was shaken, too, her head bleeding from where she'd hit the steering wheel.

Faith recovered more quickly. But with the gun lost at Liza's feet, she opted for escape. She shoved open her door and fell out onto the concrete.

Ignoring the pain that swirled inside her head, Faith got to her feet and ran toward Jonas. "Jonas? Oh, God. Jonas?"

He rose to his feet with Collier's head locked between his massive arms. The black man turned the knife he held in his fist and plunged it back into Jonas's ribs.

"Jonas!"

Jonas's startled gasp betrayed his pain, but he moved his arms in a fateful twist. Collier's eyes opened wide. They never closed again. Jonas released him and he fell to the floor. Dead.

Jonas's chest rose and fell in deep, uneven gasps. His icy

eyes were hooded as he sought her out across the garage. Tires were squealing now. Horns were honking. Men were shouting.

He held out his hand, reaching for her. Faith ran to him.

"Faith?" He collapsed to his knees. His arm dropped to his side. But his gaze still held hers. "Honey?"

"Police. Freeze." Men in uniform were swarming around Jonas, every one of their guns leveled at her bleeding—maybe dying—hero.

"No!" she shouted. "He didn't do anything. Don't hurt him!"

She heard Liza shouting behind her. But the vile words were quickly muffled.

She only knew the man whose color was draining from his face, whose beautiful blue eyes were growing too heavy to hold open. "Oh, Jonas. Please don't die."

He was within her grasp when unseen hands snaked around her and lifted her from behind. "No!" She fought against the hands that were keeping her from the man she loved. "Let me go!"

It took three men to pick her up and carry her away. To stuff her inside an unmarked car and pin her to the back seat.

She'd never gotten to touch him. She'd never said she loved him.

She pasted her face to the window, pulling at the restraining hands, keeping Jonas in her sights long enough to see the police and several paramedics closing in on him. He couldn't even move. He couldn't defend himself. Faith's eyes flooded with tears, but she angrily brushed them away to keep Jonas in her sight.

"We're The Watchers, miss. You're our first priority." The man who held her in the seat tried to explain why they were taking her away. "He'd want it this way."

"Jonas?"

"Be safe." His lips mouthed the words, but there was no rich dark sound to fill her ears and warm her heart.

He'd collapsed to the floor by the time the car left the garage and sped away from the hospital.

Chapter Twelve

Forty-two days was a hell of a long time to be alone without having contact with any of the people you loved. Faith stared out the window of her D.C. hotel room at the two gold-leafed trees in the park across the street. In spite of the bustle of midday traffic, the October rain was dreary and depressing.

How had Jonas ever survived being alone for all those years?

Oh, God, how she ached for him. She longed for one intense look from those ice-colored eyes. Or one brush of his callused fingertips in tender restraint across her forehead. Or one gruff, awkward word as he curbed his language in a boyish effort to please her. She needed a look, a touch—a soul-rendering kiss—to sustain her, and drive away her last memory of Jonas, downed and dying, so that she could be safe.

The only thing she'd been told was that he was alive. That he'd been taken into surgery immediately and put into intensive care. Her uncle Wes had recovered from Liza Shelton's cyanide poisoning as well, and he and Gran were sequestered in some other hotel in some other city, awaiting the outcome of Liza's trial.

Faith had testified before judges and lawyers and subcommittees she'd never known existed. The daughter of a rogue FBI agent, using her father's connections to exact revenge for his suicide and sell top secret weapons research to the highest bidder was a woman that everyone wanted a piece of. Liza Shelton had been charged with treason, four charges of conspiracy to commit murder, and two attempted murders. With Faith's account of William Rutherford's death, her identification of Jermaine Collier—whose real name was Clyde Avery—her explanation of the information on the disk and her account of some key memories of her father, Liza Shelton would be spending the rest of her life in prison.

As soon as today's verdict was announced.

Faith breathed in deeply and let the curtain drape back over the window. The agent guarding her this afternoon was already diving into the elegant lunch prepared by this five-star hotel's restaurant. She shook her head when he offered her a plate, but picked up a bottle of water and carried it to the couch where she curled her legs beneath her and turned the pages of the magazine she wasn't reading.

Even the buzzer of the hotel room's door couldn't startle her from her lonesome-hearted depression. She nodded when the agent jumped up from his lunch and motioned her to stay put. She listened to the brusque exchange of voices when he opened the door without really hearing any of the words.

But she did sit up straight when a different man walked into the room. She guessed him to be about fifty years old. The arrogant posture of his shoulders made him seem taller than his six feet or so of height. He had short, dark hair and dark-framed glasses that gave him an air of intelligence and authority.

"I'm George Murphy."

He smiled and held out his hand. Faith slowly stood and moved toward him to shake his hand. This was Jonas's friend. His boss from The Watchers who'd given them information to help them survive. "Mr. Murphy. Why are you here?"

For one god-awful moment she thought he'd come to tell her that Jonas hadn't survived his wounds, after all.

"Liza Shelton's been found guilty," he announced without any setup or fanfare. "You're free to go."

Faith hugged her arms around her waist and braced for the bad news. "You didn't answer my question."

"We have a mutual friend. And he needs your help."

THE SETTING WAS familiar as Faith steered her rental car around the twists of White Horse Road. There were glimpses of autumn gold among the tall lodgepole pines, and the hazy evening air was heavy with dampness that would turn to snow by nightfall. But the steep slopes of the mountain still rose in a formidable barrier on one side and dropped off into a carpet of green treetops on the other.

She checked her map and drove past the driveway to Jonas's old cabin. George Murphy had told her that Jonas was refurbishing an older, even more remote place farther up the mountain. He didn't need the reminder of Sheriff Prince's dead body to wake up to each morning.

Idly, she wondered if Jonas's perspective on mornings had gotten any worse. The magnitude of prejudice and misperceptions he faced every day would have crippled a lesser man.

When she found the right driveway, Faith slowed the car and turned. She hoped she was doing the right thing. According to George Murphy, Jonas had pretty much given up on work and people and life. The beast of the mountain was wasting away, pining for something he'd lost.

But Jonas Beck had never given up on her. Not once. She wouldn't give up on him, either.

She parked her car at the base of the drive and walked up as Murphy had suggested. She found Jonas beside the quaint, sturdy cabin, chopping wood with a powerful fury.

He was dressed in his jeans, work boots and wore gloves. But he had shucked off his flannel shirt, and a mixture of sweat and the bracing, cold air beaded across his wide, muscular back.

She made no sound. None at all. But she was ten feet away when he spun around, brandishing the ax like a weapon. "Get the hell off my..."

Faith boldly stared, drinking in every detail as he stood in shocked silence. He truly was a battered warrior, standing bare-chested and damp with sweat. The pink skin of the newly healed bullet wound in his shoulder, the marks of stitches across his rib cage, and the scar that cut across his left cheek stood out against the healthy tan of a man who'd been working outdoors.

He was the most beautiful sight she had ever seen.

"Liza Shelton's in prison," she stated simply, wrapping up the nightmare she'd endured.

"I heard." His hungry blue eyes dropped to the record book she carried in her hand. His words were a harsh, pain-filled growl. "If you've come to pay me back, I won't take a penny."

So he wanted to talk tough, huh? Faith felt the oddest urge to smile. She knew now that it was all a sham. A protective front to guard his big, beaten heart. She planted her hands on her hips and gave him attitude right back. "I'm not here to pay you anything. I'm here to collect what you owe me."

"What?" He buried the ax in the chopping stump and reached for his shirt. As he pulled it on, he asked, "What do I owe you?"

"The truth." Faith took a deep breath of the clean mountain air and put her own heart on the line. "You're hopelessly in love with me, aren't you, Mr. Beck?"

A muscle leaped in his jaw and he looked away, high into the sky. Faith caught her breath when his beautiful blue gaze came back and collided with hers. "Do you know how hard it was for me to let you go?"

She took that as a yes. Faith released the breath she'd been holding and almost laughed. Her mule-headed hero could be so noble. "How hard are you willing to fight to have me stay?"

Jonas listened to the challenge in her voice. He memorized the golden, wind-tossed waves of her hair and the pretty eyes shimmering with a sheen of unshed tears. Her jeans hugged the curve of her hips and the length of her legs. His body tightened at the ripe swell of her breasts pushing in uneven breaths against the zipper of her dark green jacket. And his heart beat hard with the promise of hope.

But twenty-some-odd years of thinking of himself as a devil-eyed monster wasn't a curse that was easily broken. She was still ten feet away, and she hadn't said the words he most needed to hear. "I don't want you to stay out of some sense of obligation. I'd have taken that bullet for anyone I was hired to protect. Keeping you safe was the right thing to do. I'm a hard man to live with. I still have a lot to learn about manners and patience and—"

"You stubborn son of a bitch."

Not the words he'd expected to hear. Not from those lips. "Faith—"

"I love you." She was walking toward him now. No, marching. Striding. Advancing for battle. Jonas pulled up to all six feet six inches of himself, bracing for the fight he saw in her eyes. "I need you. To hold me. To be there for me. To need me. I need a rock. A soul mate to make my life complete." She was right there in front of him now, boldly looking him in the eye. She poked a finger against his heart. "I." She had the nerve to poke him again. "Love."

He scooped her up in his arms and never let her finish the sentence. "I love you, too, honey."

He claimed her lips and plunged his tongue inside to taste the essence of her love for him. He tunneled his fingers into her hair and cupped the sweet curve of her rump with a possessive need that softened into humility as her arms wound around his neck and her lush, hot mouth gave back every bit of passion and love and welcome that he craved.

The hard shell of hurt that had closed off his heart to the world shattered into a million pieces. She wrapped her legs around his hips and he carried her up onto the porch and into the cabin. He laid her on the quilt on top of his bed and lost himself in the miracle of kissing and loving and being loved by Faith.

Night had fallen by the time his sated body found the willingness to rest. Faith dozed peacefully in his arms, snuggled close, one hand resting with gentle acceptance against the new scar on his cheek. Badges of honor, she'd called them, as she'd kissed each wound. Not marks of shame or fear.

He was still too awed by the blessing of her love to sleep himself, so he was awake and ready to listen when she stirred against his chest.

"Jonas?" She stroked her fingertips across his lips and he kissed each one. "You're going to marry me, aren't you? I mean, Wes and Gran raised me to be a lady, and sleeping with you all the time just isn't—"

He brushed his knuckles beneath her chin and tipped her mouth up for a long, lingering kiss. When he finally pulled back, he was smiling. "I'm going to marry you."

And then he actually laughed. It felt good. It felt right. "No one else will argue with me." And then Faith was laughing, too. And then they were making love to each other all over again.

He had a feeling laughter would never hurt again.

Later, in the earliest hours of the morning, Jonas got up and opened the curtains of the east-facing window of his bedroom. He climbed back beneath the covers and pulled Faith into his arms, his soul at peace as he watched the sunrise.

And they loved happily ever after.

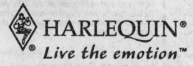

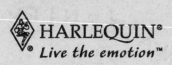 

Harlequin Books and Konica present
The Double Exposure Campaign!

Expose yourself to Intrigue. Collect original proofs of purchase from the back pages of:

UNDER WRAPS 0-373-83595-7
GUARDED SECRETS 0-373-83593-0
WHISPERS IN THE NIGHT 0-373-83596-5
KEEPING WATCH 0-373-83594-9

and receive free Konica disposable cameras, each valued at over $5.99 U.S.!

Just complete the order form and send it, along with your proofs of purchase from two (2), three (3) or four (4) of the featured books above, to: Harlequin Intrigue National Consumer Promotion, P.O. Box 9047, Buffalo, NY 14269-9047, or P.O. Box 613, Fort Erie, Ontario L2A 5X3.

---

093 KIL DXHU

Name (PLEASE PRINT)

Address   Apt. #

City   State/Prov.   Zip/Postal Code

Please specify which themed gift package(s) you would like to receive:

❑ I am enclosing two (2) proofs of purchase for one free Konica camera
❑ I am enclosing three (3) proofs of purchase for two free Konica cameras
❑ I am enclosing four (4) proofs of purchase for three free Konica cameras

---

Have you enclosed your proofs of purchase?

Remember—the more you buy, the more you save! You must send two (2) original proofs of purchase to receive one camera, three (3) original proofs of purchase to receive two cameras and four (4) original proofs of purchase to receive all three cameras.

THE DOUBLE EXPOSURE CAMPAIGN
One Proof of Purchase
SEPTNCPPOP2

Please allow 4-6 weeks for delivery. Shipping and handling included. Offer good only while quantities last. Offer available in Canada and the U.S. only. Request should be received no later than **December 31, 2003.** Each proof of purchase should be cut out of the back-page ad featuring this offer.

© 2003 Harlequin Enterprises Limited

Visit us at www.eHarlequin.com

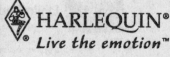